BROKEN MUSIC

The year is 1919 and the population of Great Britain is still struggling to its feet after the atrocities of the First World War. Progress is slow, even in the village of Broughton Underhill, on the edge of the Black Country. Gradually, soldiers return, wounds begin to heal and people try to move on with their lives. But for the Wentworth family, this proves to be impossible. Former police sergeant Herbert Reardon has returned to the village determined to find out what happened the night Marianne Wentworth was drowned in the lake all those years ago, when the war was just beginning.

BROKEN MUSIC

by

Marjorie Eccles

Magna Large Print Books
Long Preston, North Yorkshire,
BD23 4ND, England.

British Library Cataloguing in Publication Data.

Eccles, Marjorie
    Broken music.

    A catalogue record of this book is
    available from the British Library

    ISBN   978-0-7505-3173-3

First published in Great Britain in 2009 by Allison & Busby Ltd.

Copyright © 2009 by Marjorie Eccles

Cover illustration by arrangement with Allison & Busby Ltd.

The moral right of the author has been asserted

Published in Large Print 2010 by arrangement with
Allison & Busby Ltd.

Magna Large Print is an imprint of Library Magna Books Ltd.

Printed and bound in Great Britain by
T.J. (International) Ltd., Cornwall, PL28 8RW

PART ONE

Early March 1919

Chapter One

The crow flies up from the valley on steady wings, making straight for the group of stunted trees crowning the summit of the hill. The one he alights on is a spindly thorn, not tall enough for a nesting place, and a skeleton into the bargain, having been struck by lightning two years previously, but that isn't why the crow has chosen it. From his perch, he surveys the immediate terrain with a bright, cold, practised eye, on the lookout for small animals or birds, worms, insects, anything that moves. Or better still, carrion.

He waits, unmoving, biding his time. Directly below him, out of sight, are caves hewn by pre-historic ancients out of the soft red sandstone of the hill. And below that, the village of Broughton Underhill, sitting comfortably as it has done since Saxon times alongside the shallow river which rises at the bubbling springs and the holy well of St Ethelfleda, and after that winds through the length of the village, at one point on its way broadening out to form the lake of the big house, Oaklands Park.

Down there, the March afternoon is still, cold and quiet, so quiet its everyday sounds float up to the hilltop: the children's voices as they tumble noisily out of school, and the district nurse's bicycle bell as she makes sedate haste towards the imminent arrival of a new baby; the sound of the church clock striking four, and faintly, the jingle of the harness as old Harry Packer and his great draught horses, busy with the spring ploughing in the ten-acre field at the home farm, turn the rich red earth.

Nothing stirs up there on the hillside. Nothing catches the crow's beady eye. After a while he gives up and, with a hoarse croak, spreads his wings again and glides on the thermals back down into the village.

The crow was there again, hunched on the washing-line post in the back garden of the rectory, as he had been intermittently for days, like a black Puritan parson, when Amy took the corn out for the hens. It was a task she hated. Senseless creatures they were, screeching like flustered, hysterical old women. The slightest thing agitated them but they had to be tolerated, providing as they did much needed eggs and the occasional boiling fowl.

The hairs on the back of her neck rose when she saw the big bird and she clapped her hands to frighten it away, but only succeeded in provoking the silly hens to further squawks; with the same hard, unblinking stare the crow went on regarding her efforts to scatter corn from her basket as far as she could, in order to keep the hens from her feet. She would have crossed herself if she'd been a Catholic, or if she hadn't thought her father might be watching out of his study window.

Florrie said crows were bad luck, they brought infection, they were omens of discord, and even death, and after the last years no one wanted any more of any of these, thank you very much. Well, yes, Amy thought – but I for one don't intend to go on being miserable now that the beastly war with the Germans is over, now that I've turned eighteen and might begin to make up for what I've missed while it was on, stuck here in this dreary backwater. All very well for Florrie to sniff. But I don't ask for much, really ... dresses that I haven't had to make over myself; some real jewellery, not just that childish string of corals and the pearl ring that was Mama's; pretty shoes, she thought longingly, scuffing the toe of one hated, serviceable lace-up into the scratched, dusty wasteland the fowls had made of the backyard; some soft, embroidered underwear, scent, parties and dances. And later, a nice house, and pretty little babies... And, of course, a husband. She shivered deliciously at the frisson that ran down her spine.

One of the brave, handsome men returned from the front, he will have to be. One of the survivors, young and eligible. There's going to be a scramble for those who are left. Of course, it's ridiculous to think of me, Aimée Wentworth, having the ghost of a chance among all those girls (although some of them are practically old maids now, having waited all these years!); those girls who are rich, ready to grab, not as choosy as they had been before the war.

But I, too, have assets ... and I've seen how young men look at me.

Amy forgot the crow, excitement making her pulses race faster as she gazed, unseeing, at the gloomy old trees crowded behind the house and

11

nourished these not altogether unattainable dreams with a mental list of her considerable attractions. True, she had no money, and she wasn't at all clever, like Nella or Marianne – but what man wanted a clever wife? Just look how Nella had thrown her chances away – that certainly hadn't been clever. Amy herself had other assets – sparkling hazel eyes and the rich, waving red hair she had inherited from her mother, a well-curved little figure; she knew perfectly well how appealing her glowing looks were, and would be even more so if she had the right clothes to show them off. She had a good temper, an ability to laugh often, naturally pretty manners, and knew how to behave: she hadn't wasted her time during the hours spent with her honorary aunt, Lady Sybil, and Eunice, at Oaklands Park, but had listened and learnt, even while they were only knitting those everlasting scarves and socks for the Tommies on the front line, or boring old squares to be made up into blankets for Belgian refugees from scraps of leftover wool.

And by no means least, as their grandmother never let them forget, there were the family connections which still meant a great deal: their mother had after all been a cousin of Lady Sybil's, a Greville like her, and before her marriage to Papa, had come out herself. Though much good it had done her, thought Amy, who had scarcely known her mother and had never been allowed near enough her father to really know him, either.

But yes, my turn will come, and I *won't* let it slip from my fingers, she vowed, her chin taking on its stubborn tilt, already aware that luck was

12

what you made it. Aunt Sybil will have time and opportunity for social life again, once the last convalescent soldier has gone away, the hospital is closed and Oaklands restored to what it was before the war. There'll be house parties and tennis parties again and Eunice will want me and Nella to be invited, especially now that Grev won't be there. Grev, and ... and ... the others. But don't think of that.

Amy never allowed herself to be despondent for long. She wholeheartedly agreed with Florrie: if you don't look after yourself, nobody else will. And anyway, if the worst came to the worst, she thought defiantly, tossing her red curls, she had the means in her power to *make* what she wanted happen.

But the thought of this was a little bit too daring, even for Amy, and she swished round to go indoors, clapping her hands and whirling the empty basket at the black harbinger of doom still eyeing her from the washing post, just to show she wasn't to be intimidated by a mere crow, but he didn't move. Until she turned away; then, with a rusty caw that sounded suspiciously like a cackling laugh, he flew away to busy himself with the mice in the church belfry.

The afternoon sun had grown lower in the sky when, sated with mice and on his way back to his roost, the black bird paused to rest on a bedroom window sill of the Greville Arms, but no one noticed; there were things of more importance going on in the room. The publican's firstborn, nine-pound baby had not long ago uttered his first cry in the world – or rather, a lusty shout, thought his exhausted but exultant mother, smiling... Oh, yes, his father's son all right, she thought fondly. Another Sam Noakes. Strong as an ox, a lot of noise, but soft as butter. She and her baby gazed at each other and Mattie found in this new little face total recognition, and fell in love all over again.

They hadn't been married when her Sam had enlisted with the Worcesters right at the beginning of the war. Couldn't keep him back, though he was mithered about leaving his widowed father, bad as he was with rheumatism. But Walter Noakes, a veteran of the war with the Boers, had been as eager for him to go as Sam himself. 'What? Let the bloody Kaiser stamp all over us? Not likely! You get out there, son, and wipe the floor with them Germans! You'll be home by Christmas, see if you won't.'

Some hopes! Four years later, they were still fighting, all those men of the village who'd joined up together and seen action in all the worst of the war – at places with unpronounceable names, that the Tommies called Wipers, Pop, Armenteers... Sam, lucky Sam, big flaxen-haired Sam with his muscles honed from all that helping his uncle in the smithy next door in his spare time, had miraculously gone through it all with only minor wounds and a dose of trench fever, until the Blighty one at Neuve Eglise. Shrapnel tearing through the flesh of his leg, that was, a bad enough wound to get him a ticket home and a brief sick leave, but not bad enough to prevent him being sent back to the front afterwards, as the daily lists of those lost began to fill page after page after page in the newspapers.

Just two weeks they'd had together, during that last home leave. She, fearful, he persuasive: 'Come on, girl, I'll take care of you – you'll be all right. Say yes.'

'All right,' she'd replied. He hadn't said he might never come back, he didn't need to, with nearly everyone they knew losing sons, fathers, brothers, cousins, and the news from the front blacker than ever.

But in spite of his promises, she'd found herself pregnant after he was sent back to the front. Heads were shaken, of course they were, but Broughton had never been overjudgemental about the 'mishaps' that happened from time to time in their village; they were two healthy young folk, after all, and Sam was a hero, wounded and going back to the front and all. She'd had to leave her job up at the Big House, but she would have done that anyway to come to live at the pub and help out, to look after Sam's father and wait for the baby. A few months later, the miraculous happened: the tide was turned against the Germans and they were forced to retreat, the Armistice was signed and Sam was safe and one of the first to be sent home, just in time to put a ring on her finger before their baby should be born.

Sometimes, Mattie could scarcely believe her good fortune. That she, Mattie O'Hara as was, one of the seven O'Haras brought up in the two-bedroomed cottage at the end of Water End Lane, had not been left alone with a child to bring up, and that her man had come home whole in his body and right in his mind, not like some. And that, God willing, she would never know poverty again now, it being in the nature of things that innkeepers, while never becoming rich, maybe, were never short of business. And more than that: in time, the smithy next door would come to Sam, his Uncle Ted being childless.

The afternoon sun poured in and the baby's greedy little mouth found her breast and latched on to it, his eyes closed in total abandonment as he began his first attempts to suck. Mattie leant back and was content.

The district nurse felt the shadow of the crow across the window as she came back into the room. She wasn't superstitious, but this had been a good birth, easy for a first one considering the baby's size, and she was taking no chances. She put down her can of hot water, dropped the armful of clean sheets on the end of the bed and marched to the window, but she was too late, the black bird had already gone, flying home on strongly beating wings towards Oaklands Park.

For a while, he seems to pause over the small lake in the grounds, turned to sheet gold by the dying sun. His glance appears to rest meditatively for an instant on the old, broken-down boathouse and the rotten posts of the old jetty still standing above the water, and the sombre conifers surrounding the lake, and the red cliff of the Hill rising above. He wasn't alive at the time of the happenings there, but perhaps some atavistic memory stirs in him. Neglected, like everything during the last few years and never very sturdy, the

16

boathouse itself now looks ready to follow the jetty into the lake.

Warrant Officer Jack Shawcross, 1st Battalion, Duke of Wellington's Yorkshire Regiment, lay on the bed that had been wheeled out on to the terrace, the blankets rearranged around him by Nurse Wentworth before she went off duty. He watched the colony of birds noisily settling on their nests in the tall, leafless elms opposite, their branches a black tracery against the cold sunset. Rooks or crows, he could never be sure which birds they were, though he had plenty of time to observe them, with nothing much else to do but look into the blank void that was his future. Wondering whether it was possible to be so broken, and yet find the possibility of going on.

At night, when the roaring dreams and sweats came, and the agony in his non-existent legs began, he tried not to think about golden-haired Emily, the girl he'd been engaged to, and the last letter she'd sent him.

Chapter Two

1901–1905

The Wentworth family had not always lived here at Broughton, in the gloomy rectory. When the children were young, they had all lived in Worcester, in a pleasant house called White

Lodge, just off the cathedral close. They had a pony and trap, the little girls went to a small school run by the genteel daughters of Canon Wigmore, they had a large garden to play in, a pretty house to live in, a handsome father, the Reverend Francis Wentworth, and a beautiful, much admired mother.

Mama had been – well, a less vibrant version of Amy, delicately pretty, with large hazel eyes fringed with dark lashes and an amazing cloud of hair of that shade of red she had passed on to all of her children, in varying degrees. Nella's most lasting memories were of her reclining on the sofa in the drawing room, looking too fragile to hug, but palely smiling, smelling of violets and always wearing lovely, becoming clothes. Sometimes she read them stories, or played the piano for them to sing to, but they were not encouraged, in general, to pester her too much in case their boisterousness should bring on one of her headaches, or fainting fits.

Their papa, a tall man like William was to become, extracting his fob watch from his top pocket after half an hour of their company, seeing Dorothea reach for her smelling salts, would suggest, 'Perhaps it's time for you to go and play now, children, and leave Mama alone to rest for a little while.'

Mama, smiling faintly, would add, 'My darlings, you know how I love having you all around me. But my head ... your voices. Just a little ... piercing, I'm afraid.'

But sometimes, Nella did not really believe that Mama *did* like having them in the drawing room

– or not when Papa was there.

Guiltily, they would creep out into the garden, followed by Queenie, their shaggy English sheep-dog puppy, and for a while play as quietly as possible, so that the noise they made should not reach as far as the drawing room. But after a while natural high spirits would prevail and William would persuade his sisters to embark on one of his adventurous games, climbing into the orchard over the wall, for instance, where they weren't supposed to go because it didn't belong to them. Nella, small and quick, ready for anything, would in any case usually do whatever William suggested, but Marianne, more often than not, preferred to be alone, lying on the grass or rocking gently on the swing, her red-gold curls, fine and soft as spun sugar, spread like a curtain over her shoulders, not doing anything in particular. Dreaming, as usual.

Amy had been born when Nella, the youngest, was four, in January, 1901, on the same day that the old queen died. Everyone expected her, like so many other baby girls born on that day, to be named Victoria, in honour of the queen's memory, but Dorothea had already chosen names for her unborn child – Amyas if it should be a boy, after her father, since William had been named for Francis's father, and Aimée if, disappointingly, it should turn out to be another girl. Aimée it was, but no one now ever bothered with the fancy, Frenchified pronunciation Mama had no doubt intended, except Amy herself, as she grew older. Dorothea was not there to enforce it. Four years after Amy was born, she gave birth to another baby daughter who died after just two days, and then she herself followed, leaving a legacy of guilt behind: with her son and elder daughters, feeling that if they had been better children, quieter, their voices not quite so *piercing,* their mama might not have died; and with their father...

Well, who knew what Francis felt?

No one except, perhaps, Eleanor Villiers, Dorothea's mother, and she could only suspect. Dorothea had never been strong, and Eleanor's late husband, an otherwise sensible and down-to-earth doctor, had been neither where his daughter was concerned. Amyas could deny her nothing, she could do no wrong, with the result that Dorothea – pretty, spoilt, and difficult into the bargain – had really never shown much sense.

Even in her own pain over the loss of her daughter, Eleanor could find room to pity Francis's obvious agony, but all the same, she thought, lips tightening ... a delicate mother, four children already! In the first place, William's difficult birth had nearly cost his mother her life, and a strained three years had followed, during which Eleanor had prayed that he would be their only child, but then another two babies, first the peaceful Marianne, then lively, energetic little Nella, appeared in quick succession, and later Amy, none of them easy births. That should certainly have been the end of it. But when it came down to it, Francis, despite his splendid appearance in the pulpit, the eloquent sermons, delivered with such conviction in his mellifluous voice and listened to with such respect, hadn't shown much sense, either. He, a man of the cloth, a man of high principles, should surely have shown some restraint. And surely knew it.

After Dorothea died, Eleanor decided she had better stay on with the family to help out, not only from a sense of duty and because she was in any case lonely in her recent widowhood and needed something to fill her life, but because she loved her now motherless grandchildren, and there was little prospect of their father, wrapped up in his own troubles, offering the guidance they needed.

They were to leave Worcester and the cathedral, and their house, their school, their friends, everything they had previously known. Only Florrie would go with them, for she was to be four-year-old Amy's nurse. She was far too sensible a young woman to remain a parlourmaid, said Grandmama Villiers, their dear Grandy, who would be giving up her own house to come and live with them when they moved.

'But I don't want to go away!' declared Nella passionately, stamping her foot. 'I *won't* go if we can't take Queenie!'

'Now, now, Fenella, don't be silly!' Grandy spoke severely. 'Of course Queenie will be coming with us; she's a country dog, you know. She'll love it at Broughton Underhill. And so will you when you get there.'

Nella was absolutely determined she would hate it. It was all going to be quite horrid, strange and new; only for lucky William would it make little difference. His life was now centred on his prep school twenty miles away, and they said he could just as easily make the journey from there in the holidays (and later from Rugby, where he was to go when he was old enough) to their new home, which would be the rectory at Broughton Underhill.

'Does that mean, Father,' William asked, when they were summoned into Papa's study some two weeks after the funeral, 'that you'll be rector there?'

No, Francis told them. He would not be the rector. In fact, he would no longer be practising as a clergyman at all.

So *that* was why he was wearing a stiff collar and a tie, instead of his clerical dog collar. The children had absorbed, if not fully understood, through scraps of conversation picked up, and hints given by their mother, the belief that their father was settled here as a member of the cathedral chapter until one day he would be appointed dean, or archdeacon, or possibly bishop. This last they could well believe, their father being such a God-like creature. But what they had just heard was a puzzle, unmapped territory. Nella looked at her sister but Marianne, almost as though she hadn't heard, was far away as usual, dreamily watching a robin on the window sill outside who seemed intent on attacking his own reflection in the glass. Nella was still feeling mutinous about the move, though she had been somewhat reassured by hearing that at least their grandmother would continue to be with them. So much had changed and become alarming lately, but Grandy was always the same: kind – though quite strict, and sometimes rather sad since Grandpapa, and now Mama, had died.

22

'Father...' William began, then hesitated. Twelve years old and already big for his age, muscular and athletic, untidy, his hair flopping over his forehead, he stood rigid and pale, the freckles on his nose standing out. He was growing up fast and had sensed things in the atmosphere, was nothing if not courageous – and had learnt more from the boys at his prep school than not to call his father the babyish 'Papa' any longer.

'What is it, William?'

'Oh, nothing ... it doesn't matter ... it's nothing, not really, sir.'

'William, you know me better than to believe that will serve as an answer.'

William went from white to red. Shuffled his feet. 'Is there...? Have you...?' He stopped and then came out with it in an embarrassed rush: 'Is there ... anything *wrong*, sir?' There was only one reason, William had discovered, why clergymen parted company with the Church. Disgrace. And the whispers, like the ones that had followed the tutor at his school who had disappeared one day, never to return.

Francis's deep, dark gaze was bent on him. 'Not in the eyes of the world, if that is what you are trying to say. It is entirely my own choice, and what is wrong is a matter between me and God.' His frown, and his tone, remote and far away, forbade any further questions.

Nella held on to Marianne's hand, as much to reassure Marianne as herself, for she often felt as though it was she who was the elder sister. William stood straight as a ramrod. They looked at their father, speechless, not understanding, their eyes begging for an explanation which Francis struggled for but was not able to give, since he barely understood what was happening himself. He turned his back and in his turn looked out of the window, then said in a curious, hoarse voice, without turning round, 'That's all, children. You may go.'

Papa had never been a very *jolly* sort of father, not the sort who picked you up and gave you rides on his shoulder, made jokes or played French cricket with you in the garden, like other people's fathers did, though he sometimes smiled and patted you on the head. He was never unkind, or even very stern. But he was not the sort you could talk to, and his authority and rightness were not to be questioned. Outside the family, people spoke of him with a little awe, although everyone said he was not only the best-looking, but the most looked-up-to clergyman on the cathedral staff as he strode round the close with his quick, impatient stride, heels ringing, the skirts of his cassock flying.

But after Mama died, he had shut himself away for days in his study, and when he emerged he had become a different and rather frightening man. He hardly smiled at all, spoke rarely, and when he did he sometimes offended people.

He was, in fact, so rude to Nanny Rudd that she upped and left – or was sent packing, according to Marianne. Although she went about with her head in the clouds, as Nanny so often accused her, Marianne always remembered everything she heard – or overheard. This time it was what Nanny had said to Florrie (who wasn't Florrie

24

then but still Greenwood, the parlourmaid), and though Marianne didn't really understand it, she knew it had made Grandy very angry. 'Well, I don't care, I'm sure, Florrie!' Nanny had said. 'I can't live in the same house as that man a minute longer, anyway! Wouldn't even look at his own baby, poor mite – can you believe that? It wasn't *the child's* fault she died,' she had finished, inexplicably. 'He's a man, after all, and we all know–'

'That's quite enough, Nanny,' Grandy had said sharply, entering the room just in time to hear this last.

So Nanny departed, and Nella had declared, 'I don't *care* that she's gone,' using the absolutely forbidden phrase ('don't care is made to care, miss!') since Nanny herself had used it. 'She's a beast! And you're not to scold me for saying that, either, Marianne!'

'I wasn't going to,' said Marianne mildly. 'I agree with you, she is.'

Nanny Rudd hadn't been comfortable or kind, not like the nanny of their friends the Collins girls. She was strict and sharp and had strong fingers that dug into their scalps when she washed their hair, and pulled it back painfully when she tied their black bows. She saw to it that everything they wore was starched: their pinafores, handkerchiefs and even their drawers. Itchy britches, Nella named them. She was only nice to William, even when he was cheeky or disobedient. But then, nearly everybody was.

Broughton Underhill turned out to be a small, straggling community of some three hundred souls, a village situated in a valley between two ridges of hills and dominated by the largest of them, Broughton Hill, known simply as the Hill. The brisk climb to the top was strenuous, but the view from the top was worth it. On the one side the green Worcestershire countryside rolling towards the distant Welsh mountains. On the other, half a dozen miles away and spreading outwards as far as the eye could see towards Birmingham, began the industrial sprawl of the Black Country, which William, home from school and full of the history he'd learnt there, informed Nella had once been a great forest, the hunting preserve of kings. Land which was now despoiled, riven by canals and railways, punctuated with smoke stacks and great glass-work cones, its trees cut down years ago for fuel, its rich ores mined to feed blast furnaces and steel mills.

Sometimes, the more restless young men left the village to seek work in the nail and chain shops, the iron foundries of Cradley Heath, Halesowen or Blackheath, the glass works in Stourbridge and Brierley Hill, or they went in the other direction, to the carpet factories in Kidderminster, looking for betterment, or purely from a sense of adventure. But mostly people stayed: there was usually enough work on the Oaklands Park estate and the farms, up at the gravel pits or the brickworks, and if you worked for the estate, they looked after you for life. Apart from that, there was nothing much else in Broughton: some small houses and cottages, the schoolhouse and the Greville Arms, the smithy next door, the church of St Ethelfleda and the gloomy rectory where the Wentworth family were to live. And of course, the Big House itself, Oaklands Park.

Amy had only the vaguest recollections of the family's first arrival in Broughton. Nella laughed and declared she could have had no recollections at all, since she was only four years old at the time; she only thought she had, from the stories she'd heard so often of that day when they had all arrived there. But she must have remembered some things, since she could hear in her mind, quite vividly, Grandy's shocked exclamation at her first sight of the rectory, dark and forbidding, its tall, dilapidated chimneys vying with the square church tower for height, looking as though it were being pulled back into the clutches of what seemed like a forest of ancient and forbidding dark yews behind it, planted too near the house. It was a huge barn of a place, built at a time when rectors regularly had families of ten, eleven or more. Missing slates, peeling paintwork, collapsed guttering...

Inside it was worse. Dusty, moth-eaten curtains; dark wallpaper, stained and discoloured by damp; old furniture from earlier decades, most of it no doubt the unwanted property of previous incumbents, since the huge pieces were all but immovable, left stranded about the place like beached whales. It was piercingly cold.

Worst of all was the big stained-glass staircase window which increased the gloom of the high, cavernous hall rather than lighting it. Mrs Villiers speculated on the nature of the rector who had chosen such a highly unsuitable subject for a window in a rectory. Susannah and the Elders.

Who wanted to be faced every day when they came down the stairs with two lecherous old men spying on a young woman bathing in her garden? The girls giggled when they saw it, but fortunately the window was so dark and gloomy, and further obscured by the huge yews outside, that the subject could only be discerned properly on close inspection.

This unprepossessing house had become their new home entirely due to the elderly incumbent of St Ethelfleda's, the Reverend Wilfred Dorkings, having endured a particularly bad bout that year of his annual bronchitis, after which he had no option but to give up the struggle and live with his niece, the village schoolmistress, while still continuing as rector. Father Dorkings was a saintly bachelor who cared nothing for luxury (unless it was candles and incense in his High Church) and had lived mainly in the kitchen and his study, where he also slept, not even noticing the depredations which time, damp and neglect had wrought. Since he made no complaints to Lady Sybil, in whose gift the rectory and the living of St Ethelfleda were, the state of the house had gone unnoticed, and when she received the letter from Francis Wentworth (who had been a significant presence in her life since she was a child, her cousin Dorothea's husband, and a frequent visitor to Oaklands) telling her of his abrupt and astonishing abandonment of the ministry, and his having nowhere to live, she had made the offer of the now empty house.

On their arrival Eleanor Villiers, having summed up the situation in one look, set her lips in a firm line. 'Very well!'

The next day, in a violet silk gown trimmed with ecru lace, her many-tailed furs dripping over her shoulders and clasped together over her bosom with the beady-eyed mask of the unfortunate little animal who had provided them, her best towering grey velvet and moiré hat skewered firmly to her hair with an outsize pearl hatpin, her first action was to have old Strudwick, the verger and sexton, harness the pony into the trap and drive up to Oaklands Park, taking the reins herself. She had known Sybil since she was a baby and, outraged at the dirt and discomfort they were expected to be grateful for, had no compunction in giving her a piece of her mind.

What had she been thinking of, she demanded, sitting very upright in the comfort of Lady Sybil's warm, flower-scented drawing room, sipping Earl Grey from delicate Crown Derby china balanced in her hand, what could have possessed Sybil to offer such a backhanded gift – nothing more than a hovel, when it came down to it, she added, exaggerating for good measure – to a bereaved, motherless, penniless family? This last was a further exaggeration. Francis was not, in fact, entirely penniless: he had a private income, though only just about adequate to cover William's school fees and the day-to-day expenses of looking after his family – and there was in fact nothing backhanded about Sybil's offer, though it had indeed crossed Eleanor's mind to wonder about the mixed motives which had caused her to offer the house, and Francis to accept.

Sybil was mortified. 'Really? As bad as that, is

it? I must confess I haven't had occasion to visit the rectory for years. I will certainly see that something is done at once.'

For all the fashionable clothes, the society manners, she hasn't really changed, Eleanor thought, she is still the same generous, impulsive, careless girl she always has been – in fact, she has turned out better than ever anyone would have expected, considering the circumstances of her upbringing. Sybil's mother had died when she was a young child, and her profligate and unheeding father, John Greville, Earl of Broughton, as careless of his only child's welfare as he was of his inheritance, had left her in the care of a succession of indifferent nurses and governesses who turned a blind eye to her roaming the countryside, wild as a deer, with the gamekeeper's son, until this state of affairs became no longer tenable even to her father. She was sent to live in London with his sister to be transformed from a hoyden into a young lady, relieving him of responsibility for her while he pursued his gambling and, under a mountain of debts, let the house slide into shabby and disgraceful ruin. The estate itself remained in better case, the earl having his reputation of being one of the best shots in England to keep up. Although he had found it necessary to sell land off piecemeal to stave off his debtors, the woods and coverts remained well managed and maintained.

Despite her protests, Sybil's eventual debut into society was a success, if measured by the whirl of her activities, the friends she made. She was never a beauty, her features were too strong for that, but she was lively and popular and learnt how to dress well. It would have amazed no one if she had sold up and never returned to the dereliction that was Oaklands on her father's death, but in fact she had confounded everyone by marrying a rich industrialist much older than herself, whose money enabled her to restore the house to its former glory. Arthur Foley was a self-made man and something of a rough diamond, but he had a kind heart and Mrs Villiers wouldn't have been surprised if he hadn't had something to do with Sybil's offer of the rectory.

She was wrong in this. Sybil was, in fact, taken aback by a situation she hadn't truly known to exist, and aghast at how her neglect of her rector must have appeared. Moreover, the picture painted by Mrs Villiers had brought back to her what it was like to live in a run-down house – a hateful memory never far from her mind – and she promised to make amends, by way of despatching workmen to repair the roof, to paint and paper, hang new curtains and do anything else that needed to be done. Incapable of doing anything by halves, she went on to suggest that the two eldest girls, Marianne and Nella, might be allowed to share her daughter's governess for their lessons. Miss Osgood only had Eunice to teach, her brother, Greville, being away at school, of course.

Much mollified by all this, Mrs Villiers forgave. She thanked Sybil warmly, and added that she thought Francis might well agree to this solution to the girls' education, something he appeared not to have taken into account.

Her visit to Oaklands had in fact been most

satisfactory, she decided as she drove the pony trap back and into the stable behind the rectory but even so, she could not imagine how they were ever going to make this house into anything resembling a comfortable – even a warm – home.

But she and Florrie (who was already beginning to take on the indispensable role she was soon to occupy: nanny, housekeeper, cook, and dispenser of comfort, brisk advice and support) set themselves the task of creating order out of chaos and, as women do, quite enjoyed it if the truth be told.

There wasn't much they could do about the cold. The bedrooms were worst of all, stifling in summer but so icy in winter that the flowery patterns of hoar frost, actually inside the windows when the children woke, were sometimes still there when they went to bed at night.

Lady Sybil, however, had crowned her generosity with one hitherto unimaginable luxury: a bathroom was installed, with hot water provided by the kitchen boiler and stored in a huge copper cylinder that loomed like a leviathan in one corner of the bathroom, a great comfort on which all three girls, despite being expressly forbidden to do so, would perch in winter while Marianne told them stories she had made up, huddled together like birds on a chimney pot to get warm before diving between the icy sheets and curling up into a ball to conserve any warmth they'd managed to gain.

In a small village like Broughton Underhill, where nearly everyone was someone else's sister, parent, brother-in-law or cousin twice removed, newcomers were of intense interest and the Wentworths were at first objects of much speculation. Francis was, in fact, remembered by many as a frequent visitor to Oaklands, as a child and later, when he had spent weekends there taking part in the shoots, both before and after his marriage, and when word got around that he was in holy orders, it was believed that he was there to offer assistance to the ailing Father Dorkings and to be ready to step into his shoes when he retired. Instead, here they had a clergyman who rarely darkened the doors of the church, and never ministered; a gentleman who was obviously of somewhat straitened means, yet who was not visibly employed. His tall figure soon became a familiar sight, tramping interminable miles over the hills, that great woolly sheepdog at his heels, and eventually it came to be accepted that he was unlikely to be seen much in church, alongside the rest of his family. Mrs Villiers saw to it that they, at least, attended the services every Sunday. The children were often about the village, where they were liked for their unaffected manners, especially little Amy, who chattered to everyone and was given sweets and patted on the head because she looked so pretty.

Eunice, with whom the girls now shared lessons, was pretty too, a sweet-natured creature, but so shy and timid with anyone she didn't know well, it was painful to watch. She was a delicate little girl who suffered from a bad chest and indeed looked as if a puff of wind would blow her away.

Grev they only saw when he was home from Shrewsbury. An intense boy, very highly strung, his dark eyes too big for his pale face, he was doted on by his mother. Funny Grev, people said, so odd, but so talented. He was always playing some musical instrument or other – the piano, or the cello, or whatever his fancy had settled on at that particular time – and had already decided what he was going to be when he grew up: Greville Foley, composer, he told them, matter-of-factly. He was constantly scribbling at little pieces of music he was creating and became impatient with his sister and Nella when Marianne alone showed any enthusiasm for being allowed to play these with him. All three girls were of course taught the piano as a necessary accomplishment for young ladies by Miss Osgood, but Marianne was the only one who persevered beyond practising scales and learning to play simple pieces.

Mrs Villiers had once hoped Francis would find his salvation in marrying again, but that hope soon perished, though salvation of a sort did come when Father Dorkings, growing more frail, managed to persuade Francis (though only Father Dorkings knew how) to assist him in the parish, acting as a sort of unofficial curate, until someone could be found to take the old rector's place so that he could retire. However, no other clergyman could be persuaded to accept a living where the rectory was occupied by someone else, and this unsatisfactory situation – to Eleanor at least – continued, though Francis gave no indication as to whether he found it so or not.

But all that was before the war. A war which had begun in some obscure corner of Europe and gathered momentum until it involved the whole world, changed the face of Europe and wiped out a whole generation of young men. Yet, even when it was over, after four long years, and peace had come at last, there was no question for the Wentworth family of returning to life as it had been ... that life had ended abruptly, gone for ever, with a tragedy that had nothing to do with the war.

Life as they knew it had ended on that cataclysmic day at the beginning of August, in 1914, when the world was already swinging crazily round on its axis, out of control, as if it were the great lump of clay Joel Rafferty threw on his potter's wheel before getting it centred and shaping it into submission. Such a clamour, an upheaval, so many things happening at once. The country turning to preparations for war and all that entailed. The huge thunderstorm that night, like a prelude to the thunder that would presently roll over Europe. All of which had seemed at that time almost an irrelevance, shocking as that might seem now, of less importance then than the personal calamity which had altered the lives of the Wentworths for ever.

The day they had lost Marianne. The day the music stopped.

Chapter Three

1914

But the world did not stop. Marianne had gone, for ever, but the world rumbled on, the war gathered momentum. And in the end there was no question, as far as Nella was concerned, of staying meekly at home while every young man of her acquaintance was marching off to war, eager to defend poor little Belgium from its arrogant invaders, the Germans, who had marched through neutral territory on their way to northern France and thus to Paris. Since she was prevented by her sex from becoming a soldier, she had done the next best thing and taken herself off to enlist as a VAD nurse. She had screwed up her hair, put on a severe felt hat 'borrowed' from Florrie, and added years to her age in order to appear old enough to serve in France when she'd completed her training, and though she knew the doctor signing her up had not believed her, the shortage of nurses, plus her earnestness and determination, must have carried her through.

She began her training in a big London teaching hospital where she learnt that windows must be opened three inches during the day and two at night, and to straighten the castors of beds so that they were not a quarter of an inch out of line, that a speck of dust was a sin, to make hospital corners when tucking in the sheets, and to obey Sister at all times. She did not see a wounded soldier until troop trains arrived bringing the hundreds of wounded and dying men from the battlefield they called the Somme.

Enormous as the shock of this was, it did not prepare her for what she encountered when she was sent overseas to nurse the casualties there. 1916. Flanders. Plunged straight into the thick of it with her fellow nurses, there she had the first taste of what war really meant.

Dear Father, Grandy and Amy,

Well, here I am at last, on active service, after a seasick crossing over the Channel which I will not upset you by describing. I have been assigned to a camp hospital, comprising long lines of camouflaged marquees which serve as wards, with tarpaulin passages connecting them. I am billeted in a bell tent with my friend, Daisy Musgrave. (You remember her, my fellow VAD who trained with me in London.) It's all very military, but our tents are quickly becoming our home, with all our own things around us.

Like everyone else, I have brought too many clothes and personal possessions with me, though no doubt there will come a time when I shall be very glad to get out of uniform and into civvies for visiting the town when I'm off duty. Daisy has carted a gramophone with her everywhere, through thick and thin. She plays the latest dance music all the time and teaches me all the newest steps.

Don't worry about me – we are well fed and watched over and chaperoned within an inch of our lives. We thought the hospital rules in London were strict but that was nothing to what they are here!

To keep up the morale of the men, there are concerts and sing-songs which we nurses are graciously allowed to attend, and jollifications organised for the men who are well enough, often with soldier dancing comically with soldier at these, because nurses must not partner them. Nurses must not dance with other nurses, either ... nurses must not wear their own fur collars around their necks to keep out the icy wind as they run from their tents to the wards ... nurses must not, ever, consort in public with officers ... nurses must be saints, not human beings. So you can see how difficult this must be for me!

I am lucky to be bunking up with Daisy. She's awfully nice, such fun and never grumbles, though this nurse's life she has chosen is harder for her than for most, since she comes from a very grand family, and has never before needed to lift a finger to help herself. (Unlike me, with a sensible grandmama who has always brought us up to be useful around the house; thank you, Grandy!) She is very pretty and has lovely thick fair hair which is a great trial to her and keeps slipping down because she's always had a maid to pin it up properly before. But she never minds when she has to do the jobs everyone hates, and she's better than anybody at keeping the boys' spirits up. They call her Sister Sunshine.

We VADs are all known to the Tommies as 'sister' much to the fury of the pukka, qualified sisters, which must be galling for them, after all. Their rank is very important to them, after the years of training, hard work and little pay they've had to endure to reach it. They keep up their self-importance by ordering us about as if we were children, and not very intelligent ones at that, but we are used to this by now and most of them relent when they get to know us. "Your assistance is not without its drawbacks, Miss Wentworth," was all Sister Johnson said to me when I dropped and broke a syringe the other day.'

In the letters home which Nella wrote for those Tommies who were not able to write for themselves, they spoke jokingly of the rain, rain, rain, which would not drain away in this low-lying land, and played down how it filled with mud the bomb craters, and the overflowing trenches they were compelled to fight in; they did not mention that men, guns and horses were regularly drowned in the thick ooze, and did not speak of the horrific wounds and the deaths of their comrades; nor of the stink of death and corruption from unclaimed, unburied bodies, and the latrines which could be smelt half a mile away.

And neither did Nella mention the shock which had awaited her and her fellow volunteers. She was only one of the many young, half-trained girls, for the most part gently raised, living previously sheltered lives, most of whom had never even seen a half-dressed man before, never mind a naked male body. Having to do for them the intimate things which might help them to survive, nursing the sick and wounded in improvised, primitive and often filthy conditions which would have horrified the strict training hospitals they had so recently left. Cutting off mud-caked uniforms before they should set like cement, in order to tend stinking, gangrenous wounds and horrifying internal injuries, dressing the stumps of limbs lost by red-hot shrapnel, which could slice through an arm or a leg as easily as a piece of spaghetti; it all became second nature.

'*But I've left my best bit of news until last,*' she had concluded that first letter. '*Grev is working here, too! Can you imagine how astonished we both were – me, especially? He was the last person I expected to see.*'

In one of those happenings which are called coincidences, but which happened all the time in the random chaos of this war, she and Greville Foley had found themselves working in the same unit, she nursing and Grev as a non-combatant stretcher-bearer, a job which earned the respect of everyone, since it meant plunging out into no-man's-land in the thick of enemy fire to bring back the wounded and dying. Unarmed, not trained to use weapons or handle ammunition, their only defence a white brassard, or armband, with a scarlet cross on it.

Chapter Four

Now, four years later, and with the end of the war and Oaklands as a hospital ceasing to exist, Nella's work as a nurse was coming to an end, and there was an alarming gap stretching in front of her, an emptiness she couldn't think how she was going to fill.

'Why don't you carry on nursing, become qualified?' Miss Inman had suggested. 'We need more women of your calibre in the profession.'

A life devoted to the alleviation of human suffering sounded worthy and lofty, and many of

40

the other temporary nurses she had served with were seeking in it an escape from what might well now be a life of idle, enforced spinsterhood, but Nella didn't feel that was justification enough. She had volunteered and done her duty willingly, and not only because she had found in it an antidote to the restlessness which had consumed her before the war. But now she was, in effect, back where she had started: even in those pre-war days she had upset a good many people by rejecting what she had seen as the aimless life projected for her, its sole object to get herself married as soon and as well as possible.

Oaklands Park was a Queen Anne house built of brick that time had turned to a warm rose pink, in its approach looking smaller than it actually was, being tall and narrow at the front, flat-faced and shallow-roofed, four storeys high, but stretching out a long way towards the back. Wall shrubs spread out at its base, seeming to anchor the tall house to the ground and prevent it looking top-heavy, while climbing the walls were Virginia creeper and roses – Gloire de Dijon, Albertine, Zephirine Drouhin (a bad choice, this – a rose of a vibrant pink colour that clashed horribly with the brick, but kept because it was thornless, had a rich fragrance and bloomed continuously). Where the carriageway from the road ended, the hundred-yard-long drive began, running ruler straight towards the front steps between a double row of yews, with grass stretching either side behind them, in turn flanked by matching herbaceous borders against brick walls, until the drive swept into a circle round a central fountain and then continued round towards the back.

Nella emerged from the back door with her usual haste, passed the stables and the carriage house now used to accommodate motor vehicles and ambulances, and made for the arched wooden door set in the old brick wall, struck anew by a glimpse of the disorderly aspect of the ornamental garden at the front. The borders were overgrown, with last year's growth not cut back, the gravel was grass-grown and weed-infested; the roses on the walls, taking advantage of neglect, lolled unsupported and unpruned; the shaggy yews nearly touched each other, almost begging for their annual clip into the neat candle-flame shapes Lady Sybil had always been so particular about. Trimming them was a four-man-and-a-boy job and there was only Hughes and his garden boy now, where once there had been six men employed to look after the gardens, three of whom would never return.

Hughes had left a basket of vegetables for her outside the potting shed. Despite all the odds, he'd managed to keep his kitchen garden in good shape. The glasshouses might be empty of the peaches, nectarines and grapes, the hothouse roses and stephanotis which had filled them before the war, but the neat rows of cabbages, potatoes and onions were what mattered now, and kept the family in fresh produce, with some to spare. Compared to those unlucky beings in the towns and cities, Broughton Underhill, accustomed to being self-sufficient, had never gone hungry in the wartime years; they'd never

had to queue miserably for even the bare
necessities as food became scarcer and dearer.
Sugar and tea rationing had hit them as hard as
everyone else, and meat and dairy produce had
been commandeered by the government, but
what farmer was going to deny his family and
friends a bit of butter, enough milk? In one or
two backyards the odd clandestine pig rooted,
hidden from officialdom – while snaring rabbits
and hares and taking a game bird or two for the
pot was an inherited skill for some in Broughton,
and easy enough when lame old Scuddy Thomas
was the only help the head gamekeeper had, and
they both turned a blind eye, anyway.

Nella picked up the basket of parsnips and
carrots and let herself out through the wicket
gate that opened onto the ancient oak woods
which had given the house its name. She hurried
on, and as she reached the stile, the clock over
the old stables chimed the half-hour and for a
moment she hesitated, but then she climbed the
stile steps and perched on the top rail, pulling her
red-lined cloak around her. It wouldn't hurt to
snatch some time to herself.

A strong, cold wind blew across the fields and
she impatiently tucked back into the confines of
her uniform cap some escaped strands of the
slippery dark chestnut hair, less red than that
their mother had passed on to all the rest of the
family. Her mind jumped back again to what had
happened this morning, when she'd first heard
from matron the name of the doctor who would
be arriving within the next day or two to replace
the present MO, who was leaving the army for

good. Captain AD Geddes. Duncan Geddes. Yes, of course it was him, no mistake. And in a world which had for so long been so very dark and grey, a secret warmth flooded her.

She'd done her best to put the implications of his imminent arrival out of her mind while she worked, without conspicuous success, it had to be said. Panic touched her every time she thought of how she might react when they met. Even his name had stirred up feelings she thought she had controlled, despatched firmly into the past. What fate had sent him to Oaklands, of all places? Fate? Surely not. The thought that she might be working here must almost certainly have entered his mind.

She gazed, seeing and yet not seeing the familiar view which had shone like a glimpse of remembered Heaven beyond the mud and devastation in Flanders: rolling pastures and meadowlands extending to the ha-ha which protected the gardens of Oaklands from wandering cattle; to the left the big house itself, the figures on the terrace made tiny by distance. A tranquil, timeless scene. Transformed in autumn by the gold and amber of beech and oak, the trees were as yet bare and leafless, waiting for the true spring and the haze of bluebells that would spread beneath their feet. The dying sun was low and red in a cold green sky. A white flock of seagulls had flown inland, beautiful in flight, raucous and screaming as they followed the plough, scavenging for worms and small creatures fleeing from the blades as the earth was turned. The rows were arrow straight, a matter of pride and habit for Harry Packer, who'd learnt to plough a furrow trudging with his father behind the huge and heavy, patient Cleveland bays when he was thirteen. Still going strong at eighty-two, he should have been enjoying a comfortable retirement by now, but like his old 'osses, was still in harness and proud to be so – 'till the boys come home'.

In front of her, beyond the stile, lay the path that led across the field and down to the lake. Nella could look at that dark stretch of water now without trembling inside, but she still couldn't make herself pass through the stile and take the short cut from Oaklands to the rectory which passed by the lake. She, and all the family, were marked by what had happened there; they, and the others, too: Steven Rafferty, Eunice, Grev especially. And perhaps Rupert, though how would they ever know about Rupert?

From here, to the left, you could see the terrace at the back of the big house, and just about make out the distant figures on it. Once, a lifetime ago it seemed, scented women with stay-boned waists and pouter-pigeon busts, sweeping skirts and high-necked lacy blouses, had sat drinking Earl Grey from delicate Crown Derby china, with nothing better in the world to do than make flirtatious conversation with the men in stiff collars dancing attendance on them, ready to refill their cups or ply them with pretty little cakes and cucumber sandwiches, and pay them delicious, silly compliments. Unaware of the looming catastrophe which would shortly change their privileged world for ever. Now, behind the French windows that opened onto the terrace, Lady Sybil's once elegant, flower-filled drawing room, with its white marble fireplace, French porcelain and silk lampshades, was denuded, still part of the convalescent hospital it had been turned into at the beginning of the war.

Those women with their elaborate clothes, hair and jewellery seemed a distant dream that might never have happened; there were only nurses there now, noticeable from here by the white sails of their headdresses. And, of course, the men wearing the lurid hospital blue suits, white shirts and scarlet ties meant to proclaim their honourable wounds. Red, white and blue, the colours of patriotism. A stirring word which had summoned ardent young men in their thousands, eager to do their bit; an admonition that now had a hollow ring for those whose cost had been their limbs, their sight, their livelihood ... for some their sanity.

Nella could see them strolling or limping on crutches by the overgrown parterre, sitting in wheelchairs, reading or simply talking, with empty jacket sleeves, and trouser legs pinned up over missing legs, learning to readjust their lives. That would be Warrant Officer Shawcross lying in the bed she had wheeled out into the afternoon sunshine. She hoped Nurse Burkin, inclined to be too busy to be thoughtful, would remember to take him inside and give him an extra blanket before he became too chilled; it was growing late and he soon felt the cold, not being able to move about, though he never complained. Perhaps Eunice, kind, shy little Eunice, would see to it if she came in to talk to the patients, or read and write letters for them, as she had taken to doing, unasked.

Nella jumped down from the stile and wrapped her cloak more closely around her, picked up her basket and walked briskly on towards the rectory. The crows settled in their nests in the bare elms and the sun slid behind the belt of oaks that hid the village from Oaklands.

Joe Strudwick, verger, sexton and general handyman, had almost finished digging the grave for the funeral later that week of old Mrs Cromer as Nella pushed open the lychgate, and was leaning on his spade by the heaped earth in the corner, taking time for a smoke before going into the rectory for his tea, after which he'd be off home. He raised his hand to his cap when he saw Nella, and began to pack up his tools. She waved back and walked on.

The evening meal was nearly ready. The time was always arranged to suit Nella's working shifts, however awkward the hour, and as she opened the kitchen door, she was greeted by the homely smell of something savoury simmering gently on the hob, and the spicy scent of an apple pie Grandmama Villiers herself had made, she who had once barely known what it was to enter a kitchen.

Nella sensed something expectant in the air the minute she walked in. Grandy was wearing her neat, tucked-in little smile, and Florrie, sturdy, dour and unflappable as usual, was humming tunelessly under her breath, a good sign if ever there was one. As for Amy, curled up in Florrie's rocking chair by the fire, shoeless, polishing her fingernails with a tortoiseshell-backed nail buffer, she could hardly wait for Nella to get inside the door before making the breathless announcement that there was a letter on the dresser. 'Guess who from?'

'*And* there's a bacon hock Percy Troughton left when he brought the milk,' added Florrie, at the sink, draining potatoes and picking up the wooden masher. 'What a day!'

Nella was already making a beeline for the dresser.

'It won't disappear if you wait to take your outdoor things off, Nella,' said Mrs Villiers.

'And that hideous cap,' Amy added, swinging her foot and admiring the curve of her instep.

Nella absently snatched off the offending cap, universally hated by all VADs as well as Amy, leaving a red mark where it had rested low on her forehead, slipped off her cloak and began to read the letter eagerly, leaning against the dresser. She read the short message through, twice, then folded it and put it down carefully.

'Home. He's coming home.' William, home again! She spoke softly, quietly, otherwise she would have shouted for joy and felt perhaps she wouldn't be able to stop.

'But not just yet,' said Amy. 'He says he has things to do first. What things are more important than coming straight home?'

'He's going to Sussex, he says. I expect he's gone to see the Beresford parents.'

'Oh.' Amy flushed. She knew William and his friend had been right through the war together,

48

right until Piers Beresford had been killed, just a few weeks before the Armistice was signed. There was a moment of silence. But then Nella couldn't help grabbing her grandmother round the waist and whirling her around. Everyone was beaming, even Grandy, whose smile was usually as neatly controlled as her greying hair and the upright carriage of her little figure. And Florrie, who scarcely smiled at all. William was suddenly there, in the room amongst them. Tall and broad-shouldered, his thick thatch of foxy hair flopping untidily over his forehead, his eyes crinkling at the corners when he laughed.

'How very fortunate we are,' said Mrs Villiers softly.

Florrie, red from the fire, suddenly found a reason to examine the bacon more closely, forking it up and letting it hang suspended, dripping over the pot, pink and succulent, the skin glistening golden brown, before flipping it expertly onto a plate. 'Well, it's a nice bit of bacon,' she remarked after a minute, 'and bit's the word all right, though I suppose we should be grateful for what we can get, and I dare say the stock'll make some good pea soup.' She removed the rind and began to slice the meat from the bone – it was mostly bone, and pathetically small for five people. 'Make short work of this, Mr William would,' she went on, eyeing its proportions with resignation. 'The major, we shall all have to call him now, I suppose – fancy!'

'I don't imagine he'll want us to call him anything of the sort, Florrie, if I know William.' Mrs Villiers divested herself of her apron, hung it tidily behind the door and patted her hair. 'It's more likely he'll want to forget the army as soon as possible.'

'Hmm. Well, major or not, it'll be grand to see him again, and I'm sure Strudwick'll be glad of someone to help bring in the coal, not to mention seeing to that pile of leaves blocking the gutters. He don't fancy ladders nowadays, says he's getting too old.'

Eleanor Villiers smiled again, not envisaging immediately co-opting William into the role of handyman, though he'd always enjoyed energetic work, making himself useful, but thinking more of the warmth he would bring into the house, the vitality and sense of purpose. She for one would not be sorry at that. It was time to put the past behind them, and not only the war years but the unresolved mystery which the enormity of the war itself had overshadowed.

Amy was delightedly imagining the excitements that were sure to follow William's return.

The last time she had seen him she'd been a little overawed at her giant of a brother, so much older, so dashing in his army uniform, his Sam Browne gleaming, his peaked cap at a jaunty angle. Second Lieutenant William Wentworth, all geared up and ready to fight the Hun, trying to look serious and responsible, the effect spoilt by his big, cheerful smile, the freckles on his nose and the fact that he was just twenty-one. Straight out of university, his studies abandoned. How brave, Amy thought, how daring to do that. No wonder Papa had been so – disappointed. But no wonder, either, that William had been a hero, mentioned in despatches. She hugged to herself the warm, comfortable feeling that they were all to be together again, the whole family ... all except Marianne, of course. But Marianne had been gone for so long now, her image was already fading, and the sad feeling was hard to maintain, although the way she had died – and the guilt, and all the rest of it – still frightened Amy when she thought about it.

But there was always Nella. Her two elder sisters had been so close in age, talking and laughing together about things Amy didn't understand, that Amy used to feel excluded, but it was different now, had been ever since that night when Nella had cuddled Amy to sleep in her own bed, at the end of that awful day when Marianne had been found dead.

Nella removed her apron and drew on the cardigan her grandmother had thoughtfully set to keep warm for her on the rail over the boiler, and snuggled into its comforting warmth. 'Father's seen the letter, of course? What did he say?'

'You know your father, Nella. He's pleased – who wouldn't be? – but of course he won't show it.'

'No, I don't suppose he would.'

Another silence fell, this time of a different kind, an unease settling over the room like dust, a small cloud dimming, if only slightly, the joy of the moment. Francis Wentworth, who was against fighting for any reason whatsoever, had not been delighted when his only son had left Oxford before taking his degree. As a member of the Officers' Training Corps, both at school and university, William had had no difficulty in obtaining a commission, determined not to be left behind in the jingoistic fervour (as his father saw it) to fight for king and country when all his friends were doing the same; but the habit of non-communication between father and son was too strong to be broken and typically, after voicing his initial protests, Francis had shrugged and retreated into his books.

The big wooden clock on the wall gave its usual irritating whirr before bonging out a slow, unmusical five. Mrs Villiers said briskly, 'Well, time we were eating. Do stop fussing with your nails, Amy, this is *not* the place for that sort of thing. Put your shoes on, and give Florrie a hand with the dinner things. Make sure those plates are hot, Florrie.'

Florrie, having set aside her own portion, and a bit for Strudwick, which could be supplemented by that leftover sausage, juggled a pile of plates that were burning her fingers; there was no need for reminders – unless the plates were red hot from the oven, the food would be cold in a few minutes in that icebox of a dining room. Why they didn't eat in here, she couldn't think; they all congregated in the kitchen, or in the little parlour, for much of the time anyway, since they were the only really warm rooms in the house. The girls would have welcomed the idea, Florrie was sure, but she was equally certain that, although some standards had necessarily slipped during the war, the idea of dining in the kitchen would never have remotely occurred to Mrs Villiers. She had only recently given up changing for dinner every night.

'Will Father be joining us?' asked Nella, folding a cloth around a vegetable dish to carry it to the table. You could never be sure whether he would or would not.

'Not today,' replied Mrs Villiers. 'He'll have something in his study, perhaps, later.'

Nella and Amy exchanged glances. The atmosphere lightened perceptibly.

Chapter Five

Some hours after the telegram from William had been received, Francis Wentworth had finally abandoned his attempt to write his sermon, called for Queenie the Second, daughter of the first much lamented Queenie, and set out for a tramp over the hills.

He strode through the village, and walked steadily up the Hill. As he climbed higher and continued along the ridge, the wind grew keener, so icy it brought tears to his eyes and so strong it threatened to lift his tweed cap so that he had to jam it more firmly onto his head. Here, up on the brow, the trees bowed and swayed to their own wild songs. There was a smell of new earth and the clouds flew before the wind. He walked quicker, to keep warm. It was cold enough for snow. After a mild start, this March looked like turning into what they called around here a blackthorn winter: that unexpected snap of very cold, frosty weather just when the blackthorn blossom was giving promise of spring, which could nip the early flower buds and blight fruit in the bud. Nevertheless, the icy air invigorated him and soon his stride had achieved an effortless rhythm, with Queenie bounding along in front of him, stopping occasionally with her nose to the ground, sniffing for rabbits while his own thoughts whirled around in his mind.

The war which he had so bitterly opposed had at last, at last come to an end, and the son who had gone off so gallantly was coming home.

He was a little afraid of meeting William again. There were bridges to be built, and as yet he had no idea how that was to be accomplished. He and William had parted at the beginning of the war, not in anger, that was true, but in an uneasy truce. Francis had been unable to accept the war, and still could not, but had found no ally in his opposition to it except for young Grev, who had been as passionately opposed to it as he was, and who had yet died a hero's death in the midst of battle. He could hardly bear to think of that talented young life, extinguished.

He wondered, often several times a day, how he had allowed himself to drift into the situation in which he found himself. He was still comparatively young. Not in the mirror, perhaps, where he saw a bitter man robbed of his youth. Would he ever entirely rid himself of the legacy of those years following Dorothea's death, when he had struggled through a slough of despond, finding no one who could give him the spiritual assistance he needed, the absolution from guilt? He had not felt able to approach his fellow clergy for help, nor even his bishop – especially his evangelical bishop, projecting, as Francis had scornfully thought then, his own threadbare spirituality on to the world in general by writing popular books so that he had no actual time to spare for his flock. How do we misjudge others!

He was all too aware of his own major weakness, a reluctance in himself to face up to things, a wish to run away and hide, especially after his darling Dodo died. His mother-in-law, however, had not been prepared to let him get away with anything of the sort. She demanded tartly what he was going to do about his children, reminding him of his responsibilities to them, and since he knew they were not to blame for the punishment God was inflicting upon him it had pulled him up short: this period in the wilderness was a penalty he alone had to pay. And so, after some deliberation, he had written to Sybil.

He often wondered if that had not been the greatest mistake of his life.

He walked on, a prisoner of his dark thoughts, until presently he came to the wall which marked the boundary of Hatherley's lands, lying spread out below him on the descent into the next valley beyond Broughton. He cupped his hands and drank from the icy stream that tumbled down the hillside and found a spot where he could hitch himself onto the wall which dipped below the brow of the hill, out of the wind, while Queenie plunged about, muddying the edges of the water, happy with her own pursuits. He made sure the gate in the wall was shut. In the field below sheep and their new young lambs were grazing, a large flock spread over the hillside, and she could not always be trusted with sheep.

It had been nearly four years ago, twelve months or so into the war, when Father Dorkings had at last died, and the jovial bishop had come to see Francis. They had been given a good lunch by Mrs Villiers, repaired to the study, and after an almost indecently short interval the bishop had told him forthrightly that hiding here didn't mean he could hide from God. That he had no right to wallow in self-pity any longer. That ordained ministers were needed as chaplains to the forces in the front line and there was therefore no one to replace Father Dorkings. That it was time Francis pulled himself together, stopped running away and prepared to take his place as rector. Francis had felt as if he were a schoolboy being lectured by the Head.

He was offended by the simplistic approach to his problems, when he might at least have been entitled to put forward all his complex theological doubts in a scholarly exchange of views. More to the point, how could he stand up in the pulpit and offer comfort and advice to his congregation, when he had none to give? What could he give his parishioners, he asked, especially at this appalling time? What about his doubts as to the rightness of the war, and the place – or absence – of God in it?

'Do you think, then, that we don't all have such doubts? Do you think that any of us know the answers? But we carry on.'

The good bishop departed, leaving Francis in a state of confusion that bordered on hysteria. Had he been given no alternative, or was he still left to make a decision? Was the bishop really saying that God had not yet forgiven him, that he must expiate his guilt in this way, carry on for form's sake, as others seemed able to do, despite doubts and uncertainties?

He had given in. The lace and the incense that Father Dorkings had so loved disappeared and the village had a rector again. His parishioners did not expect too much, after Father Dorkings's unworldly ministry, and a hunting parson before him, and Francis began to feel, if not happy, then at least a little more at peace with himself. And no one but he – and God – knew what was in his heart.

In the wide bottom of the valley, the slow-winding stream curved round the Hill as it left Broughton and meandered off to join, eventually, the great Severn. Tucked into a fold of the opposite hill was the original farmhouse belonging to the Hatherleys, now several centuries old, low and red-roofed, looking as though it was some natural growth of the land. It was now occupied by tenant farmers, while situated dead centre of the valley was the very large and extremely ugly house which Hatherley's grandfather had built and moved into when he became rich on account of allowing the railway, a mile or so distant, to pass through his outlying farmlands. Landscaped gardens and a parkland surrounded the house. The whole valley looked as serene and well tended as the gardens themselves.

As he watched, Gervase Hatherley himself emerged from the house, his black retriever at his heels. Even from this distance, he looked self-important and was growing somewhat portly, though he could not yet be forty. He was dapper and correct as always in tweed knickerbockers and Norfolk jacket, a gun over his shoulder.

Ever since William's telegram had arrived, Francis had felt an astonishing compulsion in himself to go out and shout the news to the first person he met that his son was coming home, but he had not anticipated that person being Hatherley, and felt quite able to restrain himself. They had known each other a long time, from when he, Francis, had been a frequent visitor to Oaklands and Gervase Hatherley and his father had also been invited to join the shoots there, though at that time Francis had never taken much notice of him, dismissing him as a pleasant enough, mild and rather dull young man, ten or more years younger than himself. He was extremely wealthy, now a Justice of the Peace, and his standing in the community was high. It was nearly five years since he had come to Francis, asking permission to marry Marianne.

Francis had been more outraged at this than his daughter, who had hesitated, then professed herself well disposed towards Mr Hatherley, though she did not think she could marry him, but please, would her father not speak of it again – a request Francis had been only too happy to agree to. He could not, however, forget it, and had constantly tormented himself ever since by wondering whether his beautiful daughter would not still be alive had she been safely married to Hatherley. Should he not have considered the material advantages such a match would have brought, and tried to persuade her into it? It might have been possible. For all her sweet dreaminess, that daughter of his had not been devoid of common sense, when it came to the essentials of life.

Marianne ... the one of all his children who had done most to capture his heart. Marianne, with her dreams and ambitions. Who had died without ever knowing how proud he was of her, what his hopes were for her future.

There in the cold, dying light, out there alone on the empty hillside where nothing moved but the sheep, and the branches of the bare trees as the wind soughed its mournful music through them, he felt his familiar grief touched with a pang that was almost a physical ache. He did not at first recognise it as emptiness and loneliness, but as he turned and walked home in the gathering dusk, and saw the lamplight glowing from cottage windows, he thought of his solitary supper and his books awaiting him in his cold, monastic study, and decided suddenly that he would join his family that evening within the warm circle of firelight in the little parlour the girls had made their own.

He took his boots off in the porch at the side door. The fur underneath Queenie's belly was thick and tangled with drying mud, and she patiently allowed him to clean her up and towel her dry, pushing her black button nose into his face and trying to lick it, her long ears and fringe almost obscuring her blunt face. There were lights in the kitchen, and a dim lamp that was always left burning in the hall. The house was only relatively cold after the iciness outside and there was a smell of food, and he saw a light from under the dining room door which told him they had already started supper. Florrie would bring him something into his study, as soon as she was aware he was home, and for a moment he was tempted to leave it like that. But then he quickly cleaned himself up and popped his head round the kitchen door to let her know he would be joining the rest of his family.

Marianne had come to Francis quite unexpectedly, one day, when they had been living in Broughton Underhill upwards of five years and he was at his favourite occupation, dressing the leather bindings of his books. There had been a small but determined rap on his study door. 'Come in,' he called, not looking up.

Queenie the First had lumbered up from her blanket in the corner of the room she had appropriated as her own and loped across the floor, swinging her short bobtail to show her welcome. Since coming to Broughton, she had made it clear she was Francis's dog, sitting patiently by the door, waiting for him to take her out on one of his long, solitary rambles, following him everywhere and taking up permanent residence in his study. She was not as boisterous as she had been when she was a puppy, but all the same, her huge shaggy bulk nearly knocked Marianne over, tall as she'd grown lately.

Francis looked up. 'Well, Marianne?' He had a book on the desk in front of him and was patiently working oil into the smooth leather with his thumb, then polishing it with a soft cloth. The only things Father Dorkings had taken with him when he went to live with his niece at the schoolhouse were his books, leaving rows of empty shelves in his study. But Francis had more than enough of his own to fill them, books precious to him which had been carefully packed and transported here. The orderly rows of morocco bindings gleamed opulently, a silent reproach to the rest of the room, which was monastic in its austerity. A desk and chair, a table and a battered old sofa that had belonged to Father Dorkings, and that was all.

Marianne perched on the sofa, running her fingers through Queenie's fur, watching the gentle ministrations of her father's long hands. 'Why are you doing that, Papa?'

'To keep the bindings supple.' He indicated the bottle of thick, yellow oil. 'It's called neat's-foot oil, and it's made by boiling the feet and shinbones of cattle.'

'How perfectly horrid!'

'But that means it's a natural lubricant for leather.'

'Oh, yes. I see that.'

There followed an awkward pause. Marianne, very pale, her soft-spun hair, bright as a new penny and making a halo round her face as she looked down at her now clasped hands, said nothing. Queenie laid her big head on the girl's knee, looking with soulful eyes through her fringe, and nudging Marianne's hand with her nose, asking to be stroked. For once getting no response, she padded back to her corner and subsided with a sigh on to her blanket. 'Well,

61

child, was there something you wanted?'

Marianne took a deep breath. 'Papa, may I borrow one of your books?'

'A book?' he repeated as though it was an alien word he did not recognise, surrounded as he was by them. 'What do you want a book of mine for?'

'Well, I've read all the ones we have – hundreds of times.'

'What sort of book?' he asked helplessly, with a baffled glance at his collection of first editions and philosophical dissertations and religious treatises. Although he had no experience of the sort of literature girls of her age liked to read, Francis could not imagine her wanting to peruse any of the tomes on his shelves from choice. Nevertheless, he felt a distinct stirring of pleasure that she should have come to him to ask.

His children did not often do this. He endeavoured to be just and fair with them, and as they grew older he found it somewhat easier to talk to them, but in no way could they be said to communicate easily. The situation pained him; it was an impasse he did not know how to break. He felt that sharp little Nella, in particular, as she grew older, had become judgemental. And Amy: Amy, who was growing so startlingly, painfully like her dead mother. The same delicate features, the same curve of the mouth, above all the amazing mane of thick hair, a deeper, richer red than Marianne's. Also a little silliness, perhaps, which in Dorothea he had smiled at indulgently and rather liked. Sometimes he found it difficult even to look at Amy, at other times he loved her so much he thought his heart would break all over again. As for William, now eighteen – well, that pained him most of all. Something came between them, something awkward and stiff. They had been apart for most of the boy's formative years, while he was at school, and the gap widened as he grew older. Never having known his own father, who had died shortly after he was born, Francis had no experience of how fathers were expected to deal with their sons, and no instinctive knowledge either.

And now, here was his eldest daughter, the quiet, dreamy one, the one he understood least of all, asking for books.

'What sort of book were you thinking of?' he repeated cautiously.

'I don't really know. One that ... one that ... well, as a matter of fact, Papa, I really want to study how books are written,' she admitted shyly, struggling with her own confusion.

'Doesn't Miss – er – at Oaklands teach you?' he asked, taken further aback.

'Not enough,' Marianne said, quite firmly this time. In fact, Miss Osgood, Eunice's governess, whom she and Nella shared, had little notion of education as such but had taught them all she had been taught herself, which meant just enough to be useful to them in the social milieu in which they would find themselves when they grew up, and no more. Mostly, this meant being taught how to write polite letters, read the few novels she considered suitable, and learn a smattering of schoolgirl French and the basics of what she called pianoforte.

'Maybe you could teach me, Papa.'

'I?'

'You teach Steven Rafferty,' she pointed out, referring to the boy he had been persuaded to coach for Common Entrance. This was something instigated by Eleanor, part of her ongoing campaign to induce Francis to take up what she considered some useful occupation, and something, moreover, which would bring in a little extra, and certainly not unwelcome, addition to the small private income which was growing less adequate as his children grew up. She had regarded his acceptance of her idea as a major triumph.

'Well. Well,' said Francis, endeavouring to digest the notion that he might have fathered a bluestocking, 'that's a little different, child. Unless you'd like to learn Latin and Greek, like Steven?'

'Oh no, no, that wouldn't be any use to me.'

'It will if you want to get into Oxford, or Cambridge – and if you want to learn, I assume that's your aim.' He had no objection to women being educated, as long as they didn't expect to be allowed to take a degree, as the boy Steven's mother, Mrs Rafferty, seemed to think they should.

'No, Papa, I don't want that. I thought if I read what other people write, I may find out how to write properly, myself,' she explained. 'I've decided, you see, that it would be a good thing if I became a writer, and I want to learn how to do it.'

If she had said she wanted to become prime minister, Francis could not have been more astonished. 'My dear child.'

He found himself in a dilemma. What was he expected to offer her, then, if not the classics and other subjects dear to his heart? All this was quite beyond him. And then, he had an excellent idea.

'Why don't we ask Mrs Rafferty?'

Steven Rafferty was a brilliant boy, despite the slightly goofy appearance caused by the bottle-bottomed spectacles which constantly slid down his nose, to be pushed back with an absent forefinger, his unruly hair and the peculiar clothes his mother made him wear, but which Steven himself never noticed.

'She hasn't an atom of sense, that woman, look at her own clothes,' declared an exasperated Mrs Villiers, who liked yet despaired of clever, opinionated, high-thinking, eccentric Mrs Rafferty – who worked with her husband – making pottery, of all things. Nothing of any use, mind, just odd-shaped vases and bowls which Joel Rafferty threw on his wheel and put into the big kiln and Amarantha decorated with slip in funny patterns, though village rumour had it they sold for a fortune in London. If this last were true, which Mrs Villiers doubted, then it certainly wasn't reflected in the way they lived – in a tumble-down, higgledy-piggledy cottage down Hoggins Lane, near the brickworks.

But the house, where kindly Mrs Rafferty, in an embroidered velvet tabard over a linen smock, made lovely soups and scones and other delicious food with her droopy sleeves dangling messily over the mixing bowl, was a magnet for Steven's friends, as fascinating as the pottery itself, with its dominant kiln, the heavy, magically malleable clay, and the big wheel. Mrs Rafferty never minded what you did: she let you eat bread hot from the oven, or made big jugs of lemonade which she generously dispensed with chunky squares of sticky gingerbread, and when she wasn't working in the pottery with her husband, or cooking, was usually too busy reading to mind what Steven or any of his friends got up to. She let it be known that she had studied for three years at St Hilda's College in Oxford, and had the university allowed her to take a degree, who knows where she might have been by now? But she had married Mr Rafferty (a silent man who had once been something in the City and had given it up to be a latter-day William Morris, with the idea of founding an artists' colony, though so far they hadn't been able to persuade anyone else to join them) and life had brought her to where she was, and she would make the best of it. She was a member of the Women's Social and Political Union and from the moment she arrived in Broughton she had harassed the village women to join in the struggle for the vote. Not for them? Nonsense, even the mill girls in the north were joining in, some of them actually making speeches. Her pleas fell on deaf ears. She had only one ally in the village: Miss Bertha Dorkings, the schoolmistress, the rector's niece, who wore tweed costumes, sensible felt hats and a collar and tie.

His parents' liberal views had meant that Steven had been educated by her at the village school until a worried Amarantha told Mrs Villiers that her friend Miss Dorkings had been reluctantly forced to admit Steven had outstripped her ability to teach him anything further. And that was when Mrs Villiers had suggested Steven might come to Francis for coaching for his Common Entrance, something Francis had occasionally done in his Worcester days.

'But Mrs Villiers, the expense...'

'My son-in-law would not overcharge you, I am sure, but of course, I realise there would be the school fees afterwards...'

That problem was solved by Miss Dorkings confidently asserting that she would eat her bally hat if Steven didn't get a scholarship, which would take care of the fees. In view of Miss Dorkings's hats, one hoped that would not be necessary, and of course, Steven had disappointed no one, taking the exam and passing it with ease.

Chapter Six

After the surprises and shocks of the previous day – the arrival of William's letter, the possibility of Duncan Geddes again shooting into her life like an arrow from the past, and not least her father joining them for supper and afterwards round the fire in the parlour (not in one of his silent moods but joining in a game of cribbage and even suggesting opening a bottle of wine as a celebration of William's homecoming) – Nella had slept rather late, perhaps as a consequence of the unaccustomed wine. But more likely because of the thoughts that would not let her sleep for ages. People, and places. Ghosts. The years in France. The Somme massacre, when the killing turned to slaughter, when the dead numbered not thousands but tens of thousands. The hospital where she'd met Duncan Geddes, a Scot with a relaxed and humorous approach that came like a breath of fresh air into the hitherto unimaginable horror that the war had fast become.

'A humorous Scot? Are there any, darling?' laughed her friend, Daisy. She made a joke of everything. There was, after all, no call to lose one's sense of humour, even if being a VAD volunteer had turned out to be less a matter of mopping the fevered brows of handsome young subalterns than finding oneself up to the elbows in blood, guts and other unmentionables, working until you dropped and every day witnessing mutilation, agony and death.

But like everyone else, Daisy, too, was charmed by Dr Geddes, though the lazy, casual attitude of the handsome, dark-haired doctor with the laughing blue eyes (who turned out to be only half Scottish anyway) was misleading. It was too easy to misinterpret the way he never appeared to hurry, as anyone who worked with him soon found out; then, the blue eyes acquired a direct, searching look which on occasions could be distinctly intimidating. Operating on the wounded, he became a different person: taut, his hands quick and sure, entirely focused, compassionate, as Nella discovered, working hours and hours at a stretch with him, as convoy after convoy of casualties from the latest front-line battle were brought in. Working mechanically, efficiently, in the primitive operating theatres, swabbing, dressing, stitching the stumps of amputated limbs and torn flesh. Afterwards, his stint finished, lines of deep fatigue etched on his face, he would stretch his arms, yawn, crack a joke and let his smile conceal his feelings again.

And later Nella, weary to the very marrow of her bones, would crawl under the blankets with those images of him in her mind and, felled by exhaustion, drop immediately into a deep, dreamless sleep, until she was awakened for yet another endless repeat of the whole appalling, nightmare performance.

Last night, she had again fallen asleep to the sight and sounds of star shells bursting like fireworks in the night sky, the crump and thud of big guns. She woke late, dragged herself out of bed and made a quick breakfast before leaving for Oaklands, where there was likely to be a heavy day ahead, after which she was due for a spell of night duty. Although some of the men were now almost ready to go home and make what best they could of their lives, the running down of the hospital and the gradual transfer of patients when places could be found for them in other, permanent hospitals, certainly didn't mean that day-to-day nursing could be neglected. There were still many who faced months, perhaps years, of care, and needed careful nursing.

Leaving the house, she drew her cloak warmly together as she shut the rectory gate and hurried through the churchyard. It was no warmer than yesterday but the wind had died down in the night and the morning gave promise of a lovely day, fresh, cold and sunny. Frost had crisped the grass at the edges of the path and between the graves, and the tight-budded stems of the thousands of daffodils which had naturalised themselves under the trees stood to attention, a hard and frozen battalion. They would only need a few days of sunshine before bursting into flower and giving the dull churchyard its few brief weeks of glory.

A movement at the church door drew her glance. Early service at St Ethelfleda's didn't start until eight o'clock and the church door would still be locked – Amy said the Gypsies were back again – so surely it was far too early for anyone, however devout, even Miss Aspinall, to be waiting in the porch. It was not Miss Aspinall, but a man who was standing there. When he saw her, he began walking towards her; at the point where the two paths converged he stopped, saluting her as she drew near, drawing off the close-fitting smooth leather motorcycle helmet he wore.

With a shock that left her cold and bewildered, she realised who it was. 'Sergeant Reardon!' The policeman.

'Miss Wentworth. So you recognise me after all this time. Not many people do, nowadays.' His tone was challenging, as it always had been, but it held a new edge of defiance.

'Of course I do.' Recognition had come to her, in fact, mainly by the way he walked – dogged, hands behind his back, and by something familiar in his shape and the Cock Robin tilt of his head, as if permanently on the lookout. She might not have known him otherwise. Burns, she thought. The mutilation was horribly familiar to her, as was the surge of pity and outrage such sights still brought. One side of his face was puckered with scars, pink and shiny, made the more shocking by comparison with the other side, which was almost normal, apart from a slight tautening of the skin. He had been a good-looking young man. He was lucky he hadn't been blinded. She knew better than to sympathise, however; that was the very last thing any of the wounded men wanted, something she well understood. *'Don't dare be nice to me,'* she used to declare fiercely as a child, *'or you'll make me cry.'*

'What brings you here, Sergeant?'

'What better place to stay, for a few days' walking? I intend to book in at the Greville Arms, if they can accommodate me.'

'Walking?' She stared at him. 'Really?'

'Yes, really. I do actually enjoy walking, Miss Wentworth. But let's say there's also a matter of unfinished business, while I'm here, as it were. Loose ends.'

The only business he had been concerned with here had no loose ends. A verdict had been given, the police had withdrawn, case closed. But she didn't pretend not to understand him. Conflicting emotions chased each other through her mind: bewilderment that the police were apparently ready to reopen a hurried investigation they had patently never had enthusiasm for in the first place, and a kind of dread, which she couldn't explain.

'I see you're not pleased at the idea. Well, I didn't expect you would be, any of you.' He was an alien figure in his motorcycle gear, a heavy coat and breeches, the helmet and big leather gauntlets in one hand and a pair of goggles dangling from his wrist.

'None of us could be delighted at the prospect,

Sergeant. It's been four and a half years, and we're still trying to come to terms with what happened.' (But never to accept it, she thought.)

'Not Sergeant any longer, or not for the moment, at any rate, just plain mister. I'm out of the police now. Maybe for good. I haven't quite decided whether to take up my old job again yet – it would be my own choice if I did,' he added, as if to dispel the notion that the police would be unwilling to inflict his disfigurement on the general public.

'I'm afraid I don't understand why you're here, then.'

Herbert Reardon, ex-police detective sergeant, ex-army sergeant, had found himself strangely unable to forget that last case he had worked on before joining the army. It had come back to him, haunted him to be more precise, at odd, un-expected and mostly inopportune moments throughout the war: in those tense, nerve-wracked silences in the front-line trenches while they waited for the heavy shelling to start again from the other side; when he was wading thigh-deep through the disgusting black hell of thick mud, parts of other men's corpses and the huge bloated rats that fed on them; during brief, temporary lulls in the fighting when he was lying, half awake, almost too exhausted, mentally and physically, to grab a few hours' sleep; and latterly, between operations in the hospital when they were doing what they could with his mutilated face. It was the unutterable waste of lives – sons and brothers, husbands and fathers, boys barely out of the schoolroom – which invariably led him back to that other untimely death. That lovely young girl, before the war, found dead in the far-off, by then almost unimaginable beauty of a sweet English summer morning. Though she hadn't been lovely anymore when he'd first seen her. By that time, twelve hours in the water had robbed her red-gold hair of its lustrous shine, her skin of its pale radiance, her body of life. He had, however, seen the photographs her distraught family had produced. In life she had been beautiful, a remote, pre-Raphaelite maiden, in death a Millais *Ophelia*.

It was indeed partly because it wasn't in him to leave anything unfinished that he had decided to come back here, but also because he felt that she, the victim, did at least have the right to have her pointless death explained, a basic human right denied the men who had died, equally pointlessly, for nothing, during the insane war that had for so long held the world in its fist. He had never been satisfied about Marianne Wentworth's death.

Reardon was a loner, with problems of his own to sort out. As yet, he hadn't much idea what his future was to be. The only child of elderly parents, he now had no relatives or dependents, his father, the owner of a small printing works, having died while he was at the front, leaving him a tidy little sum which would last him until he made his mind up what he wanted to do with the rest of his life. He was still not much above thirty, and if he did not in the end rejoin the police, he thought he might travel: to India maybe, China, take the golden road to Samarkand, explore unknown continents. A passionate self-improver, he wanted to study other peoples, other religions, see if he might begin to make sense of what the world had come to, and why. He had first suspected the non-existence of God when, as a young boy, he had seen his mother die agonisingly of cancer, a suspicion reinforced later in his police career, when he'd seen how men were brought to dishonesty, brutality and violence through poverty and ignorance. Had there been a God, He would surely never have allowed that. Nothing in the futile and inhuman slaughter of the last years had made him revise his opinions, but maybe, somewhere, there might be some sort of an answer.

He knew that there was no question of the police reopening what it had suited them to write off as an open-and-shut case. Even supposing – and there was in his mind no certainty about this, yet – supposing he did take his old job back, he would not be allowed to resume enquiries. He was sailing close to the wind even now, in taking this on himself. And in any case, he admitted in the privacy of his own thoughts, finding answers might prove an impossible task. But he was damned if he wasn't going to try.

'If you are not back in the police, do they know what you are doing?' Nella Wentworth asked suddenly, very sharp, seeming to have followed his thoughts with an accuracy which for a moment disconcerted him.

'No,' he answered honestly. 'It's a matter of personal satisfaction, wiping the slate clean. For you and your family, as well as for me.' And perhaps a feeling that he had been spared, when so many others had not, to have the chance to right a wrong, he added to himself. It was on the cards that he might have come anyway, in the police again or not, just for that last. It was wrong that a young woman whose life had barely begun should lie in her grave with her death unexplained. It had officially been recorded as an accident, but did anyone actually believe that? Not many, if he was any judge. The circumstances of her going to that remote spot, alone, at night, when her family believed her to have been safely tucked up in bed, then accidentally falling into the water, were too bizarre for anyone, let alone Herbert Reardon, to believe. Most of the people he had spoken to during the all too brief investigation seemed to be of the same opinion. They were certain she must have gone there deliberately in order to take her own life, to drown herself in the lake ... and what else would make a young girl take such a step but that tired old cliché ... a man, disgrace? But the doctor who had been called in to examine her had pronounced her *virgo intacta*, no doubt mightily relieved that he would be spared having to pass anything else on to her grieving parents.

There had been one parent only, he recalled, Francis Wentworth. The Reverend Francis Wentworth. Not a man to like the idea of suicide, which was a mortal sin, his daughter dying with a total loss of grace. An accident had been far more acceptable than suicide. It was not the right time, yet, to put forward darker possibilities.

The sister was looking at him oddly and for a moment he thought he had her. 'Won't you help, Miss Wentworth?'

Nella huddled into her cloak. She felt frozen to the marrow of her bones. She said wearily, 'I

75

don't see how you can possibly ask that – and I don't in any case see how I or anyone else could help, after all this time.'

'You can talk to me. That's going to be my problem, getting people to talk, to remember.'

'We all talked to you, four years ago. Told you everything you wanted – or needed – to know. I think you'll find you won't be welcome here.'

It might have been a smile that crossed his face. 'I'm well used to that.'

She said suddenly, 'Look, I can't stay. I'm going on duty. I shall have to run as it is, or I'll have Matron on my tracks.' To emphasise the point, she threw a glance at the church clock; it was true, but that wasn't why she didn't intend to stand here talking pointlessly to Reardon. The truth was that this going back into the past was more than she could bear. 'I've no more to say. Goodbye, Mr Reardon.'

He fell into step beside her, slapping the big gauntlets hard against his thigh, and then laid a hand on her arm to detain her. 'Please. Don't go just yet.' His eyes, in that ruined face, wore the bright, piercing look she remembered from before. They gave her the same queer feeling she'd had on first encountering him four years ago, when she'd been reminded of the time they had come across a fox terrier pulling a screaming rabbit from its burrow where he'd chased it. She had thought then that this was a man, terrier-like, who would hang on like grim death until he arrived at a conclusion that satisfied him. That he would try to force them to admit the truth, however unpalatable. Now she saw something else in his eyes and for a strange moment thought it might be compassion. She shook off his hand and began to walk rapidly on.

'I'm sure you mean well, but I really don't want to hear any more. It was an accident that should never have happened, but it was long ago. Can't we be allowed to forget?'

He suddenly stepped in front of her, so that she was forced to stop. 'Miss Wentworth, don't you *want* to know the truth?' he asked, and heard the intake of her breath.

The truth? What was he insinuating? That Marianne's tragic death had *not* been an accident? That the old, crumbling jetty by the boathouse had not collapsed under her weight so that she'd been unable to save herself? That it had been deliberate? Marianne, creeping out at night, jumping into the black waters of the lake to drown herself? Never! She had been so happy those last few weeks. Glowing from all the attention, aware perhaps for the first time of her sexual attraction. It had changed her, certainly, made her secretive and even a little distanced from Nella for the first time in their lives, but not even remotely in a way that indicated she might choose to take her life.

'What do you mean, the truth? It was unbearably hot that night. The coolest place in the village was down by the lake. I've no doubt my sister couldn't sleep and that's why she went down there.' She was aware how lame that sounded. Well-brought-up young ladies rarely went out alone, late at night or otherwise.

He said deliberately, 'If that was so, I don't suppose she was the only one out in the cool of

77

the evening. But nobody ever came forward to say they'd seen her.'

'The lake is on private land. The only people likely to have been around are those who had no business to be there. Why don't you ask the Gypsies? They're back again, down in the Leasowes. Goodbye, Mr Reardon.'

He stood back, and let her go. A few minutes later, already halfway to Oaklands, she heard the diminuendo of his motorcycle engine on the quiet air.

She was late for duty by now, and without realising what she was doing, she found herself taking the dreaded short cut past the lake: the path her sister had taken that last night. But her mind was now so full of the vivid, painfully resurrected recollections of those last days before Marianne died that it scarcely mattered.

Not that the whole of that golden, carefree summer had ever been too far from her thoughts since its terrible, unthinkable ending...

Chapter Seven

1914

Or had they all been golden, those pre-war days? It had seemed so. Tennis. Croquet on the Oaklands lawn. Tea under the big cedar, and Grev plucking the strings of a lute. Summer muslins and one's hair up for the first time. Echoes of laughter. Lying on the grass in the hot sun. Wandering down to the lake in the valley because it was cooler there, surrounded as it was by the dense pines and the tall red sandstone cliff which threw a black shade onto the water, and from which Rupert made those spectacular dives. Long, endless days, unspooling like silken thread as though they would go on for ever.

But like a nub in the silk was the appearance of the Gypsy boy. He was seventeen or eighteen, perhaps, though it was difficult to tell exactly, his tribe generally being wiry and not tall in stature. He was usually barefoot, wearing cut-down breeches and a red handkerchief knotted round his neck, with straight black hair and deep-set eyes, as lean and brown-skinned as if he'd been carved from some tree, a savage, mangy dog or two at his heels. Wherever they were, the crowd of them, there he seemed to be, too, going about his business, whatever that might be, just beyond the periphery of the activities of their charmed circle, although in actual fact his presence didn't really bother any of them, except Rupert.

Long before his arrival at the rectory, Rupert had been the object of much interested speculation by the girls, especially by Amy. At thirteen, she was just becoming aware of young men and the impression she made on them. 'Rupert von Kessel. How romantic. Do you suppose he speaks English?'

'Of course he speaks English, you goose!' Nella had laughed. 'He was at Rugby with William for five or six years, so it isn't likely he wouldn't.'

'Well, William's been over to stay with Rupert's family in Salzburg and *he* doesn't speak German!'

'He'd hardly do that, after only a few weeks, would he? I don't suppose this Rupert wears lederhosen, either. Though he looks as though he might.'

'What are lederhosen?

'Leather shorts with braces, worn by hearty types who stride over the mountains grasping an alpenstock–'

'What's–?'

'Nella, don't tease the child,' said Marianne.

Amy tossed her head. 'It doesn't matter. *I* think he's very handsome.' She gazed at the photograph William had sent: brownish, inexpertly hand-tinted, so that Rupert's hair was bright yellow, his cheeks an unnatural shade of pink. But it didn't disguise the fact that he was tall and well made, very much the same build as William, most probably athletic like him, too, a product of school games, at which they had both excelled.

'Sorry, Amy dear, I *was* only teasing – but he looks too boring to me.' Nella remained unimpressed. She thought the photograph, a family group taken at Rupert's home in Salzburg the previous year, one of the times when William had stayed with them, was typical of what she imagined Austrians to be – stuffy and stiff-necked, Rupert's two older sisters as elaborately dressed as if for a royal garden party, sitting as if they had pokers down their backs; his brother, a dashing cavalry officer, resplendent in a scarlet and gold-braided uniform straight out of a musical comedy. His mother was extremely fat, and his father grim and unsmiling.

'And I'm *not* a child,' Amy said, still gazing at the photograph. 'Why do you two always think me such a baby? You're just as bad as me anyway, Marianne. You hope Rupert will carry you off back to his castle in Austria and make passionate love to you and–'

Marianne, who was never angry, stood stock-still, white-faced. 'You've been prying into my notebook!'

'No ... I ... it wasn't prying.' Amy was suddenly frightened. 'You left it open on the parlour desk ... and I just ... happened to see it.'

'Now, Amy, that's a fib for a start,' Nella said.

Marianne kept her notebooks in a private box in a drawer in her room and *never* left them lying around. She had never let anyone read them, either, except Mrs Rafferty, and not her lately. She had long ago stopped telling stories to her sisters. She said nothing more, however, except, very quietly, 'Don't ever do that again, Amy. Ever. Do you hear me?'

Rupert, in fact, turned out to possess a kind of devil-may-care charm, and to be even more handsome than his photograph. He had acquired a patina of Englishness during his several years of public school education – where his father, a rich banker, had sent him because he had business interests in England and thought an English education for his son would be a distinct advantage to him – and his accent had by now almost disappeared, unless you listened very carefully.

Nothing could quite disguise the fact, however, that he was not an Englishman born and bred, though to do him justice, he never tried to make anyone believe he was. He was very obviously exceedingly proud to be a member of the great Austro-Hungarian Empire, and on occasions it even seemed to amuse him to make himself appear more foreign than he really was, to emphasise his foreignness with wry remarks, and cultivate a slightly ironic tone and a dry self-mockery.

Nella saw that it made life more comfortable to pretend to laugh at oneself before others could do it, but she thought the habit quite irritating: it underlined things you might not have noticed if they hadn't been forced upon your attention, but she kept her opinions to herself. He was her brother's friend, and it was bad enough that in the current climate of opinion, the guest at the rectory was already being looked on with suspicion, by the villagers, and most of the local gentry. Von Kessel, what sort of name was that? Probably German, a sympathiser with the Kaiser, and who wanted to be on friendly terms with *him,* the way he was acting? Arming Germany to the teeth, picking quarrels with his cousin, the King. What was that ... not German, but Austrian, this young fellow? Well, what was the difference, when the two nations were thick as thieves?

But in actual fact, Nella had good reason for being quite glad of the diversion his visit brought about, hoping it might draw the attention from her. She was not in her grandmother's good books at that moment by her refusal to comply with the suggestion their aunt had made quite suddenly one evening after supper at Oaklands. Would it not be a good thing, she asked, if Nella and Marianne should share Eunice's coming-out functions in London the next year? She, Lady Sybil, had already put several arrangements in hand. There would be Eunice's big dance to attend and invitations to other innumerable social events, with all the advantages that would bring the girls. Marianne had only smiled at the suggestion and murmured vaguely, 'How kind, dear Aunt,' which meant nothing except that she would not commit herself before considering all the possibilities and deciding what to say.

Nella, however, was too horrified to be tactful. The very idea made her feel as though all the air had been sucked from her body so that she could not breathe. Before stopping to think, she had cried out, 'Oh no, absolutely not! I simply can't *imagine* anything I should detest more.'

'Fenella!' said her grandmother, shocked.

'I'm ... I'm sorry.' And, belatedly, she was. She knew her outburst would be seen as ingratitude for all that Aunt Sybil and Uncle Foley had done for them.

But their aunt only smiled and shrugged her slim shoulders. Her one great beauty was her eyes, almond-shaped, thickly lashed and of a darkness that seemed to reflect the colours of the elegant dresses she wore, so that one could never be quite sure what colour they were. She was wearing a simple topaz silk that particular evening, and her eyes were flecked with pinpoints of golden light. Nella hoped it wasn't a danger signal; she and her aunt had crossed swords on occasions before now. Lady Sybil was inclined to sweep everything and everyone before her in her enthusiasms, and she did not like to be opposed – and this coming out of Eunice's was the road to getting her married off, which she was as inflexible in her determination to achieve as any other society mother. But Nella had learnt early that if you stood up to her, Sybil bore you no ill will and perhaps liked you better for it. 'No need to apologise, child. I like a girl with spirit.' She laughed, her warm, rich laugh, and Nella released her breath. 'Though you might be sorry later,' she added. 'Most girls would jump at the opportunity.'

Most girls, perhaps. London for the season, glittering social occasions and beautiful clothes (all generously and willingly provided for them by Uncle Foley, presumably, who was rich as Croesus, and had already provided them with too much, which was another reason Nella hated the idea).

'Oh, I believe Nella will come round, Sybil, when she's had a chance to think about it,' Mrs Villiers said, with her eyes severely on Nella, steely for once in her determination that this chance should not be rejected.

Nella, however, vowed to stand her ground. She had no intentions of being cajoled, nor even influenced by the pleas of poor little Eunice, who was as horrified at the prospect as Nella herself.

'Do say yes, Nella! You can't think how much I admire you for refusing, but it would mean so much to me if both of you were to join me,' she begged. All those parties and dances would be sheer torture to her, she would be expected to make herself pleasant and agreeable to various strange young men in order to catch one of them as a husband; or worse, she would be a failure, and come out of her first season having failed to catch any of them.

Nella thought that Eunice's shrinking from this sort of exposure might be a chief factor influencing Lady Sybil's offer to herself and her sister: that with the support of her two dearest friends, Eunice would be sure to find the courage to plunge into the social whirl and find it was not so painful after all. As she constantly reiterated, Eunice wasn't the first girl to be terrified at such a prospect, but as far as she was aware, none had ever been destroyed by it yet.

'I'm sorry, Marianne,' Nella said later, 'I'm too impetuous, I've probably spoilt your chances, too.' It had belatedly occurred to her that her sister might, after all, not see things in the same light as she did, might in fact quite welcome the idea of going to parties and being surrounded by young men, which she undoubtedly would be. There was no doubt she had lately come to enjoy being the centre of attraction. Amy might not have been so far wrong, after all, in suggesting their romantic sister was dreaming of a prince who would capture her heart and carry her off. But Marianne just smiled composedly and told Nella to leave it be for the time being, things had a habit of working themselves out if you let events take their course.

Chapter Eight

'What was that man doing here, Francis?' asked Mrs Villiers, that same afternoon, coming into his study.

Francis, startled by the rapid knock on his door and the entry of his mother-in-law, was for the moment nonplussed. 'Er ... what man?'

His pretence was ludicrous, as if he had so many visitors that he could not remember – he, who still had few callers, even among his parishioners, perhaps especially among them. After working in the rarefied atmosphere of the cathedral precincts, she knew that he found the duties of a parish priest difficult, though she had begun to hope that he was beginning to be accepted. The work itself was not demanding. St Ethelfleda's parishioners had never been enamoured of the genuflexions, lace-on-the-altar and incense-swinging, otherworldly ministry of Father Dorkings – nor of the parson before him, who had never been able to offer much comfort or practical advice – and had therefore learnt not to expect too much of their incumbent. Most of them asked for little more than a sermon on Sunday, marriages, christenings and burials. The occasions which demanded most of him lately – and to do him justice he did not seek to shirk the burden – had been when he had to call on wives and mothers whose husbands and sons had been lost in the trenches, or at sea.

Eleanor knew her son-in-law had never been amenable to her plain speaking; it made him retreat into his shell, but there was no way to put what she had to say gently. 'Come, Francis, you know very well I meant that man Reardon, the detective who was sent here when ... when Marianne was found. He was here not an hour ago.'

Francis had been writing something in a large notebook with stiff covers and now he blotted his last words, carefully rested his pen on the inkstand on his desk, and folded his long, shapely hands, giving himself a moment before replying.

'Florrie didn't recognise him,' Eleanor went on. 'And she wouldn't have let him in, since he refused to state his name or his business, had it not been for...' She stopped and began again. 'He had very obviously been in the war.'

Florrie had believed him to be someone come upon hard times, reduced to begging, or selling matches on street corners, like so many more in these difficult days, when the number of unemployed was beginning to assume frightening proportions. The disillusion with the government was creeping through the whole country and had percolated even as far as Broughton Underhill – a sense of outrage that rehabilitation for men and boys broken in the war and opportunity for everyone were not happening. It did not help to be told that the war for which they had given up so much had nearly bankrupted the nation. The promised land, a fairer and more equal life for everyone, was as much a mirage as it had ever been.

'No,' Francis said with a sigh, 'Florrie would

not recognise him. He has been terribly wounded about the face.'

'Yes, Francis, I saw that. I spoke to him. Poor man...' she said softly, and paused, before going on spiritedly, 'nevertheless, that doesn't excuse what he intends to do. He must be told to leave at once. We cannot have him going round the village, asking questions. Opening old sores,' she added more quietly, looking at his face with pity. This silent, haggard man was not the son-in-law she had once known, the man her daughter Dorothea had fallen in love with and adored. He had always been startlingly handsome, in that dark, ascetic way. She had, sometimes, in the old days, thought him a little vain. But now...

'How do you know this? When did you speak to him?' he asked.

'Florrie told me about him when she came back from answering the door. I was curious and I made it my business to be out in the garden as he left. There are still a few late snowdrops under the trees by the gate, and I stayed searching for them so that he would be bound to pass me. But ... Francis, after you let him out and closed the door, he went looking for her grave and stood there until I went over to him. I asked him his business, and he told me something I find quite extraordinary. That although he is not yet back in his job with the police, for some reason I could not fathom he is making further enquiries into what happened to Marianne... I imagine I am telling you something you already know, of course. He must have told you the same thing.'

'Did he tell you why?'

'Exactly what I asked him.' She hesitated, then added quietly, 'He seems to think that it was no accident. But we all know that it was, don't we? Which is what I told him.'

'Do we know that? How do we know?'

She looked at his ravaged face with pity, paused for a moment and then said plainly, 'Are you suggesting that your daughter would commit suicide, Francis? *Marianne?*

Quite apart from suicide being regarded as a sin in some quarters, it was a tragedy that always left guilt behind it – those who were left asking why. Had it in some way been their fault? What could they have done to prevent it?

He said, 'Maybe that is something we shall have to learn to accept. Maybe it is God's will that we should ask ourselves why.'

Not for the first time, Mrs Villiers wondered if Francis was not a man who welcomed the burden of guilt on his shoulders, shouldering it until he sagged beneath its weight.

The day on the ward was as busy as Nella had predicted, and even more of a strain because, try as she would, she could not keep her mind entirely on what she was doing. Despite being so late, it had been a mistake to take the short cut to Oaklands, past the lake, but even if she had not, the memories could now no longer be shut out, not after that conversation with Reardon. As she mechanically performed her duties, took her meal breaks, joked with the patients, they crowded in on her: people, things she had forgotten, some things she never would forget...

Chapter Nine

1914

Out of all that time, one blisteringly hot July day at the beginning of the holidays stood out as the forerunner to everything that followed.

They had taken a picnic down to the lake: the three older girls and young Amy, who had pestered until she was allowed to go with them. Grev had been there, too, home from Paris, where he was studying musical composition at the Conservatoire; William, of course, and Rupert, who was working in London now but had come down with him to stay at the rectory for the long vac after a climbing holiday they had spent together in the Tyrolean Alps. Steven Rafferty had also been persuaded to leave his books and come along.

At first, when they reached the lake, they took turns in messing about for a while in the old punt in defiance of admonitions to the contrary, but the idea turned out to be better than the reality: the punt was so old it leaked excessively, and perhaps it *was* dangerous, and Steven especially was a very inept punter, so the idea was soon abandoned.

After a while, young Amy wandered off with a small basket to look for the wild raspberries that grew in the shade where the scorching sun did not reach, and all the boys except Grev donned bathing costumes and plunged into the water. Grev raised a languid eyebrow and professed himself quite happy to watch, thank you very much. He was home for the summer, bowling the girls over with his suddenly acquired self-possession and startling good looks, his dark hair falling romantically over his brow and a glint in his amused eyes. He was slim, even slight, but he had muscular forearms and the strong, sinewy wrists of the dedicated pianist. It was as if he had emerged from a chrysalis, from being a not very prepossessing schoolboy to becoming an assured and handsome young man of the world. He languidly professed to abhor all forms of physical exercise, especially the kind which had been forced on him at school, although he enjoyed tennis and riding, at which he was nearly as expert as his mother. He watched the others, as they climbed on to the rocks that surrounded the lake and began to dive off the ledge cut into the steep sandstone cliff above the dark water, with an amused indifference that seemed to the girls the epitome of sophistication. All the same, they themselves envied the young men their freedom to swim while they, young ladies now, were forced to be content with dangling their feet in the water. The idea of mixed bathing might have been taken up on the decadent beaches of southern England but it had not yet percolated to Broughton Underhill.

It wasn't long, however, before Steven, very conscious of his skinny white body and the borrowed one-piece bathing costume which didn't properly fit, came out to join them, wrapping his long, thin frame in a towel and rescuing his spectacles from the pocket of the shirt he'd left on the grass. He soon grew restless with being a mere spectator and, producing one of the books he always carried, he propped himself up on his elbow and began to read, a much more congenial occupation.

Nella twisted a stem of grass and chewed it, her eyes on Rupert and William, racing each other to the far end of the lake. William got there first and turned to continue the race back, but Rupert climbed out on to the warm rocks, from where he made some tricky somersault dives before beginning to climb higher. Nella watched the tanned, athletic body for a while until her attention was drawn away by Steven's reply to some question of Marianne's about his mother going up to London to meet some of her political women friends. 'Who, the suffragettes?' she asked.

'They don't like being called that.'

'Why not? It doesn't matter what they're called, I think they're admirable. I wish I could join them.'

'What, smashing windows and being force-fed in prison? Come off it, Nella, you wouldn't like that.' This came from William, now hauling himself out of the water just in time to hear this last, shaking drops all over the girls, expecting them to shriek, which they disappointingly did not. 'You'd be much better off listening to Grandy and looking for a husband who'd take all that nonsense out of your head.'

Nella pulled a face. 'Well, at least they're doing something.' She knew he was only trying to provoke her – he knew very well, and sympathised with, the restiveness in her which had been growing over the last few months. She was aware that she must do something about her future, but unable to make up her mind what it should be – though it would certainly have nothing to do with wasting her time on social fripperies and looking for a husband, in the way that both her grandmother and Lady Sybil thought appropriate. When she found a man she could marry, it would not matter a fig to her who he was: her partner in life would be someone who could share her dreams, and her hopes, and who would not object to her finding some form of worthwhile and fulfilling work – though what this might be had not yet manifested itself.

'Anyway,' said William, suddenly serious, 'those women will soon have more to worry about than getting the vote, if the news is anything to go by.'

'If you're going to be tiresome and talk about that archduke business again, I for one don't want to hear,' put in Marianne drowsily. 'Don't let's spoil the afternoon.'

She lay on her stomach, in the shade of a tree, half dozing in the heat, with only her still-bare feet and legs in the sun, for fear of burning her fair skin. The sun had already brought out the faint band of freckles across her nose. What did the assassination of an Austrian archduke in Sarajevo by a hot-headed group of Serbian patriots, shocking as it was, have to do with Britain? There was said to be big trouble brewing in Europe and the Balkans because of it, but then, when was there not? They were always fighting over there, those people with unpronounceable names in countries no one had ever heard of.

'Marianne,' said Steven, looking up, 'it's serious this time.' He removed his glasses and polished them with his shirt tail, prepared for a good discussion. 'Austro-Hungary has declared war against Serbia over that – and make no mistake, we could all be drawn in. Germany will support Austria, and then Russia and France – and Britain – won't be able to stand aside.'

Grev said lazily, 'Oh, come on, Marianne's right – let it alone, Steven, for now.'

'We can't be like ostriches, hide our heads in the sand–'

'Let it alone, before our fearless foreign friend decides to join us again.'

Steven opened his mouth, and then shut it. It was a delicate subject where Rupert was concerned. They were all uneasily aware that if ever it *should* come to war, unlikely as that seemed to most people, Rupert would be on one side while they were on the other.

Eunice said suddenly, 'Oh goodness, look!' A bluff in the rock had hidden Rupert momentarily as he climbed, and it wasn't until he called out to make sure they had all seen him that they realised he had been heading for a ledge to one side, much higher than the one they'd previously used.

'The idiot.' His veneer of sophistication slipping, Grev stood up, shouted and waved his arms. His voice carried clear across the lake and Rupert must have heard what he shouted but he stood there poised, until, like a wasp in his black-and-yellow striped bathing suit, he executed a perfect swallow dive.

Grev watched until he surfaced and began to

swim towards them. He let out his breath. 'He should be careful, the fool, there are dangerous rocks down there.'

'No use telling Kess to be careful,' William grinned. 'He wouldn't listen. He leads a life of unutterable recklessness, trying to outshine his arrogant soldier brother with his bravery.'

Grev laughed shortly. 'Well, of course, they're all arrogant, these Teutonic types. Obsessed with the unshakable sense of their own superiority.'

'A sweeping statement, that, isn't it?' commented Steven, peering over his glasses.

'True, though. Why otherwise would they be arming themselves to the teeth,' Grev went on, ignoring the interruption, forgetting his previous wish to have the subject dropped, 'spoiling for war?'

'Well, you wouldn't be in it,' Marianne said, smiling at him. 'Grev's a pacifist,' she announced to the others. 'Aren't you, Grev?'

'I won't fight, if that's what you mean.'

'Not even for your country?' asked William, colour touching his cheeks. Issues were rarely complicated with William. Choices were between what you saw as right, and what you knew to be wrong. If it came to fighting for the honour of his country, William would be there with no questions asked. Perhaps because of this, Nella had sensed something not quite right growing between her brother and his friend Kess this summer: a dissension that sprang partly from the uneasy political situation, but also, now that William was up at Oxford and Rupert working with his father's business interests in the City, both spreading their wings, meeting new people and imbibing new ideas, it seemed to her questionable whether their undemanding school-boy friendship would survive. They were two very different personalities and their camaraderie had developed mainly through the close quarters of school for so many years, and through participation in the same, mainly sporting, activities. They had lived closer together than many brothers and now, if things came to ahead, they were likely to find themselves on different sides. She believed this was not a thought either had brought out into the open.

Grev was saying shortly, 'Not for anything would I kill another human being, William. It's my belief that is totally wrong. Ask your father. He agrees with me.'

They all fell silent, knowing that was the last thing William would do. He said stiffly, 'No sane man wants to kill another human being, but don't the ends sometimes justify the means? What do *you* think, Steven?'

Steven said nothing for a while. Then he said mildly, looking from one to the other, 'Oh, I'm not qualified to give opinions on that subject. I wouldn't be allowed to fight anyway, with my eyesight.'

'Lucky you.' Grev shrugged to indicate the matter was over and dropped down next to Marianne. Her mass of red curls was loosely gathered into a knot as a gesture to it being officially 'up', and he teasingly extracted one of the long pins that held it, twisting the strand of hair which was released, letting it curl around his finger.

She turned her head sideways and gently took his hand and released the curl, looking at him under her lashes, her mouth curving in a slow smile.

'Here he comes!' Grev murmured as Rupert swam towards them with a powerful crawl. Reaching the shallow edges of the lake, he waded out and sat on the grass, dripping and raking water out of his hair.

Grev said stiffly, 'I don't suppose you know this, but I should warn you the cliff at the bottom end of the lake goes right down beneath the water, and there are some pretty dangerous rocks not too far beneath the surface.'

Rupert shrugged. 'Yes, you can see them when the sun is out. The water's very clear.'

'Well, as long as you're aware.'

Rupert only smiled, then he said suddenly, 'That Gypsy boy's there again.' And sure enough, there he was, further along the bank, under the trees, whittling a stick. 'Does it not make you uneasy, being watched all the time?' he demanded when nobody seemed to find his remark worthy of comment. He looked round at them all, his eyes coming to rest on Marianne, and on Grev, who had pulled out a second hairpin so that another long curl fell against her neck.

'Give it back, you tiresome boy,' Marianne demanded with a laugh. She held out her hand for the hairpin, but he held it teasingly out of reach. Rupert's eyes rested for a moment on her glorious hair, glittering in the sun, then he stood up abruptly.

William said suddenly, 'Pin your hair up,

Marianne. You might as well be a Gypsy yourself.'
He was sometimes very strait-laced, William, and
took his responsibilities as elder brother seriously,
but he was rarely sharp. There was a silence.
Marianne's eyes widened in hurt surprise, then
dropped, and she twisted her head until Grev let
go, and she could pin her hair more securely.

Rupert wasn't looking at her anymore, but was
busily making signs to the Gypsy. If the boy saw
him, he took no notice and went on sitting where
he was. In the end, Rupert cupped his hands and
shouted to him to be off.

'Leave him alone, Kess,' William said, more
easily. 'He's doing no harm.' Grev shrugged and
turned the other way, staring impassively out
across the lake.

'He's trespassing,' Rupert said. 'Spying on us.
And I suppose, of course, you're going to let him
get away with it? How very English!' He added
with a smile and a raised eyebrow, 'My father
would have these Gypsies, these *Zigeuner*, driven
off his lands.'

'What is there to spy on? Besides, I know him,'
Grev said. 'He's Daniel Boswell, his family has
travelled to these parts for years.' He stood up,
and deliberately strolled the hundred yards or so
towards the boy, and when he reached him,
stopped to speak. Far from ordering him away,
his gestures implied he was inviting the Gypsy to
join them. Rupert flushed under his tan. But the
boy shook his head, stood up in one graceful
movement, whistled to his dogs and disappeared
into the trees. Grev came back and flung himself
down on the grass again.

'What did you say to him?' Steven asked.

'I asked him to join us,' he said blandly, as if it were not the last thing any Gypsy would have done, 'but he says he has better things to do.'

'Poaching, no doubt.'

'Only for the pot, Rupert, I hope, and he's welcome to that.' He selected one of the wild raspberries which Amy had set out so enthusiastically to gather, though after half an hour, hot, scratched and insect-bitten, she had given up; the fruits were so tiny, however hard she picked, the small basket never seemed to get any fuller. All the same, the results of her labours were delicious, sharp-sweet, ripe and juicy. Holding the berry delicately between his long musician's fingers, Grev dipped it into sugar and held it out for Marianne. Obediently, she opened her mouth and her small white teeth closed round it. Their eyes met and held. A slight tinge of colour touched her cheeks. Then she laughed and, looking at Rupert, he deliberately picked up another of the fruits and fed it to her. Rupert jumped up and dived into the water, swam showily to the other side, and when he reached it, Nella saw him begin to climb to the same high ledge again.

With held breath, they all watched as he dived and emerged safely once more, then climbed to poise himself for yet another dive. Nella closed her eyes and lay back, unable to watch anymore. The sunny afternoon had become sultry and full of tensions, with Marianne somehow at the centre. She realised, with a shock, what had actually been going on for weeks. Marianne and Grev, a perfect pair, their heads bent together over the piano. But also Marianne with Rupert, playing tennis, laughing together. And come to that, Marianne with Steven, discussing a book his mother had given her, which she had found difficult to understand. Mrs Rafferty was at last growing impatient with her. Marianne was neither offended nor deterred. But neither did she make any progress into authorship. She went on endlessly scribbling in her notebooks, with nothing ever coming to fruition, so perhaps Mrs Rafferty was right to be impatient.

Did Marianne, wondered Nella, opening her eyes and staring at her sister, see these young men who surrounded her merely as romantic characters, grist to her mill ... or was she, perhaps, just flirting a little? More than a little – pitting them one against the other? Marianne?

Rupert dived again, another perfect dive, followed by another climb. It was evident he intended to go on until he dropped from exhaustion – or killed himself. Even William was looking alarmed. He met Grev's eyes and they began to pack up the picnic things. Nella helped them. They shouted to Rupert to tell him they were leaving and after another defiant dive, deprived of an audience, he followed.

Afterwards, Nella only saw the Gypsy again in the distance. There was no doubt it was pleasanter, knowing he wasn't hovering in the background.

The same tribe of Gypsies, with their brightly painted caravans, their exotic womenfolk, colourful clothing and gold earrings – worn by the men, as well as their women – had been an inter-mittent part of the village life for as long as Nella could remember, their comings and goings, like the seasons, in accordance with some mysterious pattern known only to them. They were objects of curiosity, tolerated as long as they didn't set up camp too near the village, if not trusted an inch by anyone: even the unworldly Father Dorkings had locked up the silver and emptied the poor box daily when they were around. While feeling sorry for the filthy, hungry-looking children with beseeching black eyes, whom their Gypsy mothers taught to hold out begging hands, the village women were careful not to leave their doors open behind them when they went indoors for a few coppers to buy clothes pegs and sprigs of lucky white heather. Snared rabbits and a poached pheasant or two were a hazard of life when they were about – and nothing more, after all, than certain villagers were known to be guilty of – and they were useful, though unreliable, at pea-picking and potato-harvesting. But tolerance grew thin when clothing disappeared from washing lines, even in broad daylight, and vege-tables were pulled from the gardens, cows milked during the night. That was a sign for the Gypsies to disappear again.

As they had, at the first sign of trouble, the day after the tragedy. Silently packed up and dis-appeared in their horse-drawn caravans with their scruffy wild dogs running behind, leaving no trace of themselves except the ashes of their fires. No one had ever expected them to have the face to come back.

Chapter Ten

Although a detective sergeant, as he was at the time of Marianne Wentworth's drowning, Herbert Reardon hadn't been let into all the finer details of the investigation. The salient facts had remained indelibly in his memory, but now he needed to find out more. Enquiries told him where he might find the inspector who had been in charge of the case: now retired and living in the Quarry Bank district on the other side of Stourbridge.

This was familiar country, the area where he'd been born, and he knew where to leave his motorcycle, in a little-used alley at the end of the steep street where Henry Paskin lived with his sister. He gave a delighted, tow-headed urchin a silver thrupenny bit to keep an eye on it. He felt a distinct pang of nostalgia for his own childhood – though truth to tell, he'd been glad enough to leave it behind – as he stepped around a group of pinafored little girls playing hopscotch on the pavement and watched a ragged-trousered lad trying to shin a lamp post, where no doubt he would remove the gas mantles out of mischief, if he managed to get to the top. Reardon grinned and ignored him; it was no business of his to stop the little varmint, now.

Henry Paskin's sister was standing on a pair of wooden steps that were placed on the pavement outside one of the brick-built terrace houses that lined the street, vigorously polishing glittering windows that showed starched white lace curtains inside. The doorstep had been ferociously whitened, and the brass doorknob and letter box polished so you could have parted your hair in the reflection.

A thin, sharp-featured woman with a red nose that indicated she might have digestive problems and a short temper, Emily Paskin wore a crossover pinny to protect her clothes, and a sacking apron to protect her pinny. What hair was not covered by a dust cap bristled at the front with metal curling pins. He stood, waiting until she should acknowledge him, not anxious to disturb her in her work, knowing how women like her could be when they were interrupted from 'getting on', having had his ears boxed many a time by the aunt who'd taken care of him after his mother died, just for that.

'Well?' she demanded presently, knowing he was there, but not stopping her attack on the windows, except for a sideways look, swiftly averted, that was becoming very familiar to him.

'Miss Paskin? I'm looking for your brother, Henry,' he returned, after this less than welcoming salutation.

''E's out.'

'When will he be back?'

'Gawd knows.'

'No idea when, Miss Paskin?'

'What d'you want with him?'

'I'll tell him that when I see him. Is there anywhere where I might find him?' he asked, resisting the impulse to tell her more plainly that it was none of her business. She was beginning to annoy him considerably.

'Up the cut, fishing, where else? Spends half his life there, he does, anent the Delph Locks. And don't you go 'ticing him down the Glassmakers,' she called after him as he thanked her as politely as he could and made his escape.

The filthy canal, a pram wheel protruding through other rubbish onto its oily surface, looked an unappetising place in which to seek your dinner. He'd thought his senses blunted by what he'd had to eat out there in the trenches, but he wouldn't fancy any fish that came out of that lot, Reardon thought, as he parked his motorcycle and slithered down the bank at the side of the bridge on to the well-trodden towpath.

Henry Paskin was sitting on the canalside on an upturned wooden box, his pipe in his mouth, bundled up in an old coat, with a floppy flat cap pulled well down over his eyes and his rod propped beside him. He might have been asleep but for the occasional puff of smoke from the pipe that protruded from under the cap brim. Reardon stopped beside him. 'How do, Henry.' He wouldn't have dared call him Henry in the old days, but the war, and the fact that neither was now in the police, were great levellers.

Henry lifted his cap brim, and stared. 'It's Herbert Reardon,' Reardon said.

'Young Bert.' After a second, a great paw was extended. 'God Almighty, what they done to yer, old cock?'

'Same as was done to a lot more,' said Reardon,

and sat down beside him, amongst the dried stalks and stems of last year's weeds, and the trampled and dusty grass.

'Bloody war. Oh ar. That bloody war.'

No more would be said on the subject, but that suited Reardon. The direct approach, typical of Paskin, who had been too old himself to fight, made him feel much better. It was the sympathy, or the embarrassment, that got you down. He'd always liked working for Henry, who was slow and broad-spoken, who liked people to see him as a plain, Black Country bloke, and laid the accent on thick – when he remembered. He lifted his elbow a sight too often, but he was the best policeman Reardon had known. 'How d'you find me then?' he asked.

'Your sister told me you might be here – with a bit of reluctance. Seemed to think we'd end up in the boozer.'

Henry grinned. 'Her ain't so bad, our Em. Don't mean half of what her says.' He paused and pocketed his pipe. 'Looked after me like a mother, since Ada went, and her knows I haven't touched a drop since then, believe it or not. What yer after, then, Bert?'

Reardon watched his mittened hands dive into his fishing basket and rummage about amongst the lines and hooks and maggot tins, presently emerging with a bottle of cold tea, which he handed to Reardon, and a hefty packet of door-step sandwiches wrapped in newspaper, which he proceeded to divide. 'Have one of our Em's sarnies. Plenty for both on us.'

'Thanks.' Reardon's hands were already numb.

A cold, sneaky wind crept along the canal and a dankness floated up from the water. He took a swig out of the bottle and passed it back, wishing he had his own Thermos. 'God, it's perishing out here. How do you stick it?'

'I'm used to it,' Henry shrugged. 'Well?'

'Remember that last case we had, before the war, that young woman in Broughton Underhill?'

'Ar, I do.'

Reardon put him in the picture and Henry chewed and listened and then became serious. 'Whose damfool idea is it to rake all that up?'

Reardon avoided a direct answer. 'I don't know about raking it up – was it ever rightly settled?'

Henry raised his eyebrows but didn't press his question. Silently, he wrapped the remains of his sandwich in the newspaper, extracted his pipe and a rubber pouch from his pocket, knocked out the still-smouldering dottle and with deliberation repacked the pipe and lit it. Clouds of rich tobacco smoke wafted across the scummy surface of the canal.

'It weren't up to me, Bert, that. I were pulled off the job by old Tightarse Gifford,' he said at last, referring to their revered superintendent at that time. 'You know as how he was always one for a quiet life. Retired now and writing his memoirs, last I heard,' he added with a sardonic laugh. 'Mind you, for once, I thought he had it right. We was all of a mucker at the station what with the war starting and orders coming from here, there and the next place, didn't know where we was at – and there were nothing to say it weren't an accident, so what were the use of hanging on?'

106

Reardon finished Em's sandwich: full-bodied, tasty cheese, plenty of it, and sharp pickle, when he'd anticipated a filling as thin and begrudging as Em herself. She was rising in his estimation. 'Trouble is, there's not many believe the accident theory, Henry.'

'So they'd rather believe it was suicide, then?' Henry shook his head. 'Come on, cock, that won't wash. Suicide's a stigma nobody wants.' He paused, eased his belt with his thumbs. He had grown a paunch, despite allegedly being off the beer. 'Specially when it involves a young wench like that. 'Tain't right, young 'uns going afore the old folk.' Reardon remembered it wasn't only his wife, Ada, that Henry had lost, but also a son at Gallipoli, and that was probably why Ada had died too, of a broken heart, it was said. 'Mind you, I'm not sure I believed she'd fallen in, all accidental like, meself.'

'So you do think it was suicide?'

'I didn't say that. Although you've seen – we've all seen – youngsters doing away with theirselves for no reason anybody in their right mind can see. Feelings run high when you'm that age. Every little trouble seems a big 'un.'

'True enough. Except that nobody seems to think Marianne Wentworth had any troubles.'

'That's what they all say.'

'She left no note.'

'They don't allus, do they?'

In the distance a narrowboat piled high with coal was negotiating the last of the series of locks, emerging with its gaudy paint bright in the sun. The slow-plodding carthorse that would resume pulling it was already patiently waiting to be hitched up again, cropping what grass there was near the towpath, with the bargee's wife standing by its side, knitting, apparently as impervious to the cold as Henry was.

'So ... if she didn't kill herself, and if it wasn't an accident, there's only the other thing left.'

''Owd on! There were no indications of foul play, remember.'

'Maybe we missed something.'

'Look at it this road,' Henry said after a minute. 'Facts: last seen, previous evening, going to bed late after a party. Found, morning after, eight o' clock, by the gamekeeper's dog, floating under the jetty, her frock caught on the rotten posts. Questions: Why did she go out on her own that time o' night? Why did she venture out on to that jetty when everybody knew it was a death trap? Why did she go down to the lake at all? Answer to that one: To meet somebody.'

'Do you know that she did?'

'We never knew she didn't.'

Reardon digested this confirmation of what his own mind had told him all along. 'So you're agreeing with me, Henry?'

'I didn't say that, neither. What I am saying is, you'm on a hiding to nothing trying to shift it otherwise.'

'Who was questioned?'

'Everybody she knew – or them as was left. Them young blokes – that young Foley from the Big House, and the Austrian bloke, them as she'd been running around with all summer – they was already off, same day.'

'I remember. A bit funny, wasn't it, that?'

'Not when you think how everybody was rushing to join up. One on 'em yourself, if I remember right.'

That was true enough. Reardon had queued, like hundreds more, outside the recruiting station, fired up with patriotism, the spirit of adventure and, in his own case, the feeling that he was lucky to have got as far as he had in the police, and wasn't destined to get much further, except by filling dead men's shoes, so he might as well try something else.

'Of course,' Henry added thoughtfully, 'there was them gyppos an' all. Her sister thought one their lads had his eye on Marianne. But they'd made theirselves scarce even before word got round that she'd been found, and we never caught up with 'em, though it ain't hardly likely a wench as well brought up as her would've gone out in the dark to meet one of that lot, anyroad.'

'They're back in Broughton Underhill, her sister told me.'

'Just goes to show then. I've no love for the likes of them, skiving lot of toerags they are, but they wouldn't show their faces again if they'd owt to be afeard on.' He said suddenly, 'I did hear as how you weren't back in the force, yet.'

'I've only been home a week or two. I'm not sure whether I want to go back at all.'

'Bollocks, of course you want to go back! You were all set to be a bostin' copper. You know a recommendation for your promotion came through just after you'd gone?'

'What?' Reardon stared. He'd always been ex-

109

tremely ambitious, and had he known that was in the offing, might he not have been so keen to rush off?

'Thought not. Well, it did, and I know for a fact they had their eyes on you, them upstairs. Don't go chucking away all you'd gained for nowt. But take my advice and pack this little lot in – if it gets round you're doing this off yer own bat, that's you finished.'

Reardon knew Henry was right: without authority to back him up and allow him to ask questions, this was highly likely to be the case. He watched as the barge, now fully through the lock, stopped about fifty yards away. It looked as though it was being moored. Dinnertime, it smelt like. 'I believe the constable in the village is still the same one who was there then?'

Henry sighed. 'You allus was pig-headed. Well, if you won't listen to me, go careful. Village constable did you say?' He laughed. 'Ted Bracey. He'll be there till he's pensioned off. You can ask him what he remembers but I doubt you'll get much out of him. 'Tain't in his interests.'

Reardon scrambled to his feet and held his hand out. 'It's been good seeing you, Henry.'

Henry nodded. 'You an' all.' As Reardon turned away, he added, 'You can try asking that game-keeper. The one as found her – name of Naylor, if I remember right.' He held out a mittened hand. The fingers stuck out like sausages. 'And good luck, cock, with everything.'

Chapter Eleven

Gentleman of leisure, who ever would have thought it?

It was a question Arthur Foley often asked himself nowadays. The idea doubly tickled his puckish sense of humour – not only that he, Arthur Foley, should be classed as a gentleman, but also that he should have the leisure to sit and contemplate the notion. Having worked all his life, from when he'd entered his father's engineering works as a boy of sixteen, to the day last year when his doctor had warned him that it was high time he retired and left his business in other hands, a life of idleness had been to him an inconceivable concept. However, for the sake of his wife and daughter he had lately done his best to come to terms with it. That heart attack at the beginning of the war had been a warning which he had ignored, in view of what faced the country, and he had continued to work non-stop, having turned over his foundry and machine shops to the casting and machining of metal bomb casings, the only thing he had been able to do, at his age, to help the war effort. But now his doctor had persuaded him that he owed it to his family to obey orders and be a little more circumspect. Reluctantly limiting himself to being driven over to the works two or three times a week, and following the regime his doctor dictated, he had to admit he was beginning to feel fitter. But decidedly underoccupied.

'Damn all doctors!' he muttered. He looked at the books lining his study wall without enthusiasm, guiltily aware that he ought to use this unlooked-for spare time to try and make up some of the deficiencies of a grammar school education which he had endured rather than benefited from, and of a lifetime thereafter spent in industry, in which there had been no space for what he called falderals. He knew, realistically, that he never would. He was a man of practical skills, with a hard head and a talent for managing men and making money, and that was the sum total of Arthur Foley. Books had always been something of a mystery to him, the world of pictures and paintings was uncharted territory, and he did not understand as much of music as he would have liked, despite the efforts to show him how to appreciate it made by Grev, whose whole world it had been.

He knew it was generally assumed that he had married Sybil for her position in society, and that she had married him for his money, but this was to understand only half the situation. At an age when he'd thought himself past all that sort of thing, he had fallen headlong in love with the glamorous, fascinating Lady Sybil Greville the moment he saw her (at a charity event to which he had been invited by a hostess anxious for him to head her subscription list). He had decided there and then, in his pragmatic way, that his only chance was to make himself necessary to her through his money and went about it with his usual no-holds-barred strategy. In the event, he was the one who had been bowled over by her ready acceptance of his proposal.

There may have been sceptical eyebrows raised at the whirlwind romance between this Arthur Foley, who was, perhaps *not quite*, and Lady Sybil, but on the whole the county approved her sensible choice, he knew that. How else could she, left an orphan, have kept up the lifestyle to which she'd been accustomed since birth? Theoretically she could have married anyone she chose, but when it came down to it, even her sparkling personality and undoubted pedigree were not enough to persuade the scions of the aristocracy, preoccupied with their own lack of finances, to take on the burdens she represented. Her feckless father had died, leaving her an heiress to nothing but debts, a dilapidated house and a run-down estate, much of which was due to be sold to pay off death duties. By marrying Arthur, Sybil had got herself out of a very deep hole, and she never forgot it. She had provided him with constant affection, home and a family: first there was Grev, whom he loved dearly, and then his little golden-haired Eunice, who was his pride and joy. He had achieved standing and a certain amount of respect in county society (as if he cared a fig for that!) although his money and his generous contributions to charity had no doubt helped, he thought wryly. It never occurred to him that much of the respect accorded to him might have had more to do with his own qualities than for his position as Lady Sybil's husband.

But let 'em think what they wanted, she had brought to their marriage warmth, tenderness and grace, and had continued to make him the happiest and most contented man on Earth. Showering her with what worldly wealth he had was the least of it. He would have climbed up and given her the top brick off the chimney if she'd wanted it.

Sybil had been forced to pull herself together before she went to find her husband. The news she had to tell him was good, but it was going to be difficult for both of them to receive it with as much joy as they should. When she was dressed, she sent her maid, Edith, away (what *was* she to do about Edith? she worried yet again, working the treadmill of her thoughts, then pushed the worry determinedly aside). She inspected herself in the mirror, appalled at the signs of her own distress. How too dreary she looked! With a sigh of dissatisfaction she tweaked down the jacket of her sober tailor-made. It was all very well for the government to preach economy and stick up posters declaring that dressing extravagantly in wartime was not only bad form; worse, it was unpatriotic. Throughout the war she had been willing to obey, but really by now, she was quite sick of wearing grey, and seeing everyone else wear it, as if that would have helped the soldiers in any case. She had always prided herself on being well turned out. And what was the use of a wardrobe full of beautiful, pre-war clothes waiting to be worn again, if not to cheer oneself, and everyone else up? There didn't seem to be much cheerfulness about yet, six months after the war had ended. Nor much incentive to do anything, now that her hard work was no longer needed.

Despite everything, the war had been good for Sybil in many ways. After Grev's departure – and especially after that desolate time when he had been posted missing, believed killed – she put everything she had into occupying herself with the war effort. Being busy and active had helped to give her something to think about while her heart was slowly breaking for her beloved son over there in France. She no longer had the time to think, a thousand times a day, if only...

She had been too old to see active service, though she would have been one of the first to rush off and drive an ambulance, despite her age, if she had not felt her responsibilities were at home with Arthur, after his heart attack. Instead, she had thrown herself first of all into organising help for Belgian refugees, and when the necessity for this became a little less urgent, she had further secured for herself a post working under Gervase Hatherley, their neighbour, who was concerned with the administration of military hospitals in the area. She wore a Red Cross uniform and enjoyed the work, although it was quite hard and demanding. She hadn't turned a hair when Oaklands itself was commandeered as a convalescent hospital and long huts to serve as wards sprang up like mushrooms in the smoothly tended grounds. Only part of the house itself was given over to the hospital – the ballroom and the large dining room as specialist wards, smaller rooms as sitting and rest rooms for the patients and accommodation for the hospital staff– but all the same, she saw to it that valuable furniture was carted up to the attics, along with silver and other valuables in trunks and tea chests, there to be stored for the duration of the house's occupation. The best pictures were removed, twenty-foot-long curtains were caught back and their nether portions encased in holland bags. Sybil was leaving nothing to chance, having heard tales of the soldiery. Soon, now, it would all be restored to the family. Meanwhile...

She looked at herself again, resolutely dismissed all thoughts of Edith and blotted her tears. She tidied her hair, dabbed scent behind her ears and on her wrists, and thus fortified, set forth with straightened shoulders to find Arthur in his study.

At the other end of the village, on the summit of the Hill, under the very same windswept thorn on which the crow had previously perched, sat Herbert Reardon.

He had left his motorcycle at the foot of the hill, behind a hedge, and climbed the rough path at a good pace. Despite his recent long spells in hospital, he was in good physical shape once more. He had always been tough; the desperate conditions he and all the other men had suffered during their time in France and Belgium had not been without its effect on him, but he was still a young man and his splendid constitution had helped him through the traumatic months after receiving his terrible burns; latterly, in hospital, between operations, he had kept himself fit with self-imposed exercises. He was still breathing easily when he reached the top.

He sat on the stony ground, his heavy coat providing insulation from the cold, and ate the sandwiches his landlady had provided. They weren't as good as Em's. The beef she'd managed to get from somewhere wasn't half bad, admittedly, but the bread was grey and gritty, the product of austerity flour, and the margarine was thinly scraped. Still, there was plenty of mustard, and he got them down with the help of the tea from his Thermos, though awful as only his landlady knew how to make it.

He had a week, possibly a little more, before him, to undertake what he had come to Broughton Underhill to do.

After his meeting with Henry Paskin he had suddenly known that his mind was made up. Inspector, eh? That had made a difference. He knew what he was going to do (and perhaps had intended to do all along) and had acted immediately, before he had the chance to think better of it. He had made application to rejoin the police and was once more a member of the Worcestershire Constabulary – or at least, he would be at the beginning of the next working week. It wasn't without regret that he'd abandoned the idea of world travel, but one day perhaps he might take it up again, who was to say? It was Henry who had brought it home to him how much police work was in his blood, that it had always meant more than simply a lucky escape from work in a foundry or a factory, and how rewarding he had always found it, all in all, despite the obstructions to promotion. And perhaps the answers to the large ethical questions the war had posed were not, after all, only to be found in distant lands, philosophies and religions, but equally here at home. As an unencumbered single man, and not likely ever to be anything else now, he would not lack opportunity to read and pursue as much as he wished the questions that puzzled him.

He had been warned that he would in all likelihood have to start in the uniformed branch all over again, but he knew his war experience, if it had done nothing else, had given him a different and a broader perspective, which would not be a bar to his ambition of once more becoming a detective. Meanwhile, during the interim, he believed if he was discreet enough about what he thought of as his private business here it need not come to the ears of officialdom.

He had already made a tentative start on his enquiries, though what he had achieved hadn't amounted to much. After that meeting in the churchyard with Marianne Wentworth's sister, Nella, the nurse, he had successfully booked himself in at the Greville Arms for a few days, starting from tomorrow, and then, before going to find Henry Paskin, he had decided to return to the rectory and call on the Reverend Wentworth. The meeting with him had turned out to be inconclusive, though in actual fact he had expected nothing less. A queer fish and not half, he had thought the reverend on the day Marianne had been found, and saw no reason to change his mind now.

After the rectory door closed behind him, propelled by some compulsion, he had paid his respects to his daughter Marianne's grave, and silently renewed his promises to her. All in all, he wasn't entirely dissatisfied, so far. Despite Nella's apparent dismissal of what he'd said, he believed that when their conversation had sunk in she might decide to be more forthcoming. Intuition told him her hostility arose because she was afraid he would find out whatever it was she was concealing. Maybe she would come round and see sense. Maybe he could talk her into it. We shall see, he told himself.

And that youngest sister now – Amy, wasn't it? – how old would she have been in 1914? Thirteen, not old enough at that time to have been questioned too closely, and talking to her now might not be much use. It all depended on how good her memory was. On the other hand, though only having caught a glimpse of her as he left the rectory, he had a feeling he might not be wasting his time with her. That practised glance had shown him a bright-eyed young woman who noticed things – and wasn't above a bit of eaves-dropping, he thought. She'd been standing under that gloomy stained-glass window in the dark hall when he'd come out of the reverend's study and the sharp look she gave him convinced him she'd overheard what had been said. She'd been watching him in the churchyard, too, he was sure.

A few minutes later, almost as if his previous thoughts had conjured her up, he saw Amy Wentworth again, walking down the village street far below him, swinging a basket, unmistakable with that red hair showing under the tam she wore. If she was going shopping, she'd be dis-appointed: the village was deserted, curtains drawn and blinds down in respect, for the funeral of an old village biddy later that afternoon, he'd learnt. He understood how much store folk set by that sort of thing, and for that very reason had decided to abandon his enquiries until the next day as soon as he'd learnt about the funeral. He saw Amy pause before the shop, which he could have told her was closed, then turn impatiently round and begin walking back home.

The arrival of the eleven o'clock snack he'd been recommended to take (small meals at frequent intervals, rather than the large breakfasts and even larger dinners that he'd been used to all his life) made a welcome diversion to Arthur Foley's thoughts. That said everything about his situation, he thought, when a cup of tea and a bun was a highlight of the morning. But it had become something to look forward to; it broke up the day, especially when it was accompanied by his wife bearing Nella's good news of the telegram announcing that William was coming home, at last.

'It'll be good to see the lad again,' he said spreading plum and apple jam on to one of Mrs Cherry's plain scones. The apple, added to make up for a lack of sugar, diluted the rich colour of the jam to an unappetising pale pink, but it tasted rather better than it looked. 'Liven things up at the rectory, he will.' For the girls, maybe, but as for the rector... Arthur said nothing, however. His opinion of Francis Wentworth he kept to himself, as always. What sort of faith was it that was lost at the first setback? And seemed to have been found again so easily?

She smiled, 'Knowing William, I'm sure that's true.'

He knew that she'd been weeping, and why. Briefly, he touched her hand as he accepted another cup of tea from her, admiring her self-control, wishing, with an almost physical pain, that she would allow him to comfort her. But, close as they were, this was one area where he could not reach her. Poor Sybil. It was hard for anyone, and perhaps even harder for her than for most people, to show delight at the homecoming of returning heroes when one's own beloved son would never come home again. *Missing, believed killed.* Perhaps the worst verdict of all, because without proof, it fostered desperate, unrealistic hope: that Grev might after all, in the face of all evidence to the contrary, have survived, having perhaps been taken prisoner, or become shell-shocked and wandered off, wounded, lost his memory... anything at all. That he might still turn up. It was a cruel hope, because just occasionally, such cases were reported.

She walked to the window, her glance sweeping, too quickly, past the silver-framed photograph of her son, not one of him in uniform, just a snapshot caught when he was sitting in characteristic pose, one knee drawn up, pencil and music score in hand, under the old cedar on the lawn. She stood for a moment looking out over the sadly neglected garden, absently fiddling with the forsythia in a pewter vase on the sill, the few branches she had brought in for the warmth to force into bloom. He had been plagued recently

121

by the thought that all was not well with his wife. Not ill – Sybil had a magnificent constitution – but not quite the ticket, a euphemism that disguised the fact that in actual fact he was worried about her... seriously worried. Then she turned to face him again and when she next spoke, it was of something quite other, in the way she had of relegating anything upsetting to a separate compartment of her mind. 'I've just been having a little talk with Eunice, the silly girl. The sooner I get her presented and off our hands, the better.'

'Eunice?' he repeated with a smile. 'You want to get rid of our little Eunice?'

'Oh, Arthur, you know very well what I mean! She's so against coming out next year, I'm afraid she'll do something really silly, like – like, well, I don't know, I'm sure. Throwing herself away simply out of sympathy on one of those soldiers she's always talking to, or something – which, incidentally, I wish she wouldn't do. I know she means well, the dear child, and I'm sure the men do appreciate a little civilised female conversation, but it doesn't do to give them ideas, you know. That young warrant officer, Shawcross, they tell me he thinks the sun shines out of her. And she...' She paused. Her face paled. 'She wouldn't do that, would she, Arthur?'

'Of course not, Sybil, she hardly knows the young fellow. Do calm down. Eunice wouldn't do anything so reckless.' And had other ideas, anyway, he suspected.

But Sybil was very much afraid she might. Eunice had grown so independent – cut her hair, shortened her skirts, taken up smoking – since

122

she had found herself working with her father during the war, at first just helping out when his office manager enlisted and then gradually taking on more and more responsibility until Arthur declared her indispensable. The hard work seemed to suit her and had overturned everyone's opinion of her as a girl who was not strong, which now seemed to have been engendered largely by her delicate looks and her ability to catch cold easily.

But now the office manager had returned and claimed his position back, as he had every right to do, and Eunice was at a loose end. There was no telling what she might take it into her head to do. Still the same dear girl, but for all her sweet gentleness, Eunice had always been stubborn, Sybil thought. And self-sacrificing. And the time she spent with young Shawcross... Oh, dear God!

But the possibility, too terrible to envisage, was already being pushed to the back of her mind, another idea having taken its place. 'I know! We must make some sort of an occasion out of William's return. Some sort of party, not too big. A dinner party, perhaps, no more than twelve, I don't believe there will be enough young men otherwise for Eunice to meet. I can think of several who are home by now,' she added, casting her mind down the list of suitable candidates she had already drawn up for when the London season, as it was sure to do, regained its pre-war splendour, with the nagging reminder, all too often in her mind, that Eunice was already twenty. She refused to think that she might well have a real battle on her hands now, as far as

Eunice herself was concerned. 'It will be something for us all to look forward to. No doubt Mrs Cherry can be persuaded to rise to the occasion and stretch the rations to provide something a little special in the way of food...'

But thinking of Mrs Cherry's spectacular pre-war prawn soufflé, she shook her head and sighed. So many eggs! A crown of lamb, or a saddle? Impossible to get hold of unless one pocketed one's principles and bought expensively on the black market. Iced puddings – but all that sugar and cream! Champagne? Well, Arthur probably still had that at least in his cellar. But really, it was too bad. The war over for six months and still everything austerity this and austerity that. Everyone was being told that there could be no return to the indulgent life they had all led before the war, but one might have expected some sort of return to civilisation by now. And we were the ones who had won the war! 'I expect we shall have to make do with carrot pudding or something equally dreary,' she said with a sigh.

'My dear Sybil ... aren't you being a little premature, planning something like that?'

'Not in the least! If we wait for things to return to normal after this terrible war, we might wait for ever. I'll see to it right away. Meanwhile, you must speak to Eunice, Arthur – she listens to you where she certainly doesn't to me.'

'I'll see what I can do. But remember,' he added with a smile, 'the party's supposed to be for William, not Eunice.'

'Dear Arthur, I know I can rely on you.' She kissed the top of his head, delighted to have found something to busy herself with. He reached up and caught her hand and pressed his lips to her wrist, allowing them to stay there until she met his eyes and curved her lips into an answering smile. He might be sixty-three, with a dicky heart, but he also had a wife who was an ardent and desirable woman. They were still well pleased with each other.

Amy realised her mistake as soon as she saw Miss Aspinall's closed door. It was almost always, except on Sundays and in the worst weather, propped open by a seven-pound weight that had a ring in the top to lift it. From her front room Miss Aspinall, a neat, tidy little body, sold humbugs, liquorice bootlaces, penny sherbets and pear drops, as well as home-made treacle toffee in a flat tin from which she cracked off a generous ha'porth with a little toffee hammer. A genteel lady come upon hard times, she insisted that it wasn't a *shop* she ran, but an establishment for selling confectionery; The Shop was the one on the corner kept by the Eastwolds, where you could buy anything from a quarter pound of boiled ham to a pair of moleskin breeches, a tin bath or a gallon of paraffin, post a parcel or buy a stamp.

The Shop, in fact, had been Amy's main objective, with a mission to buy stamps for Nella, and anything nice to eat, if by some miracle any such thing should suddenly have appeared, but that was already closed too – and all the cottage windows in the village had their curtains decently drawn as a mark of respect; it was the funeral, of course, in a couple of hours, the time of which she had entirely forgotten. She should have remembered, she thought, turning back towards Church Lane and the rectory. Neither Florrie nor Grandmama had been around to remind her when she set off, and without doubt, her lapse would have been noticed in the village, despite the closed curtains. She was very sorry, she had liked old Mrs Cromer, and was mortified at her thoughtless blunder, which would do nothing to bolster the impression she was trying to give nowadays of being the grown-up and responsible Miss Aimeé Wentworth, no longer little Amy from the rectory, everyone's pet.

'Amy!'

She'd been so absorbed she hadn't heard the bicycle behind her, though it made enough noise, a ramshackle old piece of machinery that was typical of Steven Rafferty. He braked to a halt, flung a long leg over the crossbar and began to walk beside her, pulling off his tweed cap so that his springing black hair leapt up in a crest. 'Well, Amy, aren't you pleased to see me, or even a bit surprised?'

'Of course I'm pleased, but not surprised. Your mother told us she was expecting you.'

The occasions on which Amy had seen Steven lately had been few. Getting from Cambridge to Broughton had never been easy, and what with half the trains being commandeered as troop trains, it had been a desperate undertaking during the war, hazardous as to its duration and unpredictable in the way of timetables. She was suddenly struck now by the change in him from the bespectacled, gangling, ill-clad youth he'd been before the war. He was wearing a soft collar and a tweed suit and a college scarf flung casually around his neck, that somehow suited the typical academic air there had always been about Steven, even as a boy: slightly absent-minded, serious. Already by now he was a little stoop-shouldered, quietly spoken, but with an added air of confidence. True, he still towered above her (even though she was an inch or two taller than Nella, now), still wore thick spectacles, but when he took them off to polish them with his handkerchief – the same old habit – she noticed for the first time what very nice brown eyes he had. 'How are you?' she asked belatedly.

'I'm very well, thank you. There's no need to ask how you are, Amy. You look blooming, my dear. You've put your hair up. Quite the grown up young lady, now,' he added in a sober, elderly sort of way.

Oh, Steven! She burst out laughing but he didn't look abashed, as he would have done once, just watched her with a slightly quizzical smile. He had meant the remark as a compliment, she knew, really, but that pedantic way of putting it was so typical of Steven. 'My old hair, it's such a bother. I think I'll cut it off, like Nella.'

'Don't!' he said, quite sharply, then added, with a smile, 'It won't be Amy, without that lovely hair.'

She dimpled, and wished she had on a prettier hat than the old grey tam she had jammed onto her curls, and the cape with the tatty rabbit-fur collar. As he went on polishing his spectacle lenses, she observed him with further interest. Really, without his glasses, he'd actually become

– well, not good-looking, he would never be that, he was altogether too bony, but not bad. 'How long are you here for this time?'

'I'm not entirely sure. The Institute's closing down, since there's no need for it any longer. I'm trying to arrange to go back to college – lecturing or some such – if they can find a place for me,' he added, somewhat diffidently.

Desperate to get into the army like everyone else of his generation, he had been turned down, as he had predicted, because of his poor eyesight. But, though filled with shame at being left at home when all his contemporaries were fighting, he had made the best of it, used his brilliant physics degree to get himself employed on scientific research, and for the rest of the war he had been one of the boffins working on various highly secret and sensitive projects at a scientific institute in Cambridge, set up for what precise purposes Amy had never known.

'Yes, your mother told us what you were hoping for,' she said with a smile. 'We all wish you success, but I don't suppose there's much doubt they'll want you, is there?'

'Oh, I don't know!' he replied, cautiously. 'I don't count chickens.' He was still as unassuming about his achievements, as modest about other people's good opinion of him as he always had been.

'I would have thought they might welcome you with open arms, in the circumstances.'

He flushed slightly and Amy bit her lip, regretting the last few words. Did he think she was referring to the vacancies left by all those

128

clever young men, students and dons alike, who had jettisoned their studies and their careers to fight for their country and would never return to finish them, and that they'd have to make do with what was left to replace them? That wasn't what she had meant at all – rather that it appeared to be just the sort of career that seemed expressly designed for Steven, the Prof, as they always used to call him. To make up for her mistake, she told him about William coming home and saw his face light up.

For a moment he seemed quite overcome, at a loss for words. 'William? Really? Well. Quite like old times.' He stopped, rather abruptly. Poor Steven, it was his turn now to feel he'd put his foot in it. He was thinking of the other two in their little group, Amy could tell, who would not come back. *Their* group, she emphasised to herself, not me. I wasn't one of them, I was still too young. A pest who tagged along, a baby, they thought me. But I wasn't a baby. I knew what was going on.

They fell a little silent. He was walking with her up Church Lane, though it was not on his way home. I'll bet he hasn't realised, she thought. 'Will you come in and say hello to the others, Steven? Have some tea?'

'Oh, er, no thank you.' He looked around, blinking at finding himself where he was, and she laughed. 'I'll pop in later. Do bring William down to see us. My mother will be so glad to see him again – and you, of course.'

'Oh, yes,' replied Amy uncomfortably. She had a vague idea clever Mrs Rafferty disapproved of her.

He turned his bicycle round and prepared to ride off. For a moment he said nothing, then suddenly, he smiled at her. 'Poor Amy. You haven't had much fun these last years, have you?'

His unexpected sympathy brought a warmth to her face. Funny old Steven. He was being very nice to her – but then, he always had been kind, waiting for her when she fell behind the older ones, unable to keep up, on the occasions they'd been compelled to have her in their company, sticking up for her when she said something silly or childish that made the others laugh. She gave him one of her most dazzling smiles. 'Well, Steven, it's all going to be different now, isn't it?'

'I hope so. Goodbye, Amy.' With a ring of his bell, he was off.

Chapter Twelve

'A party! Oh, a dinner party and I've nothing to wear!' Amy wailed.

'Nonsense Amy, you have your pretty blue muslin.'

'Which I've had since I was *thirteen*, Grandy! Besides, it's far too cold, yet, for muslin. If I have to wear that, the dress won't be the only thing that's blue.'

'Amy, Amy,' her grandmother remonstrated.

'We can't *go*, we've nothing to wear, any of us!'

'Don't exaggerate,' said Nella, 'of course we have.'

Amy spun round to her sister. 'All right, then, what do *you* intend wearing?'

'Me? Oh, I don't know – anything. I suppose it will be my dark blue. It's suitable, and I shall be quite warm and comfortable into the bargain.'

'It might be suitable, but it's frightful. You should never wear dark blue, it doesn't become your colouring. And besides, I should think you'd be sick of it, by now. It's exactly the same colour as your uniform.'

Nella paused. 'Well, I haven't anything better. Anyway, it doesn't matter. Nobody will notice what I'm wearing.'

'Oh yes, they will! Everybody always notices what everyone else is wearing. And you know Aunt Sybil's and Eunice's dresses will be the last word.'

'A new dress isn't the be all and end all,' Nella said impatiently, suppressing the thought of how long it was since she'd had anything new.

Amy didn't answer. An idea had popped into her head, and she wondered if she dare...

'We could all do with something new to wear, child,' put in their grandmother crisply. 'But we shall just have to make the best of what we have.'

Amy took a deep breath. 'Why should we, with all those beautiful things in Mama's trunk? What good are they doing, all shut up?'

Speculation passed between them, each of them thinking of Dorothea's clothes and other possessions, lying for years between folds of tissue paper in a chest in the attic. Mrs Villiers, especially, was thoughtful. 'Oh, very well, I'll ask your father,' she said at last, without the least hope of success. It would be tantamount to asking permission to violate a shrine.

Amy braced herself. 'No, let me. He's more likely to say yes if I ask.'

Another silence. Nella thought yes, he might. Mrs Villiers pursed her lips. There was no denying that Francis would do more for Amy than anyone – if Amy would let him. But the truth was, she had grown to avoid her father whenever she could, for what reason Eleanor had never been able to fathom, almost as if she were embarrassed, or even a little scared, in his presence, though it had to be admitted that his dark silences could intimidate anyone. That Amy was willing now to beard him in his den said a great deal about the poor child's longing for a few new clothes, although, young and self-absorbed as Amy could still sometimes be, compared with Nella, their grandmother did not believe this was mere vanity – just that she hadn't been thrown into maturity, as her sister had, by the terrible experiences of the war. She could not wait to grow up, of course – but who could blame any young girl for that?

And when Amy emerged from the study ten minutes later, she was beaming. 'I knew it would be all right. We can go ahead,' she said, relief at having faced her father making her dance up the stairs, light as a leaf.

Mrs Villiers lifted her eyes as they followed her. 'I do believe you could charm the birds off the trees, miss.' She did not know what it had cost Amy to approach her father.

Most of Dorothea's clothes were impractical, since she had had no need of any that were not, never having been one of the world's labourers. Amy pulled out the dresses greedily, stroked the silks and velvets with sensuous fingers while wrinkling her nose at the smell of camphor, pouncing on a sophisticated emerald and black shot satin gown with black lace sleeves and a fall of the same lace round the low neck – though more in hope than expectation – and which indeed Mrs Villiers was immediately compelled to veto, not only on the grounds of its unsuitability for a young girl, but also because it was one Dorothea had worn on an unusually grand occasion at the bishop's palace, and Francis would be sure to remember it.

In the end, Eleanor chose for her a simple deep ivory crêpe de Chine to which Amy, seizing the advantage, added a coffee-coloured georgette which she declared she must combine with it. 'Because of course it will mean a complete remake,' she said, scooping up an armful of pretty underwear while she had the chance, and adding some flesh-coloured silk stockings and a pair of bronze satin, high-heeled slippers with two delicate straps over the instep to her booty. 'Everything's hopelessly out of date.'

Nella sighed. 'Don't bank on it. It might be a party that never was.'

'How can you be such a wet blanket!'

Because this invitation, for one thing, had been an unofficial one until William arrived home – and there was as yet no indication when exactly this would be. For another, even Sybil was aware that many of the homecoming soldiers were regarding the price they had paid for victory as too high to warrant the blowing of trumpets.

'There's no guarantee William will be in the mood for social occasions, Amy.'

'Yes, I do know, Grandy, I haven't forgotten,' Amy replied, sobering. 'But it's not going to help anybody if we all go around in sackcloth and ashes, is it?'

Nella felt contrite. 'You're right, Amy, dear, of course. Help me to choose something, too. We don't want to be seen as the church mice at this feast.'

She hoped Amy would not be disappointed, but very much feared she might. Not altogether because William might not wish for such a celebration: she did not really think even the war would have changed his amenable good nature, and whatever his private thoughts, he would go along with it, she was sure. It was more likely to be Eunice who could be the one to put a spoke in the wheel. No one, knowing Sybil, could believe that this affair she hoped to arrange for William's homecoming was entirely altruistic. It was a typically impulsive and generous gesture on her part, but it would also provide an opportunity for Eunice to become reacquainted with those who had been marked down for her by her mother before the war. But the war had changed everybody. Eunice was not the biddable girl she had been then.

And especially don't expect William to be the same boy who left home, Nella wanted to warn everyone. She had seen the change in him, the last and only time they had met in the wartime years, just after her arrival in France. Knowing which hospital she was attached to, he had sought her out when he had an unexpected two-day leave pass. By then he was already, at twenty-one, a captain, though this was not so unusual. Promotion came quickly at the front: officers, leading their men, were prime targets for the enemy guns.

Accustomed as she was by then to seeing men in every stage of battle fatigue, she had been shocked by his appearance. 'It's nothing,' he said. 'We were entrenched in a place they call Bellyache Wood, with a so-called medicinal spring. The name speaks for itself.' He had laughed, but there was more to it than that. His big frame was wasted, his hands shook from time to time, his face was gaunt, his eyes haunted, as all their eyes were – boys who had seen and lived through horrors that no human being should have to witness. Neither she nor William had any idea that was to be their last meeting during the fighting, that he would soon be sent out on the Gallipoli campaign, suffer dysentery and fever, and after the huge and humiliating Allied defeat there, be sent back to France again.

Just a few hours they'd had together. 'What will you do when all this is over? Go back to Oxford?'

No, he would not go back. He had been destined for the law, and politics thereafter, but now he was totally disillusioned; it was the politicians who had got them into this mess. After the war, it was practical and useful people who were going to be needed, people like their uncle, Arthur Foley. 'And women like Eunice,' he finished with a laugh. 'You could have knocked me down with a feather when I heard what she was doing, helping to keep his business going. Surprising girl. She writes to me every week, you know.'

'To me, too – though not every week,' Nella smiled.

But perhaps I have been wrong about that, she thought now.

The responsible work Eunice had done helping her father had brought about a huge change in her. Who would ever have predicted what she would become? She had taken the load from Arthur's shoulders, become his prop and mainstay, running the affairs of the works so capably and efficiently. She had always been ready to help lame ducks, take other people's burdens to heart – but Nella was rather afraid that she had now become prone to arranging their affairs, too.

What was Aunt Sybil going to think when she learnt of the plans Eunice was making? To spend some time in Paris, perhaps to find some work there! A scheme Nella had only learnt of by chance, when she and Eunice had been having a cup of tea together before Nella went home after finishing her shift.

'Paris? Work? Are you mad, Eunice? It must be worse over there than here in the aftermath of the war!'

'Oh, I don't know, there must be something I could do,' Eunice said, sitting on the edge of the table, swinging her pretty little foot. She looked sideways at Nella. 'Why don't you come, too? It's what you need.'

'I've had enough of France, thank you. Whatever made you think of *Paris*?'

'Oh, nothing special.' She looked evasive, and

somehow troubled. For a moment, Nella thought she was going to give her reasons for this extraordinary decision, but then she smiled, and shrugged. 'I was talking to that doctor of yours, Geddes ... he spent some time there before he came to England, didn't he?'

'Did he?' Nella asked, wondering just what Eunice meant by 'that doctor of yours'. Yours, the hospital's, or yours, Nella? She had evidently lost no time since his arrival in getting to know him. The hospital's, of course. Eunice never made double-tongued remarks.

Amy had a good eye, and quick, clever fingers, and seams were soon unpicked, the pieces carefully aired, pressed and recut into what she considered more fashionable styles. For the next few days she treadled away so furiously on the old Singer that the dresses were finished at least a good two or three weeks before they were likely to be needed – assuming they ever were.

Her own dress was disappointingly not the one she had envisaged, sliding seductively around her hips, but a compromise. At least it gave her the slender silhouette she longed for: a long, short-sleeved V-neckline tunic from the coffee-coloured georgette, worn over a long, narrow shift cut from the ivory crêpe de Chine, with a creamy silk rose she was told must be tucked demurely into the neckline. Compromises are rarely entirely satisfactory, however, and when she tried it on, she twisted this way and that to see herself in the mirror. It felt homemade, she declared, tugging at the seams, and still smelt, a little, of mothballs, though anyone could see she was secretly delighted with herself, as well she might be, thought Nella.

'It looks neither home-made, nor smells in the least of mothballs. You look absolutely sweet, Amy!'

Amy glowed. She decided that if she put her hair up in a Grecian knot, it might not be so bad. And there was in the trunk a gold bracelet she might be allowed to wear, high on her arm... 'Well, you look lovely, yourself – and much more elegant than I ever could,' she replied generously.

Nella had once thought the time would never again come when clothes, when looking and feeling one's best and generally being a woman again, would matter, but yes, she did like the look of herself in the simple, bronze-gold heavy silk Amy had unerringly selected. It had scarcely needed any altering for Nella, not much more than a few inches off the hem, but its rich colour was lovely, and the burnt orange bandeau Amy wound around her hair did add a glow to her pale skin. It needed only the long rope of dark ambers Mrs Villiers slid over her head. But she mentally consigned it to the back of her wardrobe; she could not envisage wearing this finery in the foreseeable future.

Amy said, 'What will you wear, Grandy?'

Mrs Villiers replied dryly that there would be enough with two belles of the ball and her pearls and her black velvet would suffice very well, thank you.

Sybil was similarly preoccupied with the party,

addressing envelopes ready for posting when William came home and she had judged his reaction to the idea. She frowned as the gold nib of her fountain pen spluttered slightly over the address she had just written. Oh, bother! How too tiresome. She wiped the nib carefully on her flannel penwiper in its shagreen case and looked again at the envelope. Would it pass muster? She did not want to waste any of the last of her best pre-war stationery, creamy and thick as card, by rewriting it. There was no indication when supplies would be resumed.

Tapping the pen against her teeth, she glanced across to the big chair in the corner, where Eunice was daintily curled with her feet up and her softly waved head against a cushion, ostensibly reading, but with that small, secret, puzzling smile which hovered around her mouth whenever she thought herself unobserved, and which told her mother she was paying no attention to what she read and was thinking of something else entirely.

She frowned and turned back to her list. It was not promising.

There were all the Wentworths, of course, including the guest of honour, William; herself, Arthur and Eunice, which made eight. She considered the remaining names and reluctantly decided against very rich, handsome and immensely tall Henry Summers-Gently; though at the top of her list, pre-war, he had never at the best of times been the most amusing conversationalist, and now that he'd returned home from France he hardly spoke at all, stared into the distance and sometimes looked as though he might be going mad. It was the duty of every responsible mama to see her daughter settled, and he was a good match, but one didn't want to marry off poor Eunice at any cost; what she really wanted for her child was a good man like Arthur who would look after her in case – her thoughts faltered – in case anything should happen to her, or to Arthur. For a moment she stared blindly out of the window. Then, determinedly, she took up her pen again.

Gervase Hatherley? Well, no. Perhaps not. He was simply too boring to be regarded as a potential son-in-law. In addition, dear Nella would be one of her guests, and it was obvious that, no doubt because he had been so very devoted to poor Marianne, even the sound of Hatherley's name was painful to her. Sybil knew she avoided situations where she was likely to meet him. It really looked as though the possibles were boiling down to George Featherstonehaugh, who had come out of the war having suffered nothing worse than something utterly disgusting called trench fever, which was apparently caused by the bite of a louse – but perhaps one wouldn't mention that – and to pleasant, handsome Freddie Anstruther. She put a mental star against this last name. Yes, Freddie could be a strong contender. He had a nice, obliging nature, had survived the war with only a shoulder wound and much gallantry, had inherited a large house and estate not too far away, and several thousand a year to go with it. He was a bit of an ass, but his only major fault, that Sybil could see, was that he was likely to talk of nothing else but how soon hunting could be resumed, which was frightfully tedious, but one couldn't have everything. Of course, his sister, Gertrude, would have to be included, a woman with a face like a boot who had been something terrifying in the Ministry of Food during the war. Which made a total of eleven, and left her short of a man. It looked as though she would have to invite Gervase Hatherley, after all. But that might be just too embarrassing ... oh, dear!

This dinner party was proving a little more than Sybil had anticipated. Well, I've started it and I must go on with it, and I'll do my best to enjoy it, she thought. Her matrimonial ambitions for Eunice were only part of this proposed junket; she was genuinely pleased with the opportunity to celebrate William's homecoming, but she could feel no sense of joy. Would she never cease to feel that everything was dust and ashes since the loss of Grev? People thought her hard because, when he was believed to have been killed, she had never, in public at any rate, shed a tear, although the thought of him being blown to pieces, his body parts never found, was sometimes more than she could bear. Yet, she must still go on. She was still only forty-two and must manage to go on for the rest of her life. She pressed a hand to her temples.

'We must decide what you are to wear, Eunice,' she said at last, forcing herself back to the matter in hand and handing her daughter the list to look over.

Eunice looked up. 'Oh, I don't care what I wear. All that's such a bore,' she replied, though in fact she found the selection and wearing of pretty clothes anything but a bore, and she very much wanted to look her best at this particular party; it was simply that she increasingly felt if she did not stick up for herself her mama's ambitions might swallow her up. She wanted to say all this marriage-making was rot, that no one was going to bother with that sort of thing anymore, but she knew the last wasn't true: there would always be women like her mother, on the lookout for their daughters, although Eunice conceded that her mother genuinely wished to see her happily settled; the trouble was, happiness to her certainly included freedom from anxiety about money.

Sybil said suddenly, 'I think I'll take a walk, Eunice.' It was no good, she simply could not concentrate, with this other thing on her mind. 'I have rather a headache and perhaps the fresh air will do me good.'

Eunice, contrite, put aside her book. 'Would you like me to come with you, Mother?'

'No, no, just a few minutes' fresh air, that should clear it.'

'Are you sure? You do look awfully pale.'

'Dearest child, I'm quite sure, thank you.'

'In that case...' Eunice put the list down, unread, smiled at her mother and said she thought she might walk along to visit the convalescents. She was aware of her mother's eyes following her, knowing that these excursions were something else of which Sybil highly disapproved, but could find no adequate reason for stopping.

Whenever Sybil was troubled, one of the things which helped her was to walk around her garden.

She called it her garden but was under no illusion that it really belonged to Hughes, her head gardener. He was a tyrant who had not, before the war, allowed her to do anything much more exacting than deadhead the roses – under his supervision, of course. He would listen to her suggestions, nod, and then act upon them or not, as he felt fit. She was sure he had been quite glad that her war work had left her with no time to interfere, allowing him to concentrate on his vegetables.

She took deep breaths of the fresh, cold air as she walked around. It was better to think about the garden than this other dreadful business, which was beginning to make her feel less alarmed than it had at first, but more angry. She bent to pull a dandelion in the lawn. It snapped off, as Hughes always warned her they would. The two of them kept up a running battle which she'd rather suspected he enjoyed as much as she did, truth to tell, about what was to go where and how, especially since he usually won, and was often proved right. But she'd won over the philadelphus he'd attacked so ferociously with the pruning shears early one spring. There were no arching branches dripping with heavenly perfumed white flowers that year. He kept silent, but thereafter the shrub had been pruned at the proper time.

She was sad to see how neglected everything now was. What havoc the war had wreaked, even in the thousand little everyday, but important, things that made life worth living.

She paused to speak to some of the recuperating soldiers who were making a start on helping to restore the garden to its old beauty, under the direction of that formidable sergeant major, Broadbent, with his jaw half blown off. Sybil applauded his courage and tenacity in herding his volunteers, but to get the garden in good order again it was going to take a great deal more than goodwill, which was the most many of them could yet manage. None of the men was yet in the prime of health and this sort of work needed strong men, but it was a start, they had already made a difference, and in any case, she understood very well that it wasn't the garden itself which was the object: it was the contribution to the men's well-being which it would make. Not only by physical exercise, but with the feeling of damp, crumbly earth beneath your fingers, watching the yearly miracle, the cycle of life start again, the understanding that war could not destroy everything.

She came to a decision. She had a problem, and the problem must be faced and not just put aside. She must do something about it.

There was always a distinct brightening when Eunice came into the wards. A pretty face, a smile and a word for everyone, perfumed and prettily dressed, she was a change from the eternally busy, uniformed nurses and brought a breath of fresh air and femininity into the wards.

She spoke to one or two, then went to sit by Jack Shawcross, to whom she made daily visits. He was the son of a Huddersfield mill worker who'd won a grammar school scholarship, become a bank clerk, enlisted in the ranks at the beginning of the war and had risen rapidly to warrant officer, all of which were absolutely wonderful achievements, though her mother probably would not see it that way. Sympathetic as she was to all the men who had ended up here at Oaklands, Sybil was not able to keep a trace of disapproval from her voice whenever Eunice mentioned the young soldier. She would have been astonished, not to say delighted, at the nature of the conversation which followed, and to hear Eunice's bracing tone when sat down by his bed.

'I've brought you a book, I hope it isn't one you've read.' He glanced briefly at *Diary of a Nobody*, shook his head and murmured his thanks.

'It's very light. I think you'll find it amusing. Have you replied to your dear Emily's letter yet, Jack?'

'No.'

'That's not really fair, is it? She must be waiting for an answer.'

'Then she'll have a long wait. I won't have anybody marrying me out of sympathy.'

'Why don't you try to have a little sympathy for *her*? Hasn't it ever occurred to you that she might love you? It's wrong, you know, and not like you, I'm sure, not to face up to things, to make two people unhappy. Wouldn't it be tremendous, if you went back home and got your old job back...?'

His face twisted. 'Are you pulling my leg?'

'Don't make bitter jokes like that, Jack, please.'

'How do you suggest I should manage such a thing, then? Peg legs, I suppose you mean.'

'*You* can do it, if anyone can. You're a hero;

they've given you the Military Cross for what you did, and I know how you got it – going out into no-man's-land to bring a wounded comrade who was caught on the wire, under enemy fire–'

'Yes, and he died after all, and I lost my legs. Who's told you all this rubbish?'

'Sergeant Major Broadbent, and it's not rubbish. You're a hero to him, too.'

'How did I come to be in the same hospital with that fool? He talks too damn much.'

It was a familiar conversation, and never got much further than this, but Eunice kept faith with herself that it would, one day. She rose and laid a hand on his. 'Think about what I've said, Jack. And do try to have some thought for your poor Emily. *Courage, mon ami.*'

He hesitated. 'I'm sorry I was rude, I'll try to do better next time. Goodbye, Miss Eunice, and thank you for the book.'

She hurried away before he should see the tears filling her eyes.

After his impromptu lunch on the Hill, Reardon, leaving his motorbike where it was behind the hedge, had wandered down the village street until he came to the humpback bridge, the oldest of the three bridges which spanned the shallow, winding river. Two further wooden bridges also crossed it, for there were houses and cottages clustering either side, but from here he had a good view of the police house on the main street, so that he could observe the comings and goings, while remaining discreetly stationed out of sight.

He leant against the stone parapet. After the

winter, the water had risen to the level of the banks either side, though nowhere was it a deep river. Flooding, he had been told, was no unusual event: it regularly rose and spread out across the water meadows, along the street and into the cottage gardens, but in its retreat leaving behind a rich silt, wonderful for cabbages and dahlias, roses, beans and rhubarb. Bracey's garden certainly testified to this. From here Reardon had a good view of its flourishing vegetable patch, garden hut, chicken run and a pigsty beyond.

It was very quiet, the occasional sounds of the village were muted: the clop of a horse towards the smithy and the subsequent ring of the anvil, a woman shouting a greeting across a garden to another. The two shops were closed, until after the funeral. The children were still in school, the men at work. The clock on the squat tower of the church struck the half-hour.

The church and the tall-chimneyed rectory and the Greville Arms were the only large buildings in the village, with the bulk of Oaklands Park in the distance. Looking across the river towards the big house, you could see the small lake belonging to Oaklands, curving around the base of the Hill. They called it a lake, but it was in fact a backwater of the river, fed also by a spring that rose in the woods surrounding it. He watched a long-legged heron fishing in the shallows. Along the banks willows grew, their arching branches dipping to the water. The grass was starred with some little, shining gold flowers he thought were celandines. Emerging from winter, the bright day looked new and hopeful, the village peaceful and uneventful, and for a moment, part of him understood why Ted Bracey had dug himself in here. He was nearing retirement now, a man originally from a Devon village, Reardon remembered, used to an easy, undemanding countryman's existence. One that would never suit Herbert Reardon.

Yet somewhere in this new world, he too must find a place. Alone, of course, he would always be alone, what else could he expect?

He looked up and at that moment saw his patience was to be rewarded. Ted Bracey came out of the house, helmeted, steering his bicycle with one hand, the other still buttoning up the neck of his tunic. He mounted and began to make his slow, stately way towards the centre of the village. Reardon easily caught up with him. 'Morning, Constable.'

Bracey slowed even more, and became official. 'Morning, sir,' he said, touching his helmet.

'You won't remember me, but we've met before, Constable. The name's Reardon. That case here, just before the war, that young woman who drowned, Marianne Wentworth?'

After a moment's slow inspection of him, Bracey replied in his slow West Country burr. 'I do remember you. Sergeant Reardon. What brings you here again, then?' he asked, dismounting and wheeling his bicycle. Reardon did not disabuse him regarding his status, but walked by his side.

'I needed a holiday and remembered this as good walking country. Maybe you could recommend some good walks?'

'Don't do much walking meself.' Reardon could believe it. Bracey fitted into his tight uniform like a sausage into its skin. 'You want to ask the rector about that. He's the one who does the walking round here.'

Reardon had been wanting to steer the conversation around to the Wentworths and now it was Bracey himself who had done it. He wondered if it had been done on purpose, but he decided that was perhaps overestimating the constable's powers of perception, though he was obviously wondering what Reardon wanted. 'Would that be the Reverend Wentworth? Father of the same young woman we've just mentioned? Odd case, that. Never got to the bottom of it, did we? You can't get many like that around here.'

'And thank the good Lord for it.'

'Amen to that. All the same, I don't suppose it's been forgotten.'

'Nine days' wonder. Nobody wants to remember it, now, poor young lady.'

'But in your capacity, you must recall it. I mean to say, that sort of thing was out of the usual run for you, wasn't it? Pub keeping open too long, unlicensed guns, abrogation of fishing rights by strangers from the towns, that's about it around these parts, isn't it? You're very pleasantly situated here, very comfortable life, I reckon.'

'Mustn't grumble.'

Reardon saw what Henry Paskin had meant about Bracey: a leisurely life in Broughton Underhill inducing in Bracey a certain disinclination to bestir himself, or to disturb the status quo. The constable stopped and leant his bicycle against the garden wall of a cottage, propping himself up beside it. He gave Reardon a look that could only be called old-fashioned. 'Don't mind me asking, but are you here, official like?'

'Not at all. Holiday, as I said.'

'So why all these questions?'

Reardon had prepared for this. He hesitated, then asked, 'Remember Gifford, the superintendent in charge of the case?'

Bracey nodded. His chins wobbled. He loosed the tight collar of his tunic. 'Retired now, hasn't he?'

'He's writing his memoirs. And this was one case that was puzzling.' Both statements were true, but he hoped Gifford would never hear that he seemed to have acquired a self-appointed amanuensis.

'That so? Well, what is it he don't remember? It'll all be down in the records somewhere, in black and white,' Bracey said, preparing to set out again. He was sharper than he looked, if no more inclined to put himself out.

'The facts, yes. It's what's behind the facts that matters, though, isn't it? What did you know of the Wentworth girl?'

'I knew who she was, of course, but I don't think more than half a dozen words ever passed between us. Time of day and so on. Nothing more.'

'Nobody seemed to want to talk to us at the time. In fact, it was all a bit hushed up, wasn't it?'

'Just as well. They wouldn't have liked it else, up at the Big House.'

'Oaklands Park? What had it to do with them?'

'Happened on their land, didn't it? And that jetty wasn't safe, everybody knew it, should have been taken down or repaired years before, not left to rot all of its own. They didn't want no blame.'

'Well, you see, that's the problem. If Marianne Wentworth knew it wasn't safe, why did she run out on to it? What was she doing down there at all, in fact?'

Bracey produced a pipe, looked at it for a moment, then put it back in his pocket. 'You married? Children?'

'No,' Reardon said shortly.

'Then you won't know about young women, growing up. I've two daughters of my own, both married with their own families now, and I tell you, there's no knowing what they'll do at that age. It wasn't the first time. I've seen her more than once going down there when she thought that nobody was about.'

'Who did he meet down there?'

The constable shrugged his massive shoulders. 'Now how should I know she *did* meet anybody? None of my business.'

'Well. I should think, as the village policeman, it was very much your business.'

'Look here, Sergeant Reardon, I'm here to keep the peace, not to go shoving my nose into other folks' concerns. I've already said more'n I should, and I hope it won't go down in Superintendent Gifford's memoirs.'

'I can certainly promise you that, Constable,' Reardon said, as Bracey nodded, mounted his bicycle and proceeded in a stately manner down the street.

Chapter Thirteen

Young Master Noakes had scarcely yet made his appearance into this troublous world, but his mother was already up and about again. Mattie, young and strong, couldn't abide the idea of lying idly in bed when there were things to be done. A whole month, the conventional lying-in time, wasn't even to be thought of. Her mother had never had that luxury and she'd been none the worse after seven children. As a concession, she had promised the midwife she would rest as much as she could, and for the sake of her Sam and Baby Sammy, she was keeping to her word – cooking bacon and eggs for their guest could hardly be classed as hard work.

Herbert Reardon was enjoying a breakfast such as he hadn't seen before the war.

He had made the right decision to seek accommodation here at the village pub, rather than use his motorcycle to travel back and forth to Dudley every day, he thought as he munched the last pieces of crisp bacon and black pudding, mopped up egg yolk with his fried bread and prepared to embark on the toast and ... real butter, by God, if he wasn't mistaken! No bread and scrape for the village of Broughton Underhill, or at least not for the Greville Arms. He poured himself a last cup of tea. Unfortunately, there was barely a scant teaspoonful of sugar in the bottom of the basin, but sugar was still scarce as gold dust and you couldn't expect everything.

It had, of course, occurred to him that he was being given special treatment, although he did wonder why, because he knew he must have been recognised by now, despite his face, marked down for who he was. A stranger, who was asking the sort of questions he was asking, it wouldn't have taken long for two and two to be put together.

They'd given him breakfast in a small parlour off the main bar, a shining-clean room (as was the rest of the public house), and lit a good fire. He sat back with his tea and was just about to put his feet up on the fender when the young land-lady came in. 'Everything all right, sir?'

'Best breakfast I've had in years. You do yourselves well in Broughton Underhill.'

'Not to say that – but we like to give our guests the best of what we have.'

She was a well-spoken young woman with a kind of Irish beauty – pale skin and dark hair, very blue eyes. He liked the way both she and her husband met his gaze fairly and squarely, though he was getting used to people avoiding it, and didn't blame them. It was some time before he had been able to meet his own reflection himself.

'Can you spare me a moment or two, Mrs Noakes?' he asked as she began to clear away his breakfast things with movements that were quick and efficient.

Unfortunately, he seemed to have timed his request badly. At that instant what sounded like the cries of a very young baby began somewhere

153

in the back regions, but she answered, smiling, 'I can if you can give me about ten minutes. My baby needs seeing to first.'

She picked up the tray, balancing it on her forearm while she opened the door with her other hand, practised movements that were too quickly done for him to get up and help her. In almost exactly ten minutes, she was back, smoothing her apron and standing in front of him. He motioned to her to sit down. 'I dare say I'd better explain who I am.'

She sat down neatly and crossed her ankles, her hands, large and capable, work roughened, clasped together on her lap. 'I know who you are, Sergeant Reardon, and I can guess why you're here.'

News had got around as quickly as he'd expected. No doubt he'd been the subject of interested speculation in the bar last night. He'd given the idea of a drink there a miss and gone to bed early. 'It's not Sergeant anymore, Mrs Noakes. I'm not yet back in the police force.' (Factually true, if deliberately misleading.) 'Which might make you think I've no right to be stirring matters up again, poking my nose in.'

'Why should I think that? It's about Miss Marianne, isn't it? It was a mystery how she died, and if it's cleared up ... well, I can't see it matters what way. I know how it looked, but I never did think it was right, the way everything was so rushed. The police couldn't get out fast enough. Crying shame, it was.'

'There was a war just started. Things were in a turmoil.' He trotted out the explanation, though

154

he was gratified, if surprised, that someone at least had shared his doubts. 'So you knew Marianne Wentworth?'

'Oh, yes. I've lived in Broughton all my life, and I worked up at Oaklands before I married and came here – went as nursery maid when I was fourteen. Miss Eunice was already seven or eight but her nanny was too hoity-toity to manage the nursery without help. I was used to a houseful of brothers and sisters so a job like that – only one little girl, and a brother that was only home for the holidays – seemed a bit like heaven to me. Besides, she was a lovely little girl, Eunice. She looked like a picture book fairy and was no trouble, though I'm not saying she didn't have a mind of her own...' She smiled. 'I'm sorry, all that's not what you want to hear, but anyhow, that's how I knew the Wentworth girls. They used to come up for their lessons with Miss Eunice.'

'What can you remember about Marianne's accident?'

She looked down at her hands for a moment, then raised her eyes. 'As you said, it was a very confusing time, but I remember it like it was yesterday. How could I forget it, with everything that was going on that time? My Sam and his mates going off together – in the Terriers they all were, and couldn't wait to get in the fighting, you know? Silly beggars, men are, if you'll excuse me. Women don't see it like that, most of us, at any rate. If only they'd known! But there was that much excitement being whipped up... Well, anyway, some of us went up to Kidderminster first thing to see them off on the train – me and Phyllis

Hobbs, and one or two more. Lady Sybil gave me time off, which was very good of her, considering.'

'Considering what, Mrs Noakes?'

'There was a party that same evening, one her ladyship had arranged for Mrs Villiers's seventieth birthday. Any excuse for a celebration, that was always Lady Sybil! It had been planned for some time, and she refused to cancel it just on account of all the war news. There was a deal of work to be done, so it was nice of her to give me most of the day off, but she was always considerate. Mind you, I had to make up for it when I got back to the house, straight into my cap and apron and get stuck in.'

He had thought her quiet and reserved, but once started, she seemed glad to let come out what had evidently been on her mind for some time. He wished all witnesses were the same. 'Family affair, was it, this party? Lot of guests?'

'Twenty-eight at table there were. Family, a few special friends, and all the Wentworths. And the other two boys, of course.'

'Which two would that be?'

'The Rafferty boy, Steven, from the pottery, and that German ... Austrian, I should say, that was staying at the rectory. They'd been together all summer, all the young folk, Mr Greville home from his music studies in Paris, and William Wentworth down from Oxford. There was always a lot of coming and going between Oaklands and the rectory. Well, of course, they were such close friends, more like family ... and it was a lovely summer, that one before the war, if you remember. There was tennis and picnics and swimming in the lake, all that sort of thing, sometimes larking about in that dangerous old punt, till Mr Foley had it taken away. I bet he wished he'd had that rotten old jetty taken down, too, afterwards. The young ladies didn't swim, of course. If they had, Miss Marianne might have saved herself...' For a moment, her eyes clouded, the she said, 'There was no harm in it, you know. At least...'

'What?'

'I suppose were was a bit of feeling between Mr Greville and the foreigner.' Her mouth set in a disapproving line.

'Rupert von Kessel,' he said, digging into his memory.

'I think that was the name, yes.'

'When you say 'feeling' what do you mean, exactly?'

'Oh, they used to argue about whether there was going to be a war and what they'd do if there was. Dead against joining in, Mr Greville was. And then, there was Miss Marianne. I think that Austrian...' She hesitated. 'All the young fellows liked her, but she wasn't a bad girl, you mustn't think that. I reckon, if things had turned out different, her and Mr Greville might have made a go of it ... but then, she'd have had sorrow to contend with. You know he joined up and was killed? It surprised us all, I can tell you, when he went off and enlisted like that, even though he went as one of those – you know, noncombatants. Because he was as much against the fighting as the rector was, you know. And especially him going off with his father poorly as he was – Mr Foley. They said it was all the excitement of the party, but I reckon it was more to do with Mr Greville than anything – and then on top of it, Miss Marianne, of all people, being found like that next morning.'

She was losing him. 'What are we talking about, Mrs Noakes? What was wrong with Mr Foley?'

'Why, he had a heart attack! The night of the party, he was taken bad. The house was in an uproar. They called for Mr Greville but he was nowhere to be found. We were told the next day, he'd already gone off and joined up, without telling anybody.'

'Even though he was so against the war?'

'Even so, and that was what was so queer. He'd taken his mother's motor car and driven over to Birmingham and enlisted there. Left the motor with the stationmaster to be picked up.'

And von Kessel, Reardon remembered, again dredging his memory of the case, had made a hurried exit back to Austria at the same time, having left his departure until practically the very last minute – just before Britain had declared war against Germany ... although his own country, Austria-Hungary, if Reardon remembered rightly, had not been involved in the conflict for perhaps another week. It had been foolish in the extreme, with a reckless disregard for his own safety, to leave his going so late, but when had hot-blooded and careless young men of that age ever listened to caution? Reardon didn't give much for his chances of having got out of the country, however. More than likely he had been intercepted and imprisoned as an alien. He made a mental note to investigate this.

So, both young men had disappeared in a great

hurry, at the same time. And the very next morning, Marianne Wentworth had been found in the lake.

'Well, thank you very much, Mrs Noakes. You've been very helpful.'

'I don't know that I have, really.' She stood up and then said, uncertainly, 'You wonder how I could've known all this...? Well, servants see and hear a lot, you know, though if you're a good one you keep what you hear to yourself. They say things in front of you, the gentry, as though you're deaf and blind, look through you as though you're not there, some of them, pass you cleaning the stairs as though you didn't exist. The Oaklands folk aren't like that, none of them, but all the same, you pretty much know what's going on. Well, anyway...' She stood up.

'Thank you, Mrs Noakes.'

'You're welcome.' She nodded and left him.

Sam was in the taproom when Mattie went through, polishing the pewter tankards kept on hooks behind the bar, all of them different, each of the regulars having their own.

'What did he want, Mattie?' he asked suspiciously.

'What everybody thinks he wants – to know about Miss Marianne.'

'Are the police opening that business again, then?'

'He's not in the police now.'

Sam stared. 'What's in it for him, then?'

'He didn't say. And I didn't ask.'

Her husband leant across the bar and lifted her

159

chin with one great forefinger. 'Well now, Mattie, don't you go getting yourself involved in this. I know what you think about all that business of the rector's daughter, but it won't do no good. I'll have a word with him.'

'Don't be stroppy with him, Sam.' Despite his flaxen hair and his blue eyes, her husband, with his big shovel hands and the muscles and sinews developed with working in the smithy, could be intimidating at first sight, to those who didn't know him, and he'd become prone to arguments against authority since he'd been in the army. 'Poor chap. Whatever could've happened to him out there?'

'You don't want to know about that,' Sam replied grimly, as he always did. He would never talk about his experiences; none of them would, those who had returned. They never said in their letters, either. It was as though they had entered into a conspiracy to keep their womenfolk from knowing what it had been like, though sometimes Mattie had thought it was worse, imagining. 'Don't you worry, Mattie m'duck,' he said now, 'I wouldn't think of causing no trouble with him. He's all right, I can tell.'

If Sam said so, Mattie was happy enough with that.

And that night, Sam joined Herbert Reardon in the parlour after another tasty supper of tender chicken and fresh vegetables, followed by apple pie. He came in with two pints of the strong, home-brewed ale that the Greville Arms was famous for, reckoning Reardon wouldn't want to join the locals in the bar. What they talked about, far into the night, Mattie didn't know, but she could guess, she heard it often enough since her husband came home.

Sam had gone into the war not caring much about politics or politicians, except for his admiration for the visionary Lloyd George and his Liberal reforms. What working man didn't admire him? Dole for the unemployed, pensions for the old folk, and support when they became sick and infirm? Sam had believed in the great man's grand promise after the war that Britain could be made into a land fit for heroes to live in. Believed it for a while. Dust and ashes now, when the bloody government, who had managed to find millions a day to defeat the Germans, left the same heroes – crippled, hungry and despairing, without jobs – to beg on the streets.

Chapter Fourteen

A few nights before, Nella had started a spell of night duty. She had long since found that, even in a convalescent ward, it wasn't the easy option people thought it, with men asleep all through a quiet night and nothing much to do. Most of the patients at Oaklands were, or had been, serious cases, and few nights went by without someone reliving the horrors they would never speak of during the day. Then, they kept up a cheerfulness, and the sense of humour which had kept them going throughout the worst of what war could do.

161

But the unguarded night for many was tormented by wild dreams of fighting for breath in the gas-filled trenches; or the terror of being drowned in six feet of mud, or buried by debris, being caught on the wire and left wounded when they were sent on what was virtually a suicide mission, over the top, straight into the face of the enemy guns.

Sometimes it was just sufficient to hold their hands until the terror had abated somewhat, or simply to listen – it was easier to talk in the dark. And there were the quiet periods, of course, when it was possible, with the aid of a lamp turned low on the desk at the end of the ward, to write up notes and patients' records, when most of the men were asleep or if not, lying quietly, waiting to get through the night.

It had been one of the quiet nights in the ward which had once been the ballroom, towards midnight, and Nella was waiting for Burkin to arrive and relieve her so that she could take her break, when the ward suddenly erupted. She rushed to investigate the uproar.

Sergeant Major 'Bomber' Broadbent was one of the living legends in the hospital. Reputedly a terror for discipline on the front line, though fair-minded and personally fearless, he was a treasure to the nursing staff. He'd lost the fingers of his left hand and half his jaw, and was having to learn how to speak so that he could be understood, but that didn't prevent him from chivvying those men who were well enough, exhorting them to join in activities to pass the time and keep up morale – entertainment's between themselves, whist drives, anything he could think of. His current project was to involve any of those who were able to wield a hoe, or pull a weed, in a campaign designed to make a start on smartening up the Oaklands gardens. He was stoical about his injuries and didn't normally cause any trouble, but the noise was coming from the direction of where he slept at the far end of the ward. When Nella got there she found that he had rolled out of his bed onto the floor and was kicking up his legs, not shouting in pain, but singing, roaring like a bull.

'Sorry I can't help you, love. It's me bunions, see,' said Taffy Davies, who made terrible jokes, from the next bed. He had had an amputation of his right foot, and most of the muscles and bones in the same leg were shattered, too.

*'Ighty-iddle-de-ighty, take me back to Blighty,
Blighty is the place for me!'* roared the sergeant.

'Stow the hymn-singing, chum! Give us a bit of hush, for Gawd's sake,' came from the other side of the ward, an injunction taken up by several others until, all at once, quiet descended like a blanket. With a soft jingle of keys and a steely glance Matron had arrived on the scene to investigate. Five foot tall, Miss Inman ran her hospital strictly according to Miss Nightingale's principles and many more stringent ones of her own, and all of the men, not to mention some of the doctors, were terrified of her.

'Nurse Wentworth, this man is drunk! Where did he get *this*?' she demanded, picking up a now empty whisky bottle that lay on the floor beside Bomber and holding it fastidiously at arms' length from her starched bosom.

163

'Visiting day today, Matron. You know how it is.'

'Yes, I do know – and so should the visitors. Haven't they been warned often enough not to bring drink in to the men? They might be convalescent, but they're still patients. Nurse Wentworth, get him back into bed immediately. I'll send someone to help you.'

'That's all right, Matron. I'll give nurse a hand.'

A male voice sounded behind Nella; a pair of strong hands appeared to help heave the dead weight of the big soldier into bed.

'In that case, I'll leave you to it.'

'Yes, Matron,' Nella replied to her outraged, departing back. 'Come on, Bomber.'

'Oh, you're a lovely girl, Sister. Give us a cuddle, Sister. *Ighty-iddle-de-ighty, tickle me up me nightie...*'

'You've blotted your copybook with Matron this time,' Nella said, trying not to laugh. 'Just as well she didn't hear that.'

'I expect she's heard much worse,' commented her helper.

The task of getting him into bed accomplished, quite suddenly the sergeant major stopped singing, his head fell back and immediately he began to snore loudly.

'Don't be too hard on the poor bugger – begging your pardon, Sister,' Taffy Evans remarked, 'but the whisky does him more good than his medicine, you know. Lovely tenor he'd have, though, if he'd learn to sing proper.'

'Would you like a hot drink, Taffy?' she asked, tucking the sheets around the snoring sergeant major.

'No, thank you, love. Time all of us got some beauty sleep.'

'Goodnight, then.'

Her helper was still standing by the bed. She turned and smiled at him. 'Thank you, Captain Geddes.'

'A pleasure, Nurse Wentworth. Quite like old times.'

Of course she had known before she saw him who it was that was offering to help her. She didn't need to turn around to know the owner of the voice with the soft Scottish burr, though one didn't expect the new MO to be doing duty rounds with Matron; perhaps he was getting the feel of his new position. And at least it had eased the potential awkwardness of their first meeting. He accompanied her to the door, held it open for her to pass through. In the corridor, he faced her. 'It's so good to see you again, Nella. And looking better than the last time I saw you.'

'Well, that wouldn't be difficult, the state I was in,' she answered, tucking a stray strand of hair under her cap, knowing she sounded prickly and defensive, though what she said was true. When she had arrived back in England after the exhausting demands of the previous years and that last, debilitating illness, she had been looking like a scarecrow, without Amy telling her so. She looked up and found him smiling.

'You haven't changed in the least.' She wondered what that meant. 'I wrote to you when I heard you were ill.'

'I never received it.' Nor ever saw you again. 'What happened to you after that?'

165

'What happened? What happened to all of us. Passchendaele happened. I was simply one of the lucky ones.'

The third battle of Ypres would be known for evermore as Passchendaele, from the tiny village, the struggle for which over half a million men were wounded, died, were reported captured or missing. 'We were both lucky,' she said soberly.

Despite the exhausting years he had spent in France, he appeared much as he had always done, relaxed and casual, a smile in his blue eyes, though he looked older: his face was thinner, and there were lines which hadn't been there before. 'I'm only here for a short time,' he said. 'Just long enough to see to the closure of the hospital before I say goodbye to the army. Splendid place to convalesce, isn't it?'

'You should have seen it before the war.'

They had reached the dispensary, which she was making for in order to prepare the medicines for her first round in the morning, before the patients' breakfast and the end of her shift. 'I hope we might have a chance to talk, Nella. There's a good deal I have to tell you. Can you make it soon?'

'Yes, of course,' she replied brightly. 'There must be a lot of news to catch up with. In fact, I'm due for a break in half an hour. Shall we say the nurses' sitting room?'

For the next half hour she wrote up the patients' notes and reports and didn't have much idea of what she wrote. Duncan Geddes had brought the past with him, peopled by sad ghosts and painful memories.

Chapter Fifteen

1916

Flanders. A small town on the French Belgian border whose unpronounceable name she couldn't now remember. Once it had been near the front line but by then, as fronts shifted and moved backwards and forwards, from place to place, each side struggling for a few miles' advantage which neither ever seemed to gain permanently, the shattered town was at present several miles away, attempting to resume something of its normal life, or as much as it could hope for. It was crammed with army personnel on leave, seeking a brief respite and some relief from the intolerable strain of being under constant fire. There was little to do, but everyone was grateful for clean beds and baths, and a decent night's sleep, able to hear the guns only as a not-too-distant, monotonous crump rather than as if in the next room. It was also a relief from army food – almost any sort of food was in short supply, but the Belgians generally knew how to make the most of what there was.

Nella was staying there with Daisy Musgrave.

The day before they came, after giggling over a little blonde VAD who had daringly cut her own hair and looked like a badly shorn duckling, they had cut off their own hair and then wept together when they saw their crowning glories lying on the floor of the tent. But the tears were short-lived. Long hair was impossible when there was neither time nor hot water to wash and dry it, and when it was expected to be kept tidily pinned up under every condition. 'A much overdue decision, Nurse Wentworth,' Daisy declared in the voice of Griggs, a mutually detested sister, and they subsided into giggles.

The two of them, for their few days' leave, were sharing a room in a small hotel in the bomb-shattered town, and had arranged to go out to dinner that night. However, during the day Daisy had come across a young captain, one of the scores with whom she had often dined and danced the night away in London and in grand country houses, in the palmy days before the war. She seemed to know half the officers in the British Army, so many of whose names later featured in the frighteningly lengthening casualty lists. They all adored her, loved her not only for her feminine company but the feeling she gave them that life could still offer some sense of fun and gaiety. She flirted outrageously with them all, but it meant nothing; it was only this young man who brought colour to her cheeks, and sometimes tears to her eyes when she read his letters, and whose name had become exceedingly familiar to Nella.

'Would you mind, darling?' she asked. It was obvious she meant not only the cancellation of their dinner arrangements, but also that she wanted Nella to make herself scarce from their shared room.

'Daisy, you mustn't!'

'Yes, I must,' she replied fiercely, and looking at the pretty face from which all smiles had vanished, Nella said nothing. Unlike her young man, if Daisy were found out, her contract would be terminated and she would be sent home in disgrace, but Nella was not as shocked as she would have been once, nor did she feel she had any right, or wish, to judge. Morality had a different slant here for men in the trenches, and for some of the women, too, taking the reckless 'eat, drink and be merry, for tomorrow we die' attitude, a possibility that became more like absolute certainty as the war dragged on. She had arrived in France an innocent, as she now saw it, but by now there was no room for shock at anything, after what she had seen and experienced.

She left their room in the cold winter's evening before George Chiversleigh should arrive and wandered disconsolately out to look for somewhere to have dinner alone and unnoticed, and in the half-destroyed *place*, with ruined buildings on every side of it, and the fountain in the centre nothing but a heap of stones, she almost bumped into Captain Geddes. Their surprise was mutual. Neither had known the other would be here; in fact they knew little of each other's activities outside the tented lines of the hospital where they worked as part of a professional team.

'I was looking for somewhere to have supper, Nurse Wentworth. They tell me there's a good place along the end of this street. If you haven't already eaten, why don't you join me?'

She was out of uniform, wearing the only civilian clothes she had brought with her (of which she was heartily sick by now, though anything made a change from her uniform) but she hesitated, until he added, with a sudden laugh, looking at her hair, 'No one will recognise you. Oh, I say, I'm sorry, shouldn't have said that...'

'That's all right, I know,' she said. Her hair looked terrible, but she was hoping she'd be able to find somewhere to get it cut a little better while she was here.

'But if anyone does, by any chance, and sees fit to report you, refer them to me and I'll tell them I needed to talk 'shop' with you – which happens to be true.'

That explanation would not save her if the senior superintending nurse happened to find out, but suddenly, the risk seemed worth it. She let him take her elbow and guide her to a small *estaminet* tucked into a corner, which had evidently had a miraculous escape when the *hôtel de ville* next door, its roof now half missing, had been shelled. She followed him, amused that with a few words and a smile, he was able to command a small corner, screened from the packed and noisy main room by a high bench. If anyone noticed them passing they didn't make it obvious.

She still found herself a little constrained. There was almost no opportunity for personal conversation in the day-to-day nursing routine, or in the desperate conditions where they worked; there they were simply a skilful doctor and another competent nurse, doing what they could under impossible conditions, but within that environment there had grown a certain easy familiarity between all of them who worked together. A brief

170

smile, or a nod, when they had accomplished something difficult, perhaps saved a life, a stoical endurance when they failed. Here, away from the familiar routine, it was different.

The place was very small, and very warm, and crowded with service personnel. He ordered their food – there was no choice, they had to take what was on offer – and a bottle of red wine was brought to their table by a young girl while they were waiting. After he had poured them each a glass, he came directly to the point. 'I really do have something to say to you. Let's get it over and then we can enjoy the evening. It's about young Foley I wanted to speak. I gather you knew him in Civvy Street?' She nodded. 'What's wrong with him? Is he *asking* to be killed?' He must have seen that kind of sheer recklessness that Grev was showing often enough, and understood it perhaps as being a refusal to admit to danger in case their terror, and even cowardice, became apparent, but obviously he felt in his case it was something more. He was looking steadily at her. 'Or is he looking for a Blighty one?'

That wasn't something one said lightly and she was glad of their secluded corner and the noise that surrounded them, which made it impossible for anyone else to overhear. 'A Blighty one' meant a wound sufficiently serious to be sent home and because of this, despite its severity, was often welcomed. More than that, a self-inflicted injury, or one deliberately courted by men who had reached the bitter end of their tether, was not unknown. An arm above the parapet of the trench which the ever-vigilant German snipers would be unlikely to miss. 'Accidentally' shooting oneself in the foot. It took courage, but better the grim prospect of losing a hand or a foot than stay in that hell on Earth, where one was more than likely to be dead or maimed for life the next day, anyway. Such an action was, however, regarded as a serious offence, marked down as an act of cowardice, punishable by court martial and most likely a firing squad. Was it sublime courage that drove young Foley on, or was it cowardice? he was asking.

She replied, as steadily as she could, 'You don't understand. If you were a musician, as Grev is, you would *never* deliberately put yourself in the way of anything that might injure you to the extent of ruining or jeopardising your career. But he's not in any way a coward. He always swore he would never fight if war came, but don't you see, what he's doing, going out night after night to bring the wounded in, is far braver?'

'Yes, he's brave and fearless and all that, God knows how many lives he's saved, but he can't carry on like this. I don't like the look of him at all. Yet he's refused all leave so far. I've recommended he be sent home, whether he wants it or not. What are the odds on him surviving if he carries on like this?'

'I don't know,' Nella said. She couldn't deny what he was saying, that what Grev was doing was an idiocy, because she'd seen it with her own eyes. He was unsteady, he had a wild light in his eyes, indeed, a kind of madness. 'I can tell you, though,' she went on hesitantly, 'that something happened, before the war, something personal and very terrible, and it's made him extremely unhappy.' She found she could not go on. She took a sip of her wine. It was so rough it made her cough, but it gave an excuse for the tears which sprang to her eyes.

'It concerned you, too,' he hazarded, and looked contrite. 'Look here, please don't feel you have to speak of it. I am so sorry.'

'That's all right. It was my sister, you see, she died, accidentally drowned. Grev was very fond of her. I think it's thrown him a little off balance.'

She had never spoken of Marianne, and the way she'd died, to anyone before, afraid of the embarrassed pity such a revelation would call up. But he said nothing more, simply stretched out his hand and covered hers. It was a nice hand, big but well shaped, strong. She had seen those same hands expertly performing terrible, by now routine operations, little miracles, a thousand times. The contact steadied her.

'I wouldn't have mentioned anything,' he said eventually, 'except that I feel a certain degree of responsibility for him.'

'I'm worried, too, but I don't know what I can do.'

The bar was overheated, khaki uniforms mixing with the locals, the smell of food mingling with Woodbines and French tobacco and too many people squashed into one small, hot room. The decibel level of the noise was making it hard to have a serious conversation. A group of young subalterns at the bar, none of them much more than schoolboys, were making asses of themselves after too much to drink, and an old Belgian in a beret, from his place at the bar, spat

accurately into the fire. In the corner a gramo-
phone played what seemed to be the same tune
over and over again, though it was impossible to
make out exactly what it was, with all the noise.

The arrival of the young woman with their food
bridged the awkwardness that followed the
exchange. The Belgians could generally find
something palatable, and this time they were
given fried potatoes and steak, with a sauce, bread
and some cheese. He seemed to have accepted
that the subject of Grev was closed. 'Bon appétit,'
he said, smiling and raising his glass.

At the bar, an altercation had arisen. Madame
in charge had decided the young officers were
getting out of hand and was demanding they
should leave, which they were not inclined to do,
but after a certain amount of good-humoured
protest, at last they tumbled unsteadily out of the
door. In the relative quiet they left behind, the
gramophone could at last be heard, scratching
out the newest popular tune, a sweet nostalgic
melody that was on everyone's lips, being sung,
whistled and hummed, everywhere. Would she
ever hear 'Roses of Picardy' again with but a
wrench of the heart?

It was just two nights after that conversation
over dinner that Grev went out under heavy fire
with three other stretcher-bearers. It was a night-
mare attack, star shells exploding into the night
sky, the deafening sound of guns, the screams of
the wounded, men falling like swatted flies. Two
of the stretcher party were killed but the bodies
of the other two, one of them Grev, were blown
to bits and never a trace was found. Only one of

the countless numbers with no known grave. Quite literally blown to pieces, so that there was literally nothing left, not even a cap badge or an identity disc, to identify them.

Chapter Sixteen

In the room which was designated as the nurses' sitting room, Duncan Geddes sat with his legs to the fire, onto which he had thrown another couple of logs. It was a charming room which he had been told had always been known simply as the garden room. It had dark, wood-panelled walls, chintz covers on the chairs, blue and white china, several bookcases and low, wide windows overlooking the drive and the once glorious herbaceous borders. There was no one there tonight except him.

On the small table in front of him was a tray of tea which a flirty little nurse had been delighted to bring him, though obviously rather intrigued by his request for two cups. He hoped Nella would not be held up, or the tea under the cosy would be cold.

He remembered the little quirk she had of liking her tea very hot, scalding almost.

It had been wine they'd drunk, though, not tea, in that little *estaminet* where they'd had their first meal together. She had taken a gulp after he'd been so crass as to bring up the subject of young Foley which had upset her so much, and the wine had gone down the wrong way. He had cursed himself for his blindness: he had realised before that she was fond of Foley, a distant relative of some sort he believed, but he hadn't suspected the extent of her regard, or realised she might be in love with him. Of course. He had been astonished how deeply the thought had hurt him, until she had told him it was her sister that Foley had loved.

It had been impossible to pursue his original concerns about the young man after that conversation, though they were still there. Morale was at rock bottom generally, between men who saw no point in going on, and he had seen the same question in Foley's eyes that he heard being asked more and more: what were they fighting *for?* Why should they obey orders that no longer seemed to have any point to them, allow themselves simply to be used as cannon fodder? And who could blame them? It was something he asked himself, often, operating on mangled flesh, and even in his dreams removing shrapnel, dressing amputations, trying to put together men who would be better off dead, and often were before he had time to finish. But he had so far kept his thoughts to himself; he had no time to waste railing at the blind stupidity of generals and the old men in Westminster, playing their war games.

The embarrassment at the gaffe he'd made with Nella was still, to this day, vivid in his mind, as was the whole scene. The shape of the wine bottle, the candles on the tables, the ubiquitous check cloth, not very clean. The drunken young officers. 'Roses of Picardy'. Slabs of beef on their plates, more meat than they'd seen for years.

Nella having difficulty with it, and finally pushing it away. 'Aren't you hungry?' he'd asked.

'I think this is horsemeat.'

He was amused, but she pointed out that he wasn't eating his, either.

'It does taste as though it's chased many a man up a tree. Or died of old age. How very English we are,' he went on, pleased to see her smile. 'The Continentals think us mad, preferring to go hungry rather than eat horsemeat. Although there are worse things I've been offered, I can assure you.'

'McConachie's?' He laughed; the tinned stew was a staple of their rations, like bully beef and biscuits, not like mother made but welcome if you were hungry enough. 'Any other delicacies you were thinking of I'd rather you kept to yourself, thank you,' she added, with a smile.

'What would you really like to eat, right now, then, if you had the choice?'

She closed her eyes for a moment. She had thick, dark lashes that lay in soft crescents on her cheeks. In that unguarded instant, he saw the lines of strain, the exhaustion on her face and felt an overwhelming tenderness towards her. He suspected that she had, like many others, added a year or two onto her age in order to be accepted for service overseas, but he knew her to be one of the best of all these young women who had voluntarily come out here, delicately nurtured, sketchily trained, then thrown into this obscene war. They had learnt to flinch at nothing: the most hideous of wounds, the inhuman damage a shell could inflict on a human body, the stench of gas

177

gangrene. He had seen Nella on the point of fainting, many times, but she had held on, gritting her teeth, swabbing festering wounds, hurriedly applying dressings, mopping brows, while all around lay more wounded men on stretchers, groaning in pain or waiting for attention in silent agony.

'Right now?' she was saying, answering his question. 'I don't have to think. A fresh, new-laid boiled egg, some brown bread and butter, a pot of tea—'

'Tea that really tastes of tea, not paraffin, or stew, or the last thing that was cooked in the billycan—'

'Oh, *yes*. Tea. Earl Grey, or even Lipton's Breakfast.' Her eyes had lit up, the fleeting, three-cornered smile he had begun to look for widened into a laugh. He had found her to be full of courage and endurance, but now he caught a glimpse of the young woman she might have been, before the war had robbed her of laughter, a woman full of warmth and fun. 'And very hot, in a china cup, of course.'

'A china cup? What's that?'

Yes, it was the simple, honest things one had missed most, the simple, honest things.

He had not been honest with her, out there, and it was something he bitterly regretted. He had missed his chance when it was there, failed to take that one step which might have changed his life, and hers; it was far too late now, but he could at least tell her the truth, as soon as it was opportune. There were other things he must tell her, too, that were going to hurt her unbearably, more than he had already hurt her. Moreover, it

178

would not be Nella alone who would suffer. He was by no means a cowardly man, but his heart misgave him at the thought of what he must say, and it's inevitable consequences.

One of the logs he had thrown onto the fire had burnt almost through, leaving the other precariously balanced. He stretched out a toe and kicked it into place, then for good measure added another log to keep the blaze going, just as the door opened and Nella came into the room.

She had finished her reports, handed over to Burkin, told her what had happened with Bomber so that she could keep an eye on him, before she came to meet Duncan Geddes. She was glad he couldn't see how wildly her heart was beating under the starched bib of her apron. Immediately, he sprang up and pushed a comfortable chair nearer to the warmth.

'I see you've made yourself at home,' she said, noting the tea tray and the cup and saucers one of the other nurses must have brought for him; he had always been able to charm people into doing anything for him, men as well as women, nurses and orderlies alike.

'I am not finding it difficult to get back to this sort of civilisation again. I can't tell you how good this is, Nella.' He took her hand and held it, a small hand, rough-skinned and red with Lysol and hot water. She withdrew it quickly, embarrassed as she had always been at the state of her hands, and reached out to lift the teapot. 'No, no, I'll pour. You sit back.' She settled herself obediently against the cushions and he handed her a cup of tea.

'I've only about fifteen minutes.'

179

'Sarn't major all right now?'

'Sleeping like a baby when I left – a rather noisy baby.' She sighed. 'Poor Bomber.'

'Difficult night, eh?'

'Not until he started up. He must have had the whisky bottle in bed with him.'

'Who's to blame him? I read his notes, poor devil.' She nodded. 'They'll all be gone soon, and then what? What will you do?'

She shrugged 'I don't know. Get a job, I hope, but that won't be easy. There aren't enough jobs even for the men coming home.'

Someone had placed a bowl of hyacinths on the polished, dark oak table – Eunice or Aunt Sybil, no doubt – and their heavy fragrance filled the room. There were two lamps, either side of the fireplace, throwing golden circles of light onto the ceiling. The fire crackled comfortably. She would have liked to close her eyes and sleep.

'And you? What will you do?'

'Return to my old practice.'

She said evenly, as lightly as she could, 'You don't see yourself as a Harley Street surgeon, then?'

'Not quite,' he smiled, 'though something of the sort has been suggested.' He might have been tempted, after his time in France, which had gained him more experience in four years than he could have gained in half a lifetime, to specialise, and carve out a lucrative, glamorous and perhaps brilliant career for himself in reconstructive surgery, and indeed this had been put to him several times, but he shrank from it for more reasons than he could explain now. For one thing, he was not

180

ambitious for himself, and certainly not in that direction. And he was certainly not in need of money. 'No, I shall go back to my miners.'

He had told her a little of his background. The son of a hard-working Presbyterian doctor in a poor district of Glasgow, after leaving medical school in St Andrews he had gone as a junior partner to a practice in the little group of coastal towns and villages in the North-East coalfields, south of the Scottish border. There, in Lillington, he had seen what poverty was. He learnt that miners crawled on their bellies in two-foot-high coal seams, turning to lie on their backs to hew out the rich coal, which was then exported at a profit to the coal owners, while the wages of the miners themselves were cut to the bone. Some of them were forced to live in shanty towns, their children running wild, out of reach of the school-board man, absent because they had no shoes to go to school in. Money for doctors' bills was non-existent. He had been brought up with notions of service, and he intended to go back into the practice, which had been kept going for him by old Dr Hedley, brought out of a comfortable retirement for the duration and not anxious to be kept away from it any longer than was necessary. He hoped, with the money he now had, he might contribute something, however small.

Paris. He ought to mention Paris, prepare her. At that moment a nurse opened the door, then, seeming to sum up the situation, backed out and closed it. No, perhaps now was not the time, with interruptions likely at any time. 'Nella, I have to speak to you, but I can't say what I have to say when you have to be on duty in a few minutes. Will you let me talk to you, privately, somewhere where we're not likely to be disturbed?'

She said evenly, determined not to read between the lines, 'There's nowhere here in the hospital that's very private, or anywhere in Broughton, for that matter, unless you go for a walk.'

'Then how about the one which takes in that famous view from Broughton Hill that Matron's been telling me about?'

'Very well, if you must,' she said at last, then smiled, the quick smile that had always turned his heart over. 'But I'll warn you, it's a stiff climb, and unless you're prepared for a fourteen-mile tramp, we shall have to turn round and come back. It's a much better walk in the opposite direction, up to the holy well. That way you can make a circular tour, and besides, it's prettier.'

'I don't mind turning round. The view never looks the same on the way back.'

For a long moment they looked at each other. 'We'll see. If we can manage to get time off together.' She lifted the fob watch pinned to her apron. 'Now I must go.'

Chapter Seventeen

Reardon could see it in the distance, the place where the Raffertys lived, as he walked down Hoggins Lane, a little-used track which, until a new road into the works had been built, had been the main entrance to the small brickworks situated a mile further along the lane. Sam Noakes had told him where to find it – 'It's known as Rafferty's Cottage, but don't expect to find a cottage.'

The building ahead, a large, low-roofed, brick-built edifice, was certainly not a cottage, and whatever it had once been, it had seen better days. Its paintwork was peeling and one of the window shutters was hanging loose, giving it a decidedly lopsided appearance, but it had to be the place he was looking for. Sam had said one half of it used to be the old brickworks' counting house, the other half a storage place for light materials, until the distance of both from the main works came to be seen as a disadvantage by the owner and a newer, more convenient building was erected at the same time as the new entrance to the works was created. Joel Rafferty had rented the disused property when he and his wife arrived from London, had built his kiln in the storage side and converted the counting house to a domestic dwelling. Behind it were several smaller, almost derelict buildings. Again according to Sam, the Raffertys had originally envisaged these as housing for other artisans who might make up his proposed community, but that was a hope destined never to be fulfilled.

Reardon was almost at the end of the lane when he came across a woman, dressed very oddly and gathering what looked like dandelion leaves to add to the watercress already in her basket.

'Good afternoon. I'm looking for the pottery and Mrs Rafferty.'

'Well, this is the pottery, or used to be, and I'm

183

Amarantha Rafferty. What can I do for you?'

Despite looking like nothing but a bundle of old clothes, she spoke with a quick, educated accent and looked searchingly at him as she waited for an answer. Sam had warned him she was 'one o' them bluestockings', and outlandish into the bargain, a term that served for anything or anyone the village didn't understand, but she didn't seem at all intimidating. Rather the opposite: under a bright-orange hat crocheted in chenille, from which wisps of grey hair escaped, she had a humorous mouth and kind eyes; the fact that she wore umpteen layers of clothing of various kinds and a pair of men's boots certainly made her look peculiar in the extreme; on the other hand, it was a cold, raw afternoon and the boots must have been a distinct advantage when scrabbling in streams and ditches for watercress and dandelion leaves. He put her at first at around sixty but that may have been because of her weatherbeaten complexion. She could have been a lot younger.

'You'd better come into the house,' she said when he told her his business. A trodden path led directly off the lane to what seemed to be the only door, through a vegetable plot almost bare at this season except for a few old Brussels sprouts' stalks. A pump with a water butt next to it stood outside the door, which opened directly into a huge living space, the kitchen being at one end, he saw as they entered. It was magnificently untidy. But the initial impression was immediately super-seded by one of life, warmth and colour, from the warm terracotta of the wash on the walls, to the cushions and brightly patterned shawls and covers thrown carelessly over the haphazardly scattered chairs and sofas. Large, vibrantly painted pottery plates (which he assumed were the work of Mrs Rafferty, and about which there seemed to be a great deal of eye-rolling in the village) hung amongst a varied selection of prints and paintings. But above all it was a room of books. He marvelled at the quantity, completely filling the shelves which had been erected on one long wall, and spilling over onto every other available surface, including the floor, much to the detriment of the housekeeping. But what would a bit of dust matter to a person like Mrs Rafferty, with a mind above such mundane things?

As soon as they entered she pulled off her shapeless hat and threw it onto a chair, causing an affronted marmalade cat to jump up and stalk off, tail in air, and a quantity of dishevelled, greying dark hair to tumble around her face. She threw off her outer garments and tossed them over a sofa, revealing underneath them a brown dress decorated with black Assisi work, covered with a long green tabard, fringed at the hem. She lifted a big kettle standing to one side of the great stone fireplace onto the glowing embers at the heart of the fire, where it immediately began to sing. She turned and spoke, and he was disconcerted when she said, looking directly at his face, 'I take it your injuries are a result of this last disgraceful affair?'

'They are, ma'am.' He had heard the war referred to in other terms.

'Then I am sorry for you.' With a brown, work-worn hand she touched his, warmly and unselfconsciously. 'My husband died in the war.

185

It was not a heroic death, he caught pneumonia during his field training. He was too old to have volunteered to fight in the first place, but he died believing what he had done was right.' For a brief moment she was silent, then she went on briskly, 'Well, there we are. And now, Mr Reardon, I'm going to offer you tea and some of the cake I've just made. It should be cool enough to cut by now. Will you take some? Don't say no, there's plenty. Much can be contrived,' she observed, fetching tea things and the cake from the kitchen end and cutting a large slice, 'by the use of carrots for sugar, and fruits from the hedgerows.'

'Er, quite.'

He tried the cake and found it very good indeed, though the tea was another matter. He preferred not to speculate what it was made from: dried hay, perhaps. He took a long swig to get rid of it. 'Very good cake.'

He couldn't keep his eye from straying to the books.

'You like to read?' she asked, noticing his interest.

'When I have the opportunity, and the where-withal to get hold of books,' he answered, getting up to read the titles. 'You have an interesting collection, Mrs Rafferty.'

'They are here to be borrowed at any time. Which ones interest you most?' He mentioned a few and she nodded approvingly. Suddenly, he knew what it was about her: the way she talked brought to mind Miss Calder, Ellen Calder, the young schoolteacher who had conducted the WEA French classes he had attended in the days before the war, when he had been filled with a burning desire to better himself. She had written warmly to him throughout his time in France. A young lady of serious bent, she had always ended her letters to him with a paragraph or two in French, to which she had expected him to reply likewise. It had made him smile, but it had kept him on his toes, a reminder that there was still something else out there. He hadn't yet found the courage to renew his acquaintance with Miss Calder.

'I can see you have a questing mind,' Mrs Rafferty went on. 'What are you searching for?'

'I don't rightly know.' He rubbed his nose. She had glowing, intelligent brown eyes, and he knew she understood exactly what he meant when he went on, 'I suppose I've only one question, really, ma'am: why?'

'We're all asking that. There aren't enough books in the world to answer it.'

Books, and a few generalities, kept them going through another slice of the cake, and the polite refusal of more tea, until he felt able to broach the subject of his visit.

'I can't tell you anything about what happened, but I can tell you about Marianne herself. She was a strange girl in many ways, not much like the rest of her family. Have they told you she had an ambition to write novels?'

No, he said, that was news to him.

'Hmm, well. I have been very sorry since she died to think that I might have been unnecessarily unkind to her on the subject.'

'In what way?' He could not, for the life of him, imagine Mrs Rafferty being unkind to anyone.

She got up to stir the fire and throw on a big log. Flames crackled and sparks flew up the chimney. He found it very agreeable, sitting in this strange room with the old, comfortably worn chairs drawn up to the hearth, with the fire lighting the darkening afternoon and the tea table between them, the old cat reclaiming a place by the blaze. 'She came to me for instruction. No, I am not a writer myself, not a writer of fiction, at any rate. Pamphlets and so on are more in my line. For the Cause, you know.'

He might have guessed. Votes for Women. Before the war he'd been as much against the idea as anyone, but the work women had unstintingly done during the war, men's work, much of it heavy, had changed his opinion about that – and many other men's, including some in the government. Ellen Calder herself had delivered mail, wearing breeches and riding a two-stroke motorcycle they called the Baby Triumph. At any rate the women had got the vote at last – at least, if they were over thirty or a property owner.

'Poor Marianne,' Mrs Rafferty went on. 'She'd been writing fairy stories and so on since she was a child but she was confused as to how to begin writing what she considered 'proper stories' and when her father came to me and asked me to help, I told him to send her to college, to learn from people better qualified than I, but she shrank from the idea. Well, I have read a good deal, as you can see, and I studied literature when I was at Oxford, so I agreed. It was not, I fear, a success. She came to me for two or three years and at the end of it we were really not much further. She would not apply herself, you see, and at last, I'm sorry to say, I told her in no uncertain terms that she liked the *idea* of being a writer rather than actually *being* one, if you know what I mean? It was as if she were simply writing out her own daydreams – and we all know where daydreams lead, don't we? In Marianne's case, to a lot of romantic slush,' she said forthrightly. 'And she was too dreamy or disinclined to work at it and put it together properly, not even into a form where it could be shown to someone else who might well, I admit, have had more encouraging opinions than mine. I lost patience. Those early stories of hers – fairytale romances and so on – had been quite charming, but she had come to be influenced by too many of the sort of books I regard as trash, and for that I blame that silly young woman who is Lady Sybil's maid for lending them to her.' She bent her head over the teapot and her grey tresses fell either side of her face. 'There now, I've said more than I should.'

A friendship between Marianne Wentworth, who had been, he knew, more or less related to Lady Sybil, and her lady's maid, seemed quite an odd notion to Reardon, and the idea that she should need to borrow books from her even odder, and he said as much to Mrs Rafferty.

'Oh, but I don't think they were friends at all, or not in the way one usually thinks of friends. I suppose the loan of the books had brought them together, and I don't know how that came about – except that they were unlikely in the extreme to have appeared on her father's bookshelves – but I doubt they could have been much more than acquaintances. I suppose they liked each other well enough and Lady Sybil is very liberal-minded in that way, but it should never have done for her maid to ... well, get ideas. Remember, it was before the war stamped out that sort of thing.'

The war had certainly done a great deal to smooth out social in equalities, but there was a long road to go yet and Mrs Rafferty was a great deal more naive than he had given her credit for, if she believed to the contrary, which he did not think she did. 'You're being ironic, Mrs Rafferty.' She smiled.

He knew he need not beat about the bush with this lady. 'Mrs Rafferty. Did you ever entertain the idea that Marianne's death might not have been an accident?'

She gave him a level glance. She knew what he meant. 'She did not leave a letter behind, as far as I'm aware. Don't suicides always do that?'

'Usually, but not invariably.'

She thought this over for some time. 'To be honest, yes, the notion did cross my mind, and that was what made me feel so guilty. But on reflection, I ceased to blame myself She had not been upset at what I told her, it was almost as if she didn't care. I think the writing itself had come to satisfy her, that it ceased to matter that she might never be published. Poor, dear Marianne! She had such an unrealistic view of life, not at all like the real world we live in. But to answer your question – yes, I believe that given the right circumstances ... if, say, she fell in love and it turned out wrongly, she could – well, she could have taken her life.'

'Is that possible? That she had a disastrous love affair?'

'I knew little of that side of her life. You'd have to ask my son, Steven. Just before she died, they were both part of a crowd of young people who used to be together all the time. He'll be in shortly, he's gone fishing and I hope he'll bring something back for our supper... He goes back to Cambridge in a couple of days. Will you stay and join us?'

Much as he would have liked to – he had begun to think he might have found a friend in Mrs Rafferty – he declined the offer. It never did to mix work with pleasure. But he would stay until he had seen Steven Rafferty.

Her brisk tone had made him think she wished the subject changed, but it was she, while they were waiting, who returned to it. 'As I said, after poor Marianne died, I began to question myself, to wonder if I might not have been wrong. None of us is infallible, after all. I asked if they would let me have her notebooks to go through, thinking I might perhaps salvage something, you know, that although it couldn't do her much good, then her hopes might not all have been in vain...' She broke off. 'No, I am not being altogether truthful. I was more inclined to think there might be some clue in them as to why she had died. I had been rather harsh...' Her face was troubled.

'And was there?' he asked gently.

'They could not be found. No one knew what had become of them, or seemed to care parti-cularly. Her family, I think, never understood her ambitions, much as they loved her. In fact, they

191

suggested she must have destroyed them before her ... accident.'

'Which seems to strengthen the idea it *wasn't* an accident.'

'Indeed. I refuse to believe she would ever have destroyed them otherwise, not Marianne. To me, what she wrote seemed mostly rubbish, but of course, *she* didn't believe that, Marianne herself' Her eyes, bright and alert, regarded him steadily, then she said, as if coming to a decision, 'If I were you, I should ask her family about them.'

'Ask which family?'

In the long, shadowy room the arrival of the young man had gone unnoticed. He walked to the far end and threw a large fish on to the draining board where it slithered into the sink. 'Roach,' he said, coming back. 'Not much else doing this afternoon, Ma, except tiddlers.'

He was lanky, bespectacled and quietly spoken. His mother was, she had told Reardon, pinning her faith on his hopes for a junior fellowship at Cambridge; he had a brilliant degree, he had worked hard during the war, it was only what he deserved. Steven Rafferty himself appeared to be an unassuming young man for such accolades to be heaped upon him; but that was a mother's privilege.

'Steven, how quietly you came in. This is Mr Reardon, who used to be with the police. He was wondering what we can remember about poor Marianne's drowning.'

'Oh?' He regarded Reardon owlishly through his spectacles. Then he smiled pleasantly but waved away Reardon's extended hand. 'Sorry, I'm filthy. If you'll excuse me, I'll go and tidy myself up a little.' He was wearing fisherman's waders and a disreputable old jacket, patently outgrown, presumably donned for fishing.

'Don't go to any trouble for me,' Reardon said.

'Oh, it's no trouble. Can't spoil your tea, and mine, smelling of fish.' He went outside again to wash his hands at the pump, returned and took the wooden flight of stairs in the corner in several easy strides. Mrs Rafferty went to make fresh tea. A few minutes later Steven presented himself, changed, combed and tidied, and accepted cake and tea from his mother. 'Well now.'

He listened with grave attention while Reardon outlined the position, seemingly as incurious as his mother had been about his motives in starting up enquiries again.

'I have spoken to Miss Wentworth and she seemed to think I should speak to the Gypsies.'

'Nella did? I wonder why?'

'Wasn't one of them making a nuisance of himself? Hanging around you and your friends and ... er ... having his eye on Marianne?'

'Good Lord, only Rupert – the Austrian, von Kessel – thought that, or pretended to. He made the excuse that Danny Boswell seemed to be paying too much attention to Marianne, but I think he just felt a Gypsy should keep his distance from people whom he thought were not quite the same standing, so to speak. Which wasn't the case at all. They're well known around here, the Boswells. As long as they keep their hands off other people's property, nobody minds them. All the same, it wasn't usual to do what Grev did one day.'

Reardon lifted an eyebrow.

'He went over to Danny and suggested he join us.'

'Join you?'

'I know, I know. Ludicrous, wasn't it? Especially as there was no danger of him doing so. Grev knew perfectly well Daniel would run a mile rather than join us. To be honest, I wondered if he had actually put the question to him at all, simply pretended he had. They're proud people you know, the Romanies, they value their independence and rightly resent condescension. Grev only did what he did to annoy Rupert.'

'So they didn't get on well?'

'He was William's friend, not Grev's. Schoolfriend. And I dare say *they* would have grown out of each other afterwards, meeting other people, as one does, but they were still pretty close, then.' It seemed fairly obvious that Steven hadn't much liked the Austrian, himself. He appeared to be a young man who probably took nothing on face value and might very well be a clear-eyed judge of character. 'But no, he and Grev didn't get on. There was always a feeling of thunder in the air whenever they were together, although Grev was studiously polite to him, as people are with those they don't really like, you know?'

'It must have been rather a touchy situation.'

'It was, and more so with Rupert being on the other side, as it were.'

'Tell me more.'

'There isn't a lot to say, really. Actually, Rupert was rather ... shall we say, full of himself. It was obvious there was going to be a war but he hung on here, out of sheer bravado, until the very last moment. Notwithstanding the wrath of his father, I believe.'

'What happened to him?'

'I have no idea. Other than the fact he only left on the same night that Grev left to enlist. Rather arrogant, wasn't it? But as I said, he liked to make an impression, especially on the girls. Though I don't think that worked too well.'

'Not even with Marianne?'

The grave answer came after a moment. 'Don't be fooled, Mr Reardon, Marianne had far more sense than most people gave her credit for – including my dear mother here,' he added with a smile, stretching out his hand and patting hers pacifically. 'Emotions are unreliable, don't you think? Facts are what matter more in a case like this, surely?'

'Possibly. Well, you know the facts. So what do you think happened?'

'The obvious solution is usually the right one, and if you look at it logically, what happened to Marianne must have been an accident. I think she simply forgot how unsafe the jetty was, and couldn't save herself when it collapsed.'

'And what do you think a young woman like her was doing there, down by the lake, on her own, at night?'

'Oh, I think she went to meet Grev. Where they could be alone, to say goodbye properly.'

'Hmm. Have you any idea why Greville Foley should have changed his mind about joining the fighting?'

'Who knows? But what happened the previous

evening probably had something to do with it. There was a supper party at Oaklands – and it ended in an altercation. We, my parents and I, the hoi polloi, were actually invited.' He smiled deprecatingly, disarmingly, with a lifted eyebrow.

'What Steven means is, we were not in the habit of receiving invitations to Oaklands, but it was Mrs Villiers's seventieth birthday – the girls' grandmother you know,' Mrs Rafferty intervened, 'and we were invited as her friends. But let's not mince words, Steven, it was more than an altercation, it was a fight. Rupert more or less accused Grev of being a coward and Grev proved he was not by knocking him down. They shook hands afterwards, but I'm afraid it did rather break up the party.'

'As I must break up this meeting, Mrs Rafferty, and you, sir.' Reardon wanted now to be alone, to assess what he had learnt. 'Thank you for the cake, and the conversation. It's been a pleasure.'

'I hope it's been enlightening, too, Mr Reardon.'

'I'm not sure of that yet, ma'am, but I hope it may be.'

Chapter Eighteen

The Leasowes, the place where Nella Wentworth had told him the Gypsies were encamped, turned out to be on Oaklands land. Although he had indeed spent the previous day walking the

196

surrounding hills, Reardon thought he had better give more credence to his pretence of being here on a walking holiday by leaving his motorcycle parked in the yard behind the Greville Arms. He walked along the road towards the outskirts of the village and, following instructions obtained at the pub, he found the encampment without difficulty, the blue smoke spiralling up through the bare tree branches giving him the first indication of its whereabouts. He climbed over a stile by the side of a five-barred gate, but it was still hidden below the slope of the field. He paused to reconnoitre.

He had learnt a thing or two about these Gypsies while he was making his enquiries as to their location. The first was that the same family, the Boswells, had been coming back to Broughton Underhill to pitch their caravans for generations, from where they were never hounded or moved on as they were in many places. Or not until some of their more antisocial activities became too outrageous to be ignored by Ted Bracey, whose motto of live and let live was sometimes sorely put to the test by them. Apparently the old earl, in his day, had been heard to say that if they only took a pheasant or two to fill their children's bellies, they were damned welcome to them, and if they needed a place to camp for the summer, the Lea-sowes wasn't being used for anything else, and had ordered them to be left in peace. His daughter, Lady Sybil, evidently saw no reason to change that state of affairs.

As he eventually began to make the descent towards the stream, the camp came into view: several brightly decorated covered wagons drawn up together round a fire, over which a pot was suspended on a tripod, sending forth a sharp, savoury aroma which blended pleasantly with the woodsmoke. It was a quiet and secluded spot, on a curve of the stream, overhung by willows just turning green-gold, with catkins hanging from the bare black branches of the hazels. There were no men about but a group of women seemed to be washing clothes at the stream, and a few horses grazed at some distance. Otherwise there appeared at first to be no further sign of life until, as he drew nearer, half a dozen savage-looking dogs suddenly appeared from nowhere and in a moment surrounded him, snarling and leaping, teeth bared.

Not much frightened Herbert Reardon, but he didn't like the look of these at all and there was no possibility of escape. As it was he stood immobile in the centre of the ring, feeling a fool but not inclined to try moving forward, until the sound of a whistle caused the pack to sink to the ground, tongues lolling, though still keeping watchful eyes on him. After a few further undignified minutes standing in their midst came another whistle which made the dogs slink back to wherever they'd come from. Greatly relieved, Reardon moved tentatively forward. There was no sign of the person who had sent forth the command, and silence reigned, until he came into full view of the circle of caravans, heard childish voices and saw an old woman sitting on the steps of one. She was traditionally garbed, with a multi-coloured headscarf and a shawl around her shoulders, a poppy-red skirt, smoking a short clay pipe and observing him with interest as he came nearer.

Several filthy children played in the dust at the old woman's feet, but none of them took any notice of him, except for one little girl who smiled up at him, all black eyes and jet-black curls, gleams of gold from the rings in her ears: a lovely child, though he suspected that the chances of her not growing to look like the wizened old creature on the steps within a very few years were slim. He addressed the old woman. 'I'd like to speak to Daniel Boswell, if you please.'

For a long time her eyes, black as obsidian in her weather-beaten face, looked into his own, then moved over his face, as if memorising its contours. She showed neither shock, disgust nor pity at what she saw. Returning the gaze, he realised she was probably not as old as he had first thought, but rather, simply worn down by time and circumstance. Finally, her gold earrings jangling, she jerked her head sideways towards an elderly man dressed in moleskin trousers, his straight black hair falling to his shoulders, the inevitable red scarf around his neck, who had appeared from the back of the caravans. He was surrounded by the dogs, now quiet, Reardon was relieved to see, though unnervingly, like the woman, they never took their eyes off him. 'Here be Daniel Boswell.'

'What can I do for you?' the man asked, civilly enough, when he reached them.

'My name's Reardon. I'm looking for Daniel Boswell – young Daniel Boswell.' He hazarded a guess. 'You're perhaps his father?'

'No.' His black eyes were deep set in a proud, dark Egyptian face, as unsmiling as the old woman's.

To be truthful, Reardon had never had much time for Gypsies – travelling folk. They were always wanting to tell your fortune or wheedling you to buy rubbish you didn't want, generally getting into mischief. He'd personally crossed swords with them once or twice, when they'd been on the wrong side of the law. But his preconceived ideas were given a jolt by this man. He looked different. He had what, Reardon thought, searching for a word, could be called dignity. He didn't ask what the stranger's business was, but Reardon had a pretty good idea his appearance in the village, and the reason for it, would be no news to any of the Gypsies. He forbore to enlighten him, asking only, 'Perhaps you'd be so good as to tell me where I can find young Mr Boswell?'

'You be staying in the village.' It was a statement, not a question.

'As a matter of fact, yes, for the time being...'

'Then he'll find you, when he wants to. Good day, mister.'

Reardon, however much he might object to the abrupt dismissal, looked at the man's unyielding face, the alert dogs, received a strong impression he would get nowhere by any further questions, and chose caution as the better part of valour. It seemed as though he had no choice, for the moment at any rate, but to wait until – or if – Daniel Boswell the younger chose to approach him. He murmured his thanks with as much dignity as he could muster and walked back up the field, feeling with every step he took the eyes of Boswell, the old woman and the dogs still on his back. Once out of sight of the camp, he passed through the field stile again, then turned to lean on the gate beside it. Only the blue smoke of the fire was visible from here but he felt, disconcertingly, as if the Gypsies he'd left behind, out of sight, knew he was still there.

As he stood, the same barefoot little girl who had smiled at him emerged from behind the trees which sheltered the caravans, carrying a big enamel pitcher, and ran towards the river. At a point where the water fell gently over some rocks to a slightly lower level she squatted to fill the jug. The water would be as shallow here as it was in most places in its meander through the village, and so clear you could see the pebbles lying on the bed. At its edge grew the reeds and osiers the Gypsies sometimes used to make baskets which they then sold to the villagers and anyone else who would buy them. After a few minutes the child he had been watching turned with the pitcher, staggering under its weight as she made her unsteady way back to the caravans.

He sat on the step of the stile for nearly half an hour, thinking over what he had learnt so far. He was not a great deal further along in his quest and his time here was nearly up. He thought about what Steven Rafferty had told him and why Nella Wentworth should have directed him to the Gypsies. Was it because she didn't share Steven's feeling that Daniel Boswell was entirely blameless? Or did she know something he didn't,

201

something Marianne had told her, perhaps? Had something happened, which concerned the Gypsy in the days before Marianne died, that might have led up to her death?

A voice several yards to his left said, 'You wanted to see me.'

He hadn't heard anyone come close and it made him jump. He saw a younger version of the man he had been speaking to – not much more than a boy, really – sitting on the grass, one arm around his knees. He had on a brown felt hat that he wore pushed to the back of his head, but the dark hair straggling beneath it, unlike the old man's, was matted and unkempt. A pair of old corduroys were held up with a length of rope tied round his waist. Reardon had the uneasy feeling he might have been there all the time, watching him. 'Daniel Boswell?'

The boy nodded.

'The old man didn't say you were around.'

'My uncle don't like *gauje* – outsiders. What do the police want of me?'

He'd been right, they had known who he was. He said, 'I'm making enquiries into the death of Miss Marianne Wentworth, the girl who was drowned, the summer before the war, remember?'

'I don't remember nothing about that, mister.'

'You should. You were following her around, watching her.'

'Not *her*.' He grinned, showing stained teeth. 'Me, a married man with two *chaves*?'

Married? Two – babies, did he mean? Surely not, the lad before him couldn't be more than twenty-one, or two at the most – and they were

202

talking of nearly five years ago. But they married young, these Gypsies. That was why their women, often lovely in youth, grew old before their time, he reckoned. All that childbearing. No home comforts, living on the road, in all weathers. Eating nothing except what they could pinch, or get for free: hedgehogs, rabbits, birds' eggs.

'If you weren't watching her, what were you doing hanging around her and her friends? And who was it you had your eye on, if it wasn't her?'

The boy didn't seem to feel it necessary to answer, or to hurry to fill the silence which ensued. He brought a thin, rolled-up cigarette from his pocket, lit it and gazed out over the valley as he smoked. Reardon, leaning over the stile, watched him in equal silence, for the moment willing to let him take his time, and it wasn't until he'd finished his smoke that the Gypsy spoke again.

'It were the boy, the young master, that's who I was watching for. There was trouble round him. I warned him but he wouldn't listen.'

'What sort of trouble?'

'You shouldn't ask questions that there ain't no answer to, mister.'

'Come on, what sort of talk is that?'

'Danger. That's all I can tell you, 'cause that's all I ever knew. There were some kind of trouble around him.'

'And you thought you could prevent it?' The Gypsy shrugged. 'Why did you – and all of your family – leave so suddenly?'

His teeth were crooked as well as stained and the smile he directed at Reardon had something wicked in it, yet Reardon wasn't distrustful of it.

'What do you think happens to the likes of us in a war?'

'I don't know. You tell me.'

'We got out quick, and spent the time in Ireland, that's what. We have relations, other Romani, over there, they knew how to look after us.'

It was possible, at a time when the whole country was in a tumult and even ordinary people were doing all sorts of unexpected and extraordinary things. Nobody would have bothered a few Gypsies.

'The night Marianne Wentworth died. What were you doing?'

The lad grinned. 'Minding my own business.'

'Look here, nobody's accusing you of anything, Daniel. Her family have never had a proper answer to what happened to her, and they want to know.' He was stretching the facts a bit here, but since he thought it was true, he felt justified. He didn't rightly know what the Gypsies' attitude to suicide was, but he'd never heard of any of them taking their own life as a solution to their problems, and he thought they might regard it as a bad and unlucky way to go into the next world. He said, 'They don't go along with the idea of suicide. I just want a straight answer to a straight question.'

Daniel had retreated into one of the long silences the Gypsies seemed to specialise in. 'I saw her,' he said at last.

'You saw what happened?'

'She fell into the water.'

'Fell? Where were you when you saw this?'

'On the other side of the lake, in the woods on the far bank, opposite the boathouse.'

204

'What were you doing out in the woods?' Daniel threw him a sardonic look, and Reardon didn't push it.

'Well, never mind that. More to the point is ... did you try to save her?'

'Can't swim, mister.' This might have been true. Gypsies weren't very fond of water at the best of times, and Reardon had met sailors who were afraid of water and couldn't swim. 'But I run round to the other side, all the same. Waded into the water at the edge to see if I could get her out but she wasn't there.'

'Was she alone – before, I mean?'

The Gypsy looked at him. 'She was when she fell in.'

It felt as though he was drawing teeth, but Reardon schooled himself to patience. 'So someone was with her before that?'

Daniel stared into the remote distance, as though he wasn't going to answer. 'The boy from the house, the one I told you about – the young master – he was there, but after a bit he went and left her.'

'Were they quarrelling?'

'Not if you call kissing her quarrelling, they weren't. Then after he'd left her, she just sat there, on the grass. Crying, I reckon.'

'What time was all this?'

'After the church clock struck midnight.'

Reardon said, 'Did you know young Mr Foley left the same night to join the army?'

'No. I told you, we was gone ourselves afore dawn.' He saw Reardon's expression. 'We was planning to go anyway.'

He threw away his cigarette butt, and lit another. 'He weren't the last to see her, though. There was somebody else there, after him. Dunno who it were, couldn't see by then, it were getting dark. Only her I could, she had a white dress on, see.'

That was true. Reardon vividly called to mind a white blouse and a torn, dark blue skirt, black shoes, a tortoiseshell slide holding her hair back.

'Somebody else? Somebody who pushed her into the water?'

'Nah, she was the one doing the pushing. Shoved him away, she did, and after a minute he turned away and went.'

Von Kessel?

'And then?'

'That's when she ran out onto the jetty. Like a hare, and nearly got to the end afore it collapsed under her. I saw her arms go up, heard her scream. I ran but by the time I gets round to the boathouse there's no sign of her, see? So I reckon she must have managed to get out and go home – the jetty only stuck out ten feet or so.'

'A long way if you can't swim. And she didn't get out. Her skirt caught on a nail sticking out of one of the rotten posts as she went through and kept her under the wreckage. Ben Naylor, the gamekeeper, found her at eight the next morning – or rather his dog did.'

'Well, we was on the *drom*, on the road, long afore that.'

Was he telling the truth? Would he admit what he'd seen to the Wentworths? 'Will you swear to this?'

And what good would it do, he thought in the

206

same instant – the word of a Gypsy? Daniel Boswell could stand up in a court of law and swear with his hand on the Bible and wouldn't necessarily be believed. Liars, thieves and vagabonds to a man, they were, to everyone. No doubt they had their own code of honour, but if so, it wasn't one most people recognised. The Gypsy knew this as well as he did. He looked at Reardon steadily and said nothing.

There was the possibility that he *was* lying, of course, but Reardon's instinct told him that in this instance he was telling the truth – as far as it went. He had nothing to gain by lying. But although he'd denied knowing who the second individual speaking to Marianne had been, Reardon was certain he did know ... and equally sure he would only get it out of him if he wished. He held out his hand to the boy. 'Thank you for talking to me.'

Daniel looked uncomfortable as he stood up, nodded, but did not take Reardon's hand. Then he turned and melted into the bushes.

It looked as though Steven Rafferty had been right. Greville Foley and Marianne had indeed said their goodbyes at the lakeside before he had rushed off to enlist. But who was the other person Daniel had seen? The Austrian, Rupert von Kessel? Neither Foley nor von Kessel was here to tell the tale. One was dead and the other ... who knew what had happened to him?

But ... why should whatever had passed between Marianne and that other person, whoever it was the Gypsy claimed he had seen, have made her run headlong onto a jetty she knew to be unsafe, other than with the intention of throwing herself off it? Only the rotten boards under her running feet had saved her from suicide, technically speaking. Marianne Wentworth's death had, in the strict sense of the word, been an accident. It was what her family wanted to hear. It was, however, only a half-truth, when there was still no explanation, as far as Reardon could see, as to why she might well have *wanted* to kill herself. Daniel Boswell had seen her and Greville Foley kissing. Had she thrown herself into the lake in despair at his decision to enlist? He shook his head. She may have seen herself as the heroine of a romantic story, as Mrs Rafferty had suggested, but modern young women were tougher than that.

There was no excuse for him to stay here in Broughton Underhill any longer. With no evidence to the contrary, what he had feared had turned out to have no basis in fact. No one had been involved in Marianne Wentworth's drowning except herself – or only insofar as they'd contributed to her state of mind. The outcome as far as he was concerned was unsatisfactory, there were still flaws. But he had pushed his self-appointed questioning here – and his luck with authority – to it limits and the best he could do was to leave it at that; let the Wentworths go on regarding it as an accident, if that was what they wished. They might even come to believe it in time.

PART TWO

End of March 1919

Chapter Nineteen

The crow's morning flight takes him towards the
village again, away from Oaklands Park and
across its lake. It is a sharp, bright, chancy morn-
ing, he has a strong wind behind him, and the
sun is dancing on the water, except where the
dense pines throw deep shadows across the far
end. Nothing appears to be unusual, bar the
activity going on at the point where the path from
the big house joins the one from the village at the
lakeside. There, a small crowd of men – police-
men, and a doctor – is milling around a young
woman lying on the bank. Pulled out of the
water. Drowned. It appears that the lake has
claimed another victim.

But no, this woman hasn't drowned, although
she is very wet and is indubitably dead. Again,
the body has been found by the gamekeeper, Ben
Naylor, who is sitting miserably on an outcrop of
rock near the edge of the lake, his head in his
hands. Coincidence, or something more sinister?

The crow flies on, neither knowing, nor caring.

'Do we know who she is?' Reardon asked.

Ted Bracey mopped his brow and ran a finger
round the inside of his tunic collar. His best
uniform, donned in deference to the seriousness
of the incident, seemed to have grown uncom-
fortably tight since he'd last worn it. More than

that, he'd had to bicycle along here from the police house; exercise like that could kill a man of his age, on top of a heavy breakfast. 'She's Lady Sybil's maid, Edith Huckaby. He'll tell you about her,' he added, with a jerk of his head and a sideways glance that fell just short of a meaningful wink towards Naylor.

She was young. Mid twenties, perhaps. Slim and with a quantity of glossy black hair. Whether she had been pretty or not was open to question: being bludgeoned to death did not leave a corpse looking at its best. Her clothes were good. She was, in fact, extremely well dressed, in an elegant costume too fine, one would have thought, for a lady's maid, or for rough walking through the woods, for that matter: a well-tailored, double-breasted coat and skirt, in a fine, fawn wool cloth, unsuitable shoes and a saucy hat – a taupe-coloured ruched velvet toque trimmed with a veil and a bunch of velvet Parma violets, which had presumably fallen off when she had been struck on the head, it lay wet and ruined next to the little fox fur the doctor had removed. A poor thing that looked, too, bedraggled with the heavy rain which had fallen during the night, and stiff with blood.

It was a lovely, though lonely spot. Why had she come down here? Possibly twelve or fourteen hours or so since, according to the doctor, which made it roughly between seven and nine o'clock the previous night when she'd met her death. A cold, dark, and wet night it had been, too.

'No umbrella?' Reardon looked around but couldn't see one.

'Wouldn't have been much use, in a wind like

that. Got up summat desperate in the night, it did,' Bracey replied. 'Heard it did a lot of damage.' There was plenty evidence of this in the debris of torn-off branches, leaves and twigs everywhere littering the ground. March was roaring itself out, the cold, still start to the month having given way to milder but rougher weather.

The doctor gently unpinned and handed to Reardon the brooch which had fastened the high-boned collar at the neck of the victim's blood-soaked georgette blouse, a gold heart shape with the letters MIZPAH set diagonally across it. Jewellery like that had been very popular during the war, the letters a Biblical reference which apparently signified: 'May the Lord watch between thee and me when we are absent one from another.' She wasn't married, or at any rate wasn't wearing a wedding ring. Perhaps the brooch had been a token given to her by a soldier sweetheart who had never returned.

'Well, that's it.' The doctor gently straightened her clothes at last, making her decent again after satisfying himself that there were no obvious signs of sexual assault. Her underwear was fine white lawn, delicately trimmed with ecru lace. 'No other injuries. It looks as though only one blow was sufficient to kill her, with some sort of heavy, blunt weapon, I should say.' He pointed to the single wound on the temple, above the right ear, the skin and the skull beneath cracked like the shell of a boiled egg, with pieces of splintered bone protruding through the clotted blood and tissue. 'She probably didn't see it coming and fell to the ground immediately. There don't seem to be any indications she tried to ward off the attack... You'll need confirmation of all this, of course, it's not my field of expertise.' The doctor was the medical officer in charge of the convalescent soldiers at Oaklands Park, a Scot who'd introduced himself as Geddes.

'The pathologist will examine her, naturally,' Reardon replied. 'We just required immediate certification of death, and since the local doctor's away, and there was a hospital with doctors handy... You know how it is, red tape and all that.' Even when the body lying between them was as unmistakably lifeless as this one was, officialdom demanded medical confirmation.

The doctor nodded absently, looking down at the young woman. 'Unlucky place, this ... another life... God, what a hideous waste it all is.' They fell momentarily silent. Doctor on the front line, Reardon had thought straight away, as soon as they'd met; responding to an emergency without question. A quick, professional glance at his own face, a nod to one he recognised as a comrade, and then down to the business in hand. Without words, even without the evidence of Reardon's scars, the two men had known that instant empathy which linked all those who had fought at the front, perhaps always would. They were both familiar with death in most of its forms, but Reardon knew what the doctor had meant: was any death less than hideous? Especially when it robbed a young person of all the life they had before them.

'Well, then, Inspector,' Geddes went on, standing up, the knees of his trousers wet through from kneeling on the drenched grass. 'Now that

I've certified she's dead, poor woman, and if there's nothing else I can do...?'

'Thank you, doctor. Much obliged for your help.'

At that moment a constable came to tell them that the ambulance had arrived and was parked as near to the lakeside as they could get it. Hats and helmets were removed, Naylor rose from his seat on the rock, and they all stood silently until the body was placed on a stretcher, carried up the slope and away. Reardon replaced his hat, Geddes picked up the bag he'd brought with him and held out his hand. Reardon shook it and watched him go, with interest, wondering how he could have known about that other death at the lake.

He put into an envelope the brooch and a pretty little red-stoned ring he'd taken from the victim's finger after her soft, grey suede gloves had been removed, and looked for the sergeant, but he was busy directing the search of the area in the hope of finding the weapon, which could have been anything at this juncture – a heavy piece of broken branch, of which there were plenty lying around, a rock, even – though recognising either would be a hopeless task. Anything bloodstained would have been washed clean by the torrents of rain that had come down during the night. Reardon beckoned a young constable and passed him the envelope. 'Effects of the deceased. Give this to Sergeant Wheelan when he has a minute, will you, Spooner? We need to get them valued.' The 'gold' of the brooch was almost certainly pinchbeck, and maybe the red stone was just glass, but he didn't think so. He turned once more to PC Bracey.

'What about the gamekeeper?'

'Ben Naylor? Lives in that cottage up there.' He pointed to a building just beyond the fork of the path. Bracey was readier with his answers than he had been on their first encounter, now that Reardon was here officially. 'Keeper at Oaklands, man and boy, his father afore him. He's not a bad sort, on the whole. Bit of a sobersides, keeps hisself to hisself and walks five miles to Lower Broughton every Sunday to the Methodies, and five back. Mind you...' Again that same knowing glance, another shrug.

'Wait for me, will you?' Reardon left Bracey and walked over to the gamekeeper, who had resumed his position on the rock, still holding his cap between his hands, staring at the ground. His dog was sitting in uneasy obedience by his side, a black and white collie bitch with yellow eyes which had slid back and forth all the time from the body while it was fifteen yards away and who was still making low, whimpering noises from the back of her throat.

'Mr Naylor.'

'Yes?' Naylor sat up. He was older than Reardon expected. Older than Edith Huckaby by perhaps twenty years or more, but big and strongly built, with a head of springing curls flecked with grey. Grey-faced too, now, under his outdoor tan, unsmiling. As he would be, in view of what he'd discovered. A potent reminder of that other morning, when he and his dog had set out on their routine inspection walk of the grounds, the dog had sniffed around, plunged into the lake and commenced tugging at the body of Marianne

216

Wentworth, caught under the wreckage of the jetty by her skirts. Reardon hadn't met Naylor before. It hadn't been down to him to interview him at the time of Marianne's death and he hadn't got around to speaking with him before he'd left Broughton Underhill, a couple of weeks ago.

The last thing he had expected was to be back in the village so soon after leaving it, as he'd thought, for good. It was uncanny, the way this case had come up, just after he had started back with the police. Edith Huckaby. The young woman who had shared Marianne Wentworth's passion for books. He experienced the same, almost superstitious tingle down his spine as he had when the first news of this case had broken.

He had, contrary to his expectations, been welcomed back into his old division at Dudley, if not with open arms, then at least with an encouraging acceptance. Never having actually resigned from the police when he joined the army, it turned out that they were prepared to let him take up again as inspector – *acting* inspector – until (or if ever) the rank he had previously been recommended for, unknown as it had been to him at the time, should be confirmed. He could not quite believe his luck, but he was after all experienced, and his records, both with the police and the army, were excellent, they said. He knew a more likely reason was that they were still seriously short-handed, as they had been throughout the war, and with the same unrest over poor pay conditions that was fermenting in the police all over the country, the prospects of finding men – or at any rate, the right kind of men – to fill the spaces left vacant by those trained officers who had given their lives in the service of their country were not good. His old superior, Superintendent Gifford, had of course retired – without too many tears being shed by anyone – and the man who had replaced him was new to Reardon, but below him was a man called Kelly, whom he liked and respected, and who had been promoted to chief inspector.

Chief Inspector Kelly was a big, untidy man of Irish descent, with a roughly hewn face and a pugnacious chin. Permanently overworked during the war, the heavy responsibilities he'd taken on had grizzled the wiry dark hair at his temples and added lines to his already craggy face, making him seem older than he was. 'You didn't enlist with the RMP, Reardon,' he had said. 'Why not?'

Reardon shrugged. He had never been sorry that he hadn't volunteered to join the military police. Doing so might have saved him from the front line, but general keeping-of-the-peace duties or controlling ambulance convoys hadn't seemed very heroic, nor would he have had any stomach for rounding up the drunk-and-disorderlies, men who, after all, only sought a few hours' alcoholic oblivion from the nightmare of the trenches; still less for patrolling the lines to catch deserters, often terrified young lads of no more than fifteen or sixteen, who'd lied about their age to get into the army and ended up crying their eyes out and wishing with all their hearts they'd never left their mothers, poor little devils.

'Wasn't sure I'd ever return to the police, sir.'

'It might have been better for your prospects if

218

you had served with the Redcaps. Still, it might be overlooked...' Kelly smiled slightly. It was not the first broad hint he'd dropped, and it reinforced what Henry Paskin had said. Reardon grinned sardonically. Don't count chickens, Reardon, the mills of the police, like those of God, grind slow. What was of more immediate satisfaction to him was the fact that he had not been returned to the uniformed branch, as he had feared, but reinstated as a plain-clothes detective once more.

Meanwhile, he suspected they hadn't quite worked out what to do with him yet, and that was why, when this case had been reported, Kelly had decided to send him here.

'Broughton Underhill, where's that? Aside from being at the back of nowhere? Weren't you on that case there with old Paskin at the beginning of the war – the one where the girl was found drowned?'

Yes, I was.

'Right, then. Since you're no stranger to the place, you might as well get yourself over there and start on the spade work. I'm due in court for most of today, and maybe tomorrow as well.' He jabbed his pencil into the blotter on his desk several times, then he said, 'Look here, I'm going to go out on a limb with this, Reardon, and assign this case to you. I'll still be in overall charge, but I'm snowed under at the moment – fact is, my family hardly remembers they have a husband and father – so it's up to you, as long as you keep me informed. It's not far to come back now and again on that motorbike of yours, though you'd better find yourself some lodging there till the business is finished.' He added that he would spare as many constables as he could to get the enquiry under way, after which Reardon and a sergeant would be on their own, with any assistance they could manage to get from Bracey. 'I'm sending Sergeant Wheelan with you.'

That was a bonus, a gesture from Kelly that Reardon really appreciated. He knew Wheelan well – or Wheely, as he was known to all. He was another, like himself who'd worked with Paskin, and had an accent nearly, if not quite, as thick. A patient, middle-aged man with a wealth of constabulary experience and local knowledge behind him, comfortable with his rank as a sergeant and unambitious to go further, he was as solid as the Rock of Gibraltar, and almost as big. Next to Wheelan and his experience, Reardon knew he was still a babe in arms. Although he might be regarded as having the imagination, far-sightedness and ambition the sergeant lacked, Wheelan had a comfortableness and a sturdy common sense that was equal to any amount of what Paskin had called 'fancy ideas'. He was already supervising a detailed and well-organised search of the area. Reardon left him to it and walked towards Naylor.

It still tugged at his conscience, the 'coincidence' of another dead woman being found here. Could he afford to disregard the implications of this body being found, just after he had started up enquiries again about the death of the first? He wasn't sure how that made him feel about himself but he knew that he must not let past events, his own feelings about the Marianne

Wentworth affair, cloud his judgement. Yet ... if it was true that the past always had a bearing on the present, could Edith Huckaby, who had known Marianne, have been murdered because she was somehow connected with her death? He reined in his imagination. There was some way to go yet before that could be assumed. However important Marianne's drowning had become to him, in some undefined and unasked-for way, it was the present case which mattered. Who had killed Edith Huckaby, and why?

When he reached the spot where Naylor was crouched on the rock, he introduced himself and said, 'I take it you knew this poor young lady. What do you think she was doing in the woods last night?'

The gamekeeper threw a sardonic glance towards the constable. 'Ted Bracey been talking? Coming to see me, of course. But she never turned up.'

'Weren't you worried?'

'Not specially. Edith was a law unto herself. Anyway, she could never be sure whether she could get away or not.'

There was shock over what had happened, a natural sadness, something like despair, perhaps, but not, Reardon thought, grief.

'What was she to you?' he asked bluntly.

He thought Naylor was going to refuse to answer. An unwavering glance from steady brown eyes was directed at him but then the gamekeeper shrugged. 'All right, she sometimes ... visited me. When she could. Look, I've been a widower fifteen years and more. I loved my wife, none better, God

221

knows, but–' The dog whimpered and he bent down to soothe her. 'All right, Fern, my girl, it's all right.' His big hands were gentle on her head, stroking the silky fur, until presently her trembling ceased and she became quiet. 'Edith was willing enough. She knew what she was doing.'

'Not enough to realise the danger of being out alone in the woods at night, apparently.'

'There is no danger – not normally. Nobody comes round here.'

Suddenly, Naylor stood up, took a few rapid strides towards some bushes and retched violently several times. After a while he moved towards a little, clear stream trickling down through the red sandstone rocks, cupped his hands and drank, wiped his hands over his face. He came back, his face even greyer. 'Sorry. It's just ... she was beautiful, you know. Not just pretty. I didn't hardly recognise her when I found her. I...' He passed a hand over his face again.

'Take your time.'

'I'm right enough, now.' After a moment, he said, 'She wanted us to get married and go away from here, you know. She was sick of being a lady's maid. But Edith could never see the difference between what she wanted and what was possible. For one thing, I told her I'd never go away from here, never, and nor would I. I know no other job, and I asked her what she thought we'd live on. She said she had some money coming.'

'Money? Where was she expecting that from?'

'She said she had an old aunt who wasn't badly off. I suppose she meant some sort of legacy but...' He shook his head. 'She didn't come from rich folks, not Edith, she was an orphan, convent raised since she was a child. I think it was just another of her imaginings. She read too many daft books.'

'You mean the sort she lent to Marianne Wentworth – the girl from the rectory?' Naylor stared, uncomprehending, until Reardon explained, 'I was here on that case, before the war, when she drowned.'

The gamekeeper shook his head. Evidently word of Reardon's previous activities in the village had not reached him in the lonely, secluded life he led in his cottage up in the woods.

'I don't know about her lending books to Miss Marianne. Why should she do that? And if she did, what's it got to do with now?'

Reardon let that pass. 'Did you stay in, all last night?'

'As I said. I was waiting for her.'

'And you never went out at all?'

'No, I didn't,' said Ben Naylor. 'And I didn't kill Edith, neither.'

'Where on earth can she have got to?'

Lady Sybil drummed her fingers on the gleaming, dark-red bonnet of her husband's Daimler Marlborough as it stood on the drive, engine idling, waiting, as she was herself. Eunice could see she was doing her best to curb her impatience, although her mother was not a patient woman. There they were, standing outside the front door of the house, ready to be driven to Birmingham by Garbutt, Father's chauffeur, to catch the London train. Ready as they had been for ten minutes, and still no sign of Edith. Nor had there been all morning. It had been an extraordinary few hours, with no Edith to help Sybil dress and do her hair and oversee the last-minute packing. Eunice had done her best to help her mother, who was unusually quiet, saying she hadn't slept much because of the storm.

Eunice perched on the stone balustrade that stretched either side of the steps and lit a cigarette. Quietly composed, slender legs crossed, she looked exceeding pretty in a blue tweed travelling costume, her thick, honey-blonde hair arranged in a new wavy bob under a dark-blue velour-felt hat, becomingly turned up at one side and orna-mented with a diamanté arrow. 'I'm sure Edith will be here soon, Mother – and we really do have plenty of time. There's a porter waiting to help us on the train, and our seats are booked.' She knew this because she had arranged it all herself, one of the things she had taken to doing lately, quite enjoying the experience and finding that her mother made no objections, since it did, after all, make life so much easier. 'Please don't let it upset you, you'll bring on one of your headaches.

'My dear child, what *do* you mean – one of my headaches? You make me sound like one of those tiresome women who are permanently on the verge of a migraine, rather than just having the occasional bad head lately!' Eunice was relieved to hear her sounding more like her usual self. 'And it's not likely we shall have any time to spare at all, with Garbutt at the wheel,' she added, with a lifted eyebrow and a glance towards the chauffeur, who was fortunately out of earshot. Eunice knew her mother would actually have preferred to drive herself, as she'd become accustomed to doing; she enjoyed being in control of such a powerful beast as a motor car, and the feeling of speed as she drove along the roads around Broughton. Garbutt, on the other hand, could not be persuaded, no matter how he was urged on, to exceed what he considered a racy twenty miles an hour, so that there was always a slight feeling of tension in the motor car when he drove her mother.

However, there would have been no one to bring her car back from Birmingham had Sybil driven herself and in any case, there was more room in the Daimler, considering the amount of luggage they were taking, plus all the extra she fully intended to bring back. Having searched her extensive and long-unworn wardrobe for something suitable to wear at this forthcoming party, she had immediately rejected the idea of wearing any single one of the dresses hanging there. In the mysterious way that fashion had of creeping up on one, especially when there were more important things to occupy oneself with, it was borne in on her that sweeping skirts and tightly corseted waists were as dead as the dodo, that those enormous hats – 'but so delicious, darling ... and *so* becoming!' – were gone for ever and that the skirts women had shortened during the war would never go down again. She had looked at her daughter and acknowledged that she was better dressed than she was herself. A visit to her dressmaker in town, immediately, with Eunice to help her choose, was suddenly a necessity. They could catch up with some visiting, perhaps take in a theatre or two. That new Diaghilev production, perhaps, or *Chu Chin Chow*.

For the tenth time, she looked at the little jewelled wristwatch she wore. Garbutt stood to one side, unaware of, or ignoring, her growing impatience. The maid who had been sent to look for Edith yet again ran down the steps and said Miss Huckaby still couldn't be found anywhere.

'How tiresome of her! She knows what time we are to leave. Very well, we'll go without her. When she deigns to turn up, she can follow as best she may, take the next train and join us in London. She knows where to find us. I trust she will have a satisfactory explanation to offer when she does arrive.'

As far as Eunice was aware, Edith, to do her justice, had never before, in all the years she had been employed as her mother's maid, neglected her duties in the slightest, and simply to disappear like this was ... extraordinary, to say the least. A little stab of unease made her wonder if something was really wrong, though her mother appeared to have no such qualms, which was unlike her. She was always concerned with the welfare of any of the servants, especially someone as important to her as Edith was.

'Eunice, we're going to miss that train if we don't go immediately. And Garbutt ... please try to remember we have a train to catch.'

Finally, they were bowling down between the straight double row of yews and out into the long drive which led to the main gates and the road.

Sybil settled back in the spring-cushioned interior and endeavoured to concentrate on her plans for the next few days, until she became aware that the vehicle, rather than gathering speed, was actually slowing down. She made an exclamation and leant forward impatiently to prod Garbutt with her umbrella. This was really becoming beyond a joke. Then she saw that two men were standing in the road, waving the motor down. One of them was a helmeted policeman.

There was no question now, of course, of going up to town.

'Hold up, Mother, you mustn't faint.' Eunice was waving the little cut-glass bottle of salts under her nose. With her other hand she supported Sybil and looked anxiously into her face, which had drained of all colour.

Sybil sat up and waved away the smelling salts, a sovereign remedy for headaches, swoons and fits of the vapours which, like most women, she carried around in her bag as a matter of course but normally scorned. She dried away the tears the ammoniac crystals had brought to her eyes and adjusted her hat. 'I have no intention, Eunice dear, of fainting. It was only a moment of shock. Good God, what a thing! Who would *not* feel queer? I shall do very well now. But I think we must consider the London visit postponed. I'm afraid you'll be very disappointed.'

'Disappointed! What does that matter with Edith–'

Dead. She was dead. Pretty, silly, clever Edith. Attacked and hit on the head, they said, by some maniac, by the lake, last night. It was Ben Naylor who had found her, just as he'd found Marianne.

227

Eunice's thoughts whirled in her head.

Garbutt had already turned the car round and they were heading back to the house, where the policemen, who were following on foot, wished to have a few words, as they put it. 'We must find your father and tell him before the police do,' Sybil said anxiously. 'The shock of hearing the news, put as baldly as they have put it to us, might be too much for him.'

The motor stopped. Garbutt had made the journey back to the front door in a record three minutes.

Chapter Twenty

Reardon stood at the doorway of Edith Huck-aby's bedroom, taking in a general impression before he entered.

It was a little, inconveniently situated room at the top of the house, reached by the back stairs, but he realised immediately that, although plain and without frills, it was still a great deal better than the usual servants' quarters, presumably because ladies' maids were regarded as a cut above the other servants, and occupied a privileged position in the households of those who employed such women. It was in fact a comfortable bed-sitting room, with white starched curtains at the windows, discreetly patterned wallpaper and a white counterpane stretched tautly over the bed. Anonymous, except for the corner where a couple of well-filled bookshelves spanned one of the fireplace alcoves. It was as neat and orderly as a nun's cell, with no pictures, no ornaments and little evidence of its occupant left lying around, except for a wooden crucifix hanging over the bed. He stepped forward.

The dressing table was bare but for a swing mirror, a china hairpin holder, a fat red velvet pincushion in the shape of a huge strawberry, a little porcelain tray containing a rosary of blue beads and a half-full bottle of what, after a sniff, he decided was expensive scent. Cupboards and drawers were immaculately tidy, the latter containing the same sort of delicate underwear she had been wearing when she died. The garments hanging in the cupboard, though few, were good: skirts, blouses and two coats, all made from excellent-quality materials, such as could hardly have been afforded by a servant, however elevated. Like the clothes she had been wearing when she was found, and presumably the scent, too, he assumed they were all hand-me-downs from her mistress.

He had saved the bookshelves until last. The top one supported an electric reading lamp, and there was an easy chair nearby, drawn up in front of the small fireplace, where a fire was already laid with paper and sticks. Quite a cosy corner it would make, with the fire lit and the lamp burning.

On examination, most of the books seemed to be the sort of women's fiction Reardon never bothered to read, though the lettering on the spines showed household names that even he had heard of: Marie Corelli, Elinor Glyn, Ethel M Dell. He pulled up the armchair and reached out.

A flick through revealed most of them to be the sort of syrupy, pulsating romances he had expected, full of strong, silent heroes and breathless women, beating hearts and racing pulses, palpitating with words like 'passion', 'desire', 'throb' ... Featuring torrid love affairs, often among the desert sands and oases of some Eastern but unspecified land. In the case of Marie Corelli, there were overtones of the supernatural and the occult; no mean feat, this, considering her books managed at the same time to be highly moralistic and religious. He recalled that she was reputed to have been Queen Victoria's favourite author – and was still writing.

Picking up next a book by Elinor Glyn, she who scandalised society with her sensational novels, his eyebrows lifted as he read. Yes indeed, decidedly risqué. Scenes of illicit and forbidden love. Passion on a tiger skin. It was perhaps as well Glyn had arrived on the writing scene later than Mrs Corelli. Queen Victoria would not have been amused. He began to see what Mrs Rafferty had been driving at, if Marianne Wentworth had based her style on any one of these writers. As examples, they must have been touchpaper to one of her temperament. And what of the as yet unknown Miss Huckaby herself? What sort of wild emotions had these books stirred up in her?

Returning the books to the shelves where he had found them, he took a final glance round the room before leaving. Other than the books, the room did not seem to offer much help in revealing what sort of character the dead woman had really been. Then, not because he expected to find

230

anything, but because it was second nature for him to leave no stone unturned, he felt under the mattress before he left, and there, between the mattress and the bed frame, he struck gold. Literally, he thought, when he tipped out onto the dressing table the contents of the small wooden box and was confronted with a virtual cascade of jewellery. Rings, brooches, a necklace or two, earrings. Real jewellery too, although none of the pieces, he suspected, would be of enormous value. Taken together, however, they must surely have represented a tidy sum to a woman like Edith Huckaby. Thoughtfully, he returned them to the box and put it in his pocket, regardless of the conspicuous bulge it made, and went to interview the family.

He was shown into a small sitting room and found Lady Sybil standing with her elbow on the marble mantelpiece, looking into the fire, her hand supporting her head ... and her daughter, Eunice, sitting quietly in the corner. The shock of that horrible and brutal murder seemed to have laid its silence over this small and elegant room. He looked about him. He was not used to grand country houses and Oaklands did not have the faded grandeur he had partly expected, this room in particular being simply but rather beautifully furnished, and tastefully decorated in subtle colours and soft materials, with only a few gilt-framed watercolours on the fashionably pale walls. One of the few rooms, he supposed, which had been set aside for the family's use when the rest of the house had been generously given over as a convalescent hospital for the wounded.

An array of photographs stood on a circular table. One in particular drew his attention: a large group which must have been taken before the war, in which he recognised the Wentworth girls, including Marianne, and the rector standing next to a dark young man whose arm was linked in Lady Sybil's: her son Greville, presumably.

He turned his gaze away as she spoke his name. She was seemingly quite in command of herself now as she sat down opposite to him. He had said that he wanted to see all the family, and she told him now that her husband, Arthur Foley, had not yet returned from the brisk walk he took every day, on doctor's orders. 'But I'm sure I can help you more than he can, Inspector.' She was still rather white, but even as she spoke, she drew herself up and summoned her social aplomb, almost visibly pushing whatever she was feeling into the back of her mind. She took a seat, indicated one for him and looked at him enquiringly.

'For a start, then, did Miss Huckaby have any family, any relatives we are obliged to inform, Lady Sybil?' he began.

'I believe not. In fact, I know she had no one. Poor Edith, she came to me from an orphanage run by nuns, recommended by a friend who had also obtained a maid through them.'

'An orphanage? How old was she at the time?'

'Oh, she was grown up. She had been there since a very young child, and continued to work there as a layperson, helping with the sewing they took in from outside, making lingerie and so on, earning a little money for herself. It was a safe,

232

protected life for a girl with no prospects, but I know she had begun to chafe at the limitations.' As she spoke, she grew more relaxed, and even smiled a little. 'I suppose that's what you would call them, limitations, if you are not intending to take vows, and that was why she left.'

'How long had she been with you, Lady Sybil?'

'Seven years. She came to me when she was eighteen – only a girl, and inexperienced, of course, but she learnt fast.'

'You must have got to know her very well over that time,' he hazarded, not knowing whether to expect an answer in the affirmative. Not all employers were kindly and paternalistic, taking an interest in their servants' lives, though he imagined Lady Sybil must be, if what Mattie Noakes had told him about the people at Oaklands was still true.

She sighed. 'Not really. She was a very quiet person, she never said much about herself.'

He wondered if her ladyship had suspected about Ben Naylor.

'How did she spend her spare time? With friends?'

'Spare time?' She smiled again, a trifle ruefully. 'Well, in her position I don't suppose she had so very much time, you know, to make friends,' she replied, somewhat evasively. 'It was her duty to be there when I needed her. I'm sure I don't know what she did with herself, except that she spent hours in the sewing room. She was very clever with her needle and she liked to make her own clothes. She could alter things I passed on to her so that they fitted her better than they'd ever fitted me!'

'She liked to read,' Lady Sybil's daughter offered, rising and coming to join them from the corner where she had been sitting quietly without saying anything. Not that Reardon had been unaware of her presence. No one could be, having once set eyes on her, he thought appreciatively. She was exquisitely pretty, a small sprite of a girl, fashionably dressed, with a mass of dark-blonde hair and large soft eyes. A gentle girl, with a still, restful quality about her, but a thoroughly modern miss, he suspected, all the same. It would not do to underestimate her, he thought, too, recalling how firmly and calmly she had dealt with her mother when they had been intercepted in the drive and given the news of Edith's death.

'I see. Read a lot, did she – Miss Huckaby? The sort of books she lent to Marianne Wentworth?' he asked.

'Edith, lending books to *Marianne*?' repeated Lady Sybil, staring first at her daughter, then at Reardon. 'Where did you get that idea? Well, of course, I knew she was always reading, whenever she had the chance, and trashy novels they were, I'm sorry to say. Not the sort dear Marianne would have read, certainly.'

'They weren't all trashy, Mother. She lent them to me, as well – in fact, it was because Marianne saw me reading them that she asked Edith if she might borrow them, too.'

'Good gracious. Could you not have ordered them for yourselves?'

'There was no point when Edith already had them. She used to save up to buy them.'

The notion of saving up to buy books seemed so far beyond Lady Sybil's comprehension that it appeared to have robbed her of speech. She spread her hands helplessly, although in actual fact, what had momentarily silenced Sybil was something quite other: something she had forgotten that had begun flashing across her mind, an incident that had happened years ago, when she had surprised Edith in Arthur's study. The girl, who had only been with her for a few weeks, had been standing in front of the bookshelves ranged along one wall, searching avidly through the titles.

'What are you doing in here, Edith?'

'I'm only looking at the books, my Lady.' Sybil raised her eyebrows and the girl went on, hesitantly, 'I like reading, but I've never had much opportunity. The nuns thought reading a waste of time, unless it was the Bible.'

'Well.' Sybil herself had never had much time, or indeed inclination, for reading. 'We're not a bookish household here, either, and a good many of those we do have are on these shelves. I'm sure Mr Foley would be only too pleased to let you borrow any of them. Only do ask before you take one, hmm? Choose one now, if you like.'

Edith, however, had not, in the end, seemed interested in any of Arthur's books, and who could blame her? Arthur himself never seemed to read any of them and Sybil had suddenly doubted whether any of the long-gone, hunting, shooting and fishing Grevilles, who had initially purchased them, had ever opened the covers either. The dusty old tomes had overcrowded the shelves of the old library before it had been refurbished during the renovation of the house on her marriage, and she had ordered the surplus to be transferred to the study, regarding them as appropriate furniture. She realised now that they had probably been purchased in the first place in the same spirit, merely to impart an overall impression of culture, like the marble busts, statues and classical paintings also acquired by those Grevilles who had taken the Grand Tour.

'Well, help yourself. I'm sure you will find plenty of novels around, somewhere. Charles Dickens and ... er, so on.'

But on the odd occasion she had come across Edith reading, they were not the novels of Mr Dickens. Which wasn't any business of hers, Sybil had told herself. But...

'She had a perfect right to read what she chose, of course,' she said now to the inspector, 'and to lend them where she wished, but I'm sure, Eunice, that Marianne's father, too, would have obtained books for her if she wished.'

'Not the kind she wanted to read, Mother.'

'How very singular.' Lady Sybil was clearly out of her depth. Was it simply the notion of a maid having the temerity to read? Or spending her wages on actually buying books? But then she added softly, unexpectedly, 'Well, well. How little do we know of others, after all!' And Reardon suddenly saw what it was when people spoke of her: she was not a soft woman, but there was a warmth and generosity about her. She was also an exceedingly handsome woman, he thought, with those fine dark eyes and a thick, creamy skin, not to mention a mouth that could only be described as passionate. 'Forgive me,' she then went on, sharply enough to make him hope she had not sensed the tenor of his thoughts, 'but we do seem to have strayed from the point. What has all this to do with poor Edith being killed, Inspector?'

The entrance of Arthur Foley saved him from having to answer this. He strode in, bringing with him the smell of fresh air. A stockily built, elderly man of just above middle height, he wore well-cut tweeds and still had on his heavy brogues. He went straight up to his wife and put his hands on her shoulders. 'Sybil, my dear, I've just heard the dreadful news. Shocking business, but you're not to let yourself be upset by it, d'you hear?'

'Oh, I shall do well enough, Arthur. It's you I'm worried about.' She looked anxiously into his face, which was already losing the freshness brought on by outdoor exercise. 'Do you need your pills? Oh dear, I *told* them to leave it to me to tell you.'

'No, I'm quite all right, my dear, and they didn't tell me. I overheard them talking.'

A look of complete understanding passed between them. If Reardon had been asked, he would have said that Mr Foley did not need to worry about his wife being upset at the news. In the same way as Ben Naylor, she was shocked, yes, as was natural, but in fact it seemed to him that she had been more concerned about her gamekeeper's misfortune in having found the body than anything. He began to suspect she must have been aware of the association between the two: for one thing, she had not been in the least surprised by the fact that Edith had been out in the woods, at that time and in that place.

'Arthur, this is Inspector Reardon.'

Reardon's hand was taken in a firm grip. He looked more closely at the man and noticed deep shadows under his eyes and the bluishness in his lips of the chronic heart sufferer. The effort Foley had made during the war might not have been without its cost to him: Mattie Noakes had said he had suffered a heart attack on the eve of the war, yet he had carried on. It could not have been money that motivated him to do that, although turning their factories to munitions had not exactly been unprofitable for those who did. He sat down now close to his wife on the sofa, one arm resting on the back, the other holding her hand, very firmly. She sat a little more upright; the closeness, quiet understanding, and marital solidarity was impressive.

A solid man altogether, Mr Foley, as Reardon knew. The name Foley's, as he was growing up, had been almost as familiar to him as his own. J Foley & Son, in huge iron letters, arched over the gates of the big foundry and engineering shop in Cradley Heath, one of the biggest employers in the Black Country. He might have ended up there himself, had he not been lucky enough to be accepted by the police. He recalled how many men and women had lately been employed there on munitions, when the works had been turned over to making Mills bombs, of the type which Reardon had thrown himself on occasions, though he hadn't been thinking of Foley's at the time. Then, it had been more a matter of concentrating on lobbing the grenade into the right place, the enemy's trench, which hadn't been much different to throwing a cricket ball. Only the effect was different. He knew how many people had been laid off at the works too, now that the war had ended, although, as employers, Foley's had a pretty fair reputation. As long as you didn't step out of turn, they were known to be even-handed, and they'd kept on as many people as they could for as long as possible – but business was business, after all, as no doubt Arthur Foley, a Black Countryman born and bred, would have said. He was an astute man, he hadn't come in with the last load of coal.

Reardon thought it was time to produce his own version of a Mills bomb. He slid the little wooden box from his pocket. Any of you recognise this? No? Then allow me.' He tipped the jewels out on to a low table in front of the sofa. For a long, unnerving moment, there was silence in the room. 'Perhaps your maid Edith sold something like this to help her buy her books,' he suggested to Lady Sybil.

'Where on earth did you get those?' Eunice asked.

'Have any of you seen this jewellery before?'

'Well, of course,' Eunice replied for all of them. 'That little turquoise ring, and that garnet bracelet, the hair brooch... Mother?'

There was an even longer silence. Lady Sybil sat up very straight, her shoulders tense. 'I gave them to her, they're only trinkets, nothing of much real value. Just presents, little tokens when she'd been particularly helpful.'

Reardon saw immediately that he was not the

only one in the room who did not believe this. Eunice, after the first searching look at her mother, went rather white and began to pay fixed attention to the acanthus leaf pattern on the carpet, and Foley was looking at his wife with an expression that might have been sadness, or pity. Lady Sybil said coolly, 'The reason I gave them to Edith is really nothing to do with anyone. Whatever else, she was excellent at her job. She stayed with me throughout the war, and I thought she deserved some recompense.'

'I see.'

Sybil's colour heightened. It was evident what he was thinking – that a personal maid in wartime was an unwarranted luxury, and so it was. But Edith hadn't been able to see herself getting her hands dirty driving an ambulance or doing all the nasty things nurses had to do. Least of all could she envisage working in a munitions factory and coming out with her face and hair all yellow, or in fact doing any of the other demanding jobs women were taking on to free men to go to the front. It wasn't right that Sybil should have no one to help her, she said, especially now that she was so busy with all those hospital committees and fund-raising activities. Edith would stay with her mistress and help in her hospital work. Their eyes had met, Sybil bit her lips and in the end had found herself doing what Edith wanted. It had not been the first time the girl had shown how implacable she could be.

This unvarnished truth, however, was inappropriate in the circumstances, and Sybil decided on a more acceptable version. 'Edith wasn't

240

strong enough to drive an ambulance or anything like that, so I kept her with me, and she helped me in my hospital work. She turned out to be extremely efficient. Isn't that so, Eunice?'

Eunice raised her eyes from the floor. After a moment, she said, 'I believe so, Mother.'

'When was the last time you saw her?' Reardon asked.

Lady Sybil inclined her head. 'I was feeling rather tired last night, and in view of the journey we were to make to London today, I had something light on a tray brought to my room and spent the evening quietly in bed, writing letters. I needed Edith to help me undress, brush my hair and so on, of course, and she spent about twenty minutes, I suppose, tidying up, putting my clothes away and setting out those for today,' she added, leaving Reardon to wonder how the rest of the world managed to do these things for themselves. 'After that, her evening was her own.'

'And you, Miss Foley?'

'I saw her as I was going up to my room, after dinner. She was taking Mama's tray down to the kitchen.'

'What time would that be?'

'Around seven. We dined as soon as my father came home, about six o'clock – we always do, unless we have company. Then Father and I played a little chess before I went upstairs. Like Mama, I wanted to spend a quiet evening, getting my things together, writing a letter, reading a little, just pottering.'

'Was she in her outdoor clothes then?' Eunice shook her head.

241

'She was when I saw her, later,' Foley said unexpectedly. 'From my study window. I must say, I thought she was going to get a soaking in the woods. And pretty late it was, too, about a quarter past eight.'

'What made you think she was going into the woods, sir?'

'What made me think that?' Foley repeated. His wry glance took in the others. 'It was no secret that she was off down to see Naylor whenever she got the chance,' he said dryly, which was followed by a small silence.

Reardon rose to go. 'I'm afraid I must keep these, for a while,' he said, scooping the jewellery back into the box, 'but you'll have it back, later, of course. By the way, she was wearing one of those brooches, you know, with Mizpah written across it.' Eunice started. 'She wouldn't have had a young man by any chance, a sweetheart in the army, at any time?'

Arthur Foley shrugged, mystified, and Lady Sybil said, 'If there was, I have never heard of him – and I've never seen her wearing anything like that, have you, Eunice?'

'No,' said Eunice, colourlessly. 'No, I haven't.'

After a few more questions about Edith's personal life, friends, acquaintances, anyone with whom she might have quarrelled, all of which yielded negative answers, Reardon came to the conclusion that they had reached the point any interview got to at some stage, the point where that was as far as he was going to get for the moment. It would be necessary to interview all the domestic staff, as well as those employed in the hospital, but that would come later. He left the house and walked, via the lake, into the village to meet Wheelan for lunch at the Greville Arms and to book them both in for the next few nights. He also hoped to persuade them to let him have somewhere there which would serve as an office, since the front room of the police house, which was Bracey's office, was nowhere near big enough. He had in mind the small parlour where he had had his meals served when he stayed there, which would do nicely.

As he walked, Lady Sybil's assertion– 'She was excellent at her job ... whatever else' – still rang in his ears. Whatever else. Surely the phrase and the way she had used it implied that although Edith Huckaby did her job well, there were other things about her which were not quite so commendable. And he wondered about the Mizpah brooch. It was pretty, and had sat well at the high neck of her blouse, but why was she wearing such a thing, unless to give herself the status of someone who had a man at the front?

And what did Miss Eunice Foley know about that brooch?

Chapter Twenty-One

For the first part of the previous night, while Edith Huckaby's body was lying lifeless by the lake, the occupants of the rectory had slept – or tried to sleep – as the storm crashed over the house, the banshee wind howled down the tall chimneys and the rain lashed down in torrents. Eventually the storm rolled away, only to stay grumbling in the distance until just after midnight, when it came back with a vengeance and the household was reawakened with a great splintering, groaning crash. After the few moments' eerie silence which followed, bedroom doors flew open onto a hall which was now part of the roaring windy darkness outside. The great staircase was strangely lit by lurid flashes of lightning, and gusts of rain were blowing in through the space where the Susannah window had once gloomed over the hall. One of those ancient yews, planted too near the house and once believed to be indestructible, had been split, root to tip, by the lightning, and one half was now thrusting itself through the shattered remains of the stained-glass window like the neck of some prehistoric monster, the bitter green smell of its leaves permeating the air.

Unlike Oaklands, where a generator housed in a shed in the grounds provided electricity, here at the rectory they were still dependent on oil lamps and candles, and the lights they held flickered onto the glass which littered the polished floorboards – ruby, sapphire and golden in the light of the candles, a prettier picture in their splintered ruin than they had ever been in their completeness. The two older women, Florrie bristling with curling pins and Mrs Villiers with her hair hanging down her back in a tidy grey plait, began to rush about to see what could be done, while Francis, who rarely went to bed before two or three in the morning, emerged from his study and stood by, shocked and helpless.

'Well, at least that's the end of the nosy old Elders,' Nella said. Amy, at first overawed by the extent of the damage, began to giggle.

'This is scarcely the time for hilarity, miss! Go and get some cloths from the attic, one of you,' Mrs Villiers commanded severely. The lightning, in striking the tree, had saved the tall chimneys from being struck, but the wind had apparently blown slates from the roof for not only was rain blowing in through the glassless window, but water was also coming through the ceiling onto the half landing. 'Hurry, we shall have to get rid of the water before we can remove all that glass – though how we'll do that without getting cut to ribbons, I surely don't know.'

The brisk commands galvanised them into action and they all hurriedly retreated to throw on some clothes, after which Amy ran off with Florrie to fetch buckets, mops and brushes, Francis was despatched to knock up Strudwick, who was so deaf he had probably slept through it all, while Nella, holding her candle, flew up the attic stairs to bring down some of the torn-up rags rescued from old clothes too far gone to be of any use for anything except dusters and floor-cloths. She snatched up the whole of the accu-mulated pile from the corner where they sat – they were going to need them all – then stopped, momentarily transfixed, by what lay underneath.

It was a rectangular wooden box about fifteen inches long, six or seven inches deep, encrusted with an intricate pattern of varnished shells, the work of some Victorian young lady, no doubt. The children had found it, empty, among the other odds and ends left behind by previous occupants of the rectory and which had been banished to the attic: murky oil paintings of mournful-looking Highland cattle, up to their knees in mist, dim sepia prints of English cathedrals and countless heavily framed portraits of previous incumbents of St Ethelfleda's – and sometimes their wives and large families as well. Marianne had immediately pounced on it and it had been the repository for those exercise books with marbled covers in which she had written her stories ever since. Nella dropped the rags and cautiously lifted the lid. The notebooks, which they had never found after Marianne died, were still in there.

'Nella! What *are* you doing?' came from Mrs Villiers, distractedly waiting below.

Later, later. Hastily, she opened Dorothea's clothes chest and thrust the box in, burying it as far down amongst the dresses and furs still there as she could, and then clattered down the attic stairs with the cloths.

By the time they had cleared up what they could, there hadn't been much time left for sleep, and the following morning, bleary eyed from their disturbed night, the women sat around the kitchen table drinking tea and eating an early breakfast, while Francis disappeared into the church to inspect it for any damage which might have occurred there. They were too tired to talk much, and presently Nella left them and went first to her room to collect the exercise books she had spent what was left of the night reading, and then up to the attic to return them. She had the books in her hands and was looking at the shell box, wondering where the best place would be to hide it again, when the door opened and she saw that Amy had followed her.

'I knew there was something the matter,' Amy said. 'You've been so quiet.' Her glance went from the familiar box to the notebooks. She made a strangled little sound that was almost a scream. 'You've found them? Oh, Nella, you've found them!'

The bright, hopeful new day which had followed the storm seemed like an affront in view of the appalling event which had occurred the night before, news of which greeted Nella when she arrived at Oaklands. She was stunned by it; she moved through the day like an automaton, avoiding the gossip as much as she could while struggling with the discoveries she'd made the previous night and the feeling of disbelief that the unthinkable could have happened again in virtually the same place – albeit in a different way – even down to the thunderstorm, just as there had been on the night Marianne died.

The whole hospital was horrified and shocked by the murder, although Edith had only been known to the nursing staff as a distant figure, part of Lady Sybil's household, one who occasionally appeared among them with a message, always quietly but elegantly dressed, fastidiously avoiding coming into contact with the more unpleasant aspects of hospital life. Whenever she appeared, she had been regarded warily by the hardworking nurses: the appreciative glances of any of the men she accidentally encountered in her scented and graceful progress were enough to remind the women that they were wearing stiff, unbecoming uniforms with their hair bundled under a cap, and were smelling unattractively of carbolic, or worse. They rolled their eyes at each other. All the same, the murder sent a ripple of pity, and then unease, through their ranks when the staff was gathered together and warned by Miss Inman to avoid the woods (a favourite walk of the nurses when they were off duty), where a dangerous homicidal maniac might be lurking. One by one, the male staff, the nurses and the hospital domestic staff were then questioned by Sergeant Wheelan and his men.

Duncan Geddes, in his turn, was being questioned by Reardon, along with the matron when, out of the corner of his eye, he caught the swish of Nella's skirt as she hurried past the open door with her hands full. This dreadful news could do nothing but open old wounds for her, remind her of her sister's death. He *must* find some way to talk to her today, though he could not rid himself of the idea that she was avoiding being alone with him – and who could blame her? he asked himself bitterly. Were they ever going to get the chance for that walk she had promised – and the opportunity for him at least to clear the air? The hospital was quietly and gradually winding down but circumstances seemed to be deliberately conspiring against time being found in the still-busy daily routine which kept them both fully occupied – and now this unexpected and tragic

248

happening, which was taking up every spare minute and disrupting everything. About which it would be unthinkable to complain.

Reardon was at that moment tentatively enquiring if all the patients could be accounted for the previous night. Only a few were actually bedridden, and although he thought the chances of any one of the ambulant patients having committed this murder were slight, it was necessary routine questioning.

Duncan had guessed what he had been getting at. 'Inspector, we all experienced things in the trenches that would turn anyone's mind, and many of the men here still suffer nightmares – like anyone else who was there,' he added pointedly. 'However, this is a surgical unit, not a psychiatric one. I doubt if any one of them–'

'Even if the ward doors were *not* locked at night,' interrupted Miss Inman crisply. 'By myself.'

'Locked?'

Against the unlikely event of anyone sleepwalking.'

The notion of any of the patients sleepwalking, following Edith in the pouring rain and battering her to death, never mind the very idea of the redoubtable Miss Inman forgetting to lock the wards securely, did not in fact persist for long in Reardon's mind. All right,' he said, 'let's drop that idea for the moment.'

Duncan Geddes listened with half an ear as Reardon continued. He was still thinking about Nella, his mind worrying at ways to find an opportunity to talk to her, really talk, now that he had found her again, at last...

Chapter Twenty-Two

1917

In the late summer, there had been a curious lull after the prolonged fighting which had ended with the victorious capture of the Messines Ridge from the enemy, and a mood of tentative optimism prevailed, regardless of the artillery thundering in the distance on other battle lines. Rumours were rife that an enormous offensive was in the offing, one designed to drive right through Belgium to the coast and capture the enemy submarines which were doing so much damage to the navy. More than a rumour, if the massive influx of troops, guns, supplies, horses, wagons and tents now camped out in the Ypres salient meant anything.

Meanwhile, in the relative calm, the day-to-day nursing went on: everyday ailments, coughs, colds and mild flu epidemics, bronchitis, trench fever and the ever-present trench foot. Even, from time to time, cases of highly contagious tuberculosis, consumption, that men from poor backgrounds, malnourished and undersized, unsuspectingly carried, bringing them a certain ticket home if a less than hopeful future.

The big push eventually began at the end of July, and by the time it was two weeks old, it was only too evident that this was going to be one of the bloodiest battles of the war so far. The bloodiest and surely the wettest. It began to rain, and went on raining as no one had seen it rain since Noah, it seemed, and the mud level, on this low-lying land reclaimed from the sea, rose. Tommies stood up to their waists in mud and slime to fire their guns at the enemy. Dead and wounded men, horses, limbers and guns sank into it without trace. And into the casualty clearing station, barely six miles from the fighting line, where the medical team which Duncan headed was now working night and day, snatching whatever sleep they could, whenever possible, the casualties poured in, convoy after convoy, in numbers uncountable. The wounded and dying, grateful for any comfort they could be given, looked on the nurses as angels, the doctors as miracle workers. The nurses were surely angels, but Duncan knew he was no miracle worker. Amputating hopelessly smashed arms and limbs hour after hour, up to the elbows in blood, he felt more like a butcher.

Nella had come out of the makeshift ward one night, despatched off duty for a few hours' rest, just as dark was descending. The nightly barrage, the firework display of Very lights, bursting star shells and the accompanying crescendo of guns, was beginning. He was standing outside, snatching a few minutes to smoke a cigarette in the lee of an ambulance from the last convoy which would shortly return for yet another cargo of wounded, his cigarette a red pinpoint glow in the dark. She didn't at first see him, and stood for a moment on the duckboards over the mud outside the lighted opening as if she couldn't quite orientate herself.

251

She looked dazed with exhaustion, as they all were, by the continual demands of the work, and emotionally drained by the suffering they witnessed daily. When would it all end? she had asked, only the day before – not until both sides had annihilated each other and there was no one left to fight? She'd had no news of her brother recently and he knew she lived in hourly dread of seeing him brought in, mortally wounded.

Two weeks ago, her friend, Daisy, had been killed.

It was almost an accident, a shell tearing through the canvas walls of the makeshift operating theatre where she and Nella were assisting Duncan. She had turned to catch some light to thread a needle for him to stitch a wound. An orderly, standing two or three feet away, had moved at the precise moment when the piece of shrapnel would have hit him; Daisy fell, and died within a few minutes. She wasn't the first nurse to have been killed or injured, by any means, but this had been Daisy, Nella's friend. Funny, brave Daisy who would never again make rude remarks about Sister Griggs, or weep over the bundle of their chopped-off hair on the floor, who would never again run risks to be with George Chiversleigh. In a uniform so unbelievably immaculate it was hardly believable in all that filth and chaos, with his blonde hair disciplined to smooth silk when he took off his cap at the funeral, his face like stone and his eyes dazed and blank, George had been granted a few hours' leave to come and see Daisy lowered into her grave, watched by a crowd of weeping nurses, the coffin covered with a Union Jack. A week later, he, too had been killed. Company officers did not last long, after all.

Seeing Nella standing there, looking so lost, Duncan spoke her name gently and she raised her head. 'Captain Geddes,' she said automatically, as if still on duty, rubbing her hands, chapped and chilblained in winter, always raw with constant scrubbing and disinfectants: hydrogen peroxide, Lysol and carbolic.

'What's that you're rubbing?'

'Only a scratch.'

'Be careful.'

She nodded. Her glance went to the photo he was holding.

Creased with much handling, it was with him wherever he went, and without any conscious thought of what he was doing, he held it out to her saying, 'My son, Jamie.' He saw his words, and the sight of his wife and child, fall like a blow on her and could not believe what he had done. Apart from the unforgivable insensitivity of it, he could not have chosen a worse time.

But she seemed hardly to glance at it, and even summoned up the ghost of a smile as she handed the photo back. 'He looks very like you.' She said nothing about pretty Dolly, in her light chiffon dress, with her hand on the shoulder of their son, but pushed her hair back from her face and leant back against the wall of the hut, closing her eyes. He could not have forced explanations on her then, utterly spent as she was. She would be asleep where she stood if she stayed there much longer.

'You need some rest,' he said gently, shaking her. He took her elbow and began to guide her to the billet she now shared with another nurse. Someone came out of the ward. 'Captain Geddes?'

'You're needed,' she said.

He hesitated fractionally. Then he bent and kissed her gently on the forehead. Tomorrow he would explain.

The sight of her walking away from him was not one he wished to remember.

The following day she was forced to report sick, and was immediately despatched by ambulance to the base hospital. Infected fingers weren't unusual – dressing the filthy, gangrenous and often poisonous wounds the men suffered was dangerous, however careful you were – but this was acute. She lay, very ill, in the base hospital for several weeks, after which she had been sent home. He wondered if she knew how fortunate she was not to have died.

He carried on with his work. The carnage and suffering was beyond human belief. All for a few yards of territory, and possession of a small village called Passchendaele. It went on and on, mirrored by the never-ending struggle to ameliorate pain, to save what life they could. In the midst of it all, weary above exhaustion, he had found time to scribble one or two brief notes to her, but he never received an answer. He knew it was highly unlikely she had ever received them.

Chapter Twenty-Three

Reardon had left Broughton meanwhile and ridden back to Dudley to give the report Kelly had demanded.

'So it was blackmail?'

'If it wasn't, I don't know what else you'd call it.'

As usual, Kelly had a quick grasp of the situation, most of which he held in his memory, helped by the few meticulous notes he'd taken as Reardon brought him up to date with the case so far.

'Lady Sybil *says* the jewellery was to repay her maid for services rendered, so to speak,' Reardon said, 'but even her husband and daughter seemed to find that hard to swallow. There was nothing of any outstanding value there, I reckon, but added together – well, let's say I wouldn't mind finding a collection like that in my Christmas stocking. But I can't see anyone giving that amount away, unless they were under pressure.'

'Some indiscretion on the lady's part, maybe, that she needed to keep from her husband? This Arthur Foley's quite a bit older, you say.'

'Yes he is, but that wasn't the situation as I read it. He's elderly and not in the best of health, apparently, but it seems a perfectly happy marriage.'

And that precludes the possibility of a bit of playing fast and loose? Not from what I hear. The expected thing, in some circles, I understand.

And anyway, blackmail doesn't only apply to sexual shenanigans.'

Reardon thought for a moment. 'Any hanky-panky going on was between the victim herself, and the gamekeeper.'

'That's the man who found her – Naylor ... Ben Naylor, right? And I see he found the other girl, the one before the war, Marianne Wentworth, and in the same place, too. Hmm. Unlucky chap – or do we have a prime suspect here?'

'The verdict on the Wentworth girl was given as accidental death.'

'And Edith Huckaby was murdered for sure. Well, we'd better find anyone else, as well as her mistress, who might have had good reason to want her out of the way. The lady is capable of using a heavy weapon, I assume?'

'Physically, I dare say, but–'

All right, not much of a woman's crime, I agree. Someone could have done it for her, of course ... fancy man, mebbe, if she had one. If the blackmail had become too much to endure. No trace of the weapon?'

'Not yet. We might do better if we had some idea what we're looking for. Searching for a broken branch or a rock in that spot, I tell you, needles and haystacks aren't in it! Ten to one it's been chucked in the lake, anyway,' observed Reardon gloomily.

'The PM report should tell us more. Should be here any time, in fact.' Kelly checked the big clock on the wall. 'Doc Simpson has meetings in London tomorrow, so it's suited him to give it priority, Meanwhile, this Naylor, the gamekeeper. What about him?'

'He's been with the family since he was a boy, head gamekeeper now, following his father's footsteps. He's a widower, and has been for some time. I reckon he's a bit of a loner, doesn't mix much in the village, doesn't drink there – though he seems respected. He's a religious type, a Methodist.'

'You're not saying because he's a Methodist he couldn't commit a murder?'

'No more than I'm saying Edith Huckaby couldn't blackmail because she was a Roman Catholic. But I have to say it doesn't strike me that way, although he admits she'd been trying to persuade him to leave and find better-paid employment. The possibility of that appears to be so remote to him I doubt if he even gave it a passing consideration, never mind had a row about it. As far as I know – yet – he could've had no other motive.'

'And how many men have you known who've committed murder for no motive any sane person would consider reasonable? Come on, Reardon!'

But Reardon still thought Naylor an unlikely suspect. He was stubborn, no doubt. He would dig in his heels in an argument, but he doubted there was enough passion in him to kill. On the other hand, he *could* be one of the quiet types who smouldered until something, often a quite trivial something, made them explode. But these sort of murders, the way in which Edith Huckaby had been killed, where the killer was in close contact with the victim, were rarely, if ever, coolly premeditated. They were invariably frenzied, repeated attacks, blow after blow committed in uncontrollable anger, in the heat of the moment.

The report on the post-mortem was in fact brought in a few minutes later, by the pathologist who had performed the autopsy himself, a man in a hurry, just as Reardon was about to leave. Kelly gave it a quick scan and passed it over. Sifting through the jargon, it appeared that it had indeed been a single blow to the temple which had killed Edith Huckaby, though it had been one delivered with some force, splitting the skin and fracturing the delicate bones beneath, leaving a star-shaped wound, two inches across.

'A wound of that type, what sort of implement does it suggest?' mused Kelly.

'A police truncheon?' hazarded Simpson, a man renowned for his humour.

Kelly looked at him.

'Well, something similar, or with a similar smooth, rounded end.'

'A branch, or a smooth stone, maybe?' asked Reardon.

'Stone, maybe, but wood? Unlikely.' He shook his head. 'No fragments or wood splinters in the wound. No evidence of a struggle, either, so the end must have been quick. But close contact like that, you should be looking for a good deal of blood on her assailant. These scalp wounds, they bleed a lot. And sorry,' he finished, anxious to be off, 'that's the best I can do. I'll leave the rest to you.'

'What about other possibilities? Other than anyone known to her, I mean,' Kelly asked when he'd gone, rubbing the side of his nose. 'It was a lonely spot. And there are enough tramps, homeless, workless around nowadays, God help 'em, who might have attacked her for what they might get – just for the contents of her handbag, say.'

'She was still wearing her jewellery, and she didn't have a handbag with her. But she was on her way to visit Naylor, so I don't suppose she needed one,' Reardon answered slowly, his mind on something else. Kelly was right, of course, about the growing number of itinerants, that band of bitter and disillusioned ex-servicemen forced on to the roads by the impossibility of finding any sort of employment. But there were other types of itinerants...

'Women carry handbags whether they need them or not, ask my wife,' Kelly was remarking dryly. He looked very sharply at Reardon. 'There's something else?'

With some reluctance, Reardon told him about the Boswell tribe and their encampment in the village, and felt Kelly's ears prick up as he added, '...the same family who've been coming back to Broughton for years, except for the war.'

He had no wish to involve the Boswells again, he thought as he watched Kelly add to his notes, but he knew there was no possible way they could be left out of the questioning that the whole village would be subjected to, until Edith Huckaby's killer was found.

The meeting with Kelly over, he was once more on his bike, heading back to Broughton. Blow this for a game of marbles, he thought, but at least henceforth he would be staying at the Greville Arms. And since Kelly had seemed satisfied with how things were going so far, he hoped it meant that he would allow him to have his head without keeping such a tight rein in future.

The police were still questioning the hospital staff about the murder but hadn't yet asked for Nella, and as soon as she had the chance, she escaped for a while across the garden to the old summerhouse, the only place she imagined no one was likely to find her. It was known to everyone as the summerhouse, though it was really not much more than a wooden shed with a shingled roof which had always been devoted to the children's use, built beyond the tennis court by the big cedar in the corner before the wild garden began, a little hidden place shaded by trees, where the ground rose in a slight slope above a small, deep, reed-fringed pond.

She hadn't visited it since before the war. Was it possible, she wondered, ducking under the low branches of the dripping trees, that they had grown so much since she was last here? The shade was deeper, the silence more intense as she approached. How gloomy it was, though it had never seemed so before. Or was that only because it wasn't now seen from the perspective of child-hood, when this corner had seemed deliciously secret and hidden? Certainly the only colour now was the greenish yellow of the emerging daffodils under the beeches, and a smoulder of purple showing here and there between them where the prima donna chequered fritillaries had con-descended this year to put in an appearance. Among the reeds fringing the pool's edges, the yellow flags had spread to take up most of what had only been a small pool in the first place, and were already showing dozens of fat buds among the long spears of their leaves. Fish had once swum there, but the predatory heron which was always on the lookout had no doubt long since despatched them all.

The door wasn't locked. Inside was the same old clutter of cricket bats and warped tennis racquets, sundry odd chairs and a wooden table. The air was dry and dusty, the windows had spandrels of spiders' webs in the corners, the sills were littered with dead lacewings and the corpses of wasps. It smelt of dry wood and the resiny scent of the old cedar whose branches overhung the roof; a smell redolent of all those childhood afternoons passed here, playing games on wet days, with the rain pattering on the shingles.

The old wind-up gramophone still sat on the floor in the corner. Gently, she rubbed the dust off the name painted on the lid in schoolboy characters: GCR Foley. Grev, who'd had it at school with him. Who had soon, in France, been listening to a very different kind of music. Infinite sadness touched her, and despite the dry warmth of the summer house, she shivered.

It seemed her flight across the lawn had not been unobserved, after all. The door opened and the scar-faced man Reardon stood there, one foot in the doorway. 'Inspector Reardon,' he said, in case she needed reminding. Inspector now – so he had, after all, gone back into the police. 'I don't wish to intrude, but I did wish to see you before you went home, Miss Wentworth.'

She looked at him warily, then sat down on the nearest chair and gestured to another. The ancient cushions on the seat gave off puffs of dust as they sat. After being told that she had last seen Edith several days ago, and ascertaining that she had been at home with all her family the previous evening, he said, unexpectedly, 'I'm sorry, this business must have brought it all back to you, about your sister.' She simply nodded. 'Did you know her well?'

'Who, Edith? Hardly at all, really.'

'I'm told your sister knew her better?'

She looked startled. 'Who told you that?'

'It doesn't seem to have been a secret that they had interests in common.'

'Reading, you mean? Yes, there was that. But nothing else.'

'How did *you* find Miss Huckaby? As a person, I mean?'

She tried to keep her voice even. 'I'm sorry she's dead but ... to be honest, no, I didn't care for her much. She was sly. She listened to private conversations and then repeated them. That was the only reason she made herself friendly with Marianne, I'm sure – to find out anything she could. Marianne was naive enough to believe it was all because of those books.'

'Do you have any evidence for this?'

She looked at him steadily, wondering if she could trust him, for such a long time that he must think she wasn't going to respond at all. Then she took a deep breath and said, 'Only my sister's notebooks. We thought they were lost but they've ... turned up, after all this time. Only last

262

night, in fact. She never allowed anyone to see what she'd written and she'd hidden them, though it seems ... well, it appears she let *Edith* read her notebooks.'

Another long drawn-out silence followed, broken only by the soft scratch and patter of a bird's feet on the shingled roof. Eventually, she said, 'Well, anyway, that's beside the point. It's Edith you want to talk about now, isn't it, not Marianne?'

'Miss Wentworth,' he said gently, 'maybe this is as much about your sister as Edith Huckaby. I suspect there was something in those notebooks you think you ought to tell me about, was there not? Otherwise you wouldn't have mentioned them.'

She looked down at her shoes, the sensible black shoes she was forced to wear day after day, and after a moment or two, she said, 'She wanted to be a writer, you know ... Marianne, I mean. She wrote down everything in those exercise books – ideas for stories as well as completed stories, descriptions of people and the things she knew about them, sometimes not very complimentary. Secrets, sometimes, I'm afraid. She wouldn't let anyone see them, but last night I sat up reading right through them ... she can't mind now. Most of the stories were, well, embroideries, though sometimes not.'

'Isn't all fiction a form of embroidery?'

'Lies, you mean?' She managed a pale smile. 'I meant embroideries on real life. She would, you know, take something that had actually happened, or was happening, and write it down as though it was fiction. I recognised all sorts of situations, people too. She was careless about disguising names, and sometimes she didn't even bother. I suppose you'd call them diaries as much as notebooks.'

'So what was it you learnt from them?'

'Nothing that I didn't ... suspect ... before.'

She was starting to regret that she had begun this conversation, but now that she had, she saw there was no alternative but to go on, and maybe he was right, perhaps confronting the past was the only way to deal with the present. 'We were very close, and I loved her so much, but she was a funny mixture, Marianne. She was hopelessly dreamy, but at the same time she was very determined, and she always had a streak of practicality ... shrewdness, I suppose.' She swallowed. 'Well ... a few months before she died, she had ... a proposal.'

'Of marriage? From Greville Foley?'

She looked at him sharply. How could he possibly know about Grev? 'No. It was from a man called Gervase Hatherley.'

'Who is he?'

'He lives not far away, the other side of the Hill. He's rather rich, and as a family, we've never had much money, I'm afraid, so it would have been a good match from that point of view. But she refused him. He's quite a bit older, and to be truthful not exactly anyone's idea of a romantic hero, but he wouldn't take no for an answer, and I'm sorry to say she let him think she might change her mind and say yes. I knew there was simply *no* chance of that, but when I said it was too bad of her to let him think there was, she told me not to be too sure she wouldn't decide to accept him after all. I-I felt as though I was talking to a stranger. That was bad enough, but I had no idea, until I read the notebooks, that she'd actually been meeting him in secret – at least, once or twice she had.' Her voice choked with the misery of the horrible conclusions the thought led to...

He said gently, 'Your sister was ... innocent.'

She was grateful for his quick understanding, and suddenly found herself liking this man, respecting the integrity which had propelled him to come here and pursue the truth about Marianne dying, in the first place. And he *had* found it. Before he left the village, he had made a point of coming to the rectory and telling them how Danny Boswell had seen Marianne fall – *fall*, not jump – into the lake, and the weight of four years' wondering if she just *might* have committed suicide had been lifted from all of their shoulders. Suddenly, it seemed easier to talk to him. 'All this makes her sound very foolish, but I think it just filled the need for some sort of drama. You can't think how dull our lives were before the war. And I suppose he agreed to the secrecy because ... well, I think he would have done anything to get her to marry him, and the idea must have touched his vanity as well. But Gervase Hatherley is a very proper man, and wouldn't abide being made to look a fool if it had come out.'

'A fool, or worse? Putting her in a compromising situation like that? Meeting her in such a secluded spot, a young girl, unchaperoned?'

'I ... suppose so.'

'Do you think Miss Huckaby got to know of their meetings?'

'I don't know whether she did or not, but in view of what other things Marianne told her, it's possible, isn't it?' Despite herself, she could not keep a trace of bitterness from her voice. It was painful to know that Marianne had confided things to Edith Huckaby that she had kept from her own sister.

'Are you suggesting that she went out to meet Hatherley the night she died – and perhaps Edith Huckaby knew about it, and has held it over Hatherley ever since, until he finally snapped and killed her?'

'That would be nearly as fanciful as Marianne's stories, wouldn't it?'

'Yet you've always wondered if he had something to do with your sister's death, haven't you?' he hazarded.

'Have I? I don't *know!* I was very cross with her about keeping him dangling, like that, but I never even dreamt she'd be so silly as to meet him secretly. Until last night, that is, when I read those notebooks.'

'I can see how difficult you would find that to believe.'

That, too, hurt. But she had to say, honestly, 'No. No. Of course it was a shock to find out what had been going on, but I don't, not really, at the bottom of me, find it so difficult to believe. You never knew Marianne. She sometimes lived in another world. But I wish there had been something more in those books. The last entry I read ended right at the end of the last page and

266

was written two days before she died. She never missed a *day* writing in those books. One of them must still be missing.'

Chapter Twenty-Four

The gamekeeper's cottage stood alone on the edge of the woods, a one-storey brick-built house with a pump, a rainwater butt, an outside privy and a picket fence surrounding a garden of sorts, which Ben Naylor didn't have much patience in maintaining. A few sunflowers and etiolated Michaelmas daisies, plus a few rampant herbs, defied the weeds and came up every year, progeny of the ones his wife, Mary, had planted in an attempt to brighten the place up the first year she and Ben had married, just after his old dad had died. Apart from that there was nothing but a grey old apple tree, with one great leaning limb propped up, and a poultry run surrounded by stout wire netting. It was enough for Ben. That was how he liked to live, surrounded by silence, and the noises of the woods, and the animals who, like him, made their home there.

He opened his door to another bright morning and immediately his eyes lit on the ground outside the hen run. A fox, dammit, had had another one of the chickens in the night. Decapitated it, then left it where it was, adding insult to injury. Looking with rage at the carnage of blood and feathers, he swore again at the

267

senseless waste. He counted the rest of the chickens, one gone and the one left dead, then put Fern's food bowl and her water dish outside her kennel before leaving her chained up while he disposed of the mangled corpse – he knew he should have left the bitch outside last night, but she'd been better company than his thoughts – and went to investigate how the fox had managed to get in. With the cessation of hunting over the last years, the vermin had increased. Stop one earth up and there were twenty more.

He turned to go back indoors and saw two men walking up the path from the village, one of them the policeman he'd met before and an older, bigger man. The inspector's scars were obviously due to the war which Ben had been too old to fight in; when he saw men like that, he knew now how lucky he was to have escaped. Too old, and needed here anyway, to shoulder the management of what was left of the estate, as well as covering his own duties. It hadn't been easy, just himself and old Scuddy Thomas, but he'd done what he could. If Lady Sybil started up the shoots again, which Ben was confident she would, he was determined there would be some good sport, eventually as good as in the old earl's day.

Reardon saw the gamekeeper waiting for them, arms akimbo, as he and Wheelan approached. His glance skirted queasily past the array of foxes' brushes, decaying grey squirrels, magpies and rooks nailed to the fence, like heads on turnpikes, presumably *pour encourager les autres*. He introduced Wheelan. Ben nodded. 'Didn't expect you

268

chaps to be about so bright and early.'

'Best part of the day, first thing in the morning,' the sergeant replied heartily.

'Pot of tea on the go, want some?'

Reardon accepted the offer. 'Wouldn't say no, while we have a word or two.' They followed the gamekeeper inside. The living room was low-ceilinged, dark and sparsely furnished, with heavy old furniture and a bare brick floor on which a rag rug offered scant comfort, though it was warm enough from the stove, where a fire glowed through the open doors to give some illusion of homeliness. A harmonium stood in one corner, with an open book of Moody and Sankey's Gospel hymns on the music rest. On a bench under the small window were piled onions, carrots and potatoes, some raw meat and what might have been the skin of a rabbit or a hare, all sitting alongside a big, black pot, soot-encrusted from the fire. Reardon found himself in some sympathy with the desire that the fastidious Edith Huckaby – she of the aspirational nature and the pretty clothes – had expressed for a different life, should she have hitched herself to Ben Naylor, who appeared as deeply entrenched here as one of the centuries-old oaks growing outside in the wood, his roots as deep into the earth as theirs.

They addressed themselves to the mugs of thick, stewed, heavily sugared tea they were given from the big teapot keeping hot on the hob, minor pleasantries being exchanged while Naylor tidied away the remains of his breakfast from the bare, scrubbed table.

'Nice job you've got here,' Reardon remarked

when the gamekeeper pulled out a stool and joined them. 'Pretty much your own master, I reckon?'

'Lady Sybil lets me get on with it. She knows me well enough to know I wouldn't let her down.'

'You've worked for the estate a long time?'

'Soon as I were old enough to work at all. Started with my father.'

'So you know her well?'

'None better. We grew up together, so to speak. No airs and graces when she were a girl – and none now, come to that. I've no grumbles about working for her. Born here in this cottage and I hope to die in it.'

'What did Miss Huckaby think to that?' Wheelan asked.

'As I told the inspector here yesterday, not much. We could've been married and stayed quite content here, only that wasn't what she wanted. I could understand, mind,' he added fairly, 'she'd grown used to fine ways and this would've been a comedown.

Reardon recalled the crucifix, the rosary. And she was a Roman Catholic as well, wasn't she?'

Naylor raised a sardonic eyebrow. 'Well, she didn't go to Mass, being as there's no RC church near enough. But once a Catholic, always a Catholic, that's what they say, don't they? And I'm a Methodist, so you see how it was.'

'You said she wanted you to leave Oaklands. Did you quarrel over it?' Reardon asked.

'I'm not a quarrelling man. There's few things worth losing your temper over. Only gets you into trouble. I told her straight I wasn't going, and that was that.'

He was a difficult man to read, one who obviously kept a tight rein on his emotions. Obstinate as a mule, slow to anger, but maybe, like anger in many who kept their feelings bottled up, it could explode, given the right trigger to detonate it, Reardon thought once again. 'The night before last, when she was killed. You're sure you saw nobody that night?'

'Not even Mr Hatherley, night like that.'

'Hatherley? Who's he?' Reardon asked, as if the name was new to them.

'Mr Gervase Hatherley, his lands march with ours. He exercises his dog along here most nights.'

'Aren't there walks on his own land?'

Naylor shrugged. 'Nobody's going to stop a friend and neighbour walking along here, if that's what they want to do. He's doing no harm. He only goes as far as the lake. Sits on one of the rocks for a while, then turns back.'

'Oh, an old man like, needing to rest?' Wheelan asked ingenuously.

Naylor picked up the teapot to replenish the mugs, found it empty and put it back on the table. 'It's not that. He's a younger man than me, but see – he were attached to Miss Marianne, the one you mentioned,' he said, with a nod to Reardon. 'Hit him pretty bad, when she died, I hear.'

'What do you mean by attached? Was she his young lady?'

'Not that I know of. And I shouldn't think it likely. He's what they call a confirmed bachelor, very well respected, not short of a bob or two. Big shot around here, JP and all that. And she was only a girl, but by all accounts he thought a lot of her. Likely he thought of her as a daughter.'

'And that's why he comes down here to look at the place where she died, every night?' asked Reardon, unable to conceal the scepticism he felt.

'Can't think of any other reason he'd come this way so regular, apart from exercising his dog. But I said *most* nights, not every, and as to Monday night, I wouldn't know. I didn't go out and you can't see the lake from here. Anyways, 'tain't likely he'd be out a night like that, in that rain, much less sitting looking at the lake, is it?'

Reardon couldn't think of any other questions at the moment. Their tea was finished, and he stood up. 'Thank you for your time, Mr Naylor – and for the tea. You say this Mr Hatherley's land adjoins this estate?' he asked as they went out. 'We might as well walk on to see him while we're out this way. You never know, he might have chanced the rain. How far is it, then, to his house?'

'Follow the lake, then take a right turning where the path branches. You'll see the Gypsies' caravans on t'other side and you'll find the path skirts the base of the hill and into the next valley.' He cast a weather eye on the sky. 'Best get a move on. We're in for some more rain, and it's rough going in parts,' he added, taking a dubious look at their feet. 'Haven't you got any transport?'

The police contingent had arrived in Broughton squashed into a canvas-sided motor van, which had also transported Reardon's motorcycle, but the men had now departed in the van, leaving only the motorcycle parked behind the Greville Arms. Wheelan's deadpan jokes about it, and the size of him, led Reardon to feel it wouldn't be a good idea to suggest the sergeant should ride pillion.

'That's all right,' he said. 'The sergeant here enjoys a good walk.'

When the two detectives had left him alone, Ben Naylor finished preparing the meat and vegetables for his supper, threw them all into the pot with a handful of pearl barley and a sprig or two of thyme, and set the stew on the stove where it would stay on a slow simmer all day. He put the innards aside for Fern later, and threw the head and skin onto the fire. He whistled for the dog and set off in the direction opposite to that taken by the two policemen, up to Peddy Covert, the nearest thicket of woodland that provided shelter for game. His head was thick after sitting up late, his mind troubled in fear that he'd given something away in his conversation with the police. Neither of them were fools and he believed that neither had been entirely convinced by what he had seen fit to tell them.

Following his daily routine left his thoughts free to wander without the need for too much concentration, and with Fern running ahead of him he plodded on, planting his feet firmly on the familiar path, gun over his shoulder. What he'd told the police about his association with Lady Sybil was true but it left out most of what he felt about her. She was far more than an employer to him: he could say she was a friend without fear of contradiction from her, and one he had known for most of his life. They'd grown up together as children, running wild, in the unusual circumstances of

273

Lady Sybil's neglected childhood, not yet of an age to care about the differences of their stations in life. She was a high-spirited girl, fearless as a boy. She dared do anything. He had seen her put a dying squirrel, that had been attacked by a magpie, out of its misery with a stone on the head, and getting a bite for her pains. Ben had taught her how to look for birds' nests and take but one egg; to climb trees. Shown her where the badgers' setts were, how to imitate a bird's call, or to skim a pebble so that it bounced seven times across the lake; he had taught her to swim in it. It had been an anarchic childhood, untroubled by authority. It could not have lasted. When she began to grow up she was sent to London to her father's sister to be coached and primped and dressed and altogether be made into a young lady fit to take her place in polite society.

Just in time. By then Ben had reached the age when he was becoming susceptible to girls, and was beginning, painfully, to imagine himself passionately in love with her, to suffer all the pangs of unrequited first love, and a boy's unrealistic fascination with the unattainable. After she left, he went on with his life, and after a while he met and eventually married his Mary, a village girl who was his true and only love. Nevertheless, those childhood years were never to be forgotten. There wasn't much Ben wouldn't do for his Lady Sybil.

Mary had died in childbirth, and their longed-for child with her, ten years after they were married, and Ben had retreated into himself, with no intention of ever marrying again. Since then, he had lived alone in the house where he

274

had been born, following the same uneventful existence which had always been his. He had no problems with that but, contrary to everything he had previously believed, now that Mary had been dead so long, he had begun to feel the need of a wife. He had been brought up in a strait-laced household, where the teachings of the Bible were paramount, and anything else but married respectability was not acceptable.

Then Edith came along. What he had told the police was not strictly true. He had wrestled with his conscience over her, about marrying her and making an honest woman of her, but when he compared her with Mary, something stuck in his throat. Yet Edith, walking fearlessly through the woods to his house at night, when everyone else was in bed ... how could any red-blooded man resist what was so patently on offer?

It was she herself who had begun to suggest marriage. But ambitious as she was, how long would she be content with life in a gamekeeper's cottage, on a gamekeeper's wages? Never, he thought, and was proved right when she began urging him to leave, to 'better himself' as she put it. Garbutt, the chauffeur, earned more than he did, she said, and had an easier life. If they were to go as a married pair, lady's maid and chauffeur, they could find better-paid work than here at Oaklands. But she was not, Ben thought, what any man wanted for a wife, much less himself.

He hadn't loved Edith, but she had been, in her own way, an important part of his life. And now she was dead and he was left with another dilemma on his conscience.

Like all such directions, the distance to Hatherley's house took nearly twice as long to walk as Naylor had predicted, nearer twenty minutes than ten. The going was rough but their shoes were stout enough, if not as stout as Naylor's heavy boots, and the rain obligingly held off.

Hatherleys, the house in the valley was called, proclaiming ownership by the name chiselled into its stone gateposts. A big house of raw-looking red brick with stone quoins, uncompromisingly geometrical, standing squarely in a soulless garden: two rectangles of lawn with a raked gravel drive running between them to the front door, two stone urns, empty at this season, either side of the steps. Even the lawns were pristine, having already been cleared of the storm debris that littered everywhere else.

The door was answered by a large, youngish, capable-looking woman of commanding appearance, wearing a grey serge skirt with a dark-blue blouse tucked into her belt, and a permanent smile on her face that didn't quite reach her eyes. 'I'm sorry,' she said, when Reardon enquired if they might speak to Hatherley, 'Mr Hatherley is indisposed. He can't see anyone.'

'I think he will see us. We're from the police. I'm Inspector Reardon and this is Sergeant Wheelan.' Reardon produced his official badge, which had no effect whatever when she condescended to lift the chain attached to a lorgnette reposing on her bosom in order to examine it. The smile remained in place but she was adamant. 'I'm afraid it's still not possible. I am

276

Mr Hatherley's housekeeper. He has a heavy cold and he's keeping to his bed today.'

'You do know that there's been a murder committed around here? We need to see Mr Hatherley and talk to him.'

She replied implacably, 'He is indisposed and doesn't wish to see anybody.'

The statement was immediately contradicted by the presence behind her of a man who was descending the stairs and crossing the black and white encaustic-tiled floor of the large hall, which the open door revealed as a bare and echoing space that the presence of several large, dark and heavily framed Victorian paintings on the walls did nothing to mitigate. The handsome, red Chinese silk dressing gown he wore, patterned with black dragons, made the only startling splash of colour against the dullness of the monochrome background as he came forward.

'Let the gentlemen in, Mrs Liddington. If they don't mind catching a cold, I don't mind sharing it. Gervase Hatherley,' he announced himself with a nod, keeping his hand tucked into his pocket. 'Send some tea into the study, will you, Mrs Liddington, and a couple of aspirin?' He beckoned the two police officers to follow him into a room where a bright fire burnt and the electric lamps were lit. A black Labrador lay stretched across the hearthrug and only moved away with reluctance when ordered to.

'Dreadful day,' Hatherley remarked, as the rain Ben Naylor had predicted began, scratching against the windows. He stirred the fire into a blaze and settled into a deep chair next to it, motioning them to seats opposite. 'Now, what can I do for you? I presume it's about this young woman who's been killed. Frightful business.'

He was a grey man inside that richly coloured dressing gown: receding iron-grey hair, grey eyes in a pale, doughy face, though the pallor was probably due to the heavy cold he undoubtedly had. His voice was thick with it and his eyes, behind the heavy-framed spectacles he wore, were red-rimmed. Yet despite the cold, he remained dapper. What hair he had was well brushed, his nails neatly manicured and he wore a black silk cravat nattily tucked into the neck of his dressing gown. He was inclined to be portly, and Reardon guessed his age at around forty.

'It's good of you to see us,' Reardon said.

Hatherley waved a plump hand. 'Not at all.' His glance avoided Reardon's face and skidded past his left ear to fasten on a vase on the window sill.

'We wouldn't have bothered you, as you are, only–'

'Yes, yes, I understand. You have your duty. I cannot imagine in what way you think I may be able to help you, but I will if I can.'

'Thank you, sir. To begin with, then – we've been told you often walk down by the lake in Oaklands Park.'

'Yes, that's true,' Hatherley answered, looking without charity at the notebook Wheelan produced, and pursing his small, pink mouth. 'It's a regular evening exercise. Just the right distance to walk Caesar in the evenings.' The dog pricked his ears and raised his head on hearing his name, then let it drop heavily and went back to sleep.

278

Hatherley sneezed several times into a pristine handkerchief. 'But I didn't go down there on Monday night. I suppose that's what you're going to ask?'

'Well, I was, but if you weren't there, sir...'

'Caesar had to do without his walk. Apart from the weather, I wasn't up to it. Bed and a hot toddy was a much more attractive proposition.'

The arrival of the tea, which neither man really wanted, was not brought in by the redoubtable Mrs Liddington, but by a blushing young girl who crashed the tray down so that the milk sloshed out of the jug. She dabbed at it with a napkin and gave an apprehensive glance at her master but he appeared not to have noticed. 'Thank you, Betty.'

She poured the tea, handed round the cups, forgot the sugar, retrieved her mistake, then left, no doubt thankfully. Hatherley raised his eyebrows with a gesture implying, what can one do about the help nowadays?

Reardon said, as the door closed behind the girl, 'This is the second death that's occurred down there by the lake within the last few years. You will remember the other one, no doubt – Miss Marianne Wentworth?'

Hatherley opened the round cardboard pillbox on the tray, extracted a couple of pills and swallowed them with a gulp of tea before he looked up and said to the vase, 'How could anyone who knew her forget that?'

'I believe you knew her well?'

'Indeed I did.'

'Is that why you go down there and sit looking

279

at the place where she died?'

The man's calm did not desert him. He said evenly, 'She was a very lovely young girl, on the brink of her life. The accident was tragic, but her memory is ... precious to me.' His eyes, magnified by his thick glasses, unexpectedly filled with tears. He blew his nose.

'In fact, you had asked her to be your wife?'

'Which I believe she would have been in time, had her life not been so tragically cut short, though I fail to see that is any of your business,' he answered coldly.

'Only in so far as anything that might connect the deaths of two young women in the same place is very much our business,' Reardon said, and there followed a short silence. 'Right, then, Mr Hatherley, if you weren't there, down by the lake on Monday night, you can't have seen anything, which is what we wanted to know.' He made no move to go, however, but added casually, 'I don't suppose you knew Miss Huckaby at all, the unfortunate young lady who has been killed?'

'Well, of course not, not in that sense, she was Lady Sybil's maid. But as a matter of fact, I *was* acquainted with her, slightly. Through her mistress's war work, you understand. The young woman used to help Her Ladyship. Being on the hospital administration side myself, there were occasions when we met.'

'What was your opinion of her? Did you like her?'

'Good Lord, I don't know that I ever thought about it. One doesn't, really. When one doesn't meet them socially, I mean,' he added, at last meeting Reardon's look. 'She seemed to do her job, and Lady Sybil appeared to like her, otherwise she wouldn't have been in her employ for so long, would she?'

'Probably not.'

'All the same, one doesn't like to think of ... what happened to her. She seemed harmless and inoffensive enough.'

'Well, Mr Hatherley, I don't think we need keep you any longer, though there's just a small point we'd like cleared before we go. It's come to our notice that you were in the habit of meeting Miss Wentworth sometimes, by the lake. Is that true?'

This time, Mr Hatherley's self-satisfaction was so far upset as to cause him to swear. 'Oh, God, these bloody villages!' he said. 'Nothing is ever secret. All right, yes, but it was only once or twice – and not, I assure you, the day she died.'

'Unwise, to say the least of it, wasn't it, sir? Meeting her alone like that?'

'I would not like to think you are implying that anything ... untoward ... took place. Because if you are, I would suggest you might think of framing an apology.'

'If I've given that impression, then I do apologise, Mr Hatherley. That was not my intention.'

Hatherley would not let it go. 'I dare say you might choose to think the worst, but it was simply that Miss Wentworth did not wish to let everyone know her business – any more than I did.'

'There was a party, the night she died. Were you a guest?'

'I was. And yes, to anticipate your next question, I did walk home via the lake – to clear my

281

head. There had been quite a lot of champagne consumed.'

'What time was it when you left?'

'I don't remember. Just after eleven, perhaps. The evening didn't go on late. The guest of honour was an elderly lady.'

'No meeting with Miss Wentworth that night?'

'We had already met, at the party,' he said coldly. And in any case, I never met her at night.'

Both police officers regarded him gravely. Then they stood. 'Thank you for your time, sir,' Reardon said. 'You may hear from us again.'

'Well, Wheely?' Reardon asked as soon as they were outside and heading back along the lakeside path towards the village. The capricious rain had stopped again and they paused for a moment to allow Wheelan to fill and light his pipe. Reardon had given up smoking during the course of the operations on his face, the process had been too painful, and now he found he no longer had the desire for tobacco, though he still liked the rich smell that wafted across as Wheelan got the pipe going.

'I doubt he'd anything to do with it,' Wheelan said, sucking his pipe.

'He seemed pretty upset at the mention of Marianne Wentworth.'

'Ar, very likely. Summat tells me he'll enjoy spending the rest of his life feeling sorry for hisself.'

'That's a bit harsh.' Then Reardon laughed. 'Summat tells me you may be right, Wheely.'

Wheelan smoked on, and after a moment or

two, pointed with the stem of his pipe across the lake to where smoke rose above the trees. 'That the gyppos' camp you was on about?'

'I thought we would try to find time to go over and see them this afternoon. But first, I want to pay another visit to the Big House.'

Reardon had successfully secured the use of the parlour at the Greville Arms for the duration of the enquiry, and a small table had been found where the two officers could take their meals in private, leaving the large centre table free to be used as a desk, an arrangement which suited everyone admirably. Over bread, cheese and pickles Reardon thought about what Nella Wentworth had told him, about Marianne's secret meetings with Hatherley, not so secret as he had thought, evidently. PC Bracey, for one, had been aware of those visits of hers to the lake, though he still swore he hadn't poked his nose in, as he put it, to find out what was going on.

On the night of her death, when Danny Boswell had seen that figure, apparently arguing with her, Hatherley had, on his own admittance, been there. He said it was around eleven o'clock, but he could have been lying. He could have waited, or returned. But in either case, for what conceivable reason? Unless he had known Marianne was going to be there.

As for how it might link to Edith Huckaby's death...

She was still something of a mystery, this young woman who had been murdered, but he was beginning to find slightly disturbing the picture

283

which was emerging of the sort of person she might have been. The sad fact was that no one had seemed to actually *like* her. He was getting the impression of a rather lonely young woman with no real friends, poised as she was between the upper echelons of the family in which she could play no part and the lower servants who regarded her with suspicion and whom she most likely despised. Yet she was a young woman who must have had her dreams, her loves, hopes, aspirations. So much so that she was willing to grab the opportunity of marrying Ben Naylor, a match which seemed to Reardon could never have been made in Heaven: no two people more opposite could be imagined. It looked very much as though she had seized on him as her only chance to get out of the life that had been thrust upon her. Reardon could feel pity for her, disadvantaged from the start, with no parents, dependent upon the impersonal charity of the nuns she had lived with. Books appeared to have been her lifeline, a glimpse perhaps into the possibilities of another life, unreal and romanticised as it was (although it was something he partly understood, given his own addiction to reading, learning, and the new worlds it had opened for him). Then she had discovered that Marianne Wentworth shared her view of the world. Marianne had rashly confided in her – without the need for too much persuasion, perhaps, for she had been alone in that sense too, notwithstanding that she had been part of a loving family. Was it indeed some secret Marianne had rashly confided to her that Edith had used, and which had eventually led to her death?

Chapter Twenty-Five

Leaving Wheelan to interview Lady Sybil's domestic staff when they went back to Oaklands shortly after lunch, Reardon went to speak to Lady Sybil herself once more. He was informed by the old manservant, Ellington, that her Ladyship was not well and asked to be excused, and that Mr Foley was not available either, since this was one of the days when he was driven over to the works.

He went to find Wheelan. Leaving the house, he turned the corner and walked along the terrace, at present occupied by a few men in hospital blue, reading, chatting, playing chess, writing letters, taking advantage of the pale spring sunshine while it was still there. The last of the patients, he supposed, before Oaklands closed as a hospital. He paused for a moment before the sweeping view from the terrace. Resplendent with graceful, mature specimens of sequoia, weeping ash, and cedar of Lebanon, the calm symmetry of the lawns was now spoilt by the double row of long wooden huts which had been erected as hospital wards. Nobody paid him much attention, apart from one young man sitting in a wheelchair, his lower half swathed in a blanket, who seemed to be watching him closely. But when their eyes met, the young man turned his chair in the other direction. Reardon walked on slowly, trying to fix the layout of the house in his mind and finally found himself, having come almost full circle, by the stable yard where all the ambulances were parked, and the back door which opened on to it, standing open.

In front of him was a passage with the back stairs which led up to Edith's room, to the left were the kitchens, from whence he could hear the rumble of Wheelan's voice as he talked to the servants. There wasn't much room in this narrow back entrance, most of it being taken up by a combined coat rack and umbrella stand, top-heavy with what seemed to be a communal collection of coats, waterproofs, umbrellas and walking sticks. To his right was a door with a wooden plaque reading: Estate Office. Out of curiosity he tried the handle. It wasn't locked but appeared to be unused now for its original purpose, although the scuffed footprints on the dusty floor showed that people still had reason to come in. Dust was everywhere: on the stacks of leather-bound ledgers and a Dickensian desk with a sloping top, on the pens and an inkstand in which the ink had long since dried up. A large safe, or maybe a gun cupboard, with tarnished, fancy brass door furniture, hung on the wall. As he turned away, debating whether or not to join Wheelan in the kitchen, through the dusty window he saw Eunice Foley.

Wheelan was sitting at the kitchen table in front of a cup of strong tea and a piece of Mrs Cherry's feather-light seed cake. He hadn't tasted seed cake since he was a child and had hoped never to do so again. He disliked the flavour of caraway, and even more the seeds which had managed to get under his denture, but he munched on stolidly. You couldn't waste good cake in these stringent times, nor throw kindness in Mrs Cherry's good-natured face.

'To be truthful, she never rightly joined in, like,' that lady was saying, answering his questions about Edith Huckaby.

'Too stuck up, if you ask me,' put in Elsie, the pert blonde maid who had, like most of the Oaklands domestic staff, worked in the hospital during the war, leaving only a skeleton staff of the ancient old butler, Ellington, Mrs Cherry the cook, and occasional women from the village to make up the shortfall. There was a new addition now in the form of Jinny, a round-faced fourteen-year-old who hadn't long left school, and who seemed to be struck dumb with shyness in the face of her elders.

'Now then, Elsie,' reproved Mrs Cherry, 'no need to speak ill of the dead. Miss Huckaby was all right – for a lady's maid – though never what you might call really friendly, I have to admit.'

'Well, I call that being stuck up. Lady's maid! She barely brought herself to say hello to me when I saw her. All dolled up, she was, fox fur an' all, making sure her stocking seams was straight and her hat was on just so in her handbag mirror before she went out. Fancy, all that just to see that old Ben Naylor! That was Monday night, the night she was killed.' The way Elsie said it implied the last occurrence was more than likely to be consequent on the previous ones.

'She had her handbag with her, then? What was it like?'

'Lovely little grey suede pochette, with a kind of loop to put your thumb through, to hold it, like,' Elsie replied promptly and not a little enviously. 'Lady Sybil passed it on when the loop came off, but Edith fixed it.'

'Did she have an umbrella with her?'

Mrs Cherry said, 'I don't think she had to start with but it began to look like rain just after she'd left and then I heard the door open and shut, so I expect she came back for one ... there's a whole lot of old umbrellas and mackintoshes that anybody uses in the stand by the office.'

'Very handy. I wonder, would you mind having a look-see and tell me if there's one missing?'

'Lawks, there's that many, how would I know? Why do you ask that?'

But Wheelan didn't enlighten her. He valiantly swallowed the last of the seed cake. 'No, no, thank you, Mrs Cherry, no more. Real tasty, but I have to watch me figure,' he added, patting his comfortable stomach. 'What time was it, when she went out?'

Mrs Cherry said. 'Quarter past seven, thereabouts, it would be.'

'You're sure about that? Mr Foley says he saw her going out at quarter past eight.'

'Maybe she came back and went out again, forgot something maybe. It was just after we'd had our supper when she left, wasn't it?' she addressed the others.

They agreed and Elsie added, 'Took *her* supper up to her room, of course. She came to bring the tray back to the kitchen and left the plates for Jinny to wash up, before she waltzed off. Breath of air, she said – as if we didn't know where she was off to.'

The old manservant, Ellington, said with great dignity, 'You seem to have forgotten, miss, while you've been working on the wards, that them Upstairs are no business of yours and you'd do better to remember in future.'

'Edith Huckaby wasn't Upstairs, even if she liked to think she was!'

'She was as far as you're concerned.'

Elsie had her own opinions about that but she knew when to shut up. She was a bright girl and hoped when things were back to normal to be given the now vacant place of the head parlour-maid, who had left to work in munitions, had met and married a soldier, and was now living in Nottingham.

'Did Miss Huckaby have a key to get in with?'

'No,' said Ellington. She knew she had to be in by ten, otherwise she'd have been locked out.'

'And you didn't notice she hadn't come in?'

'Well, we wouldn't have known. The hospital keep most of their supplies in the stables, now there's no horses, and there's a lot of coming and going outside this door with the orderlies and what not. I just assumed she had come in and gone up the back stairs,' Ellington said, flushing at the implication he'd been lacking in his duties.

Mrs Cherry came to his defence. Anyway, we was playing rummy, the four of us, making a bit of noise, laughing and that, but I could see Jinny here was nearly falling asleep, poor little duck; she's not used to all the work, yet, so I sent her up to bed and we just sat talking by the fire, until

I went up to my room and he went to lock up as usual at ten o'clock.'

'So you were in here all night, all of you?'

'Except for when I took the master his nightcap,' Ellington said. 'He always takes a glass of whisky and water of an evening. I took it in at half past eight. I went to draw the curtains and make the fire up, but he said not to bother, he was going to turn in right away. He did look a bit below par and I asked him if he wasn't feeling well. Just tired, he said. Which isn't to be wondered at, seeing how hard he works.'

'So you were all in here until ten?'

'Not me, I went up before that. I need my beauty sleep,' Elsie said with a laugh.

'Need time for all that titivating with curling your hair and that, more like!' Mrs Cherry reproved her. Elsie only tossed her blonde head.

'Right, well, I won't keep you from your work much longer. Thank you for the refreshment, Mrs Cherry. Very welcome. I might need to see you again.'

On his way out Wheelan paused by the umbrella stand Mrs Cherry had mentioned, and after several moments' contemplation, extracted a large cotton one, its original black colour faded and greenish, with a handle of amber, carved to resemble the head and neck of a swan. More likely resin, he thought on closer inspection, at any rate there was no million-year-old fly or any other insect embedded in it. It was tightly furled, and when he inserted a finger between the folds, it was very slightly damp. He looked at it thoughtfully, then tucking it underneath his arm, he took it back with him to the village.

Eunice had been hurrying across the stable yard when Reardon spotted her. Her head was down, and as he stepped outside to meet her, she almost bumped into him. 'So sorry,' she gasped, 'I wasn't looking where I was going. Oh, Inspector Reardon, it's you.'

She looked distressed and agitated, with a heightened colour, far more than the near collision warranted, and he ventured to ask if anything was the matter. She shook her head. 'All the same,' he said, 'it seems as though this may not be the best time to ask if I may speak to you.'

'Of course you may,' she answered, visibly pulling herself together.

'Somewhere a little more private?'

'Round the corner, in the orangery?' She smiled faintly. 'That's what we call it, though as far as I know there have been no orange trees kept there in living memory. We used it as a conservatory, before the war.'

Now the glass-walled, glass-roofed building against the south wall was evidently in use as a refectory for walking patients able to take their meals at the hospital-issue tables and chairs placed there. The heavy pre-war perfume of tuber roses and stephanotis and the damp, earthy smell of living green plants had given way to the lingering odours of institutional food and the disinfectant with which the floors and tables had been scrubbed. It felt bare and empty and echoing, despite some dispirited plants scattered here and there, indicating that someone had made a half-hearted attempt to cheer the place up, but had clearly not made any commitment to look after them.

Eunice went to sit at one of the tables by the windows and Reardon took a seat opposite her. There was another expanse of lawn on this side of the house, and her attention seemed to be riveted on it, where the same young man he had felt to be watching him was being wheeled along one of the paths intersecting the grass. She turned her gaze away but not before he saw that her eyes were suspiciously wet. He half rose from his chair. 'Miss Foley, I can see this is definitely not the time to talk. Another time.'

'No. Please stay. I'm simply being stupid.' She lifted her chin. 'How can I help?'

She was the sort of gentle young woman whose looks aroused protective instincts in men, but he did not think her helpless. Nevertheless, 'I'm sorry to see you upset,' he said. 'Is it something to do with what has happened? With Miss Huckaby? You must tell me if it is.'

She shook her head. 'It's an entirely private matter.'

'I won't press you, then. But nothing, I'm afraid, is private when it comes to murder, Miss Foley.'

'This truly is, I assure you.'

There was a silence.

'Very well,' he said at last. 'Let's start with Miss Huckaby. She had been with your mother a long time, so you must have known her quite well. Did you like her?'

She stared at him with her big blue eyes and at last she said flatly, 'Actually, I thought she was pretty beastly. If you want the truth.'

'Ah.'

'But that doesn't mean I'm glad she's been killed.' Two spots of colour had appeared on her face, but her chin lifted and she sat up very straight. 'Do you smoke, Inspector Reardon?'

'No.'

'Then you can't offer me one. Never mind. My father disapproves of me smoking, anyway.' Her glance wandered out over the lawns again.

'Miss Foley?'

'What? Oh, I'm sorry... I don't seem to be able to... I'm not concentrating.' She bit her lip, then said suddenly, 'You're right, something *is* bothering me, though it's nothing to do with Edith. What it is, there's a soldier here, a patient, who worries me. He has been badly wounded, in fact he has lost both his legs.'

'I see. And you and he...?'

She stared. 'Good gracious, no, nothing like that! No ... but because of what's happened to him, he's broken off his engagement to his young lady. He won't have her marrying him out of sympathy, as he sees it, or because he's a wounded hero, and he refuses to believe it isn't sympathy she feels, but love. She is heartbroken, but nothing will convince him that he would be anything but a burden to her if they married. I'm afraid I have just been very cruel and told Jack Shawcross in no uncertain terms that if everyone in the same condition is to go through the rest of his life with a chip on his shoulder, well then–'

She stopped abruptly and he saw the realisation of what she was saying dawning on her. A hot tide of embarrassment spread over her face but she didn't flinch from meeting his gaze.

'Have you thought this young man might just be right?' he said, after a moment. 'It's easy enough, I would suspect, to believe such obstacles can easily be overcome, to think things like that don't matter, but will she feel the same when they have both had to cope with it for ten, twenty years?'

'I understand what you're saying, but there is no reason to believe he won't be able to lead a useful and happy life,' she said stubbornly. 'You think I am interfering in matters that do not concern me, don't you?'

'No. I believe you are tender-hearted, Miss Foley, and it does you credit, but I also believe you're mistaken.' He believed, too, that gentle Miss Eunice, with her dainty little figure and big soft eyes, was obviously rather more than she seemed. He remembered how firmly she had dealt with her mother when they had been stopped in the drive and informed of Edith's murder.

'If I loved a man, Inspector Reardon...' she began, then stopped, blushing furiously. 'Well, never mind. That isn't what we're here to talk about, is it?'

No, it wasn't, but she had disturbed him. As she talked, across his mind had flashed a bright image of Ellen Calder, with her soft skin and her bright eyes, her forthright views and her support of his determination to educate himself better, and of the letters she had written so constantly while he was away. He had read and reread them and at one time dared to imagine he detected an increasing friendliness, even affection, in them. What had started with 'Dear Mr Reardon' had become 'My dear Herbert' and they had been finished off with warm sentiments. She knew about his facial wounds and had continued to write encouragingly to him in the various hospitals where he'd undergone treatment, in much the same vein as the words Eunice Foley had used. He had briefly hoped – then had told himself not to be a fool.

'He won't even reply to her letters any longer,' Eunice was saying, 'but I've taken the liberty of writing to Emily Boothroyd myself and asking her to come down here to stay, so that she can at least make him listen to her. There, what do you think of that?'

He thought she had done a very brave, and what might turn out to be a very foolish thing, with the best of intentions, but he forbore to say so. After a moment, she said, 'Why did you want to see my mother again?'

He was more than prepared to drop the previous subject, though this was likely to prove even more painful to her. 'Miss Eunice, that jewellery Lady Sybil alleges she gave to her maid. You do realise what that means, don't you? I'm sorry, but I must tell you that I'm not inclined to believe your mother gave it to her for the reasons she said. A more likely interpretation seems to be that Edith Huckaby had some hold over her.' She looked panicky, which told him what he wanted to know. 'So you did know about it? Then perhaps you'd care to enlighten me.'

'I'm afraid... I'm sorry, I can't. Or rather,' she then added with some spirit, 'I won't.'

He said gently, 'We shall find out, one way or

another, you know, and maybe not how or in what way you would wish. Wouldn't you prefer to tell me now, in your own way?'

'No!' She pulled a dying frond from a sorry-looking fern nearby and began to shred it. The powdery brown dust on the back of the leaves stained her slim fingers and she made a great business of using her lace-trimmed handkerchief to rub it off. He sensed, over her bent head, the struggle that was going on.

At last she tucked the handkerchief up her sleeve, and raised her eyes. 'Well, after all, why not?' she asked, a little defiantly. 'You already suspect enough ... sooner or later, you'll discover the truth.'

'With your help, I hope we might.'

For a long time she said nothing. 'I could scarcely believe my eyes when you produced that jewellery,' she said eventually, 'though my mother was speaking the truth when she said it isn't really worth so very much. But all the same, for her to have given it away! That little turquoise ring was once my grandmama's! And you spoke, I believe, about a ... a Mizpah brooch Edith was wearing, did you not? Well, in actual fact,' she said with heightened colour, 'that belongs to *me!*'

'Then how was Lady Sybil able to give it to Edith?'

'I don't think she did. The clasp was a little loose, I lost it and Edith must have found it and just kept it without saying anything. Perhaps one should not blame her,' she went on, less indignantly; 'no one knew it was mine, after all, it was lost the first time I wore it. I should have waited

296

to get the clasp fixed. It was ... it was sent to me by ... a friend.'

'I shall see to it that you have it back.'

'Oh yes, please, it means a great deal.' More calmly, she added, 'Yes, I should be so grateful. As for the rest of the jewellery – well, when I thought about it being given to Edith, a lot of things became clear. You see, she had become very ... well, not to sound snobbish, but she was getting above herself, as my old nanny used to say. And my mother was allowing her to get away with it! She is always pretty lenient with any of the servants, but Edith was taking liberties which normally Mother would not have put up with under any circumstances. I couldn't understand it – until you produced that jewellery box. And then...' She drew in her breath. 'Oh, this really is too frightful – it ... it was blackmail, wasn't it?'

'Yes,' he answered bluntly. 'I realise that must be painful for you to acknowledge, but that does seem to be what it amounts to. I don't suppose you have any idea what it was about?'

There was a miserable pause. 'Yes, I'm afraid I might have. At least–'

'Was it by any chance over something that happened during the war, when they were working together?'

'Oh, no!' She was clearly startled by the suggestion. 'It had begun before then, I'm sure. Though I think *that* – I mean my mother finding her a nice easy job that would seem like war work – was all part of it. Mr Gervase Hatherley, our neighbour, who was in overall charge, told me once that he would have sacked her if it hadn't been that he didn't wish to upset my mother. It wasn't true what she told you about Edith's efficiency: she often got things in a great muddle because she didn't like what she was doing and was careless, Mr Hatherley said (muddles that apparently my mother used to sort out), though the job didn't involve much more than answering a few letters, making lists and so on.' She paused. 'These last two days I've done a lot of thinking, trying to piece things together.'

'And what conclusions have you come to, Miss Foley?' No answer. 'Well, you do know what it was all about, don't you?'

She could not meet his eyes. She looked down at her pretty little hands fingering the gold expanding bracelet she wore around her left wrist.

'Was it,' he asked gently, wanting to help her, 'to do with the quarrel your brother had with Rupert von Kessel at that party here on the eve of the outbreak of war?' He heard her indrawn breath. 'I was talking to Mrs Rafferty, and she happened to mention they'd had a misunderstanding. Will you tell me what happened then?'

'All right,' she said at last. 'I will. It might be more than time it was talked about.'

Sybil, too, lying on the chaise longue in her boudoir with a pounding headache, was thinking of that same party, which was no coincidence, because that was the day which had led up to the situation they all found themselves in now, the day when everything had started to go wrong, the last day she had ever known peace, in every sense of the word. That day which had begun so happily, as

298

a celebration of dear Eleanor Villiers's seventieth birthday, and ended with heartbreak. However she tried, she couldn't stop the events of that evening going round and round in her mind, like a record with the needle stuck in a groove...

Chapter Twenty-Six

1914

The party had been planned for weeks, and by the time the date arrived, the possibility of war with Germany was no longer a matter of mere speculation, but expected daily, and an invitation to one of Sybil's famous suppers was grasped as a welcome, if temporary diversion by all those who'd been invited.

One or two people who had commitments had been forced to cancel, yet there were still twenty-eight at table, friends, relatives and family, young and old. She had done the flowers herself: cream and pink roses, with ivy trailing among the best silver candelabra, placed at intervals down the long expanse of gleaming mahogany, the crisp napkins, each with a rose tucked into them. The food Mrs Cherry and her staff had laboured over was light, delicious and looked simply too ravishing. An airy, golden prawn soufflé, cold roast beef and chicken, a gigantic salmon in aspic glistening with cucumber scales, new potatoes, tender vegetables and salads, jewel-coloured jellies, strawberries, and not least, Eleanor's birthday cake, looking too exquisitely decorated to cut into.

All the Wentworth girls were there, of course, looking sweetly pretty in their light summer dresses. Eunice, too, who had acquired a sort of glow that night which her mother couldn't account for. William, already in uniform. And Grev, charming Eleanor, next to whom he sat, dark and incredibly handsome, smiling at the old woman with his sideways smile, turning his mother's heart with love as he always did. There was always a vibrancy, an electric current that ran through the house whenever he was here, despite those brooding, dark moods that came on him occasionally. She put that down to artistic temperament, and lately, perhaps, to the knowledge that the coming war would certainly curtail his music studies, that he would not be able to go back to Paris until it was all over. But a more potent worry to her was what would happen to him if he continued with his refusal to fight, should that be necessary.

Her glance strayed from him to Rupert von Kessel, William's friend, who was still in England. A very foolish young man, dallying over here with a kind of bravado, storing up trouble for himself, ignoring advice and the repeated telegrams from his irate father commanding him to come home *immediately*, lingering despite the political situation which was growing more and more critical by the hour. That assassination of their archduke had caused the great Austro-Hungarian Empire to bring its power to bear by declaring war on little Serbia, but Rupert dismissed this with a wave of the hand. The Serbs were never anything else but troublemakers, and the might of the Imperial army would have no difficulty in putting down this rebellion, as they had others. Rather than alarming Rupert, the danger seemed to excite him. As if it were a dare to see how long he could remain balanced on the brink. The fact that the Kaiser's Germany had ordered mobilisation in support of Austria, and that Russia had retaliated by following suit in support of Serbia, worried him not at all. But when Britain too declared war, as she must, it would certainly mean the nation would be involved in a European conflict, and where would Rupert be then? At best, he was at risk of being interned as an alien; at worst ... well, at least one German, a butcher, had already been set upon by a yelling mob, beaten up and all his meat thrown out into the street. God knew what else might happen.

Sybil had known he was likely to be an uneasy presence at this supper, but since he was William's friend and a guest at the rectory, it had been impossible not to include him, and she had prepared herself to smooth over any awkwardness, or as much as she could. She was particularly aware of General Izzard, an old friend of her father's, a darling, elderly man of great charm but little tact, whom she delighted by calling him Izzie. A veteran of the South African war, he would certainly make a beeline for William, the only man in uniform, as soon as he saw him, to air his opinions and give advice on the current crisis – and what he might say to Rupert did not bear thinking about. He was outspoken to the nth degree and she must keep them apart at all costs.

She was determined the evening was not going to be ruined by controversy about Great Britain's part in this international turmoil. She wanted it to be an evening that would be remembered with pleasure by everyone, with no arguments, especially for Eleanor, and for Arthur, too, who had his own worries about the future of his business, and who did not seem to be looking quite as well as he should this evening. A touch of indigestion, he'd said when she remarked on it, and promised to go easy on all the rich food.

'I must warn you, Izzie,' she accosted the general as he came in, 'that I expressly forbid any war talk tonight.'

'Oh, really?' He looked both astonished and disappointed. 'Can one possibly avoid it? The Belgians are going to refuse the damn Kaiser's ultimatum tomorrow, you know, and rightly so. They're neutral in all this, after all, and there's no question of them granting his troops free passage across their country into France, and then the balloon will go up all over Europe–'

'Not tonight, Izzie,' she stopped him firmly. 'I've put you between Eleanor and little Amy, so you must be nice to both. It's Eleanor's special day and it's a great treat for Amy to be invited to a grown-up occasion.'

He brightened. Eleanor Villiers was a delightful old friend with whom he had danced and flirted when they were young, and he liked children, especially one as pretty and enchanting as little Amy. Good God! She was the very image of her mother, who had always outshone Sybil. He wondered how Sybil liked that.

302

Sybil relaxed as the evening progressed. She lifted her crystal glass, not displeased with her seating arrangements as she looked around the table. Rupert, safe though looking sulky about it between Arthur and old Cousin Martha, Lady Endicott, who was extremely deaf but had brought out all her jewels for the evening, some rather grey diamonds and the magnificent Endicott emeralds, which showed up well in the light of the thirty-six candles. There was nothing Sybil liked so well as a combination of dusk and candlelight to grace a dinner table. The soft light was so kind to the ladies' faces, the flickering flames caught the prismatic cut of crystal goblets and threw intriguing shadows onto the rest of the richly furnished room. With the growing dusk outside, they seemed to be enclosed in a privileged bubble of magic.

She kept an eye on Izzie, but he was behaving himself, saying something pretty to Eleanor so that her eyes sparkled in a youthful manner that must remind him of times long gone, or perhaps it was the champagne that was doing it. It was an agreeable gathering altogether, the guests seeming to have entered in a complicity not to mention the crisis uppermost in all their minds. Even the Raffertys were mingling well, there in full force as friends of Eleanor: Joel Rafferty, who was inclined to fall into taciturn silences, and awkward young Steven, both of whom managed to look slightly crumpled in their unaccustomed evening clothes. Mrs Rafferty, however, in a curious peacock-coloured crushed-velvet dress hanging loose from the shoulders, after the Rational mode, and wearing a feathered headband which made her look rather like an Indian squaw, made up for both. She was seated next to Francis and had even managed to coax a smile or two from him with her outrageous, clever opinions, he who had once captured the hearts of so many young ladies, with his ready smile and urbane manners. He was still a handsome man in his mid fifties, but his smiles were rarer.

Suddenly, now, in her boudoir, all those years later, alone with her memories, Lady Sybil put her hands over her eyes and wept uncontrollably.

Chapter Twenty-Seven

In the orangery, Eunice was saying, 'The party was as much for William, William Wentworth, you know, as for Mrs Villiers, a sort of send-off to his joining the army.'

It had been arranged that one of his friends, a brother officer who owned a motor car, would come to pick him up after they had eaten, when they would drive together to join their unit. William fooled around throughout the supper, drank a lot of champagne and teased Eunice until she blushed, then stopped fooling, looked into her eyes and told her how pretty she looked. She wanted the evening never to end, but it did, too soon after the meal, when Piers Beresford arrived in a noisy, racy-looking motor with a strap around its bonnet. The non-family guests shook hands with William and wished him luck before drifting into the drawing room for their coffee, leaving the family to say their goodbyes in private. Rupert and William stood for several moments with their hands clasped. 'I have just made my farewells and thanks to your family, since I shall be leaving before breakfast to-morrow, to go home,' Rupert said at last. 'Grev has promised to drive me to Birmingham in his mother's car early in the morning.'

'The sooner you leave the better. Good luck, Kess.'

'You too, my friend.' William clapped him on the shoulder and Rupert walked away.

'No waterworks, now!' William warned jokingly, as the rest of them went outside. The girls and his grandmother did their best, though they could not help a tear or two as his things were stowed in the back. He hugged and kissed them all, Eunice as well, who was there because he had gripped her hand and refused to let it go. She just *might* have imagined, she thought, her eyes bright, that he had held her so tight for a moment when saying his goodbyes – but she had not imagined what she had read in his face, the emotions he had been at such pains to conceal all evening, the feelings every young soldier must have on going to war for the first time: the fear that he might never return, or would not be brave enough in the face of the enemy, the unexpected wrench at leaving his family. The revelation had been gone in an in-stant, concealed once more beneath a mask of joking. The two young men in their brand-new uniforms seemed more like a couple of excited schoolboys setting out on a larky adventure than officers in the British Army ... indeed, Piers Beresford, with his blonde curls and choirboy face, scarcely looked old enough to shave.

At last they were ready to leave, and as William was preparing to crank the motor, Francis stepped forward and uncharacteristically took William's hand in both of his, then drew his son towards him. 'God keep you, my boy,' he said, and went abruptly indoors.

With a tightening in her chest, Eunice watched as the motor started, William threw his long legs over the door and slid into the front seat, and with whoops and a cheerful wave of their hands, he and his friend roared away between the two lines of dark, pointed yews towards the road. The women watched until the motor could no longer be seen and then dried their tears. Eleanor stretched out a hand to Eunice as they went indoors to join the others, but she shook her head. 'I'll be in presently, Mrs Villiers,' she said gently.

She needed to be alone for a while and walked down into the rose garden, where its small centre pool was surrounded by a great circle of roses trained on ropes that swung in swags, one to the next, and a stone cherub in the middle perpetually spouted water onto the lily pads almost covering the water's surface. She sat on the stone rim of the pool, battling to overcome the sense of loss, the feeling of change and impending disaster. It had been another very hot day and the stones were still warm, though a slight breeze had arisen and made a gentle soughing through the trees. In the dusk, the scent of the roses was almost overpowering.

The windows of the drawing room were open

to the evening and the sound of Grev playing the piano floated across to her, overlaid with a subdued hum of conversation. The sort of music he played nowadays was not the sort most people stopped their conversation to listen to. Modern music, hard to understand, with no tune, only a series of discordant notes and plangent silences. She wondered if this might be one of his own compositions.

It was time she rejoined the others, she thought as it came to an end. She went through the French windows into the drawing room, just as Grev was beckoning Marianne to join him. Sitting next to each other on the piano stool, they began to play together a tune from *The Gondoliers*, one that all of the guests recognised, and this time listened and hummed to, smiling as they watched the young couple playing in perfect harmony: the dark, handsome young man and Marianne, looking particularly lovely tonight, in a soft cream shantung dress and a string of seed pearls. Her hair was a nimbus of red-gold round her head in the soft lamplight, and she had a cream rose tucked into it, which Eunice had not noticed when she arrived. She looked across the room and saw Rupert, watching them with a peculiar intensity. He could not play a note of music and claimed to be tone-deaf and quite ignorant on the subject of Mozart, his native city's most famous son, all of which naturally did not help to endear him to Grev. He was watching both the players intently, a slightly supercilious smile lifting the corner of his mouth.

They finished in unison and as the polite

applause began, and the indulgent smiles, Eunice turned her head and her glance came to rest on her mother. Sybil was standing, frozen, gazing at the pair. Eunice was transfixed herself. It did not take a great mind to see what was going on between her brother and Marianne, she thought, and was sorry. Marianne Wentworth, dearest of family friends though she was, could never come anywhere near being the brilliant match their mother had envisaged for Grev.

Sybil came to life and walked over to the piano. 'Charming,' she said, with one of her most radiant smiles. 'You've become very talented, dear Marianne. You must play again for us later in the evening. For the present I must see to the tables in the card room and leave all you young folks to each other. Come and see me for a few minutes before you go to bed, darling,' she added, lightly touching Grev's shoulder.

He glanced at her smiling face. 'Yes, of course I will, Mother,' he replied, with an answering smile.

'It wasn't that Mother didn't like Marianne,' Eunice told Reardon. 'She did, very much, everybody did, in fact she was rather a pet of hers. It was just that, when it comes to marriage – one has to marry the right person, as I have reason to know.' She laughed a little, but there was a hint of desperation in her voice. And Mother and Grev ... he was very special to her.'

'I think I understand,' Reardon was recalling the photograph he had noticed in the drawing room, Foleys and Wentworths together, Sybil standing proudly with her son's arm linked through hers,

308

her other arm around Marianne. Everyone smiling, except the rector, standing saturnine at the edge of the group.

'Although I must say, I was surprised. I had always thought – and still do,' Eunice added with a lift of her chin, as if convincing herself, 'that when it came down to it, Mother would not absolutely insist, as long as we found someone we could truly love.'

'And after that? At the party, I mean.'

'Oh, after that, we younger ones fooled around generally, laughed and talked, played silly pencil-and-paper games and so on, until it was time to go home.'

'I see. But you haven't told me about the fight.'

'Oh. Oh, she told you about that as well, did she, Mrs Rafferty?'

'What happened?'

'Goodness, it was nothing, really. It was old General Izzard who started it. Those who hadn't gone home were all milling around in the little room off the hall, waiting for the motors to be brought round, you know, and he started talking to Rupert – about the war. He was not very tactful and Rupert's hackles rose, I suppose, at any rate he answered very sarcastically. It wasn't at all sensible of Izzie to bring the subject up, but he *is* very old, and everyone knows how out-spoken he is, though he doesn't mean anything by it. But Grev took Rupert's remarks to an old man amiss, and in no time at all, they were at each other's throats – not literally, but exchanging insults, you know, Rupert taunting Grev about his pacifism, calling him a coward, which was certainly not true, and in the end Grev just lost his temper and knocked him down, though it was more of a push, really. It didn't hurt Rupert, I'm sure. I think he was more surprised than anything, as much surprised as Grev himself. At any rate, he apologised to the general, who accepted, though pretty stiffly. And Grev apologised to Rupert and they shook hands. So you see, it wasn't much of a quarrel at all. I'm afraid they'd both had a little too much champagne.'

'Feelings were running very high about the war at that time.'

'Yes,' she said gratefully, 'they were, weren't they?' A little colour had come back into her face. 'In any case, that was the end of the evening. Mother was concerned about my father. She thought he wasn't looking well and asked me to go upstairs with him and she'd be up later, after she'd seen the last of the guests off – the Wentworths, who were waiting for the Daimler. Papa had ordered Garbutt to drive them to and from the rectory, all of them except William and Rupert, who'd walked here, through the woods.'

'Rupert would have walked back, then?'

'I expect so. There wouldn't have been room for him in the motor. But I was upstairs with Father by that time, and when my mother came up we helped him into bed.' She laughed ruefully. 'He won't have a manservant to run his bath and shave him and lay his clothes out, you know – he despises all that sort of thing, and he insisted he was all right when we left him. But I didn't think he was, so I didn't go to bed straight away, just in case. In the end, I was about to, when I heard

Mother's door slamming with a tremendous crash, and then I heard Grev running along the corridor and down the stairs, and the front door slamming.'

'How did you know it was your brother?'

'No one else in the house ever ran down the stairs like that! He used to take them three at a time sometimes, and jump the last.'

'Do you think they had quarrelled?'

'Grev and Mother? That wasn't something that often happened.' Her lip trembled. 'But I think they must have done. I can't think of anything else that would make him run away like he did that night and do what he did. I waited for ten, fifteen minutes, wondering whether I ought to go to Mother, or if it would make things worse. In the end, I did, but Edith advised me to leave her alone. She convinced me there wasn't anything to worry about, nothing that a good night's sleep wouldn't cure. But of course, none of us got much sleep that night. It wasn't above an hour after that Father had his heart attack.'

And they couldn't find her brother when that happened because he'd already fled, Reardon recalled, but did not say so. He didn't wish to press her much further at that point; he had read unacknowledged terror in those soft eyes and she would, soon enough, have to admit the conclusions which must follow from her mother's blackmail. After a few minutes, he thanked her for her cooperation and left her. She had, in any case, already told him a great deal more than she thought she had.

311

Chapter Twenty-Eight

After he left Eunice, Reardon walked back to the
Greville Arms, taking the short cut between Oak-
lands and the village, along the same well-used
path which Edith had taken on her last night.

Reaching the point where the path divided,
where the sandstone outcropping surfaced on the
slight slope towards the waterside and provided a
convenient place to sit for a moment, he dropped
down onto it, wondering if this was the very same
rock where Hatherley sat, keeping his nightly
vigils. And where, perhaps, he had watched Mari-
anne and young Foley meeting that fateful night.
Why did he come here? Was it masochism, guilt?
Was Hatherley the figure Danny Boswell had seen
struggling with Marianne after Foley had left her?

The initial elation brought by his conversation
with Eunice Foley was diminishing rapidly. His
mind alive to the possibilities this had brought
forth, he had, for a while, almost believed he could
see where all this business had started, how it had
continued and even, possibly, how the end had
come about. His speculations as to the motive for
Edith's blackmailing were becoming certainties.
As for the perpetrator ... well, he was not at all sure
he could see Lady Sybil resorting to murder. On
the other hand... He sighed. There was always an
'on the other hand'. He would have been prepared
to wager a month's salary that she was not the

woman to submit to blackmail in the first place, either, but she almost certainly had done.

He stood up, feeling suddenly cold. Was it his fancy that the tragic deaths of two young women had overlaid this spot with a brooding, almost sinister atmosphere, or was it the picturesque, almost Gothic scene itself: the bulk of Broughton Hill opposite, the ancient caves scooped out of the soft rock looking like gaping mouths; the broken down boathouse, a total ruin now, roofless and with saplings growing through it, the rotting posts of the jetty still standing, reminding him too much of the shattered tree stumps in no-man's-land; the whole of it the epitome of the romantic fallacy almost asking to be depicted on the canvas of some artist with an exaggerated imagination?

He gave himself a mental shake, stood up and followed the path to the village, alongside the lake as it curved in an elongated tadpole shape until it joined the river at its tail.

Inside the Greville Arms, Sam was busy behind the bar of the snug, and a good smell of home baking issued from the direction of the kitchen. 'Any chance of some tea, Sam?'

'That there is. Your sergeant's just had a pot. I'll get Mattie to send in some fresh.'

He found Wheelan drawn up to the fire, papers spread out on the table, which also held a tea tray, with a plate empty but for crumbs and a stray currant or two. The sergeant jumped when he walked in as if he might have been nodding off. Reardon couldn't blame him: cosy fire, Mattie Noakes's baking ... But if he had been dozing, he

313

became immediately awake to the moment, adjusting the spectacles which had slipped down his nose, screwing the top onto his fountain pen and tapping together the papers spread out on the table while Reardon divested himself of his coat and sat down opposite, legs stretched to the fire.

Looking over the top of his spectacles, the sergeant passed over the report he'd typed out with two fingers on the Remington they'd brought with them. 'Report all up to date, er, Inspector.'

All right, all right, Wheely, what's wrong with Bert? As long as Kelly doesn't hear you. He'd have me strung up.' He'd always been 'young Bert' to both Wheelan and Paskin and anything else didn't feel right, not yet, especially since he felt himself dependent on the sergeant's experience, not to mention his capacity for taking exactly the right kind of notes, and his prodigious memory. It had crossed his mind, in fact, to wish Wheely had been with him when he had been talking to Eunice Foley. He couldn't, however, help feeling that it was those first few minutes of conversation with her (about that young man who'd lost his legs – Shawcross, wasn't it? – and which would have been impossible in the presence of anyone else) that had established a rapport between them and which had led her to trust him enough to be so candid.

'Bert, then, if that's what you want. By the way, I thought I might as well look in on them Gypsies, seeing as I was passing by the Lezzers. Nowt doing. They swear to a man they didn't see or hear a thing – for what that's worth. However, four of 'em were drinking here in the taproom and playing skittles in the alley till closing time. All bar the old bloke who seems to be the boss, Daniel Boswell – and one lad they say is bad with some sort of fever and never left his bed. The women all say they were together, and never set foot out the camp.'

'What about Danny Boswell, the young one?'

'Seems to have been in Ireland for the past week, buying horses, or that's what they say, and no reason to disbelieve 'em. As near the truth as we're going to get, anyroad.'

Reardon sighed. 'Well, no more than we expected, I suppose.' He had intended visiting the Gypsies to talk to Danny himself, but it might not matter all that much now.

The friendly, buxom woman called Mrs Jenner, who helped out in the kitchens, brought in his tea and, he was pleased to see, another plate on which reposed two fragrant, golden squares. 'Leave your tea to draw if you want a good cup, but get on with the lardy cake while it's still warm.' She nodded pleasantly and left them to it and Reardon didn't hesitate to obey. He'd sampled Mattie's lardy cake before, and though the rich, somewhat heavy confection might later induce somnolence in him also, he felt the sort of hollow inside that had nothing to do with hunger, yet only something sweet and stodgy would fill. In any case, the cold motorcycle ride across country which he was due to take yet again in less than an hour, in order to bring Kelly up to date with events, would take care of that.

While he ate, and drank his tea, he thought over Wheelan's report. Very much to the point, and faithfully recorded, word for word, he had no doubt. The kitchen staff had opened up to his avuncular presence, as people usually did.

'Hm. So Edith did have a handbag with her, after all. Where did it end up, then? In the lake with the weapon, I reckon,' he finished, answering his own question.

'I wouldn't be so sure of that one. Just you 'owd on a bit.' Wheelan produced the furled umbrella he had purloined from the stand at Oakland, explaining his reasons for doing so.

The goodly lump of rounded, polished amber-like substance which formed the swan's head and neck, seemingly meant to fit comfortably into the palm of the hand, was rather bigger than a golf ball. A good, old-fashioned umbrella, it was sturdy, with a heavy frame, and its cover was also heavy and thick. Reardon tried an experimental sideways swipe, holding it upside down with the back of the swan's head towards his imaginary objective, and found its weight gave it a good impetus. Enough, if it landed in the right place, to crack open a skull. And in all probability the right shape and size.

'That's a bit of luck. Looks like we could have the weapon, Wheely, but I reckon we'd best see what the doc, and the experts, make of it before we start counting chickens. If it is, it disposes of any ideas of a random killing.' He considered for a moment or two. 'Let's suppose Edith takes it from the stand in case it rains, and then Naylor, in spite of what he said, comes out to wait for her. They meet and have an argument, he grabs the umbrella and hits her with it.'

'There's a lot of supposing there. And how did it get back into the stand?'

'Well, if Naylor had taken it back to the house... I don't suppose anybody would've thought it odd, seeing him around the back entrance. He must use the estate office if he's been helping out with the management lately, as he says. The umbrella stand is just outside the office door. The domestics were in the kitchen, playing cards, and the hospital lot are always in and out, the door opening and shutting. It would only have needed a minute to put the umbrella back, no more.'

'No chance of much evidence from it, though, after all that rain – and anybody with any sense would've wiped the handle. Why didn't he chuck it in the lake and be done with it?'

'It might have been missed. And it was pelting down by then, Wheely, as you said. A long wet walk back to the house. I dare say he used it. With the added advantage it would wash any "extraneous matter", as our friend the pathologist called it, off the cover.'

'And him underneath it? Gawd.'

Reardon grinned. 'Maybe not. Naylor's hardly the type to care about a drop of rain. But it's a thought.' He sat for a moment, thinking, then having finished his tea and with a piece of lardy cake sitting comfortably in his stomach, he said, 'My turn now,' and gave the sergeant the gist of his conversation with Eunice.

'So Edith was there with her mistress, then,' Wheelan said, 'when this row between her and her son happened?'

'In the dressing room, anyway. Which adjoins

317

the bedroom, near enough for her to have overheard what went on.'

'And to hold it over Lady S later?'

'So it would seem. Then he storms out of the house, goes to meet Marianne Wentworth at the lakeside – and here we stumble a bit. Was it pre-arranged? Must have been, I think, and if so, it seems Hatherley wasn't the only one she liked to meet in secret. But this was at night and young ladies, however fancifully inclined, don't usually go that far. However, if we're to believe Danny Boswell–'

'A gyppo?'

'For the moment, we have to believe him. She certainly did go there, and according to Danny, she and Foley did meet. They had a tearful farewell, he leaves her, then disappears without a word to anybody. His sister confirmed what Mattie here told me earlier, that he had made an arrangement with his mother to drive the Austrian fellow to Birmingham, but he never returned. He left the motor in the care of the stationmaster, who let Lady Sybil know and held it until it was picked up. Still no word to his family until about three weeks later, when they got a letter telling them that he and von Kessel had parted in Birmingham, von Kessel to make his way back to Austria, if he could, at that stage, and Greville to join the British Army. Which in itself poses questions, in view of his avowed pacifism.'

'Jubous,' said Wheelan, 'all very jubous. Especially if he'd had a fight with the Austrian.'

'Apparently they made it up.'

Wheelan's eyebrows rose.

'Well, his sister says they did – and Greville Foley was apparently one to keep his word. And then there's this other person to consider, the one Danny Boswell saw having some sort of argument with Marianne after Grev had left her. Hatherley was at the lake at his own admission.' Reardon tried the teapot to see if there was any left. Only a few cold dregs came out, but he drank it anyway. 'There were a deal too many people around there that night for my liking.'

'What about the Austrian? Could it have been him Danny saw?'

'Von Kessel? Hmm. According to Eunice Foley, he set off for the rectory about eleven; why should he have hung around the lakeside till then?'

'But just supposing he did … young Foley could have killed him, which makes more sense of him running away.'

With surprising and gratifying speed, the information had already come through that there was no official record of von Kessel ever having been interned as an alien in Britain. Enquiries with the Austrian authorities, as to whether he had ever reached home, or indeed if he had survived the war, could well take months.

'How about contacting his parents direct? Rule him out, one way or t'other,' Wheelan suggested.

'I'd rather wait until we've gone through the usual channels. No point in upsetting his family unduly.'

Until they had to drag the lake, was the unspoken thought that lay between them.

His meeting with Kelly went on too long for

Reardon to think of returning to Broughton that evening, and he returned to his lodgings, an indifferent meal and an evening alone in the back parlour, thinking, making notes and staring at his reflection in the dark glass. A pattern was emerging to this case. He believed he had the gist of it clear in his mind, but it was still maddeningly far from complete in ways he could not ignore. He tapped his teeth with his pen and frowned.

Somewhere in the yard outside, Mrs Hingley's dog barked, invisible beyond the darkened window. Reardon laid down his pen.

It had been eight-fifteen when Arthur Foley had seen Edith go past his study window. A dark, wet night with no moon, pitch-black by then. If Foley had looked out of his window with the curtains undrawn, he would only have seen, as Reardon was seeing now, his own reflection staring at him. Why had he lied? Or perhaps he hadn't, had simply been mistaken, and had meant to say *seven*-fifteen, the time the servants said Edith had left the house, when it was not yet fully dark. Eight-fifteen was the time the butler had brought in his whisky and water.

He woke next morning in the lumpy confines of the musty flock mattress Mrs Hingley provided for her lodgers, fighting nameless fears, with an equally ungraspable depression hanging over him. It was not, nowadays, an unfamiliar sensation to wake up with, this knowledge of having journeyed, in those unconscious hours beyond his control, back to somewhere beyond the limits of human endurance. Nor was the relief of being able to tell

320

himself that was all it was, now, a nightmare past and gone. He hoped he hadn't shouted his terror, or screamed, or otherwise made an unacceptable disturbance, but there had been no banging on the wall or ceiling from any of the other lodgers.

It had rained again during the night. He stood at the open window and took deep breaths. The air was cool on his overheated face, but smoky and polluted. Street lamps were pale in the foggy dawn. It was never totally dark, here: the clouded night skies were always crimson with the reflected glow from the forges and blast furnaces below.

He made a hurried toilet then left the house that lay in the shadow of Dudley Castle, its round, grey stone towers standing on its hill, high above seven counties, feeling better despite having taken nothing but a cup of what passed as tea. Tea begrudged and water bewitched. It was time he got out of here, found a small house away from the grime, somewhere he could live alone and do for himself, he thought as he roared off on his motorcycle, comparisons with Broughton Underhill and one of the Greville Arms' breakfasts foremost in his mind.

The rush of clean, cold air, the exhilaration of speeding along on empty roads cleared his head, drove away the demons as he left industry behind and met the country roads. He didn't realise how fast he was going until he hit a patch of ice and skidded on a corner, almost coming into contact with a farm cart. It brought him up short. One motorcycle accident was more than enough.

An inglorious end to his army career he still believed it had been, never mind they'd seen fit to give him a commendation for it. He had recently been drafted into the Signal Corps, and as a sergeant despatch rider, was taking urgent messages from the front line back to base. December, 1917. Snow, ice, frozen mud. Driving along a road clogged with ambulances, the walking wounded, supply wagons, limbers and horses carrying field artillery. Swerving to avoid two Tommies limping along in front of him, each supporting the other, he'd hit a crater, which had thrown him clear, unhurt. But the motorcycle had toppled over and trapped both the soldiers underneath it before bursting into flames. No time to wait for anybody else, in all that chaos, to get to them. The only way was to lift the bike off them bodily, himself. He never knew whether the soldiers had survived. Didn't remember anything, until he woke up in the base hospital with half his face gone.

The first thing he'd done, as soon as he was free of the first of the hospitals he'd spent the rest of the war in, was to get on a motorbike again, otherwise he knew he'd never have done it.

Mr Hatherley did not look pleased to find Reardon waiting for him when he came out of his front door to where his spanking red limousine was drawn up on the gravel drive, ticking over, his uniformed chauffeur in attendance at its open door. He glanced unfavourably at the leather-helmeted figure propped against his motorcycle.

'What is it now?' he demanded testily. 'I really haven't the time to be bothered this morning. I'm due at the magistrates' court in ... less than an hour,' he said, pulling his watch out. He had still not recovered from his cold, his face was pasty and he did, in fact, look quite ill.

'I'm sorry, I don't wish to inconvenience you unnecessarily. Perhaps when your court duties are finished, you could come down to the Greville Arms, where we have our office?'

Hatherley looked even less pleased at this. 'Well then, a few minutes, but be quick about it.'

'In private, sir?'

'Come inside.' He dismissed the chauffeur with a wave of his hand. 'Ten minutes, Larkin.'

Reardon followed Hatherley into the same room as before. He switched on an electric lamp and sat by the fireplace in the same chair he'd previously occupied, but the dead ashes of the fire had not yet been cleared and the room had a cold, stuffy feel to it. He waved a hand and Reardon took a seat opposite, placing his gauntlets and leather helmet on a small table by the side of his chair.

'Now then, what's all this? I've told you all I can about poor Edith Huckaby.'

'This is not about Edith. Our enquiries are at the moment concerned with the night Marianne Wentworth died.'

Hatherley's face became suffused with colour. 'This is intolerable. I have already told you exactly what happened that night. I went home via the lakeside, but that was long before Marianne died.'

'How do you know what time she died, Mr Hatherley?'

There was a pause. 'I don't, of course, but it must have been after I left the lake. There was no sign of her while I was there. If I'm not mistaken, we have been over all this before.'

'Maybe, if you give the matter a little more thought, you might change your mind.'

'And just what, exactly, is that supposed to mean?'

'A long time after the party broke up, Marianne was seen there with Greville Foley. He left, and then later, she was seen struggling with another person.'

'And that person is supposed to be me? You think I pushed her into the water and left her to drown? Good God, what do you take me for?'

'A man who is suffering from guilt? Yes, I do think you were that person, Mr Hatherley. But I don't think you pushed her into the water. There seems to be little doubt she was alive when you left her. But afterwards, after you had gone ... our witness saw her run to the edge of the jetty in a very agitated state... Why were you arguing with her?'

There was no doubt in Reardon's mind that he had struck home. Hatherley's complexion had grown even more ashen, if possible. He suddenly stood up and walked over to a side table which held bottles and glasses, poured himself a substantial amount of amber-coloured liquid and drained the glass in one gulp. He stood, his hand on the mantelpiece, looking into the cold fire. Then he turned, his face patched with colour.

'All right.' He resumed his seat, sitting down heavily, like an old man whose knees had difficulty in bending. 'All right. I did see her. I waited for her, I knew she was going to be there because I'd overheard her making the arrangement with young Foley to meet, after the party was over. At least, what I suspected was an arrangement. I was on the terrace where I was finishing a smoke, before going home. Everyone else had left, except the Wentworths who were waiting for the car. She and Grev were just inside the French windows. Just a few words, but put together, it seemed enough: '...*tonight ... you wouldn't dare ... the lake ... yes, I would, no one would ever know...*' Something like that. I don't remember exactly, but it was enough to make me feel very much afraid they were planning something ... very, very stupid.'

'So you waited there at the lakeside until–'

'Until they both arrived, and until he left her. She had been, that night ... well, radiant, but now I could see something must have happened between the end of the party and then. I saw how upset she was, how upset they both were, in fact. Too much so for any romantic interlude, I thought. Then he ... he embraced her passionately, and left. She was in a storm of tears. I didn't know what was going on, or what to do. In the end I went over to her, asked her what was wrong and tried to comfort her. But she begged me to leave her alone. I refused at first, and said I would see her home, but she would have none of it, said she'd be quite safe. In fact, she was quite angry with me and pushed me away. And, God help me, I left her. It has haunted me ever since.'

The spirit-induced colour had left his face, and his brow was beaded with sweat. He looked wretched, and for the first time, Reardon felt pity for him. If he had told this in the first place, he could have saved everyone a lot of trouble. But Reardon had got what he wanted and kept his own counsel.

Chapter Twenty-Nine

Another night of heavy rain was followed by a morning so glittering it seemed to Amy that the whole earth had been rinsed clean. Birds sang, a hawthorn had burst into blossom overnight, and the sun dazzled from the puddles in the lane leading to the pottery. She tried to steer her bicycle to avoid them and the hem of her skirt grew soaked with brushing against the rain-soaked weeds alongside the edges, but she scarcely noticed.

'Is Steven in, Mrs Rafferty? He hasn't gone back to Cambridge yet?'

'Amy, how nice to see you! No, he's still here – he went to the village to post a letter and he took a book to read by the river on his way back. It's simply too lovely to stay indoors.'

'Oh, then I'll go and find him.'

'Stay a moment and tell me – I heard you had some storm damage, at the rectory.'

'A yew tree was struck and smashed through Susannah and the Elders.'

'Oh dear, the stained-glass window.' Mrs Rafferty tried to look sympathetic, but only succeeded in smiling. Amy warmed to her.

'Well, good riddance to the horrid old thing. The new window will be plain glass, thank goodness. It'll be so much nicer and lighter in the hall without it.'

'Yes, I suppose it might be a good thing out of

a bad one. No one was hurt, I hope?' she added, looking closely at Amy and thinking how subdued and pale she looked. Nothing like her usual bright and bouncy self.

'We were all in bed when it happened, but you never saw anything like it. Half the tree, right through the window. They had to saw the branches off where it was, and they're still chopping the trunk and the rest up outside now, Sam Noakes and his Uncle Ted. Well ... Mrs Rafferty, if you don't mind, I'll just walk down to find Steven. I have to see him, and then go back home to help. There's still a lot of clearing up to do.'

'Then take this with you.' His mother lifted a piece of oilcloth from a chair. 'It's very wet out there and I told Steven to take it with him to sit on, but of course he forgot. He'll get rheumatism, though I don't suppose he's noticed the wet.'

'I don't suppose he has,' Amy said, smiling faintly and taking the oilcloth.

'And call in on your way back. I made a big pot of soup this morning and I know you'll be at sixes and sevens at the rectory with no time to cook.' She patted Amy's shoulder and then, because she looked so woebegone, gave her a kiss.

His mother need not have worried. Even Steven could not avoid noticing how wet the ground was and he was half sitting, half propped, against what looked to be a rather uncomfortable rock, a book in his hands, but jumped up immediately when Amy came down the path. 'Amy! What brings you down here?'

'Oh, Steven!' she burst out straight away. 'I've

327

done such a terrible thing – what am I going to do?'

'Well, I think you'd better tell me what this terrible thing is first. What's that I see under your arm – the oilcloth I forgot?'

He spread it out for her and Amy sat down with her knees to her chin. He perched again on the large rock, opposite her, so that he could see her as she spoke. She hadn't bothered to put her hair up, just tied it back with its black bow, and she was wearing an old grey dress and no hat. That she – Amy! – didn't seem to have noticed how she looked was clear indication of how upset she really was. He watched her with concern.

'It was the storm,' she began, wanting to get it all off her chest before she panicked and took fright and bottled it all up inside her again, as she had done for upwards of five years. 'Nella found Marianne's notebooks, you know, the ones she was always writing in, and she's going to give them to that policeman who's back here because of the murder – oh, Steven, it's simply too awful!'

'Yes, poor Edith Huckaby. Who would have thought–'

'What? Oh, yes, Edith. Yes, that *is* shocking, of course, but...' She reached out and plucked a feathery stem of grass, running it top to bottom between her fingers, stripping it to the bare stem.

'But what?'

She looked up and her eyes were swimming with tears.

'Whatever's wrong?'

'Oh Steven, you must help me, I don't know

what I'm going to do, and you're always so ... reasonable.'

'Am I?' he said, oddly, looking down at her. 'However, I can't help if you don't start at the beginning and tell me sensibly what it's all about.'

She swallowed. 'I don't know what you'll think of me.'

He reached across and tucked her hand into his. His own hands were long and bony, but they held hers with a very warm and comforting grasp, and he smiled. 'No worse than I've always done, I don't suppose. Go on.'

'Well, you know, she discovered I'd been reading them, one day. Yes, I do know I shouldn't have done that, but I was curious, I wondered just what the big secret was. And – well, I read them again and that time she was very cross with me, I mean really *angry*, you know? I'd never seen Marianne so furious before. She said everyone in the family knew she wanted to keep her writing private and what right had I ... and oh, a lot more horrid things. She called me a silly little girl, and after that she used to stow them away somewhere secret.'

'And now, in some way that you haven't told me, Nella has found them and is going to hand them to the police–'

'That's not all,' Amy said in a small voice, scuffing the toe of her shoe into the damp sandy soil. He waited patiently, and after a moment, she went on. 'That night, after we got home from Oaklands, after Grandy's party, the night it happened – to Marianne, I mean. We went straight to bed but I woke up about an hour later feeling thirsty, and I went down for a drink of water – and there she was at the kitchen table, scribbling away. Just to tease her, I pretended to try and see what she was writing, though I wouldn't really have *looked*, not after she'd been so mad at me. After that time, she was always accusing me of prying, but this time she just told me to go away … Steven, she was *crying*. I asked her what was the matter, but she wouldn't tell me. She looked so sad, and unhappy, but then she kissed me and said she was sorry she'd been so cross with me lately, and told me to go back to bed.'

Amy herself looked unhappily down at the ground. She raised her eyes, full of unshed tears. 'When they … found her, next morning, I went into her room – not to pry, I swear, just to be there, do you know what I mean? I couldn't believe what had happened, well of course none of us could. And, you know, it was so awful, her room was in such a mess, when she always kept it much tidier than either Nella or me kept ours. The things she'd been wearing for the party were thrown all over the place just anyhow, her new cream shantung dress and her bronze party slippers and her seed pearl necklace and the rose Grev had given her, everything! It didn't seem right to leave them, somehow, so I just started to tidy things up a bit and that was when I found it.'

'What did you find?'

'The exercise book she'd been writing in at the kitchen table, the one I told you about. I think she left the house in such a hurry she forgot all about hiding it with the others Nella found. I …

330

haven't told Nella about this one.'

And where is it now?'

'In my stocking drawer, at the back. I've kept it ever since because ... because, I thought, one day, it might be ... useful.'

'Useful?'

The colour rose like a tide in Amy's neck. 'Well, I just thought if Aunt Sybil knew what I know, what Marianne had written, it might persuade her to let me ... you know, all the London thing with Eunice.'

Steven didn't let go of her hand, but for a long time he said nothing, just stared down at her. Then he said, 'There's a nasty word for that sort of thing, Amy.'

She looked chastened, sad and suddenly older. 'I know. I knew you'd think badly of me ... but I never have used it, and I never will, now. I don't think Eunice will ever agree to be brought out now anyway, and even if she does, I don't think I want to be part of it. It doesn't really seem to matter now, all that,' she added in a low voice. 'I suppose I can burn the book and nobody else but you need ever know about it. But do you think I should, Steven? Throw it away, I mean?'

'That surely depends on what was in it, doesn't it?'

'It was— No, I simply can't tell you – tell any-body – oh, I don't *know!* It doesn't seem possible that it really can have been true. Maybe she *was* only making it up...'

He said patiently, 'Amy, if you're sure you want my advice, then don't you think I should see this notebook?'

Still she hesitated. All right,' she said at last, reluctantly. 'I will let you see it. Oh, if only William were here, he'd know what to do, but he's not, and I know you'll help me.' Amy never had any doubts that everyone was ready to help her. 'Only promise me, Steven, you'll never breathe a word to *anyone* about it?' She added, almost under her breath, 'It was a very stupid idea, to think I could frighten Aunt Sybil, especially after all this time, especially now they're both dead.'

That afternoon, she stood outside her father's study as she had stood so many times before, in the shadow of the Susannah window. Only now that was gone and the space where it had been was empty, waiting for the new glass, which they said might be weeks in coming. The hall was exceedingly draughty without it, oddly empty and light, leaving nowhere to hide. Her palms were damp. She half turned to run away but she remembered the way Steven had looked at her when he said, tightly holding her hands, 'You know what you must do, Amy, without me telling you.'

'Steven, how can I? You don't know my father!'

'What can he do to you?'

It wasn't that she was *afraid* of him, she told herself, or not all the time, only when he was in one of those cold, unapproachable moods he could fall into, especially since Marianne died. And only she had known why.

She put her free hand over her breast, as if it would still the hammering of her heart, which she would have sworn she could actually *hear*, then somehow the hand seemed to find its own way towards the door and give a knock.

'Who is it?'

'It's Amy.' Her voice came out in a whisper, but it was loud enough for him to hear.

'Come in, child.'

Encouraged by what sounded to be his approachable tone, she stepped into the room that could still make her feel like a terrified eight-year-old. The musty smell of old books, the absence of anything pretty or interesting to look at, only those shelves crammed with old tomes, and the tatty old brown sofa which had belonged to Reverend Dorkings and which her father refused to have re-covered. The small, meagre fire smouldering in the grate, giving out no heat. She had no idea how to begin, but of course she might have known that in this case there would be no need for her to say anything. His eyes were drawn immediately to the marbled cover of the notebook she was clutching. But he said nothing, simply waited for her to begin.

'This notebook...' she began at last. There was a long pause. 'It's Marianne's,' she explained, unnecessarily. Another pause. He waited before making a reply until the church clock finished sounding eleven, followed, a moment behind, by the fussy little strike of the one on the mantel, then faintly, from the kitchen, more unmusical bongs. The clocks in this house never did synchronise.

'Where did you find it?' he said at last. His tone was no longer encouraging.

'It wasn't – exactly – lost, Father.'

'I see. Then where have you been keeping it?'

She stared silently at her shoes, wishing with all her heart that she had never seen the wretched book. 'Come, Amy, the truth. Why have you kept it hidden, when you knew we were looking for your sister's books?'

The habit of not lying to her father, the fear, was too strong. 'Because of what she had written in it.' There followed another long silence. Queenie, as if sensing the atmosphere, began to pad uneasily from one to the other. Amy put her hand on the dog's head, taking comfort from the feel of the thick, warm fur as she pushed her fingers through it, until Queenie drew back and went to flop down at Francis's feet. He finally made a move. Stiffly, he indicated that she might put the book down on his desk. She did so. 'Where are the other notebooks?'

'I never had those, Father, but Nella has found them, in the attic. I-I think she has given them to the policeman, to Inspector Reardon.'

His frown darkened. 'Indeed. Then will you please go and find Nella and your grandmother and ask them to come in here? You will not say anything of what has passed between us, do you understand? Leave the notebook with me.'

She fled.

'Bless you, child, what's the matter?' said Mrs Villiers, taking Amy by the shoulders and looking anxiously into her white face. 'Are you ill?'

Amy thought she very well might be. She had imagined she would feel better, after getting rid of the notebook which had lain like an unexploded bomb, facing her every time she opened the drawer for a clean pair of stockings. But she felt worse now, certain that the bomb was about to blow up in her face. All she could say was that Father wanted to see them all directly, in his study.

Nella asked sharply, 'Why?' But Amy, mindful of that cold command, dare not say.

He was standing in typical pose, looking out of the window, his back to the room, his hands clasped behind his back, when they all three went into his study, but the notebook was not in the same place on the desk where she had left it and Amy knew he had opened it and read what was written there.

He turned when they came in and said, quite gently, 'Perhaps we should all sit down.' He took his own seat in the chair before his desk; the only other chair was piled high with a dangerous tower of books and pamphlets, and since there were no other seats than the lumpy sofa, they were all three compelled to sit on it. The cushions were covered in a corded brown velvet so old and thin it had grown bald in patches; there were hairs where Queenie had illicitly curled herself when no one else was in the room, and Mrs Villiers took her seat with distaste. Nella perched on the very edge, her eyes riveted on the desk.

'It seems that we have something of a family problem to resolve.' Francis indicated the exercise book. 'The nature of which will be made clear when Amy reads to us what is written there.'

'Father, no! Oh no, I couldn't.' Amy went white, her freckles standing out like stains.

'Since you are obviously familiar with the contents, I don't see that as an impossible task.' He smiled. Amy was not the only one who was frightened by it.

'No! Please don't make me.' She began to shake.

'What is this, Francis? Why are you intimidating your daughter in this way?'

'Read it to us, Amy.'

Nella could bear it no longer. She suddenly stood up and marched to the desk. 'I'll read it, whatever it is.' She picked up the exercise book and glanced inside. 'There doesn't seem to be much, anyway.'

'Stop!' cried Mrs Villiers, also standing up and snatching the book from her in a most uncharacteristic way. 'There is no need for anyone to read it aloud. If it contains what I think it does...' She turned the cover back, skimmed over what was written in Marianne's large, schoolgirl handwriting on the first page. 'I thought so.' Her direct glance met that of Francis. 'Read it, Nella – to yourself – then we shall *all* know what we are talking about, without all this unnecessary melodrama.' Thrusting the book at Nella, she sat back on the sofa, scarcely noticing the lumps in the cushions this time.

So, it had come at last. The fear that had remained tight within her all this time, that eventually would come to light what had happened during that strained time between her daughter Dorothea and Francis. Those three years immediately after Dorothea's near brush with death at William's birth, when she had been terrified of having another child. The numerous times when Francis had left his wife alone to join the famous shooting parties at Oaklands. Eleanor had at first been pleased that he had found a way of getting rid of his frustrations by way of these sporting weekends, in the sort of male company which did not encourage introspection and guilt feelings, until she had found out that Sybil had been present at most of them, too.

She blamed herself for not taking more notice of what was happening years later, also, during that summer before the war. Marianne had looked radiant, she should have known it was the glow of a girl in love. But it was not until the night of her own seventieth birthday party, when she had seen them together at the piano, Marianne and Grev, that Eleanor had even suspected. And after Marianne's death, become convinced. Many things had still puzzled her, even so, and it was only now, after that quick glance she had given to those few damning words Marianne had written, that she realised exactly what had happened that night, how it explained everything: Grev's abrupt departure, Marianne's drowning.

She had only needed to give that first page of the notebook one quick glance. The image of all that was written there had burnt itself on to her retina, so that it danced before her eyes: Marianne and Grev, that night, had been told the truth by their respective parents, Francis and Lady Sybil. How could those two grown-ups have been so unthinking, compounding the follies of their youth with the cruelty of middle-aged necessity? If the truth had to be told (and Eleanor believed that it should have been brought out into the open long before then) ... if the truth had to be told, then it should have been done differently, not in a manner which could

337

not fail to hurt two vulnerable young people.

It did not take Nella long to read the disjointed and haphazard outpouring of Marianne's scribbled sentences on the first page of the notebook: *'Tonight, Father has ruined my life. No happiness now for me, or for Grev.* My brother! *Why did they not tell us, before? Aunt Sybil – and my father. Dishonouring my mother and living a lie all these years. A man in his position. They have both lived a lie. I promised to slip out and meet Grev tonight. In less than an hour, now. He laughed and said I wouldn't dare, but I really meant to. I cannot, not now. Yes, I will. I* must *see him again. But what are we to say to each other? How are we to carry on, feeling as we do?'*

She turned the page. There was nothing more. She stood, her face blank with disbelief, as white as Amy's, speechless, feeling as though all the breath had been knocked out of her body by a giant fist. The world went on outside: a vehicle drew up on the gravel, probably to collect the debris of the tree, the sound of sawing stopped. The front doorbell, Florrie would get it. And Nella asked herself why she, of all the people in the room, had been the only one not to know. The one who might have been expected, out of them all, to have worked it out for herself.

The policeman, Reardon, had told them that the Gypsy, Daniel Boswell, had actually seen Marianne lose her balance, her arms flailing in an attempt to save herself as she felt the rotten boards of the jetty collapsing under her, and heard her scream. But this – this thing she had just learnt – this added another dimension to the story: whatever had happened, right at the very end, Marianne must have run along the jetty, after what she had just learnt, with every intention of letting the deep water take her instantly. After all, if one did not consider it first, it could seem an easy, swift and sure way to end a life. Until it came to the point...

The set of her son-in-law's mouth showed Eleanor he had reached one of his stubborn conclusions. 'You know what I must do,' he said. 'The police must have this, since I understand they have the rest of Marianne's notebooks.'

Eleanor looked at him sitting there, the light of martyrdom in his eyes, and she thought, outraged, surely this is too much. All these years, Francis had kept it up, indulging himself in guilt for his own misbehaviour, and for Dorothea's death. Enduring patiently, paying for his sins, and making his family pay, too. He never had been able to see his way through the thorny thicket of blame and forgiveness. 'Give it to the police, Francis?' she cried. 'You will do no such thing!'

Nella was rallying, too, could scarcely believe her ears at what she was hearing. Was her father entirely mad? Providing Reardon with two ready-made suspects for Edith's murder? Edith could never have seen this last notebook, of course, but what if she had somehow wormed out the secret from Lady Sybil, and threatened to tell? She stood, white-faced, still clutching the notebook. It felt alive, like a serpent in her hand. Suddenly, she flung it, as hard as she could, into the fire.

For a moment or two it sat on the miserable little heap of coals without catching alight. There was an appalled silence in the room as they watched the covers slowly begin to curl upwards. Then at the moment when it seemed as though the pages must burst into flames, Francis thrust his hand in, snatched the book back and threw it onto the hearth.

He bowed his head, nursing his hand as if the fire had scorched it, though there had not been enough heat for that.

'I'm sorry, Father.'

'It doesn't matter, Nella. It's over. The secrecy. I would not have had any of you find out this way, but I am glad, after all, that you know.'

They were all on their feet now, standing like figures in a tableau, as Francis still sought for words, when the door opened and four pairs of eyes turned towards it. It took a moment for it to register with anyone that the person who stood there was William.

He was here. He'd come back, war-weary, but safe and sound, and he'd come straight to her, Eunice, first, before even going home. Safe and sound in wind and limb, and wholly hers in heart and mind. They had kept faith throughout the war, and William had come home to her. She felt to be enclosed in a blaze of glory.

They were standing in the orangery when Sybil saw them. Facing each other, close, close together, hands clasped. He was looking down at Eunice with an expression she could not fail to recognise. So that at last she understood a good many things that had puzzled her lately about Eunice. Something in her began to ache, but in that moment, quietly, with a barely perceptible sigh, she accepted the inevitable, relinquished the matrimonial hopes for her daughter she had cherished so long.

Chapter Thirty

'Witch', he used to call her.

'Do you know what my name means?' she had demanded of the twelve-year-old Ben. 'I do, I've looked it up. Sybil: a prophetess, fortune-teller, a witch, that's what it says.'

'I'll call you "Witch", then. T'others don't suit you.'

So that's who she'd been, Witch, in those childhood years, when he had been Ben, her boon companion. Now he was Naylor, her head gamekeeper, middle-aged, awkward, twisting his cap in his hands. 'I just wanted to say, m'lady, you can rely on me. I won't say nothing. About what I saw, Monday night.'

Ben had seen? A sudden painful lurch in her chest, and the blood draining from her extremities. She said, carefully, inadequately, through stiff lips, 'Thank you, Naylor, I won't forget that. But *you* must – *whatever* happens.' He nodded and walked away to prevent any further embarrassment. Before he reached the door she said, 'I'm sorry about Edith, Ben, very sorry.'

He turned and for a moment she thought she saw a flash of – what, anger? – in his eyes. 'Yes, m'lady.'

And then he was gone, leaving her shaken and confused. Don't panic. Rest assured. His promise meant that he still, as she did, treasured and would not deny fond memories of that idyllic, carefree, unthinking childhood they'd shared, almost-brother and almost-sister, gleeful at breaking the rules and avoiding authority. Halcyon days, in retrospect.

She had been fiercely resentful at being sent away from Oaklands by her father, when she became fifteen, to live with Aunt Charlotte and her silly girl cousins, to be made into a young lady. First her hair, then her clothes. Her complexion. Her speech. 'Lord, what has Broughton been thinking of? It's quite a little hobbledehoy! Look at her hands!' cried Aunt Charlotte, almost in a swoon with horror. Piano lessons, dancing lessons, French lessons, all of them hated. Then, being brought out ... parties, dances, lovely clothes, young men. It had suddenly become quite fun, and a little wild.

What wasn't so much fun was Oaklands. Her father had begun to take notice of her when she blossomed and he saw how she could become an asset to him, and he commandeered her to act as hostess for him at his weekend shooting parties. She had come back to Oaklands and seen with new eyes her old home's dilapidation, and grieved over it more than she did over her father's descent into drunken stupors every night, his gambling away money he didn't have, and the way both were ruining him. She saw that what was needed was money, and did her best to do what her father wanted and entertain his guests, being charming

to those he had his eye on as suitable matches –
suitable in his eyes but not in hers. They were all
wrong, in one way or another: rich but ugly;
handsome but penniless; charming but feckless.
Francis Wentworth, a distant relative of sorts, was
none of these, but neither could he be considered
as a suitor, since he was already married, with a
wife he adored and a baby son. He had the dan-
gerously seductive looks of a beautiful, unattain-
able, medieval young monk, pale and thin faced,
with an expression of suffering in his dark eyes. He
was fighting demons at that moment in his life.
Unthinkable she should allow that to continue...

In later years, she looked at Grev, and saw the
same dark eyes, the same sensitive face, trembled
and wondered that no one else saw the likeness.
Perhaps it was not as apparent as she feared. Or
perhaps those who saw it wisely said nothing. She
would give twenty years of her life, or all that
remained of it, to see that face now.

At the Greville Arms, in the office they had set up
there, Reardon heard the sound of an engine,
looked out of the open window and saw drawing
to a halt a motor car with a long bonnet and a
strap around it. A young man's motor car, a
yellow-painted, sporty Martini, covetable. Sud-
denly, every boy in the village seemed mira-
culously to appear, to stare and jostle round the
phenomenon of such a spectacle, here in Brough-
ton. A tall man jumped from it, followed by
Eunice Foley, with a scarf tied round her hat.
There was all at once much talking and laughter
and Sam coming out of the door to greet them.

343

The two men pumped hands and beamed at each other and the driver was gesturing towards the motor Sam was admiring and telling him, 'Used to belong to a friend – I went to see his parents on the way home and took it off their hands. Oh, she's beautiful, runs sweet as a nut. Nothing wrong except two flat tyres on the way, but blame the roads for that.'

He was broad-shouldered and long-legged, this tall young man, in a pre-war suit that now hung loose on him, clean-shaven and with a thatch of reddish hair that told Reardon this might be William Wentworth. The sender of the Mizpah brooch, he concluded, looking at Eunice's face.

A few minutes later, they came into the parlour. William shook hands with Reardon and said, after Eunice had introduced him, 'I got home yesterday and came as soon as I could. My sister – Nella, that is – thinks you'd like a word with me. She's sorry she can't be here herself, but she's on duty.'

When they were all seated, he said directly, 'I gather you're anxious to know what happened to Rupert von Kessel. Well, I can tell you because I wrote to him, care of his parents, after the Armistice. We'd been close before the war, you know, school and all that, and I'd spent one or two vacations with his people in Salzburg, where they'd always made me pretty comfortable, so it seemed...' He paused awkwardly. 'Well, they wrote back to tell me he didn't make it through the war.'

'I'm sorry.'

'Yes. I'd always wondered if he ever got out of England and back to Salzburg, though I felt it was more than likely he had, being Kess. One way or another. Legally or illegally, bribes or whatever was needed,' he added with a wry grin. 'He spoke near-perfect English, after all, and he had plenty of money, so it was quite possible he could have got across the Channel. And so he did, and straight away joined the Imperial Army – the Tyrolean Kaiserjäger Battalion, to be precise.'

'Those who fought in the Alps against the Italians?'

'That's right. Splendid chaps, weren't they? For all they were on the other side. Unspeakable conditions during the winter – but Rupert wouldn't have let that worry him, nor the danger, either. He'd climbed the mountains since he was a boy, with his father, and loved them... We spent several holidays together climbing there. He was killed in the Trentino offensive in 1916. Got a gong for bravery, which won't surprise anyone – if he had to go, I think that's the way he would have chosen.'

Reardon realised the laconic statement hid a lot, that it was the way this young fellow, his eyes older than his years, like all of them who'd gone through it, covered his feelings. Reardon liked the cut of his jib, as the sailors said. Young bloke, straight from public school, no doubt, and into the hellfire war, which had made a man of him, as it had done for many who eventually were lucky enough to come out of it. Officer material. The sort of officer Reardon would have been happy to serve under, never mind he was but a lad. Boys grew into men swiftly, over there.

'Thank you for coming to see us, and so

promptly. I appreciate it.'

William hesitated. 'There's something else,' he said, and now he looked embarrassed. His neck reddened above the too loose collar. 'I seem to have walked right into a family situation which might have some bearing on this wretched case you're investigating.'

He looked a good deal more uneasy about the prospect of speaking about that than about what he'd had to tell Reardon before. Death, and war, he had learnt to cope with, but family scandals were a different kettle of fish. And then, although Reardon thought he knew what was coming, William surprised him. 'My father would like to see you, if you can spare the time.'

They were told by the housekeeper that Francis Wentworth could be found in the church when they went along to the rectory an hour later.

The little, grey stone church with its squat tower stood a dozen or so yards from the main path through the churchyard, where ancient, lichened gravestones leant and where thousands of daffodils spread between the tombstones and stood thickly along the edges of the paths, a few already in flower, the swollen buds of the rest waiting to burst into bloom. 'Must be a rare sight when they're all out,' commented Wheelan, a bit of a gardener when he had any spare time.

'"*Continuous as the stars that shine.*"'

Reardon received an odd look for that, but merely smiled as he pushed open the grainy, weathered oak door of the ancient church. Inside, a pinafored woman was just getting ready to leave,

346

buttoning up her coat, picking up a basket of cleaning things. 'The rector? You'll find him up at the front.' She pointed down the nave, beyond the rows of bench pews to where several old box pews stood, their high panelling intended in less enlightened times to provide privacy and protect the wealthy occupants from draughts.

Typical church smells assailed them as they walked down the aisle. Damp, ancient stone, dry woodwork, candle wax and brass polish, and a slight smell of burning oil as they neared the front – perhaps from the sanctuary lamp glowing red over the altar.

Francis Wentworth had been sitting in his church, the old Saxon church he had come to love, in the Broughton box pew, alone with his thoughts while Mrs Wright busied herself with cleaning the brasses and polishing the lectern. Before that, he had been on his knees for an hour in front of the altar, and now he felt a kind of peace, of the sort he had not known since he first entered the ministry, a young man full of hope and fervent with the love of God. Odd, how the murder of someone he had scarcely known had brought this about, in this church where Grevilles were laid to rest. He stared at the Greville arms, emblazoned on one of the open doors of this pew, big enough to hold a family, its place prominent near the pulpit, its woodwork elaborately carved. On the wall above was a plaque to Elizabeth Greville, Sybil's mother, who had died too young. No memorial to Grev: he had borne the name of Foley, the man who had been the best of fathers to him, important in everything that mattered.

He heard a murmur of voices, heavy footsteps ringing on the stones as the two policemen came down the aisle. He rose and extended a hand, invited them to take a seat. He was well enough disposed towards this man who had finally vanquished the bugbear of Marianne's death, even though the way she died was not something either Francis or any of his family had ever really disputed.

'It seems, Inspector, that things have moved on since our last conversation a couple of weeks ago, when you spoke to us about my daughter, Marianne. I believe, since you are now looking for reasons for poor Edith Huckaby's death, you may find this ... of some use.' He spoke without a tremor but his hand shook slightly as he offered Reardon yet another of the marbled-covered exercise books which Nella had passed on to him. 'I think you will find it is self-explanatory.'

'Thank you.' Reardon took the notebook but did not offer to read it now, since he had no doubt what it contained. He had not found the others very readable, though they had demonstrated that the rector's daughter Marianne had not been discreet – and that Edith had been skilful in taking advantage of this. The relationship between the two young women had evidently been somewhat more intimate than most people had believed. Marianne had seemed to regard Edith as a mentor: *'Edith thinks this ... Edith says that...'* had appeared more than once after some piece of writing, or beside some little secret Marianne had confided to the books.

'You will realise when you read it how difficult this is for me,' the rector went on in a low voice. 'I have given it to you because I feel you should be acquainted with all the facts, and know that in this affair I am not blameless, but I trust you will not jump to conclusions because of that.'

'It is not up to me to judge, sir.'

'Certain inferences might seem obvious, but that poor young woman's death... We live in a lawless society, Inspector. Men have been trained to kill, and learnt that life is cheap.'

The scent of the flowers in a tall vase on the chancel steps, the smell of brass polish, were suddenly sickening. Reardon, who had begun to feel some sympathy for Frances Wentworth, said stiffly, 'I dare say there may be some who look at it that way, as they've always done, but I think most men who fought at the front, in spite of everything, would believe that life is very dear indeed.'

The rector said immediately, 'I apologise. It is I who am jumping to conclusions now.' He held out his hand. After a moment, Reardon took it, and for the first time in their acquaintance, saw the rector smile, albeit one that seemed infinitely sad.

Protocol had gone by the board since Oaklands had become a hospital. No pulling the front doorbell and waiting for the butler to answer it. The door stood wide open to a hall as big as the ground floor area of the average home. Reardon was about to step inside when he saw and heard the yellow Martini scrunch up the gravel drive and draw to a halt. Out of it stepped Eunice

Foley, and a sturdy young woman in a sensible hat, albeit one that did nothing to conceal the mass of golden hair that tumbled from beneath it. Eunice took her by the elbow and they disappeared around the corner with a wave to William Wentworth, who drove off again in the direction of the main road. No doubt this was the girl Eunice had spoken about, engaged to the patient in the wheelchair. She was very persuasive, Eunice Foley, as he had reason to know. No one else he had encountered since his own disfigurement had ever made him give serious thought to Ellen Calder's feelings, rather than his own, in the matter of their relationship. It disturbed him more than he liked to think.

He stepped into the hall. Doors opened off it in every direction, indicating possibilities beyond. As he stood there, orientating himself according to the layout he had earlier tried to fix in his mind, wondering which door led to the small sitting room where Lady Sybil had previously received him, a brisk nurse appeared.

'Can I help you?'

'I'm looking for Lady Sybil.'

'Sorry, I can't help you, but here's someone who will. Elsie!'

Obviously one of the household, rather than the hospital staff, a pert blonde young woman in a housemaid's cap and apron, armed with dustpan, brush and dusters, was crossing the back of the hall and came forward. The nurse smiled and went on her way and Reardon repeated his request to the maid to see Lady Sybil.

'Stay here, I'll get her for you. I think she's in

the music room.'

'No need to keep you from your duties. Point me in the right direction, and I'll find her myself.'

'No!' she said quickly. 'No, you can't do that, not the music room. You stay here.'

'Wait a moment. First, will you show me where Mr Foley's study is?'

'It's just here.' She gave him a sharp look, and pointed to a door on the right.

'I'll just take a look inside.'

'Well, sir, I don't know if–'

'It's all right, Elsie, I just want to take a look.'

She obviously didn't trust policemen, and stayed with him while he opened the door. He didn't need to take more than a step inside to see all he wanted to see – a corner room, which was a mirror to Lady Sybil's sitting room on the opposite side of the house, handsomely furnished with a bank of well-stocked bookshelves, a big mahogany desk, comfortable leather club chairs with dark-green velvet cushions and floor-length velvet curtains to match.

'Thank you, Elsie,' he said as he stepped back into the hall and she closed the door behind him. 'I'll wait here until you find Lady Sybil.'

The inspector with the war-scarred face knew. It was the second time he had looked searchingly at the photograph Arthur had taken that summer day when they, her family, and all the Wentworths had been together, for a tennis party. The first time had been when he'd talked to her and Eunice, just after Edith's body had been discovered. Something inside her did that sickening, downward

351

plunge again – her heart, in all probability.

'And how are your enquiries progressing, Inspector?' she asked as steadily as she could when they were seated.

'Satisfactorily, I believe. We are not quite there, yet, but not far off ... it's all taking us back a long way, Lady Sybil. As far back as 1914, in fact. I would like to talk to you about a party you held here about then, on the eve of the war.'

'So long ago? Surely not...'

'Past events have their repercussions. You do remember that party?'

'Of course I do. It was Eleanor Villiers's birthday, and the day her grandson left to join his regiment. So good that he is home again, at last. Dear William, we're all so fond of him.' She fumbled a cigarette from the silver box on the same small table that held the photo, inserted it into an ivory holder and lit it with an onyx lighter, trying to avoid looking at the photograph. She held out the box towards him.

'I don't, thank you. Lady Sybil, I'm afraid I am going to have to ask you some questions which are bound to be painful and upsetting... That time, the night of the party, was the last time you saw your son, I believe?'

'Need you remind me of that?' she asked in a low voice.

'I am indeed sorry to do so, but the facts must be faced if we are to find the true reason why Miss Huckaby died. I'll come straight to the point. Your son had fallen in love with Marianne Wentworth and she with him, and he left, did he not, because he learnt the truth?'

Briefly, she closed her eyes. 'What truth is that, Inspector?'

'I think you know what I mean,' he said gently. 'The truth about his birth. That Mr Foley was not, in fact, his father.'

'That is ... quite unpardonable conjecture.'

'I am sorry if you find it unpardonable, but it is not conjecture. It has come from the Wentworth family, from the rector himself, the Reverend Mr Wentworth.'

From Francis, thought Sybil. *Francis*. Her thoughts whirled. So, he had succumbed, after all. Why, when they had by mutual consent – except for that one, disastrous revelation – kept this skeleton concealed in their respective cupboards for so long? But since he had, however, seemingly chosen to admit to a secret that was as much hers as his, might she not at least have expected his support now? An almost hysterical laugh caught in her throat. So typical of Francis, another retreat into self-flagellation.

'That was what Edith Huckaby was blackmailing you about, was it not? She found out and threatened to make it public.'

She had long since ceased to feel that would matter – except to one person. Her husband, however, was not here, for which she was truly thankful.

She said, through stiff lips, 'Very well.' She knew now she had no alternative but to give what explanation she could. Keep calm, she told herself, stop this trembling inside. There is no proof, nothing. Nothing to worry about. Ben Naylor has promised to keep to himself what he saw, and if Ben makes a promise to me, he keeps it. 'Very well, Inspector...'

All evening, the evening of that party no one would ever forget, she had been uneasily aware that Arthur might not have been feeling well. To anyone else it might not have been apparent: he seemed to be his usual dryly spoken, good-humoured self, but she knew the times were worrying him, and that he was overworking, and she kept an anxious eye on him. She could have wished he had not been witness to that upsetting altercation between Grev and the Austrian in the little sitting-out room, but at least she was able to urge him to his bed as soon as the guests had gone. She and Eunice had seen him comfortably settled, and then she had gone to her room to wait for Grev.

Brushing her hair before the mirror, she heard the murmur of a few words her son exchanged with Edith, who was still tidying her boudoir before retiring to her own bed. When he came through into her bedroom, she was sitting in front of her mirror in a peach silk peignoir trimmed with black lace which she had afterwards thrown away, not able to bear looking at it. He took the silver-backed brush from her and stood behind her and began to brush the long dark hair, smiling at her reflection. It was years since he had done this, as he used to love to do when he was a small boy.

'What was it you wanted to see me about, Mother? Other than reproaching me with hitting one of our guests.'

'Well, that was unpardonable, you bad boy, and you know it.' But she smiled at him, she couldn't help it.

'I do know. But he accepted my apologies. We're friends once more,' he replied, tongue firmly in his cheek.

She took the brush from him and laid it with a nervous click on the dressing table. 'Come and sit by the fire, darling. There is something I wish to talk to you about.'

The subsequent half-hour was one she was to remember, and regret, for the rest of her life.

'Well, of course, Inspector' she finished, 'as you have probably guessed, Edith hadn't gone away when Grev came in. She stayed, and listened and heard everything. Though she never said she had, except by a look or implication.'

'But she did, however, ask for payment – those jewels, or money, perhaps?'

'Oh no, she was too clever for that. I suppose she thought if she was too demanding my patience would eventually snap, and I would let her do her worst and face the music. Especially after Grev died. What did it matter to me, then? But I couldn't do that – not to my husband. He has a weak heart, you know, and he loved Grev so much. To learn that he was not his son would have killed him. No, Edith never actually *asked* for anything. She would simply pick up a small trinket and admire it, until I got the point and told her to keep it. If I gave her an order she didn't feel inclined to obey, she would smile, and simply look at me. But yes, the word was

355

certainly blackmail.' She took a long, considering look at him. She stood up and walked across to the fireplace, and stood facing him, her arms crossed over her breast, as though she were suddenly cold. 'And then quite suddenly, the other night, I thought, this tyranny must stop.'

The long nose of Arthur Foley's Daimler emerged through the factory gates and the motor car picked up a little speed as it left behind the smoke and grime of the Black Country towns and began to bowl smoothly into the countryside and towards Oaklands. He sat back in the crimson leather interior, trying to relax, willing away the sense of doom. He had felt distinctly unwell these last few days, and that business of Edith Huckaby had done nothing to help. He was not unprepared for the eventuality that another heart attack, possibly more severe than the first, would come sooner or later, probably sooner. But, please God, not yet. Not quite yet. There were things to set right before he let go and slipped off this mortal coil.

Oh, Sybil, why did you do it?

Though she had, God only knew, danced to that young woman's tune long enough. For over four years, he calculated, viewing the affair in retrospect. If only she had seen fit to tell him, when it all began! He had, of course, known something was wrong, but not until recently had he begun to suspect just how bad it was, or what it might be. Although he was not a man to allow anything of that sort to carry on and affect his family for longer than necessary, he had refrained from saying anything as long as possible because he had hoped Sybil herself would eventually tell him.

He closed his eyes, willing himself to relax, let himself drift, and was carried back once more to the hours after that fateful party on the eve of the war, which he had endured for Sybil's sake until the guests were leaving...

Feeling a great deal better after a short rest in bed, where his wife and daughter had tucked him in like a damned invalid, deciding to get up and go along to see Sybil to say goodnight properly, talk over the party as they always did. Not intending to stay long because he realised, as he made his way on what seemed to have suddenly become an endless journey down a long, long corridor, that he maybe ought not to have tried it; that he was in fact still not feeling up to the mark after all the jollifications. Not feeling up to the mark at all. Reaching the door of Sybil's room just as Grev stormed out of it, his face white and his eyes blazing. Throwing off Arthur's hand as if it was a brand. Edith had noticed that, damn her. She was pottering about in the boudoir, preparing the nightcap she always made for Sybil on the little spirit stove kept in the corner, but her eyes were bright with curiosity (why had he never noticed before what sharp, knowing eyes she had?). Putting two and two together from what she'd overheard between mother and son, and making five, no doubt. He'd never liked the wench, an ungrateful young woman for whom Sybil had done a thousand kindnesses. Why had he not ignored her then and gone in to Sybil, after all? Because all of a sudden he had been feeling much worse – much more than just not the ticket. Hardly able to get back to his room and into bed before the pain really took him in its grip, in fact. By then panting, scarcely able to reach the bell to call for someone to help him.

Oh God, the same pressure in his chest he was feeling now, the same panic. Don't let me die now ... don't mind dying, been prepared for it long enough after all, affairs all in order ... but not now, leaving Sybil with all this. Not now. Summon up the strength from somewhere. Surprising where it comes from, when you need it most...

His groping hand found the amyl nitrite ampoules he had been told always to keep in his pocket and he crushed one in his fingers, inhaled. Better. Much better. Gradually, he was able to relax. He closed his eyes but, unbidden and un-wanted, Monday night came back ... himself at the chess table with Eunice, after their early dinner. They were talking desultorily between moves about the visit she and Sybil were to take the following day to London. He was teasing Eunice about spending his money. All pretence, of course. His beautiful daughter could have all he possessed, and more. He allowed her to let him win the game, before she went to her room to write letters and he went about his own business.

Later, a good deal later, fortified by the whisky and water Ellington brought him each night, he went up to say goodnight to Sybil. He opened the door gently. The lights were out. He whispered her name, then saw her bed was empty.

He went to look for her and found her – where else? – in the room that was almost a shrine, the

358

music room, surrounded by all Grev's music paraphernalia. Cradling in her arms like a baby the viol she had given him for a present, that Christmas when early music had been his current passion.

That had been the last Christmas Day they had all spent together – Sybil, he and the children – and the Wentworths, of course, who were practically family and always came across to Oaklands at Christmas. The huge fir tree in the hall decorated with bright baubles, silver ribbons and candles. All the women dressed in their best, Sybil outshining the rest in some midnight-blue and silver tissue creation with a diamond-held feather in her hair, dazzling not only him. Presents for all under the tree. Grev playing his new instrument for them, his dark, serious face explaining how it differed from the modern violin, how it had once been played in what was called a consort, six viols making, a whole consort. Less than six, or different instruments in the group, and it was a broken consort. A broken consort. Of the one which had made up the group of Grev's friends, two of them were gone. He stepped into the music room and walked towards his wife.

'Oh, Arthur, what have I done?' she asked shakily.

'My dearest love,' he answered in a voice no one else but Sybil ever heard him use. 'I know what you've done. Did you believe I haven't always known?'

'You see, Inspector,' Sybil said, 'things had reached the point where there was no choice. I

359

had to stop it.'

Her eyes were large and luminous with emotion in her white face. She had begun to pace the room as if she couldn't keep still. 'We had all heard that someone had once again been making enquiries about Marianne's drowning. It was supposed to have been an accident, but how could I, of all people, believe that?' she asked. 'Did you know that Grev never once wrote to me after he left? To the family as a whole, yes, but not to me, personally. That's what has haunted me, that he died without ever forgiving me ... that he might never have died at all had he not been forced away by what he'd learnt from me – though in all conscience, I cannot think what else we could have done.' She sank onto a sofa and sat with bowed head. Minutes passed in silence, but when she looked up again she was calmer, her face resolute.

'That night, Monday, I could simply stand Edith's insinuations no longer. I don't believe she was aware that I knew she went down to see Ben Naylor most nights when she was free, or perhaps she did, and didn't care. I waited until she left me and then I dressed again and went down the path and waited for her, under the trees, until she came past and then I ... then I hit her, and hit her, and hit her.' She covered her face with her hands.

'What weapon did you use? What did you hit her with?' Reardon asked after a moment.

She looked up quickly. 'With the handle of her umbrella. I snatched it from her and began to hit her. And then, I–I just did not seem to be able to stop.'

'Lady Sybil. Edith Huckaby was killed with a single blow to her skull.'

'A single blow? What do you mean? That's not possible.'

'With the right instrument, and enough force, it's entirely possible.'

'Oh. Oh, I see. It was the first blow that killed her. Then I need not have...' Her voice trailed off.

He thought, how foolish we are sometimes, all of us. Especially when it's to protect someone we love. The confessions she'd made wouldn't stand up for a minute, which she must have known had she not been blinded by the need to save her husband.

'Lady Sybil,' he said gently, 'your husband told me he saw Miss Huckaby pass his study window at quarter past eight, but that's impossible, you know. It was pitch-dark by then, he would have seen only the reflection of the room in the dark glass – and in any case, that is the wrong side of the house. Yes, I believe he did see Edith – but earlier, perhaps when he was playing chess with your daughter. And when Miss Foley left him, he immediately followed Edith.'

'No, no!'

'I believe he did it on the spur of the moment. He knew, or guessed, what was going on between you and decided to put an end to it.'

He had thought she was about to faint, but she rallied. She stood up and faced him, her hands gripping the edge of a chair, her head held high. 'You will never be able to prove it.'

He thought, a flickering thought, that she might very well be right that this, his first case, was not going to leave him covered in glory. Edith had died, possibly not through any deliberate intention to kill her, but in a moment of uncontrollable anger directed against her for the years of misery she had inflicted on her mistress ... but what was there to prove this?

Whatever she had done, whatever misery and anguish she had inflicted, however, she had not in any way deserved to die. And how far had his own self-appointed investigations into Marianne's death contributed? But this, the path of guilt and remorse, was one he refused to take. Others in this particular case had walked it before him, with what consequences?

It was something he was going to have to accept, along with the knowledge that Edith's death might well be indirectly due to his wilful perusal of the way Marianne had died, which had provided her with an even stronger hold over Lady Sybil.

At that moment, the door burst open with an unceremoniousness surely unprecedented in this house, and the abrupt advent into the room of Garbutt, the chauffeur. His round, doughy face was the colour of cold porridge. 'It's the master. Come quick, m'lady, they've gone to find a doctor. Come quick, it's the master!'

Arthur Foley was still in his limousine, slumped against the cushions. His face was livid, distorted. His wife raised him and held him in a sitting position, trying with her other hand to find his ampoules, not knowing which pocket they were in. A whispered sound came from him, almost unintelligible, uttered with great difficulty, something which sounded like '...better...'

'Yes, yes, my dearest, you *will* be better soon. The doctor will be here, any minute. Where is he, where is the doctor?' she flung over her shoulder. Her husband tried to speak again and struggled to move. 'Hush, hush, be still. Just be still.'

'No! No! ... letter ... !'

Duncan Geddes emerged from the house at speed and climbed in beside them, bending over the stricken man. Arthur Foley's body quivered, his eyes became unfocused, and finally he sank.

'Lady Sybil,' said Duncan, laying his hand on hers, 'I'm so sorry, it's too late. I'm afraid he's gone.'

Chapter Thirty-One

April had arrived and although it was still very cold, and dull today, in the churchyard it didn't seem so, with the thousands of daffodils now in bloom, spreading sunshine over the grey old stones. And in the Oaklands woods, there had been primroses in the banks, the beeches were coming into translucent green leaf, the bluebells at their feet soon to turn into a misty blue.

As Nella walked into the hall, pulling off her hat, Amy met her. 'You have a visitor, in the drawing room.'

'Who is it?'

But Amy smiled mysteriously and wouldn't say;

this new, grown-up Amy who had her hair up and whom Nella couldn't quite believe in yet. The last few weeks had changed her, as it had changed them all. Poor Amy, she would have to wait for her first grown-up party, after all, though if it mattered to her, she was hiding it very well. She added, 'I should tidy yourself before you go in. Your hair's a mess.' Nella smiled. Not so different, after all.

She slipped off her coat, and as she turned to smooth her hair in the looking glass in the hall, she was arrested by piano music coming from the drawing room. It was a sound so little heard in the house that she stood stock-still, halted by recognition that was like a blow to the solar plexus; the sort of music her untutored ear could not understand, but her mind did: slow, moody and fragmented as it was, and which sent an almost superstitious frisson down her spine.

She opened the door and found Duncan Geddes in the drawing room, his hands moving over the keyboard of what had been Dorothea's upright walnut piano. It was the one piece of furniture which had been transported here, with much trouble, when they moved, and which now sat in one corner of this plain, uncomfortable room, destined to remain mostly unplayed and looking highly incongruous with its gleaming polish and brass sconces and the rich, fringed green silk runner Dorothea herself had embroidered.

When he saw her at the open door, Duncan stopped playing at once and stood up. 'Forgive me ... I should have asked...'

She waved a hand. 'What was that music?'

364

'I'm not sure. It was already open...' He turned back the pages of the sheet music on the piano rest. 'Debussy. A prelude... *'Feuilles mortes'*. Dead leaves. Melancholy, but lovely, don't you think? At least it would be if I wasn't making such a bad fist of it... And I'm afraid your piano needs tuning,' he added apologetically.

'No one plays it now. Marianne used to, sometimes.'

There was an awkward pause.

'I came to say goodbye.'

So soon? Her spirits should not sink like this, when it was scarcely unexpected. Most of the hospital patients had now gone from Oaklands, the nurses, too, Nella being one of them, but she hadn't expected the final closure to come quite so soon. She suspected there might have been a concerted effort on the part of Matron and the medical staff to speed things up after the shocking events which had happened there lately, a feeling that the family had a right to be left to themselves at last – which, if it were true, was laudable, and typical of Miss Inman, who was rarely given enough credit for having finer feelings beneath her starched facade.

'They've started dismantling the huts, and the last patients have gone ... good old Bomber last week, and yesterday young Shawcross went to a rehabilitation centre in Bradford – accompanied by his fiancée. Did you know he's agreed to marry her, at last? He'll be in good hands, she's a sensible young woman and she's beginning to make him see his life needn't be entirely without point ... your cousin did a good job, bringing her

365

down to see him.'

'Oh yes, Eunice and her lame ducks.' Nella smiled. The pretty dress Amy had made for the homecoming party which had never happened, she would have occasion to wear after all, for Eunice and William – a William determined on a new start – were to be married after the period of mourning for her father was over. Together, they had plans to keep the Foley business going. Eunice had, after all, already learnt the ropes from her father, and men he had implicitly trusted – his shop-floor manager and his office manager – had returned home, and were willing and eager to give the support needed, if it would be the means of keeping the works open and providing employment.

They were to live at Oaklands. It would not be a house of ghosts, haunted not only by Grev, and perhaps Marianne, but also by Arthur Foley, the man who had been father to him all his life – and not least by Edith Huckaby, whose murder seemed likely to remain an unsolved mystery after the departure of the police and an inquest verdict of murder by person or persons unknown. Oaklands, which Sybil had been so looking forward to reclaiming for the parties and dances, the dazzling social life she had envisaged for Eunice, would become better than that: it would be a family home again, with children's voices soon filling the empty spaces and dispersing the shadows.

Duncan had risen from the piano stool and was leaning against the piano, hands in his pockets. 'And you – have you had any more ideas of what you will do with yourself now, Nella?'

She had thought of little else since leaving the hospital – even perhaps learning shorthand, and how to type, and then finding work in some office, though it was an idea entirely without appeal, and was certainly not how she wanted to spend the rest of her life. She had thought of asking Mrs Rafferty for advice, but she and her friend Miss Dorkings were more at a loss with themselves than she was, now that the vital objective of gaining for women the right to vote had finally been achieved. The Bill had been passed, said Miss Dorkings tartly, because the government could in all conscience have done no other than give them the vote, after women had proved themselves every bit as good as men during the war – but no doubt about it, it was also because people like their old adversary, Mr Winston Churchill, were afraid the Movement might start up again if they were denied it.

Nella shrugged. 'Something will turn up, I'm sure.' Talk about her future was too depressing. Looking around for a tea tray, she said, 'You must think us very inhospitable. Has no one offered you tea?'

'Your sister did, but I declined it, thank you.'

'Are you sure you won't have some?'

'Thank you ... very kind, but no.'

Why are we having this stilted conversation? Duncan asked himself. Perhaps tea would bridge the awkwardness of his unexpected visit, but it would only prolong the agony. Better say what he had to say as soon as possible and then he could leave.

The trouble was, he hadn't seen Nella for a couple of weeks and she had, in some way he couldn't quite put a finger on, become subtly different. Perhaps it was the dress she was wearing, of some amber-coloured wool, the colour warming her pale skin, and her thick bobbed hair, freed from the confines of her nurse's cap, swinging forward towards her cheekbones, curving around her face. She looked a little lost and uncertain, and perhaps a little older. After being so used to seeing her in uniform, quick and decisive, so sure of herself, the change was oddly disconcerting. He thought he could, in fact, only remember with any clarity one particular time she had been out of uniform, on that night they had first dined together. There was little chance of him ever forgetting that: the absurd ragged locks which had made him laugh; and the desire to kiss away the look of exhaustion and bring a smile to her eyes, which had brought the first realisation he might be starting to love her.

He said abruptly, 'I took the liberty of coming here because I desperately need to make my explanations before I leave.'

She smiled, and her chin lifted imperceptibly. That, at least, was familiar. 'Duncan, there is no need. I've told you, I understand perfectly.'

'I'm very much afraid you do not – and how could you, when we parted like that? I deserve to be punished, but at least don't send me away without some chance to redeem myself.'

Punish? She certainly had no desire to do anything of the sort, but she hoped she had enough pride not to allow herself to be hurt again, in the way he had once hurt her. Whatever had been between them was over and done with, and best forgotten. On the other hand, would she not be punishing him if she refused to listen?

'I'm sorry, but I *do* need to explain. Please, Nella, at least don't pretend it didn't matter. Not that. Please, sit down.'

'Well then...' Someone – presumably Amy when she'd shown him in – had put a match to the fire always kept laid in case of visitors, who remained mostly non-existent (at least, those deemed worthy of the drawing room), but so far it had done nothing whatsoever to alleviate the chill of the room. She knelt on the hearthrug, holding her hands to the blaze, while he folded himself onto a low stool opposite. 'I'm listening.'

He had sworn, over there in Flanders, never to involve her in the shambles that was his private life, until he came to realise it was becoming impossible not to. He had always had every intention of telling her about Dolly, though somehow he had never seemed to find the right opportunity. He'd told himself afterwards, re-peatedly, it was because he hadn't been abso-lutely sure of her that he had failed to do so; that perhaps he was mistaken in thinking she felt as deeply as he did; that she was too young and unspoilt to be drawn into the sordid chaos of his life. All of these things were possible, but he knew the real answer. The truth was that he'd been a damned coward, and he had taken the coward's way out, on that night of the war which had seemed to him to have passed totally beyond what humanity had ever before been capable of.

The mayhem all about them had brought home to him precisely how fragile was their own hold on life, and suddenly afraid of losing her, he had momentarily lost control of his senses, and blurted out the truth ... or part of the truth.

And he had lost her, anyway.

'It was a crass thing to do,' he said now, determined not to prevaricate any longer, 'showing you that photograph. I can't think what made me do it like that, except that the whole situation had been preying on my mind for months. You see, Nella, what it was ... when you and I met out there, Dolly, my wife, had already left me. Or rather, since I was in France, it was Jamie she left; took herself off and left the child to the care of his nursemaid and his old grandfather. I had been with the army about six months. She ran away with a naval officer she had met, a man named Kidson. I should have told you all this, but I was very bitter and ... to be perfectly honest, I could never be sure she wouldn't come back one day – and that if she did, I wouldn't, for Jamie's sake, feel duty-bound to try and patch things up.'

'And ... did she come back?' She had grown very tense. Her knuckles showed white, and her voice had taken on an edge of uncertainty.

'She's dead, Nella. She was in fact already dead when you and I met, although I had no idea of it then – if only I *had* known! She was killed in one of the Zeppelin raids on London, in a hotel where she was staying. I was never notified because she was registered there as Kidson's wife. Kidson himself was actually with his ship at the time of the raid, so he didn't find out for some time, and even then wasn't in a hurry to inform either me or her father of what had happened.'

'Duncan, I am so sorry.' Sorry, and berating herself for not having sensed the unhappiness that had been there beneath the casual surface; all the time when he had unfailingly met almost insuperable physical and emotional demands, and smiled and rallied his flagging team to do the same with a joke or a laugh. 'How hurt you must have been.'

Hurt? His pride, for a while, certainly. But as for Dolly ... how could he explain about Dolly? The truth was, he had fallen in love with nothing more than a pretty face and charming manners, so bowled over by her that he had not realised until too late how frivolous and pleasure-loving she was, disarming him by showing herself sympathetic to his ambitions, though only if, as he was to learn by bitter experience, they didn't interfere in the slightest with her pleasures. What she really wanted for him, he learnt too late, was to leave the coalfields and the miserable existence of Lillington's miners behind and for him to take up a fashionable practice in London, the sort some people were advising him to take up now. Whereas he, brought up with a strong Presbyterian background, had found his ambitions centred on what little he could do to alleviate the misery of the people he had found himself working amongst. Their marriage was already doomed, even before he enlisted in the RAMC.

'We met when I went as a junior partner to Dr Hedley in Lillington. Her father was a wealthy colliery owner, a widower. He wasn't a bad man, not a tyrant, like some of the coal owners, he was simply insensitive, a hard-headed businessman who doted on and spoilt his only daughter.'

All this he had intended to tell Nella after making that clumsy, thoughtless blunder over the photograph. But next morning, she had not been there, had been despatched back to the base hospital, extremely ill with that poisoned finger. And although he had managed to scrawl several hasty notes to her, she had never answered.

He told himself that there was no guarantee she had ever received them, but he was not sure whether he believed this, and because he was so ashamed and angry with himself, he felt he had no right to seek her out and force explanations on her. If ever this is all over ... he said to himself, and tried to believe it was better for the time being to let things ride. Working so near the front line, in the very heart and centre of battle, as he was doing, the odds on him surviving the war were not great anyway. He threw himself into his work, with no thought or care for his own safety. The Military Cross he was awarded meant little or nothing to him.

The war over, he had made his way home, spending a few days' leave in Paris which, amongst other things, gave him time for more sober reflection. He began enquiries as soon as he got back to England and found she was working at the convalescent hospital in her home village. He pulled strings to get himself a temporary position there.

The fire had caught hold now but he saw Nella

shiver. So far, he hadn't even noticed the chill of the room. He looked around and then, seeing nothing else, lifted a crocheted wool antimacassar from a chair back and placed it around her shoulders. She smiled and drew it around her, grateful for its warmth, as he went on, needing to finish the whole story. 'My partner, Hedley, seemed to think Dolly leaving like that helped to kill James Lowther, her father, but who knows? He died of a stroke only a few months ago, settling the substantial part of his fortune on Jamie. I was staggered to find he had also named me as trustee of a large fund to be used to provide some sort of care for the miners. He and I had always got on rather well, as a matter of fact, never mind the fierce arguments we had about the miners' welfare and so on, and maybe they helped to change his mind, I don't know. Anyway, it's a marvellous opportunity. Clinics, better medical care...' His face became animated as he spoke for a while about his hopes, his aspirations.

She listened without saying anything until he had finished. 'Why, that's ... simply wonderful. What a chance! No one could do it better than you.' Her cheeks were flushed. The light of the fire danced in her eyes. And he determined to take the plunge and say what he had, after all, come here to say.

'Why don't you join me, Nella? Together we could do a wonderful job.'

The very idea was so splendid, providing just the opportunity she had been looking for, to do something worthwhile with her life, that she could hardly believe it. Better than shorthand typing, any day! She said simply, 'Thank you. I would love that, more than anything, I think. If you believe I have the experience. But then, I could always learn...'

For a moment he didn't understand what she was saying, but only for a moment. 'Oh, dammit, I can't even get that right. Nella, I'm not offering you a job! I'm asking you to marry me.'

After that, there was a great deal of lost time to be made up, and dusk was falling, the room was in shadow, the fire had died to a heap of pink ash and Duncan was heaping more coal on it from the scuttle, when he said, his back to her, 'We should see your father.'

'Mm,' she murmured. She was in no hurry for all the fuss there would be when their intentions became known. 'In a while.' Any time now, someone was going to come in and disturb them anyway.

'We should perhaps make it now. About our marriage – yes, but meanwhile...' He stopped and added abruptly, 'Meanwhile, there's something more I have to say, which he, above all, should hear.'

'Duncan...?'

'I told you that on my last leave, before I came home, I spent some time in Paris.'

'Yes? And?' She was all attention now.

'Well, Paris is still ... Paris. Licking its wounds. On the one hand, grey and dismal, full of foreign politicians arriving with talk of peace settlements – a lot of sadness – on the other hand, everyone determined to return to the old life as soon as possible ... art, and fashion now their dressmakers have come back from the front, good food – no horsemeat there, I can tell you!' He came and sat beside her on the sofa and took her hands. 'Look,' he went on, 'look, there are tales, incredible tales, to come out of this war ... God knows, I don't want to upset you, but there's no way to break this gently. When I was in Paris, I met someone we both thought dead...' He kept a very tight hold of her hands.

Her heart began to hammer. She knew the name he was going to say without him uttering it. 'I don't believe it,' she cried. 'You're pulling my leg?'

'Would I do that? About such a thing? Yes, impossible as it is to believe, I met Grev, your cousin Grev, there.'

This time tea, dispensed by Eleanor, was drunk while they all listened to what Duncan had to tell them – Francis, remote and grave, his face impossible to read, Mrs Villiers sad, almost as if she could sense something cataclysmic was coming, and Amy barely able to conceal her excitement. Francis had asked that they should all be present.

'What about his mother?' was the first thing Nella had asked Duncan, after the first stunned moment when she'd heard Grev's name.

'Eunice is telling her. She has had letters from her brother.'

So that explained Eunice's talk about going to find work in Paris, and her hesitation. She must have been torn between waiting for William, due home any day, and the hope that she might actually see Grev again.

That night in Paris, Duncan had heard someone speak his name as he left the small but exclusive restaurant where he had dined – a farewell dinner with a doctor friend on his way home to Canada– when he felt a touch on his shoulder. He spun round, hand on his wallet, but it was no apache, no ruffian ready to rob him. There was no mistaking him, it was Greville Foley. A young man he had believed dead, blown to bits. 'Good God, it is you, Foley? I'm not dreaming?'

'Who else? You look well,' Foley said, as coolly as if they had met on a London street.

Which is more than I can say for you, my friend, thought Duncan, summing up the hollow cheeks, the skeletal frame, the feverish eyes.

They faced each other awkwardly, silent. 'How is Nella?' Grev asked at last.

'I don't know, we've lost touch.'

'That's a pity. I thought you and she–'

'No.'

Grev was all at once racked with an onslaught of helpless coughing. They stood underneath a street lamp, Duncan with his arm around the young man's shoulders, steadying him until finally the spasm passed and he leant against the lamppost, handkerchief to his mouth, looking ghastly under the yellow glare. 'Well, you see how it is with me,' he said, when he had his breath back.

Duncan had seen too many cases of TB not to recognise another when he saw it. 'How long?'

'How long have I had this, or how long have I

376

got? To the first – since I left the army, and to the second, God knows, but not long, I shouldn't think.'

'Look,' Duncan said. 'We can't stay here, talking. Come back inside with me and have a drink.' He needed one as much as the young man obviously did; they had wined and dined themselves very well indeed, he and his Canadian friend, but the shock of meeting a ghost from the past like that had sobered him immediately.

'We thought you dead.'

'I hoped you would.'

They went back into the restaurant, where the *patron*, recognising Duncan but casting a wary eye on his companion, showed them to a discreet corner. While they waited for their drinks to appear, Duncan studied the emaciated young man. Now that he was getting over the first shock of their meeting, he speculated on why, if he had indeed hoped to be thought dead, as he said, Foley had approached him. They could have passed in the street without Duncan ever being the wiser. As an ex-soldier, not in fact now dead, as presumed, and not having made any attempt to rejoin his unit, he would be considered to have deserted his post, and would face serious consequences, if he were caught. The precarious state of his health, however, seemed likely to be its own answer to that. Maybe he did not, at this stage, care very much one way or the other.

Nella said, 'Did he tell you exactly what happened? How he escaped being killed, when the others were blown to bits?'

'For some reason, when the shell that blew up

377

his companions burst, he was simply blown aside. That sort of miraculous escape happened all the time, as we both know. He did have superficial injuries – he was hit on the head for one thing, and must have lost consciousness, though for how long he doesn't remember.'

There was, as a matter of fact, a good deal Grev didn't remember, Duncan thought. How he had got to the ploughed field miles away where he eventually found himself, for instance, stumbling along, aware only of a blinding pain in his head, and the fact that he was almost stark naked, remembering nothing of the shell which had blasted his clothes off, or indeed anything that had gone before the explosion, not even who he was. The only thing that seemed to matter was the wound on his right hand, which for some inexplicable reason he knew was catastrophic for him.

Mrs Villiers said softly, 'His right hand? Grev? Dear God. It must have seemed the end of everything to him.'

Francis got up abruptly and stood in his favourite position, his back to the room, staring out into the afternoon.

Was it that wound to his hand which had pushed Grev over the edge, determined that he would never go back near the front line; which had made him stumble on for miles as all hell was still breaking loose behind him, until at last he came to a lonely, half-ruined shack where the Flemish couple who took him in had cared for him and asked no questions? Was it that which had kept him from 'remembering' who he was, how he had got there? Perhaps. One thing was sure. He had remembered enough of the French he had learnt as a student to try and pass as French. They probably didn't believe him, of course, his rescuers, but they detested the Boche, who had killed their son, devastated the farm which had been their only means of livelihood, and left them with nothing but this hovel as a refuge. They kept him for a couple of days, replaced his rags of clothing with ones of their dead son, and then he was passed on to the nuns at the nearest convent. From there, he managed to get to Paris, where he had been ever since, living with one of his pre-war tutors who was not sympathetic in any shape or form to the war.

'If he had given himself up, with a wound like that to his hand, he would have been sent home,' Nella said.

'It was bad, but nothing like as serious as he must have thought it at first. In fact, there's little wrong with it now.'

'I don't blame him,' Amy said suddenly. 'Why should he have stayed there to be killed? But why doesn't he come home now?'

Duncan said gently, 'He can never come home, Amy. There would be charges to be faced.' He did not add that it was too late for that now, in any case.

'Oh, oh, that's monstrous! The beastly war is *over*, and he was so brave!'

Francis turned back from the window. 'Yes, Amy, he was,' he said, in a voice from which all emotion had been drained, and then to the rest of them, he said, 'You will excuse me, I hope. I must go at once to his mother.'

Epilogue

April 1919

The Channel ferry steams towards Boulogne. The tall woman in black who came aboard with those others – her daughter, the young man with the red hair and the reverend gentleman – has left them below and is now alone as she paces along the deck. She walks with head bowed against the light wind, her hat pulled well down over her brow, the capacious bag she carries hooked over her arm.

She walks forward and leans across the bows, feeling the rhythm of the waves as they slap against the sides of the boat, listening to the music of the wind. They are approaching the port. What was just a blur on the horizon becomes the outline of sheds and buildings on the quayside and is rapidly becoming clearer as they steam towards the land where her son awaits her.

Please God she will not be too late. Duncan Geddes, the doctor, has told her, gently, that Grev does not have long now. Long enough, she prays, long enough to put things right between them. His last letter to Eunice had included one to her, which Eunice had passed on: a short, unrevealing note, reminiscent of the ones he used to send her from school. She was adept at reading between the lines, however, and at last he *had* written to her.

That other letter...

She dips her hand into her bag and withdraws the small grey suede pochette she had once given to Edith Huckaby, and which her husband had hidden in the gun cupboard the night she died. Only she, his wife, had heard, and understood, his dying words, what he was trying to say.

'...*the gun cupboard, a letter...*' She has not opened the envelope, addressed to the police. She knows what it contains: the confession Arthur had already made to her, when he found her in the music room that night, after he had followed Edith Huckaby and killed her. Followed her, meaning only to warn her off, to tell her plainly that her blackmail was an empty threat. But her insolence had enraged him, and with the sudden fury of a normally mild man, he had snatched the umbrella...

Only Sybil knows this. Reardon, the police inspector, suspects, but he has no proof. It lies here, in her hand. She looks into the water, grey-brown and choppy. The bow cuts through the waves, making white wings of water either side. She holds the bag tighter.

Ahead is France. Paris, where her son awaits her. Screaming, wheeling seagulls begin to surround the ferry as it nears land. One swoops down towards her in a graceful arc, and perches on the rail beside her, the feathers on its breast white and dazzling. It stays, motionless, its bright, cold, beady eye unwinking. She wills it to fly landwards, a sign of hope.

In a sudden movement, she leans further over

the rail, then drops the pochette over the side and into the water. The predatory seagull beside her gives a mournful cry and swoops after it, folding its wings as it sinks below the rail and disappears. The little bag is not heavy and for a moment it sits on the surface, before being swallowed up in the creaming waters of the ship's passage as it cleaves through the waves towards land.

The publishers hope that this book has given you enjoyable reading. Large Print Books are especially designed to be as easy to see and hold as possible. If you wish a complete list of our books please ask at your local library or write directly to:

Magna Large Print Books
Magna House, Long Preston,
Skipton, North Yorkshire.
BD23 4ND

This Large Print Book for the partially sighted, who cannot read normal print, is published under the auspices of

THE ULVERSCROFT FOUNDATION